MOVE

—— YOUR BLOOMING ——

CORPSE

ALSO BY D. E. IRELAND

Wouldn't It Be Deadly

MOVE
— YOUR BLOOMING —
CORPSE

D. E. IRELAND

MINOTAUR BOOKS

A THOMAS DUNNE BOOK
NEW YORK

A THOMAS DUNNE BOOK FOR MINOTAUR BOOKS.
An imprint of St. Martin's Publishing Group.

MOVE YOUR BLOOMING CORPSE. Copyright © 2015 by D. E. Ireland. All rights reserved. Printed in the United States of America. For information, address St. Martin's Press, 175 Fifth Avenue, New York, N.Y. 10010.

www.thomasdunnebooks.com
www.minotaurbooks.com

The Library of Congress Cataloging-in-Publication Data is available upon request.

ISBN 978-1-250-04936-0 (hardcover)
ISBN 978-1-4668-5036-1 (e-book)

Our books may be purchased in bulk for promotional, educational, or business use. Please contact your local bookseller or the Macmillan Corporate and Premium Sales Department at (800) 221-7945, extension 5442, or by e-mail at MacmillanSpecial Markets@macmillan.com.

First Edition: September 2015

10   9   8   7   6   5   4   3   2   1

To Rex, Julie, and Audrey

ACKNOWLEDGMENTS

To Amanda Lynn for thinking up the title, and to George Plumptre's book *The Fast Set: The World of Edwardian Racing* for the invaluable role it played in our research.

I can imagine few things more delightful than to be invited there for Ascot. One sees the racing in the most comfortable way, meets all one's friends (and enemies), makes—or loses—a little money, and all without any fatigue or bother.

—Daisy, Princess of Pless

If I am asked to give advice to those who are inclined to spend their time and their money on the Turf, I should give them the advice that "Punch" gave to those about to marry—don't.

—Archibald Philip Primrose, 5th Earl of Rosebery

A sensational incident, even surpassing that which characterized the Derby, took place at Ascot this afternoon during the race for the Gold Cup. Just as Miss Davison rushed at the King's horse Anmer at Epsom, so a man ran on the course at Ascot.

—A cable sent from London to *The New York Times* reporting how Harold Hewitt ran onto the Ascot racetrack and was trampled on June 19, 1913

MOVE

— YOUR BLOOMING —

CORPSE

ONE

ROYAL ASCOT—JUNE 1913

A high-pitched scream pierced the air. Startled, Professor Henry Higgins looked up from his notebook. He saw only horses, jockeys, and a sea of outlandish hats. It was the third day of Ascot Week, and all of British society was in attendance, including the King and Queen. Half of London seemed to be crammed into the paddock where owners admired their horses while trainers gave last-minute instruction to nervous jockeys. As it was Ladies Day, hordes of titled women also milled about, vying to see who sported the most eye-catching ensemble and towering hat.

One of those ladies let out another shriek. "This is insufferable," she said to her female companions as a stableboy led a magnificent black gelding past them. "How dare they allow a horse in here. The beast will trample us all!"

Higgins wrote in his notebook, *Fifty-year-old matron born in north-east Scotland. Currently resides in Hampshire.*

She shook her sky-blue parasol at the animal. "I insist this horse be removed!"

"Hush, woman," Higgins said. "You're in the paddock at Ascot Races, not Selfridges department store. The horse has far more right to be here than you do."

"How dare you speak to me in such a fashion." She pointed her parasol in his direction.

"And have a care how you wave that lace weapon," Higgins continued. "At last year's Ascot, some actress stabbed General Owen Williams in the cheek with her parasol. Injured the poor chap simply because she took fright at a horse. The addlebrained ninny."

"Of all the nerve," the lady said as her friends crowded about. "I cannot believe the ruffians they allow into the paddock."

"Oh, I suspect you've known a few ruffians in your time, madam." Higgins smiled. "Especially during your girlhood in Aberdeen."

The woman's mouth fell open.

"But several dozen years in East Hampshire have concealed much of your Scottish past. In fact, you spent your adolescence in the market town of Petersfield or its near environs." This pronouncement caused her to visibly blanch.

"Do you know that gentleman, Lady Marjorie?" a white-haired friend asked.

"I certainly do not." Lady Marjorie snapped open her parasol. "And he is no gentleman. More likely a sordid reporter spying for some penny daily."

"Hardly that, madam. I am Henry Higgins, professor of phonetics and elocution. It is no boast to say that I can place a person within six miles of his birthplace after hearing a few sentences out of his—or her—mouth. And I can place a Londoner within a street or two."

"Ridiculous." The white-haired friend shot him her haughtiest look. "You'll be performing circus tricks next, no doubt."

"And you, madam, have spent all of your life in London, much of it in Notting Hill." Higgins thought a moment. "Pinehurst Court, I believe."

She gasped. The matrons looked at him as if he had just lifted their skirts.

"We have had quite enough of your insufferable rudeness," Lady Marjorie said as she turned to go. "And I must say, that four-legged beast was preferable to a knave such as you."

Higgins tipped his hat at the departing women.

"Really, Henry, I believe there is enough entertainment today at Ascot without you baiting the ladies." His friend and colleague Colonel Pickering stood behind him, looking quite formal in his finest gray morning coat and silk top hat. He gestured at Higgins's notebook with a silver-tipped walking stick. "And you might stop writing down speech patterns long enough to watch a race or two."

"I've seen two races today, each lasting three minutes. You can hardly expect me to spend the afternoon conversing about horses and hats, which is all anyone here wants to talk about. Besides, I don't want to converse, I want to listen. During one casual stroll, I can eavesdrop on dissolute earls or bookmakers from South London. Imagine the possibilities for recording regional dialects."

"Hey, governor, why ain't you in the stands?" a familiar voice called out to them.

Higgins nodded toward the man now pushing his way through the crowded paddock. "You see, even Cockney dustmen are here."

Of course, Alfred Doolittle was no longer a dustman. After Higgins took on his daughter Eliza last year as a pupil, Alfred had come to 27A Wimpole Street hoping to shake down Higgins for a few quid. Instead of being insulted by Doolittle's blatant appeal for money, Higgins was amused by the older fellow's brash manner and colorful eloquence. As a lark, he mentioned the dustman to American millionaire

Ezra D. Wannafeller. The last thing Higgins expected was that Wannafeller would offer Doolittle an annuity of three thousand pounds if he agreed to lecture for his Moral Reform League. Soon after, Alfred Doolittle left the squalor of the East End behind. He was a respectable member of the middle class now, with a wife, a house in Pimlico, and—most incredibly—an Irish racehorse.

"What'cha two gents doing in the paddock?" Alfred said when he reached them. "I convinced my Viscount to open up his private box for us owners and our friends. No reason to stay here. He's put magnums of champagne chilling in buckets by every seat, he has."

"Champagne gives me indigestion, and the Colonel has misgivings about sharing the largesse of your Viscount," Higgins said.

Pickering frowned. "Of all the people I might ask to share ownership of a racehorse with, Saxton would be last on my list."

"Does this mean you prefer Turnbull's company?" Higgins asked in surprise. Jonathon Turnbull was yet another man who owned a share in Doolittle's racehorse.

"Good grief, I'd forgotten about him." Pickering shook his head. "My word, Doolittle, you chose two of the most scurrilous chaps in London society as partners."

"And lucky I was to get them." Doolittle adjusted his brushed top hat. Dressed even finer than Colonel Pickering, he sported a black morning coat, sharply pressed striped trousers, a black waistcoat, white gloves, and a green Ascot tie. His Oxford dress boots fairly gleamed in the June sunlight. No doubt Doolittle's Savile Row tailor bills were impressive.

Higgins thought it time for a change of subject. "I trust you have been to the stables to see the Donegal Dancer. Does the jockey seem confident of victory?"

"Aye, Professor. Not only do I have the most fleet-footed colt to ever come from the Emerald Isle, there's not a jockey better than Bomber Brody to ride him. A word of advice: get an Irishman to ride an Irish horse. The horses know the difference, they do." Doolittle had acquired the racehorse only three months ago, but acted as if he were on the Board of Stewards at the Jockey Club. "Anyway, gents, the next race begins in fifteen minutes. You don't want to be watching the most important race by jostling for a place along the track."

"The King might disagree," Pickering said. "Prince Palatine defends his title in the Gold Cup, and it's no secret His Majesty favors last year's champion. But Tracery may nose him out."

"His Majesty is wrong to think the Gold Cup is the race to watch. He ain't seen my Donegal Dancer fly down the course, now has he? Aye, and when he does, I wager he'll want to buy my beauty. But none of us will sell a single hair on his fetlock."

"That horse has a bewildering number of owners," Higgins said. "I hardly think another one will matter."

"I swear, I'd like as sell my darlin' Rose rather than surrender that sweet colt."

"Alfie! The race is starting soon!" The aforementioned Rose waved from the other side of the paddock. Doolittle's wife looked as fancy as he did, and in their racing colors besides. Higgins's eyes popped at her shamrock green dress and tricorn hat festooned with purple berries. When this was combined with her brassy red hair, Rose made quite the colorful figure.

Doolittle sighed. "Wish you gents would give a few lessons to my Rose. After all, it only took the two of you a few months to turn Eliza into a proper lady. Makes me proud to see her parading about Ascot like a blooming snob. I don't mind telling you, Rose could do with a little polishing."

Higgins shrugged. "Your wife seems to be doing fine at her first Ascot."

"Let's go, Alfie!" Rose yelled again. "Get your arse over here."

"Perhaps a little polishing might be in order," Higgins added.

"I'd best get moving." Doolittle gave an exaggerated sniff to the sprig of violets in his lapel. "She don't like to be kept waiting. And you two should get to our private box before the fun begins. Eliza is already there, eating every tea cake in sight. But I'm right offended she didn't wear the Donegal Dancer's racing colors. The least my daughter could do for her old dad is wear the green and purple of our silks."

Higgins cast another look at the vividly arrayed Rose Doolittle. No reason to tell the man that Eliza was appalled at the idea of putting together a tasteful outfit in green and purple.

"Alfie!"

"Better get hopping. Don't want the missus to be making a scene, now do we? She's already been in the champagne and we ain't even started to celebrate the Donegal Dancer's victory—which is as sure as coal dust in Newcastle."

Doolittle stepped nimbly through the crowd, tipping his hat to every other person in the paddock. "I declare, the fellow must know more people here than the jockey Fred Archer," Higgins said to Pickering. "Bold as a pirate, and charming into the bargain."

"I wish he had discretion as well as charm. How could he join a racing syndicate with Saxton and Turnbull? Half of London won't accept Saxton into their homes, and the other half has barred Turnbull. I've made certain to sit in the back of the viewing box so as not to be seen."

"At least you have Sir Walter for company."

Sir Walter Fairweather was Senior Steward of the Jockey Club and an old acquaintance of the Colonel. He was also another person who owned a share of the Donegal Dancer.

"Thank heaven for Fairweather. At least he's a decent chap. But his only interests are horses and gardening. And I would have thought he had more sense than to get involved with men such as Saxton and Turnbull." Despite the Colonel's scholarly honors and military exploits, he was still shocked by other people's bad behavior. His naïveté sometimes amazed Higgins.

"Pick, these people are part of the racing world, not the Cathedral Choir at Christ Church. Doolittle could never have acquired or maintained a racehorse on his own, so he went to people who had money and credit."

"Bad credit, you mean." Pickering frowned. "Doolittle's right about one thing. The next race is about to start, and Eliza expects us to watch it with her. But I do wish she hadn't placed so large a bet. She has five guineas on the Donegal Dancer."

Higgins winced. "By George, the girl is mad. That's everything she's managed to save up. At this rate, she'll fall into debt before her father does."

"I couldn't talk her out of it. Anyway, we'd best go. Your mother asked us to join her in the Royal Enclosure, but I already promised Eliza."

"You go on ahead. I heard an interesting turn of phrase nearby that I want to jot down."

"Very well. But if you don't make it on time, I will leave it to you to explain it to Eliza." With a last warning look, Pickering made his way out of the sun-dappled paddock.

Once he left, Higgins sidled up to a bald fellow in a rumpled suit deep in conversation with one of the jockeys. He quickly wrote down their words. Too soon the pair walked off. As Higgins headed for Lord Saxton's private box, he spotted a tall, middle-aged man a few feet away. He was also writing in a small notebook. Could he be a fellow scholar?

"Excuse me, sir. Are you a student of languages?" Higgins asked.

The scribbler looked up, his eyes wide with alarm. "Are you speaking to me?"

"Yes." Higgins held up his own notebook. "I wondered if you were copying down speech patterns as I was."

The man quickly closed his leather-bound book. "Not that it is any of your concern, but I was recording my impressions of the day."

"A journalist, then?" Higgins eyed the fellow's gray Norfolk jacket. While his suit was well made and expensive, it didn't compare to the morning coats and tailored suits of the wealthier racing fans. Higgins wished he had dressed more casually today as well. Against his better judgment, Higgins had worn formal dress to Ascot, something he rarely did. He couldn't wait to take off his blasted morning coat and top hat once he returned to Wimpole Street.

"Certainly not. Journalism is a dreadful profession." His eyes shifted from side to side as if he expected someone to disapprove of him speaking with Higgins. "I always carry a diary and Bible with me. This way I can never forget God's teaching." His voice lowered. "Or important occasions which should be commemorated."

"I only come to hear people's speech patterns. I've no interest in horse racing."

"Oh, I am not a fan of racing either." He looked offended at the very idea. "It is a foolish and dangerous endeavor. Nor do I approve of the greedy, thoughtless people who come to watch. If there is a more despicable place than a racecourse, I have yet to find it."

"If that's how you feel, it seems a fine waste of a train trip and an entrance ticket," Higgins said. The man stared back at him with a mournful expression. Could there be anyone duller than a sanctimonious fellow with no sense of humor? "I haven't introduced myself. I'm Professor Henry Higgins."

The man looked at Higgins's outstretched hand for an uncomfortable moment before giving it a brief shake. "Harold Hewitt."

Higgins grinned. "We have the same initials. In fact, you seem to have a preponderance of 'h's in your life, seeing how you come from Herefordshire. Even more remarkable, you also attended Harrow."

He stiffened. "Whoever told you that?"

"It's my job to identify where a person comes from after hearing them speak. Your intonations reveal you to be a native of Herefordshire. And you pronounce 'commemorated' as a student at Harrow would, or at least a student who was taught linguistics by Nigel Uppington." Higgins cocked his head. "But I hear a bit of London in your speech, too. You currently live in the city. Perhaps the vicinity of Chelsea."

Hewitt took a step back. "I find you rather presumptuous, Professor. If you will excuse me." He bent down and opened a black satchel that sat at his feet. As Hewitt stuffed the diary into the bag, Higgins caught a quick glimpse of the contents.

This time, Higgins stepped back in alarm. Before he could think what to say, Hewitt gave him a curt nod and marched off, satchel in hand.

With growing unease, Higgins watched the man disappear among the noisy throng in the paddock. The next race was imminent, and the very air crackled with excitement. Higgins tried to catch sight of Hewitt again but failed. Everyone now pressed forward toward the track. He had little choice but to move with the crowd.

Better find a policeman or a racing official as soon as possible. But surrounded on all sides by excited racing fans, he couldn't glimpse a single police uniform among all the morning coats and feathered hats.

Someone grabbed his sleeve. "Here you are."

Eliza Doolittle looked resplendent in a summer ensemble of palest yellow. When he and Pickering took her on as a student last year, the

Colonel replaced her few ragged dresses with a wardrobe fit for a duchess. Higgins thought Pickering spent far too much money on ensuring that Eliza was the best-dressed woman in the room. Today was no different. Her stylish gown, covered in scalloped embroidery, was as delicate as fairy dust in contrast to the large belted bow at her waist. And Higgins couldn't help but marvel at her enormous hat crowned with gigantic yellow satin roses. Tilted at an exaggerated angle on her head, it blocked his view of anyone else in the paddock.

"Honestly, Professor, I can't believe you're still dawdling in the paddock. Not that I wouldn't mind staying here myself. I don't fancy some of my dad's partners or their wives. And I hate my own dad's wife. But if I have to suffer through their company, so should you."

"I don't know why I should suffer."

"You're the one responsible for getting my father the annuity. Without that, he'd be throwing back a pint in Whitechapel right now. And Rose wouldn't be wearing a wedding ring on her fat greedy finger."

Higgins groaned. Once Eliza began to complain about her stepmother, there was no stopping her. "Isn't your cousin Jack here today? In an official capacity, I mean." Jack Shaw was not only Eliza's cousin, he was a detective inspector at Scotland Yard.

"I saw him about an hour ago. He's worried about another incident like what happened at the Derby two weeks ago. There are police everywhere."

"Where? Can you point them out?"

Eliza leaned on her parasol and scanned the crowd milling about them. "There are too many spectators in the paddock. I can't get a good view, especially with all these hats."

"They're off!" someone yelled.

"Blimey! We can't miss the race!" Grabbing his arm, Eliza dragged Higgins through the pressing throng. She didn't let go until she'd pushed her way to a fenced-in area of the paddock. Aware of the grumbling at her intrusion, Eliza gave them her sunniest smile. "Please excuse me, but my father's horse is running in this race. Wish me luck."

Several displaced gentlemen did just that. Higgins wasn't surprised. Although he was usually indifferent to feminine charm, most men considered Eliza a lovely young woman. And in her form-fitting yellow dress, eye-catching hat, and coiffed chestnut hair she seemed as ethereal as a woodland sprite. Of course, they hadn't heard the Cockney cabbage let loose with any of her favorite East End phrases.

"Here they come!"

Eliza leaned over the paddock fence. The summer breeze lifted up the long ribbons on her hat and set them sailing behind her. Higgins resigned himself to watching the race. He wouldn't be able to get a policeman's attention with all eyes on the horses thundering down the track.

The roar of the crowd grew with each passing minute. The only empty space in all of Ascot was the dirt track stretching ahead of the horses. Fans lined up ten deep along the course, and the stands were packed with people. Higgins squinted at the horses making the far turn, trying to spot a reddish-brown colt with a black mane and tail. The sun was so bright, he tipped his top hat over his eyes to see better. He was grateful for the Donegal Dancer's bold racing colors; the jockey's bright green jacket with purple sleeves made the pair easy to spot.

"C'mon, Bomber Brody! Give the Dancer his head!" Eliza jumped up and down.

Higgins heard the pounding of the hooves as the straining horses drew near.

Eliza let out a delighted scream. "He's pulling up to the lead! Do you see? Dancer is almost in first. Blimey!"

Higgins felt his heart race as the horses barreled down the course toward them. Maybe he should have put a guinea on the Donegal Dancer.

The crowd lunged against the railing. Higgins had to push a few people back or find himself squashed. He looked over to see if Eliza was unharmed. Good grief, she'd climbed onto the fence. Leaning over, Eliza pounded the railing with her parasol.

"Go, Dancer! Go faster, you bloody marvel!"

Higgins moved closer. "Watch your language, Eliza. Remember you're a lady."

The din rose to deafening levels when the horses rounded the turn. Then the traditional Ascot bell rang for the final stretch.

"Ride, Bomber! Ride!" Eliza beat her parasol to shreds.

Even Higgins got caught up in the excitement as the horses thundered past. "Go, Dancer!"

Eliza leaned so far over, Higgins grabbed the large bow on her sash to keep her from falling. "Move that blooming horse, Bomber!" she yelled.

A frenzied moment later, the Donegal Dancer crossed the finish line a nose ahead of the black gelding. As the crowd roared, Eliza threw herself into his arms.

"I love that horse! He's faster than lightning, he is. And I love the races!"

Laughing, Higgins set her down. "Does this mean you'll be spending all your free time now at the racecourse, rather than the cinema?"

"Don't be daft. I put five guineas on that animal." Eliza lifted her parasol. The silk was torn to pieces and the handle almost sheared in half. "Good thing, too. I'll need to use some of my winnings to buy a new parasol." With a shrug, she tossed it aside.

When Higgins offered her his arm, she tucked in her hand with a delighted sigh. "Wasn't that the most wonderful thing you've ever seen? Dad must be dancing a jig right now."

"And so he should. It seems your father knows something about horses after all. That, or he's damnably lucky. But now that the race is over, help me find a policeman."

Eliza looked perplexed. "Whatever for?"

"Right before the race, I exchanged a few words with a man carrying a leather satchel. When he opened it up, I got a peek at the contents. And I didn't like what I saw."

She stopped walking. "What was inside?"

"Books, a small flag." Higgins frowned. "And a gun."

TWO

"Someone should take that bottle away." Eliza laughed as her gleeful father sprayed everyone with a magnum of champagne. "He'll drench the Prime Minister next."

Wet stains now marked her expensive new dress, but she didn't mind. Such a glorious victory—and the money she won with her bet—was well worth a ruined French gown. And how lovely to be at the center of it all: the parade ring at Ascot. With the attention of the racing world focused on them, Eliza felt as thrilled as if she were the winning horse.

As for the victorious colt, the owners circled the Donegal Dancer. His damp neck wreathed with flowers, the racehorse's deep red coat gleamed like mahogany against the jet-black of his mane and tail. At some point Eliza kissed the horse's nose, a moment caught on film by a newspaper photographer. When more reporters crowded in, Eliza finally stepped back. She grabbed a glass of champagne and offered it to the jubilant jockey, who sat astride his winning mount.

"A toast to Bomber Brody!" she said, raising her own glass high.

How fortunate that one of the horse's owners was Maitland Louis Wyngarde, 12th Viscount of Saxton. Not only had Lord Saxton outfitted his private viewing box as if it were a salon, he had brought footmen to the race. Several of them now served champagne to the owners and their families. The rest of the crowd watched with envy.

Higgins refused the footman's offer of a champagne flute. "Eliza, you've danced with your father, kissed the horse, and asked a dozen bookmakers about the size of your winnings. Now please help me find a policeman so I can report the man with the gun."

"Very well," she grumbled, although she knew Higgins was right. Eliza had promised to stay only a minute at the celebration, but she got caught up in the wild joy of it all. Heaven help her, she even found herself embracing Rose Doolittle. With luck, both of them would forget that as soon as possible.

With a sigh, Eliza turned away. "I think you're worrying about nothing. This Harold Hewitt fellow probably carries a gun because he works here. Dad says when horses are severely injured, they put them down with a gun."

"Hewitt doesn't work here." Higgins sounded impatient. "He told me he didn't even like horse racing. I'm telling you, there's a suspicious man walking around the racecourse with a gun in his bag."

Luckily they hadn't gone more than thirty yards when Eliza spied a portly man lighting a cigar. "See that fellow in the brown suit and bowler? I think he's one of the Scotland Yard detectives who were at Drury Lane last month. I remember thinking he looked like a bulldog. What was his name again?" She snapped her fingers. "Detective Jeremy."

She and Higgins hurried over to the detective. Although he seemed wary when Higgins and Eliza first approached, he soon recognized her from the eventful night at the theater. He listened intently while Higgins explained his encounter with Harold Hewitt.

Detective Jeremy puffed on his cigar as though mulling the story over. "Did he threaten you with the gun, Professor?"

"I don't think he realized I'd seen it. I only caught a glimpse before he closed the satchel."

"Perhaps it wasn't a gun that you saw."

Higgins threw him a jaundiced look. "There aren't many things that look like a revolver."

The detective blew a smoke ring before replying. "You and Miss Doolittle solved a murder last month. And you both received a great deal of attention from the press. Maybe you enjoyed the experience so much that you are now seeing suspicious things where none exist."

"He thinks you're barmy, Professor," Eliza said with a smile.

"No, he thinks I'm a liar. Or worse, some sensation seeker that actually enjoyed the circus we went through last month in the papers."

Eliza heard the anger in Higgins's voice and hoped he would keep his temper in check. "Detective Jeremy, as you may remember, Inspector Shaw is my cousin, and he will vouch for our characters. I know Jack is on duty at the racecourse today. Please let him know about Mr. Hewitt. Ask him to meet us at Lord Saxton's private box."

"I'll do what I can, Miss Doolittle, but there's a reason so many police are at Ascot. We don't want a repeat of the incident at the Derby two weeks ago."

Although Eliza had not attended the race at Epsom, she knew the incident he referred to was the death of Emily Davison. Determined to bring attention to the suffrage cause, the political activist ran in front of the King's horse Anmer on his way to the finish line. She suffered fatal injuries and died four days later. Thousands had attended her funeral this past weekend in London. Feelings were running dangerously high on both sides.

"We're keeping a close eye on any woman who looks like a suffragette," Detective Jeremy continued. "Dozens have been turned away at the gate. And any suffragette already here will not be allowed to get within ten feet of the racecourse. Or the King."

She was puzzled. "How can you tell which woman is a suffragette?"

He cast an appreciative gaze over her figure. "For one, they're not likely to be dressed as you are, miss."

Eliza took offense at his comment, but held her tongue.

"Why keep an eye out only for women, Detective?" Higgins asked. "Many men also believe the fairer sex should have the vote. This Harold Hewitt fellow may be one of them."

For the first time, the detective looked concerned. "You could be right. Let me put the word out about the man, and I'll track down Inspector Shaw." He removed a notepad from his jacket pocket. "Can you describe what this Hewitt looks like again?"

Higgins reached for his own notebook and tore out a page. "I've already written it down."

Once the detective left, Eliza turned to Higgins. "You can stop worrying now. So let's have one more look at the Dancer before we head to Lord Saxton's private box. The Colonel will wonder what became of us."

When they found themselves once again among the raucous owners, Higgins shook his head. "They've turned the place into one of Dante's Circles of Hell. I should ask the police to arrest a few of them. Starting with your father."

"You're just angry you didn't place a bet on his horse." Eliza waved to her dad, who was singing "Whisky in the Jar" to an embarrassed racing official. "Next time don't be so cheap."

"Next time a Cockney flower girl asks me for speech lessons, I'll charge for them."

She laughed. "Good luck finding another flower girl who can win a bet for you. A bet that paid you far more than what my lessons cost."

"You impudent, ungrateful turnip. I've a mind to——"

Eliza stepped on Higgins's foot to quiet him as Lord Saxton headed in their direction. Although Colonel Pickering disapproved of the man, she found him gregarious, friendly, and attractive. The Viscount was tall and athletically built, with dark red hair and a ready smile for everyone, commoner or lord.

"Congratulations, sir," she said.

He winked at her, his eyes glassy. "Damn fine race, Miss Doolittle. Run by a damn fine colt." Saxton paused as if seeing her for the first time, although they'd been introduced three hours ago. "Damn fine filly, too." His smile turned into a leer, and Eliza's cheeks grew hot.

She heard Higgins clear his throat. Saxton ignored him and picked up Eliza's gloved hand. Turning her palm up, he kissed it. Before she could react, he leaned forward and kissed her on the mouth. As she stood speechless, he strode off toward his jockey.

"A shame Freddy wasn't here to see that," Higgins said in mock outrage. "Your excitable swain would have challenged Saxton to a duel—and been beaten to a pulp right afterward." He let out a dramatic sigh. "But then who knew you would turn out to be the temptress of Ascot."

Eliza rolled her eyes. "It's not hard to tempt a drunk man."

"I do apologize for my husband's behavior," a woman said.

Startled, Eliza turned to see Lady Hortense Saxton, a willowy brunette with alabaster skin and an entitled air about her. Like Rose Doolittle, the young viscountess was dressed in the horse's racing colors, but she looked far more elegant. The tulle skirt of her promenade suit was the requisite green, but above the satin cummerbund, she wore a cream-colored blouse of flowing chiffon. Even her hat was tasteful—a small green toque with but a single purple feather. Despite her conservative outfit, there was no mistaking Her Ladyship's station in life. An emerald brooch as big as a plum was pinned to her green cummerbund, and Eliza was close enough to see that the shiny handle of her green silk parasol was real gold.

"It's quite all right," Eliza said. "Perfectly understandable to kiss and embrace everyone after winning. I accidentally kissed a reporter when I first got here."

"The horse, too," Higgins added.

Lady Saxton ignored him. "Still, my husband barely knows you. I am sorry we haven't had the opportunity to speak before now. Maitland invited so many people to sit in our box, it's as crowded as the Hippodrome. I wouldn't be surprised if a street sweeper showed up. But if I remember correctly, you are Mr. Doolittle's daughter Eliza."

"I am. And this is Professor Henry Higgins."

After a brief tip of his hat, he turned away with a bored expression.

"The Professor and I teach phonetics and elocution, although I was his student only last year," Eliza said with pride.

"You seem to be in the papers with some regularity. I am fully aware of your remarkable transformation from Covent Garden flower girl to lady." Eliza heard the amused condescension in Lady Saxton's voice. "And certainly all of London read about your droll exploits last month at the Drury Lane Theatre."

"There was this murder, you see. And the Professor and I were—"

Lady Saxton shook her head. "Spare me the details, Miss Doolittle, and send my regards to the Eynsford Hills. I hoped Clara would attend the race today. She may have told you that we attended finishing school in London together, although I was two years ahead of her. Such a pity she isn't here."

"Clara wanted to come, but her mother insisted she and Freddy attend a family wedding in Brighton." No need to tell her that Clara was so furious at missing Ascot, she ripped the dress her mother had bought for the occasion.

"I heard you and Clara are friends," Lady Saxton said. "My cousin Isabel knows Mr. Eynsford Hill. He confided that he was engaged to you. If so, I extend my congratulations."

Eliza didn't know how to explain that both statements were untrue. For while she enjoyed Clara's company, an hour spent with the girl could seem like a day. And Freddy must stop telling people they were engaged. It was too soon for them to be making marriage plans. Eliza was only twenty. Of course, according to Clara, Lady Saxton was the same age as Eliza, which meant she married the Viscount when she was eighteen. Eliza couldn't imagine marrying anyone at that age, not even one of her favorite cinema stars.

"Freddy and I are not engaged. We've only been courting since March."

Lady Saxton shrugged. "I married Lord Saxton six weeks after we were introduced. How unfortunate that Clara has never had a proper 'coming out.' I know it's 1913, and everyone is going on about how times have changed. But if a girl hasn't been presented at Court, she may as well resign herself to marrying a bank clerk." She smiled and suddenly looked like the girl of twenty she really was. "I should introduce Clara to several suitable gentlemen. Maybe I can get Clara married off to a man with a title. A proper one, too, not some penurious knight."

Eliza smiled back. "Clara would be thrilled." Indeed, Clara wanted nothing more out of life than to marry a rich man. The girl would marry Jack the Ripper himself if he had a title.

Like a sudden strong breeze, Lord Saxton threw himself into their midst. Unsteady on his feet, he spilled champagne out of the glasses he held in each hand. He offered them to the women. Eliza shook her head, and the Viscountess pushed the other one away. With a careless laugh, Saxton drained both glasses before tossing them to the ground. Broken glass scattered. Eliza shook a few shards from her skirts.

"It seems we have outstayed our welcome," he announced. "I've been told by three different racing officials to leave the parade ring immediately. The Gold Cup race is due to start, and they want us to clear out before the next winner is led in."

"I don't blame them," Lady Saxton said, her dark eyes flashing anger. Even though she was at least a decade younger than her husband, Eliza thought she seemed the older of the two. Certainly she was far more sober.

"I agree with Lady Saxton," Eliza said. "We should leave."

"Lady Saxton?" He shook his finger at Eliza. "Why so formal? After all, your father and I own the Donegal Dancer. That makes us family, a racing family. I insist you call me Maitland and I'll call you Eliza."

"Maitland, really," his wife said in a tone that would freeze water.

He ignored her. "And you ought to call her Tansy. That's her nickname, you know. All the upper crust have nicknames. Don't know why, maybe to prove we are the upper crust. Anyway, she's Tansy, so that's what you call her." He looked at Eliza. "Go on."

"I wouldn't be comfortable calling her that," she said.

His expression grew hard. "But I insist. You're as good as she is, Eliza, even though Tansy thinks she's better than anyone here. Better than me for certain."

"You're making a spectacle of yourself," his wife said under her breath. "Again."

"This is how I act. I've always acted this way. You and your family didn't mind my behavior when they trotted you in front of me two years ago."

Eliza looked around for Higgins to rescue her from this marital spat. But he was busy writing in his notebook as he eavesdropped on some racing fans.

"Why don't you escort your wife back to the box?" Eliza suggested. "Maybe one of your footmen can bring a spot of tea for everyone. I'm sure Lady Saxton—"

"No, no, no. Her name is Tansy." He held up a warning finger.

"It's quite all right, Miss Doolittle. You may call me Tansy." She glared at him with a tight smile. "*Lady* Tansy."

Eliza tugged at her gloves. "Glad that's been settled. Now I think I'll just—"

"What is *she* doing here?" Lady Tansy pushed her husband aside with her parasol.

A beautiful blond woman sauntered through the crowd in their direction. Her apple green dress sparkled in the sunlight, drawing numerous stares.

"How dare she show her face here!" Lady Tansy said. "I told you I will not allow her anywhere near me!"

"Keep your voice down." He grabbed her arm. "She'll hear you."

"I hope she does hear me. That trollop, that wanton baggage you throw money at. If you must make a fool of yourself, I'd rather you choose a woman less garish and slow-witted."

"Enough," he said between clenched teeth.

Lady Tansy shook free from his grip. "As though half of London doesn't know about the pair of you. Now she further humiliates me by wearing the colors of your racing silks!"

The young woman drew near. Eliza now saw that her dress glittered with tiny green sequins, while her lacy bodice was dyed pale lilac. To complete the look, she sported a purple silk turban—something normally reserved for evening—but it looked sweet atop her honey blond curls.

"She has a right to wear them," Lord Saxton muttered. "They're her racing colors, too."

"Don't treat me like a fool!" His wife shouted so loud, everyone within ten feet turned in her direction. "I am well aware of how she seduced you into becoming a syndicate member. As she has seduced you in so much else. But I will not have it rubbed in my face!"

"I can't stop her from wearing the colors. She paid for the privilege. And please remember that Turnbull was the fellow who brought her into the syndicate, not me."

This enraged Lady Tansy even more. "You are both unspeakable cads."

Saxton managed a drunken smile. "All is fair in love, war, and horse racing."

Lady Tansy slapped him so hard across the face, his hat flew off. While everyone gasped, she stormed into the crowd.

As Eliza stood speechless, Higgins appeared beside her. "What the devil is going on?"

"I don't know exactly."

Lord Saxton picked up his top hat and waved it at the onlookers. "Nothing to worry about. My wife had too much champagne."

Stony silence greeted his words.

Instead of going after his wife, Lord Saxton bowed to the young woman in the turban.

"Why is Diana Price wearing the horse's racing colors?" Higgins asked in a low voice.

Eliza realized he was right. The woman in the turban was Diana Price, a popular musical hall singer and former Gaiety Girl. "She owns a share in the Donegal Dancer."

"I can't keep track of who owns that horse. I'm afraid I'll wake up one morning to discover I've become an owner, too."

"I'm amazed you even know who Diana Price is," Eliza said. "I thought you only went to Oscar Wilde plays."

"Proves how little you know me. I never miss a Gilbert and Sullivan operetta. Miss Price sang Casilda in a production of *The Gondoliers* a year ago. Decent soprano voice, albeit a little ragged in the higher registers."

Saxton took Diana by the arm, his head bent close to hers.

Eliza frowned. "Even a drunk seaman at the Speckled Pig wouldn't flaunt his fancy lady in front of his wife. The Colonel was right about Lord Saxton. He is a boor. I wonder why Miss Price bothers with him. He has no class at all."

"She doesn't have much class either. The fellow standing off to the side is her husband." He gestured at a somber young man in a top hat.

Eliza gave Higgins a playful shove. "How in the world do you know all this gossip? I'm beginning to think you're writing down people's secrets, not their speech patterns."

"I know Gordon Longhurst because he works for a stockbroker firm in the City. In the past, I conducted business with his late father, who worked at the same firm." Higgins stared at Longhurst, who was clean-shaven and of middling height. "I always wondered how he got Miss Price to marry him. He's just an ordinary chap with a decent income."

"And an indecent wife," Eliza murmured as the wife, her lover, and her husband now headed their way.

Higgins sighed. "I told you we should have left the parade ring a long time ago."

"Diana, this is Miss Eliza Doolittle. Eliza, this is Diana Longhurst, better known by her stage name, Diana Price." Saxton leaned even closer to Diana. "Eliza's father is the chap who joined our syndicate in March."

Diana clapped her hands. "How delightful. Do you know I haven't even met your father? I've been touring the provinces this spring and missed all the racing fun. But now I can see my lovely horse again. Where is the precious animal who won us so much money?"

"He's back in the stables," Eliza said.

Diana tossed her head in a theatrical gesture. "Then I am off to the stables this instant to visit our darling colt. I wish now I had thought to bring him flowers."

Her husband leaned in. "Best to wait, my dear. Last year's champion Prince Palatine will soon be running against Tracery, the favorite."

"How large a bet did we place on him?"

Longhurst seemed puzzled. "You never said you wanted to bet on the Gold Cup."

"But we can't come to Ascot and not bet on the favorite." Diana stroked her husband's cheek. "My sweet, place a bet for me. Please."

He took a deep breath. "Very well, but I'll have to hurry. It's close to post time."

"I trust you'll manage, Gordon. You run nearly as fast as the horses. If this horse takes the Gold Cup, we'll have won twice today. First, the Dublin Dancer—"

"Donegal Dancer," Higgins corrected.

She shot Higgins a flirtatious smile. "The Donegal Dancer and whatever the other horse is called."

"Tracery," Eliza and Higgins said in unison.

"What a strange thing to call a horse." Diana tugged at her husband's lapel. "Now run off and place a bet on that animal with the dreadful name."

Without another word, Longhurst hurried away.

"Faster, sweetheart!" Diana looked at them with a smug smile. "Gordon was a runner at Cambridge. He's so fast, the man never misses a train no matter how late I make him."

"The Professor and I should go," Eliza said. "By the way, this is—"

"Will you take me to see my horse, Maitland?" Diana smiled at Lord Saxton, who had just thrown back another glass of champagne. "I am certain there is a great deal you can teach me about horses." She pressed closer to him. "And stables."

"Diana? What in the world are you doing here?" Jonathon Turnbull marched over to join them.

An intense man, his dark goatee and even darker eyes lent him a devilish appearance. Unlike the affable Lord Saxton, Turnbull treated everyone with indifference or contempt. When they were introduced earlier this morning, Eliza couldn't leave his presence fast enough.

"I thought you were not coming to the race today, Diana," Turnbull said.

She gave a careless shrug. "I changed my mind. Besides, I wanted to see my horse run. Or should I say *our* horse. After all, you were the one who convinced me to join the syndicate."

"Diana has every right to be at Ascot," Saxton said. "Now clear off and leave us alone."

Turnbull looked at Saxton with a vicious expression. "Move away from her or I'll make you regret it. Besides, you're so drunk, you're barely able to stand."

"Even drunk, I could knock you into the dirt." He sneered, although he proved the truth of Turnbull's accusation by nearly falling over. "And Diana likes to keep me close."

Turnbull brushed her aside and stood toe-to-toe with Saxton. "I wonder a drunken sod like you even dare speak to her, let alone touch her."

"I do a damn sight more than just touch her."

"This is not the place for such an absurd conversation," Higgins said sternly. "All of you have spouses attending the race. They don't deserve to be humiliated like this."

Eliza caught a movement out of the corner of her eye. A brownhaired woman in a lavender walking suit watched them. Eliza recognized her as Turnbull's wife, Rachel. Although Eliza had met her earlier in Lord Saxton's viewing box, the woman barely spoke a word.

Diana giggled. "How exciting. Two gentlemen want to fight for my honor."

Eliza felt a wave of pity for Mrs. Turnbull. "I wouldn't think you had any honor left to fight for, Miss Price," she said in a loud voice.

Higgins made a choking sound.

Diana's silly smile vanished. "How dreary you all are, spoiling my lovely day at the races. If the boys wish to behave like pugilists, I will go off to the stables and see my horse."

When she passed Eliza, her blue eyes seemed as unfocused as Saxton's. The singer was as drunk as he was.

"I wouldn't go after her, Turnbull," Saxton said. "Not with your wife watching."

Turnbull looked over his shoulder in time to see her slip into the crowd. "Rachel! Rachel, come back here!" He grabbed Saxton by the lapels of his morning coat. "Stay away from Diana."

Cursing under his breath, Turnbull set off in the direction of his wife.

"You both should be ashamed of yourselves," Eliza said. "And if I were your wife, Lord Saxton, I'd push you in front of one of these racehorses."

He gave her an injured look. "Eliza, is that any way to talk to me? I thought we were friends. In fact, I thought we were——" His face suddenly turned as green as his racing colors. "Excuse me, but——but I think I'm about to be ill." Without another word, Saxton ran off, cradling his stomach.

Higgins looked at Eliza. "Are we done here?" he asked in a long-suffering voice.

But they'd gone no farther than twenty feet when Eliza was waylaid by an overenthusiastic Cockney fellow by the name of Billy Grainger. A friend of the Doolittles from the East End, he near talked their ears off before Higgins was able to drag Eliza away. When they finally reached Lord Saxton's private box overlooking the racecourse, Colonel Pickering greeted them with a scowl.

"About time the pair of you arrived," he said. The viewing box was now a muddle of empty chairs and trays of discarded tea cakes. "Detective Inspector Shaw and I thought we'd have to send the police out looking for you."

Jack Shaw stood leaning against the box railing, arms crossed. "This story about the man with the gun better be good, Lizzie. I won't be happy if you've wasted my time."

She hurried to give her cousin a hug. "Jack, thank you for coming. I know you're on duty and trying to keep an eye out for suffragettes and all, but the Professor saw a man with a gun. He's so upset, he won't stop talking about it and—oh look, the Gold Cup has started!"

Jack threw his hands in the air. "I give up. How about you, Professor? Have I been summoned here to watch another race, or will someone tell me about the man with the gun?"

"Hang the race." Higgins joined the detective at the railing.

Feeling a bit guilty, Eliza divided her attention between the horses and the conversation about the gun. The Colonel stood next to them, listening. None of the Donegal Dancer's owners or their wives had returned to the box. They must still be at the parade ring.

Although she hadn't placed a bet on this race, Eliza found herself caught up in the excitement nonetheless. As the horses made the turn, she got to her feet. The roar of the crowd rose to fever pitch. Tracery was in the lead as the horses hit the straight mile headed for home.

She heard Jack ask, "But what exactly did this Harold Hewitt look like? What was his approximate age? And what was he wearing?"

"Come on, Tracery," she murmured. "Run. You're almost there. You can beat that Prince."

Suddenly a man burst from the shrubbery along the track. Eliza couldn't believe her eyes as he ran onto the racecourse. She let out a cry as the horses thundered toward him. The same tragedy that occurred at the Derby two weeks ago was going to happen again. Someone was about to be trampled!

"Look!" She pointed at the man who now stood in the middle of the course, the galloping horses almost upon him. They would never be able to stop in time.

Higgins and Shaw jumped to their feet. The man waved a flag in one hand and what looked like a gun in the other.

"Bloody hell!" Higgins shouted as the horses reached the man.

Several swerved wildly to avoid him, hitting other animals. But Tracery rode right over him. Eliza screamed as the man fell beneath the horse's hooves. Another horse kicked him as it raced past. Tracery went down immediately. His jockey somersaulted over the animal's head and crashed to the ground.

Pandemonium erupted. Many spectators hissed and booed that anyone dared run in front of the horses again. Once the other racehorses galloped past, dozens of people dashed onto the field. The man and the jockey lay motionless. Tracery, now riderless, got back on his feet and continued running down the track.

After a moment of stunned silence, Higgins said, "If you want to know what Harold Hewitt looked like, he's now lying dead on the racecourse."

The trampling incident dampened everyone's high spirits. The owners had spent the past hour restless and agitated after they finally returned to Lord Saxton's box. They assumed the man had run out as yet another political gesture. If that was true, Higgins thought that being trampled by racehorses seemed a ridiculous way to champion women's suffrage.

As Senior Steward, Sir Walter came to inform them that things weren't as tragic as feared. Tracery's jockey Albert Whalley had recovered and was now walking about the paddock. There was still no word concerning Harold Hewitt, who had been taken away by ambulance. News of his death would probably follow. But none of the horses had been hurt. And Prince Palatine snagged a Gold Cup victory once again in a bittersweet win. Tracery had been a good twenty lengths ahead of the Prince when Hewitt threw himself in the horse's path.

Eliza repinned her hat. "I'm ready to call it a day."

Her father had other ideas, though. Alfred Doolittle pushed himself up from his chair, his top hat wildly askew. "Hard to believe some barking mad loon ran in front of the horses. And if he had done that to our Donegal Dancer, I'd have run over there and trampled on him meself. Then kicked him in the arse for good measure."

"Dad." Eliza sent him a warning look.

"Anyway, why turn this wonderful day into a time of weeping and wailing? Our glorious colt won at Ascot! The devil take these fools who want to get trampled. Let's pay one last visit to the Dancer in the stables so we can end the day on a high note."

"You tell 'im, Alfie!" Rose thumped him on the back.

The Duchess of Carbrey also rose to her feet. As the owner with the most exalted title, she commanded their attention with barely a word. Women who owned racehorses were frowned upon. But such was her standing that the Jockey Club turned a blind eye to the stable of horses the Duchess ran under the alias "Mr. Stirling." Higgins admired her sheer tenacity and disregard of convention. And the widowed duchess had livened up more than one afternoon tea at his mother's flat in Chelsea.

Just now, the older woman silenced all conversation with a single look. "Alfred is right. We must not allow poor misguided fools like Emily Davison and this Mr. Hewitt to ruin our great racing traditions for their own political ends. I myself am in favor of women having the vote. Certainly I have far more sense than most men taking up space in Parliament. But throwing oneself in front of a charging horse is stupidity of the highest order. Therefore, we shall do as Alfred suggests and go to the stables to cheer our champion."

Everyone rose and filed out of the viewing box. Higgins started to follow.

Eliza hung back with Pickering. "We want to go home, Professor. And your mother is still in the Royal Enclosure. I'm sure she's ready to head back to London."

"The racecourse and stables are crawling with police right now." Higgins felt guilty that he hadn't found a policeman in time. They might have been able to stop Hewitt. "I need to see if Jack's learned anything about this mad fellow."

"All right," Eliza said as Pickering gave an exasperated sigh. "But let's do this quick."

Within minutes of their leaving the viewing box, Diana Price's husband hurried over to them. "Have any of you seen my wife?" Gordon Longhurst sounded frantic. "When I came back from placing the bet, she was gone. And I haven't seen her anywhere. It's not like her to miss a race, especially one she's wagered on."

Higgins hoped she wasn't engaged in a tryst with yet another man. "She said she wanted to visit the Donegal Dancer in the stables."

Longhurst shook his head. "I've been to the stables. The police won't let me through."

Eliza took his arm. "My cousin is a Scotland Yard detective inspector. He'll let us pass."

Higgins followed behind, grinning. If only he had a pound note for every time Eliza boasted about her cousin.

True to her word, Eliza got them into the stables. Jack Shaw was deep in conversation with racing officials and waved to his men to let them through. As soon as Jack was done talking, Higgins would ask him a few questions about Hewitt.

Up ahead, Eliza, Longhurst, and Pickering entered a stall where a rollicking chorus rang out. "Three cheers to the Donegal Dancer!"

Higgins glanced into the nearby stalls. Some held curious or nervous horses; others were filled only with hay and feed buckets.

Longhurst emerged once again. His wife was not with him.

"Did you find her?" Higgins asked.

"No, and the jockey says no woman's been near the horse's stall all day." He sighed. "I can't imagine where she could be. Could you help me look for her?"

As Longhurst walked along the stalls, Higgins searched in the opposite direction. He hoped he would be the first to find her—and whatever man she was probably with. But each stall revealed only another horse, a suspicious trainer, or a tired groom. Not until he reached the last stall did Higgins stop short. A purple turban lay on the pile of straw inside.

"Miss Price?" Higgins asked. "Are you in there?" When there was no answer, Higgins swung open the half-gate and entered the stall. What he saw made him reel back in horror.

Diana Price lay crumpled on the straw, her body covered in blood. Beside her was a pitchfork, its prongs streaked with red.

"Mr. Longhurst, come here!" Higgins shouted, amazed he was able to get the words out. He steadied himself by clutching the gate.

"Have you found her?" He heard Longhurst running toward the stall. "What in the world is she doing down here? I swear, sometimes I could kill that woman."

After a moment's hesitation, Higgins crouched down and felt the woman's pulse. Clearly someone else wanted to kill her, too.

THREE

As if sensing the horror of what had happened, horses whinnied from every corner of the stables. Higgins pulled Eliza out of the way when two men carried the blanketed corpse past them. Even after they left, however, the metallic scent of blood lingered.

After Gordon Longhurst spotted his wife's dead body, his frantic cries brought the owners of the Donegal Dancer running. Grooms, jockeys, managers, and racing officials soon followed. While the men shouted for the police, Rachel Turnbull fainted at the sight of Diana's blood-soaked gown. As soon as Scotland Yard arrived, the owners were mercifully hustled into an adjacent stall and instructed to stay there until a policeman told them otherwise.

Since Higgins and Eliza could not contain their curiosity, they lingered in the corridor. But they learned little. Jack Shaw hadn't left the stall where Diana was found, and Detective Jeremy stood in front of the gate. His grim expression warned them away.

A chilling moan rose once again from the stall where the owners waited. "Diana! Oh, God, Diana!" It was Gordon Longhurst. "Who did this to you? Diana!"

Higgins frowned. How uncivilized for the poor man to be kept here like this. Eliza must have thought so as well; she stepped up to Detective Jeremy and peered over his shoulder.

"Move aside, miss," Jeremy said.

Eliza ignored him. "Jack, someone must see about Mr. Longhurst. The fellow has lost his wife. He needs to see a doctor and perhaps a minister, too. He's in a bad way."

Higgins was about to add his sentiments when Jack emerged from the stall. "You're right, Lizzie," he said, brushing straw from his trouser legs. "I should have sent him elsewhere. I got caught up examining the crime scene."

Jack gestured to another policeman a few feet away. "Detective Boyd, you and Detective Toller take Mr. Longhurst to the infirmary. Have a doctor tend to him, but keep him there until I am able to question him."

Eliza began to protest, but he held up his hand. "Sorry, Lizzie. Until I have the chance to talk to everyone involved, no one can leave."

A moment later, the two detectives half carried Gordon Longhurst out of the stall. Higgins winced. The man looked dreadful. What a damned awful day.

Once the police had taken Longhurst, Higgins turned to Jack. "Who would do such a vile thing? Killing someone with a pitchfork is unspeakable."

"There's also a sizable lump on the back of her head, along with a bruise on her cheek," Jack said. "I suspect someone struck her first, causing her to fall. The killer must have used the pitchfork to finish her off."

Eliza shuddered. "Are there any fingerprints on the pitchfork?"

"It looks as if someone wiped it clean. We'll take it to the lab for analysis."

Guilt hung heavy on Higgins's mind. If only he'd found a policeman sooner and informed them about Hewitt and the gun. They might have prevented him from running onto the racetrack, which put the horses and jockeys at serious risk. Far worse was the likelihood that Hewitt killed Diana. After all, what other suspicious person was lurking about Ascot with violent intentions? If Hewitt was the murderer, Higgins would blame himself until the day he died.

"I didn't find evidence to indicate who was with Miss Price in that stall," Jack said.

"But who would kill her?" Eliza asked. "And why?"

"As far as we know, the only dangerous man at Ascot was Hewitt," Higgins said.

"Maybe Miss Price learned about Hewitt's plan to run out on the track and tried to stop him," Jack said. "Killing her with a pitchfork seems a barbaric response."

"How much longer are you going to keep the owners in there?" Higgins jerked his head toward the stall, where a babble of irritated voices grew louder by the minute. He was glad Pickering had taken his mother home. After what happened last month, she didn't need to be involved in yet another murder investigation.

"Thank you for reminding me." Jack stepped over to the half-gate of the stall. "Ladies and gentlemen, I need everyone to follow me. My men have found a meeting room in the other building which should comfortably accommodate us."

Another hue and cry rose up.

"Protest all you like," he said sternly, "but none of the Donegal Dancer owners may leave until after I have taken a statement."

"This is unconscionable." Lady Saxton's affronted voice was un-mistakable. "Who do you think you are to treat us in this beastly manner?"

"I am in charge of investigating this murder. If you don't wish to speak to me here, my men will be happy to haul you off to Scotland Yard."

Everyone filed out of the stall. Lady Saxton threw Jack a poisonous look. Alfred Doolittle was the last one out, and he seemed a bit sheepish. "Jackie, I don't think my Rose is in any fit condition to be questioned right now."

Higgins peered inside the stall. A snoring Rose sat sprawled against the far wall, the grapes on her hat tilted far over her face. Rose hiccupped but remained asleep.

"A bit too much champagne, y'see." Doolittle shrugged.

"Blooming idiot," Eliza muttered before she stalked off.

Jack turned to Detective Jeremy. "Keep anyone but the police from going into the stall." He pointed at Rose. "And as soon as that woman wakes up, bring her to me. But try to get some tea or coffee in her first."

Relieved to be out of the stables, Higgins enjoyed the brief seconds of walking to the other building. Too soon, he found himself seated at a square oak table in what was apparently a conference room for racing officials and managers. The air was redolent with the smell of leather, pipe smoke, and tobacco, which he found comforting.

After everyone was seated in the spindle-back chairs, Jack shut the door behind him. He walked over to the head of the table and smoothed back his hair. It did little good. Jack had a mop of black unruly hair that only a zealous barber could tame. Higgins also noticed that Jack's left eye was clamped down in a squint, which the detective only did when he was troubled.

"I have been told that Miss Price was last seen by some of you in the parade ring," Jack began. "These individuals are the Turnbulls, Lord and Lady Saxton, Miss Doolittle, and Professor Higgins. After her husband went off to place a bet, Miss Price decided to visit the stables on her own. The Gold Cup race began about twenty minutes later. I need to know exactly where each of you was during that time period, as well as during the race. Who would like to go first?"

Everyone looked down at the table or stared back without expression at Jack.

Eliza cleared her throat. "The Professor and I were making our way back to Lord Saxton's private box. It took longer than planned because we ran into Billy Grainger. You remember Billy. He's a bookmaker now, but in the old neighborhood, he was a yob."

Higgins was afraid to ask what a "yob" was.

Alfred Doolittle chuckled. "Billy Boy has straightened himself out. Makes his money now without having to steal it. And with a gift of gab to set your ears bleeding."

"I concur," Higgins said. "He was an alarmingly voluble gentleman."

"Anyway, he near talked our heads off so we couldn't get to the box until right before the race started. And you were there when we arrived, so we watched the Gold Cup with you."

Jack nodded. "That you did. As for Mr. Doolittle, we've confirmed that until the Gold Cup began, several racing officials were in his company. Apparently they were trying to keep him away from the parade ring." He paused. "And the champagne."

Alfred winked at Higgins, who couldn't help but grin back at him.

"And during the Gold Cup, Mr. Doolittle and his wife watched the race while these same officials stood behind them." Jack looked at the others. "As for the rest of you . . ."

The Duchess of Carbrey shook her head at her fellow syndicate members. "I shall go next, since everyone else seems to have lost their tongue."

Higgins noticed Jonathon Turnbull's face growing red in anger. But not even Turnbull dared cross the Duchess. It wasn't only her wealth that gave Turnbull pause. Minerva Richardson Cox boasted a self-confidence that could lay waste to his customary arrogance. And as her two late husbands—and several discreet lovers—could attest, she was also a handsome woman. Although she was past sixty, her ash brown hair bore only a few strands of gray. Minerva was an apt name for her. He could easily see her as the Roman goddess of wisdom she was named after. All she needed was a sacred owl sitting atop her shoulder.

"Before the Gold Cup began, I went to the paddock to confer with my trainer." The Duchess adjusted the enormous plumed hat tilted above her coiffure. "One of my horses is set to run in the last race today. My trainer and I also watched the Gold Cup from the paddock."

Jack scribbled that down along with the name of the trainer. He then turned to an older gentleman sporting old-fashioned Dundreary sideburns and a drooping white mustache. His pinstripe trousers, gray morning coat, and brushed top hat were nearly an exact copy of Pickering's formal wear at Ascot. "And you, sir? I have been told that you are Senior Steward of the Jockey Club."

"Yes, I am Sir Walter Fairweather." The older man straightened in his chair. "Prior to the Gold Cup, I oversaw the weighing-in procedure at the stable. And during the race, I was investigating a complaint on the track."

Higgins detected a hint of East Anglian dialect in Fairweather's cultured speech. Although Higgins had first met the distinguished gentleman this morning, Fairweather was an old acquaintance of Colonel Pickering. A former professor at the University of Edinburgh, Fairweather had retired early to conduct botanical research at his manor house in Essex; that research led to a knighthood six years ago.

Jack waited for someone else to speak. "Lord Saxton," he said finally. "Where were you and your wife leading up to the Gold Cup?"

Higgins took his first good look at Saxton since discovering Diana's body. By Jupiter, the man looked worse than Longhurst. His pallor was chalk white, and his eyes red and swollen.

"I was ill," Saxton said in a hoarse voice.

"He threw up," Turnbull sneered. "We all saw how much he had been drinking. But that's what Saxton does best. He drinks. The epitome of being drunk as a lord."

Higgins prepared himself for an ugly scene between the two men.

Lady Saxton didn't bat an eyelash, however. If anything, she looked amused. Saxton surprised Higgins by nodding his head.

"It's true. I drank too much champagne." He took a ragged breath. "If I hadn't—if I'd gone with her as she asked—Diana would be alive. Diana would be alive!" A sob escaped him, and he buried his face in his hands.

Lady Saxton seemed mortified. "Maitland, take hold of yourself. You shame us all with this maudlin display."

Saxton pushed back his chair. "I'm sorry. I'm sorry—I'm going to be ill again." He rushed from the conference room, followed by one of the detectives.

Jack crossed his arms. "And where were you, Lady Saxton? Tending to your sick husband?"

She shot him a scornful look. "Anyone who was at the parade ring can attest I was in no mood to do any such thing."

"Why was that?"

"Inspector, this has already been a long, distasteful day. If you persist feigning ignorance of Maitland's very public affair with Diana Price, it shall grow far more tedious."

Eliza leaned closer to her cousin. "It's true, Jack," she said in a stage whisper. "When Miss Price arrived, they had a proper row."

"So where were you, Lady Saxton?" he asked.

"Once the unfortunate Miss Price made her entrance, I left. I was in a bad temper, as you can imagine, and went off into the crowd. I didn't even watch the Gold Cup." She sniffed. "Not that I cared a whit about it anyway."

"Then you had a reason to want Miss Price dead?"

"A banal observation."

Jack bristled. "You had a motive and no alibi during the time of the murder. How is that for a banal observation?"

Lady Saxton narrowed her eyes. "It may be banal, but it's also incorrect." She sat back with a weary air. "My husband has been indiscreet with a number of women since I married him. If I *was* the jealous murderess you imagine, I would have done away with five ladies by now. Although none deserves to be called a lady."

Higgins fought back a grin. The woman had brass enough to stare down the Kaiser.

Jack seemed a bit flustered by Lady Saxton. "Regardless, madam, you had no reason to wish the victim well."

"I am not the only woman in this room humiliated by her husband's liaison with Miss Price." She looked pointedly at the Turnbulls, who sat across the table from her.

"You're a venomous bitch," Jonathon Turnbull said.

While Lady Saxton only lifted an eyebrow at his outburst, Rachel Turnbull began to cry. The Duchess rapped sharply on the table with her gloved knuckles. "I warn you, Jonathon, such language will not be tolerated here."

Jack frowned. "Mr. Turnbull, I advise you to keep yourself in check."

"In check? An innocent woman has been murdered in the most brutal fashion, and you're bothered by my language! Why aren't you trying to find the killer?"

Jack threw his notebook down on the table. "I'm doing just that, but first I must wade through a few tales of sordid behavior. And speaking of finding the killer, where did *you* go after you left the parade ring, Mr. Turnbull?"

Turnbull leaned forward. He seemed as tense and coiled as a snake eager to strike. Higgins realized the fellow was as agitated by Diana's death as Saxton and Longhurst, only he showed it through anger.

"I feel like I'm living in a damned nightmare! As if I would harm Diana. While she was being murdered, I was trying to find my wife. More fool I to think Rachel needed me more. Neither Saxton nor I would kill such a beguiling woman. We adored Diana."

Tears rolled down Rachel's cheeks. Higgins exchanged troubled glances with Eliza, who seemed as uncomfortable as he was.

Jack's left eye squinted tighter than before. "Mrs. Turnbull, I am sorry to upset you more, but I must ask where you went after leaving the parade ring."

Eliza reached over and gave her a handkerchief. Rachel took it with a grateful but watery smile. After a moment, she regained control.

"Jonathon had words with Lord Saxton when Miss Price arrived. I was too far away to hear what was being said, but the situation confirmed rumors I'd heard." Her voice was so quiet, Higgins strained to hear. "I simply could not face Jonathon at that moment. Like Lady Saxton, I began to walk blindly through the crowd. I didn't stop until the race began. When that gentleman was trampled, the crowd grew so agitated that I returned to the viewing box." She took a shaky breath. "That's all I can tell you, Detective Inspector."

Someone rapped on the door. "Come in!" Jack barked.

A constable entered the office with a jockey. It was Jimmy "Bomber" Brody, who rode the Donegal Dancer to victory. Brody snatched off his flat racing cap and held it in his long-fingered hands, along with a riding crop. He still wore the Wrexham purple and green silks.

"You wanted to speak to me, Detective Inspector?"

"Yes, I did. Before I forget, how is Tracery's jockey?"

"Bert Whalley? Shaken up a bit, sir, but all right."

"Glad to hear it. I know you were with the others when Miss Price's body was found. But you'd left by the time the police arrived."

"Sorry, Inspector, but I have another race today. I had to meet with the trainer. Otherwise I'd be as good as dead myself." He flushed. "Sorry. That was a stupid thing to say."

"Did you see anyone suspicious today in the stables? Someone who didn't belong there?"

"That I did. The fellow who ran out on the racecourse."

"What?" Higgins couldn't hide his surprise.

"I saw the man this morning as soon as the course opened. I caught him wandering about the stalls. He weren't dressed fine enough to be an owner, and he didn't look like any trainer I'd ever seen. Seemed a bit off, too. Writing in some fool book, talking to himself. Had a bad feeling about him. I told one of the grooms to toss him out."

"You're certain this was the same man who ran out onto the field?"

"No doubt, Inspector. I saw that madman when they brought him in on a stretcher. It was him, all right." Brody frowned. "I wish I'd told a racing official this morning. Because of the trouble at the Derby, they would have thrown him out of Ascot altogether." He paused. "Is he the one who killed Miss Price?"

"We don't know yet," Jack said. "Were you here when Miss Price came to the stables?"

"I never saw her. Of course, I'd never met her before, but I didn't see any ladies in here after the race." Brody shook his head in disgust. "It's not right that strangers who have no business being in the stable come here and wander about. This sort of thing wouldn't have happened last year."

"Are you referring to the horse thieves?"

"Yes. For a time, we kept a close eye on anyone coming to the stables, but we've gotten lazy. That means it's sure to happen again."

"Someone's kidnapping racehorses?" Eliza asked.

"The first horse was stolen five years ago," the Duchess said. "Then a little over three years ago, thieves took a champion mare called Red Glory right off the Sussex farm where she was stabled. Even worse, the horse carried a foal at the time. No ordinary foal, either."

"I remember," Higgins broke in. "It was in all the papers. She had been bred with some great racing champion a few months earlier."

"Maximus," Sir Walter said. "No greater champion has graced the Turf since. Any foal with the bloodline of Maximus and Red Glory would be worth a fortune."

"But they found the mare, didn't they?" Higgins said.

"A year later, wandering along a country road in Yorkshire." The Duchess looked somber. "Thank heaven Red Glory was alive and well. However, she had already given birth. And there's been no sign of that filly or colt since." She frowned. "I suspect the foal died, or was sold off for breeding purposes. Not that it will do them any good. If you can't prove the bloodlines, a horse's offspring are worth little."

"Some racehorse owners have claimed their horse was born to Red Glory," added Brody. "But like Her Ladyship says, they can't prove it."

Doolittle leaned forward in excitement. "What if that foal was our own Dancer?"

"Alfred, you know perfectly well Calypso and Lady Carlin are the sire and dam of the Donegal Dancer," the Duchess said, not bothering to conceal her exasperation.

"Whatever happened to these horse thieves?" Eliza asked.

"Never caught," Sir Walter said. "The following year, they stole another champion racehorse called Sea Wind. Such a tragedy. Because no one could pay the outrageous ransom, the horse was found dead a month later. Another attempt was made to steal a prize mare this past April down near Lincolnshire, but the grooms scared the thieves off."

"This is awful," Eliza said. "Jack, you must find these horrible people."

"The Yard is working on it, along with a few other cases. Now getting back to today's events." Jack gestured at the jockey's coat. "The Donegal Dancer's racing colors are purple and green, the same colors of the suffragette movement. Who registered them?"

"I registered the silks, Detective Inspector," Sir Walter said. "After all, I am the Wrexham Racing Syndicate's agent. But the Duchess of Carbrey chose those colors."

Jonathon Turnbull glared at the older woman. "She never asked our permission, either. Not that I would have given it. She knows how I feel about those infernal women."

"Exactly," the Duchess said with a cool smile. "I am aware of your backward attitude about women's suffrage, which Miss Price inexplicably shared."

"I wonder if Hewitt knew they were the suffragette colors," Eliza said.

"I saw a small flag in his satchel. Was it a suffragette flag?" Higgins glanced up at Jack, who nodded.

"If Miss Price was opposed to women's suffrage, and Mr. Hewitt was a champion of it . . ." Eliza looked over at Higgins.

"But how would he know she opposed the movement?" Higgins asked.

Jack turned to the jockey. "You're free to go, Mr. Brody. I believe you're scheduled to ride in the next race."

"Yes, sir. Thank you, sir. I need to change my silks."

After Brody hurried off, Jonathon Turnbull banged his fist on the table. "We've told you what we can, Inspector. Now what have you found out about this dead fool who ran in front of the horses?"

"Oh, Mr. Hewitt is still alive," Jack said. "He was only unconscious when taken to hospital. His injuries are severe but not fatal. Once Mr. Hewitt is able to speak, we intend to find out everything possible. In the meantime, I need to know why there are so many owners of the Donegal Dancer. This is a racing syndicate, I presume?"

"Indeed it is," Doolittle said. "The Wrexham Racing Syndicate."

"Why Wrexham?"

"You should know that, Jack." Doolittle wagged a finger at his nephew. "Wrexham is the Welsh town where I was born and raised."

Jack gave a rueful grin. "You're right, I should have remembered. But how did you become part of it?"

Doolittle thumbed his waistcoat. "Turnbull and I met at a boxing match this spring. Since we were such sporting men, we got to talkin' about horse racing. Sounded like a right bit of fun, owning a racehorse. And seeing how I came into money this year, Turnbull suggested I join the syndicate. Glad I am of it, too."

"Owning a racehorse is expensive," Turnbull added. "Sharing expenses through a syndicate reduces the share of the winnings, but it also reduces the risk. I formed the syndicate after Diana and the Saxtons bought a share of the horse. It was a wise business decision."

"The only wise one he's ever made," Lady Saxton said under her breath.

Turnbull ignored her. "And I was the one who initially bought the horse. I learned through an acquaintance of Ahearn Griffith's death. He ran Derryfield Farm in Kildare. The estate was selling off his whole lot of horses, and at quite reasonable prices. I sent an agent to scout his stock, and he recommended buying the colt."

"And how could I not buy a share of a horse called the Donegal

Dancer?" Doolittle turned to Eliza. "After all, your mum came from Donegal. And she loved to dance, too. Seemed like a sign, it did."

She reached over and squeezed his hand.

"The Duchess spoke of the horse's sire and dam," Higgins said. "I assume their bloodlines are impressive."

"Lady Carlin was a champion in her own right. A blood bay like the Dancer, but without the star," Sir Walter said. "And Calypso won a fair number of races himself in his day."

"How many members are in the syndicate?" Jack asked.

"Six. No, wait. Five, now that Miss Price is gone," Doolittle said.

"Jonathon was first, and he asked Miss Price. She brought in Saxton. I became an owner after watching a few of Dancer's practice runs." The Duchess gestured at Doolittle. "Alfred joined us in March. The name was the Turnbull/Price Syndicate, but that wouldn't suffice once more of us joined. So we came up with Wrexham."

"I was the last one to become a member," Sir Walter added.

The Duchess smiled at him. "Since Sir Walter is Senior Steward of the Jockey Club, we asked him to act as our agent. He handles all the syndicate's legal and financial transactions."

"You own a string of successful horses already, Your Ladyship," Jack said. "Why join a syndicate?"

"The colt is as fine a horse as I've seen," she said. "Fine enough that I tried to buy him outright, but the others refused. I had no choice but to join."

Jack wrote in his notebook before looking up. "How are the prize winnings doled out to syndicate members?"

"We have a meeting either once a month or two weeks after a race," Sir Walter said. "After all the costs have been totaled, each member receives his or her share of the winnings. Our next meeting takes place at the Henley Royal Regatta."

"What do you mean by costs?" Jack asked.

"Trainer and jockey fees, transporting the horse to and from races, veterinarian and stabling costs, including a farrier, feed, and insurance." Sir Walter held up his forefinger. "Plus track fees and the Jockey Club fees, of course. We also pay a percentage of the prize winnings to both the trainer and the jockey."

"I'm surprised there's any money left after all that," Eliza said.

The Duchess shrugged. "It's expensive owning a racehorse. Not an enterprise to be taken on alone, unless you have the capital to sustain it."

Sir Walter nodded. "Indeed, yes. I've known more than one man who has been ruined by the Turf. Although we have taken steps to see that it shouldn't happen with our syndicate."

"How so?"

"If a member does not pay his or her share of the monthly bills for the upkeep of the Donegal Dancer within ten weeks, the member's share in the horse is forfeit," Sir Walter replied. "That share is then sold to a new owner. This prevents a member from getting too mired in debt."

Turnbull pushed himself away from the table, his chair legs screeching on the wood floor. "Are we done here?"

At that moment, a stable hand barged into the room. "Excuse me, but Her Ladyship asked for news of the other races."

Jack stuffed the notebook into his suit pocket. "Go ahead."

No one seemed to react after hearing about the winner of the Coventry Stakes, Tetrarch, and the two horses who came in second and third. Brody's mount didn't even place. Considering what had happened, Higgins wasn't surprised. It was a marvel enough spectators still remained at the racetrack to care. Then again, few people outside this room knew about the murder in the stable.

The Duchess of Carbrey rose, prompting the men to scramble to their feet as well. "Is there anything further you require of us, Inspector?"

"Not at this time, Your Ladyship. I do appreciate everyone's cooperation in what has been a difficult afternoon."

"More banal observations," Lady Saxton murmured, and swept out of the room.

"I hope she remembers that her husband is still here," Higgins said.

Jack shot him a weary look. Sir Walter gave his arm to the Duchess, and the pair left.

"Let's go, Rachel," Turnbull ordered. His wife slowly got to her feet. When they walked past the detective, Turnbull deliberately bumped into him.

Higgins saw Jack fight to restrain himself from pushing back.

"Well, I'd best see if Rose has recovered," Doolittle said. "I keep telling her to stick to gin. Champagne doesn't agree with her."

Once he left, Eliza turned to Higgins. "Maybe if she didn't drink it by the bucketful."

"So what do you think?" Higgins asked Jack.

"I don't know who would be worse to meet in a dark alley: Jonathon Turnbull or Lady Saxton."

Eliza smoothed her wrinkled dress. "You can't expect her to be upset because her husband's mistress got killed."

"Why not?" Jack said. "Rachel Turnbull certainly seemed upset."

"Mrs. Turnbull seems a tad more sensitive than Lady Saxton."

"Professor Moriarty would be more sensitive than that young woman."

"I doubt the owners or their wives had anything to do with the murder." Higgins frowned. "I think Hewitt is the logical choice."

"You may be right, but we've only begun to sift through the

evidence and question suspects. We did retrieve Hewitt's diary. The answers may be somewhere in that book."

"What type of revolver was he waving around?"

"A Webley .38 caliber." Jack pulled out a chair and sat. "Fully loaded, too."

Eliza seemed puzzled. "If Hewitt did kill Diana, why not shoot her?"

"A gunshot would attract attention," Jack said. "Even a madman might think twice before doing that. But the murder does appear premeditated. The victim was killed in a stall used as a spare tack room, which explains the pitchfork. No one would leave such a thing in a stall where a horse was stabled, for fear the animal might injure himself. If Longhurst hadn't been looking for his wife, it might have been hours before her body was found."

Higgins felt crushed again by guilt. Who else but a madman would murder Diana in the stables right in the middle of Royal Ascot? "I blame myself for this. I should have tracked down a policeman the moment I saw that gun in his bag."

"Even if you'd told me earlier, I doubt we'd have found Hewitt in this crowd."

Higgins appreciated his kindness, but he didn't believe him.

"Can we change the subject for a moment? I've had enough of murder for one day," Eliza said. Both men looked at her in surprise. "I hope you and Sybil still plan to brunch with us on Saturday. Mrs. Pearce will be most upset if you cancel again. She's cooking all your favorite foods. Besides, I've been waiting to meet your fiancée for weeks."

"I'll try, Lizzie, but I'm in the middle of this new case. I barely sleep as it is. And once Miss Price's murder hits the papers, I won't have time to eat either."

"You can spare an hour or two. I don't see how you dare marry that poor girl if you're going to leave her alone most of the time. You must find a way to mix murder and marriage."

Higgins and Jack laughed.

"I've put away a few men who did just that, my girl," Jack said.

She ruffled his hair. "You'll come, won't you?"

"I'll be there, and with the lovely Sybil, too."

Eliza suddenly shivered.

"What's wrong?" Higgins asked.

"What sort of person runs a defenseless woman through with a pitchfork?" She looked at her cousin. "If Hewitt isn't guilty, you have to catch whoever did it, Jack. A monster like that is sure to kill again."

FOUR

Damnation, man! The correct pronunciation is ee-lab-or-ate, not a-lab-rat!"

"I'm sorry, Professor."

"Start again from the beginning, Mr. Wallace."

Higgins scowled at his pupil, who was the recent heir to an uncle's photographic supply company. Formerly a minor clerk, James Wallace needed to improve his speech and manners for his new elevated station in life. The young man once again pushed his wire-rimmed glasses farther up his nose. An annoying habit, Higgins thought. And the fellow was most unremarkable. Indeed, he was so average in height, features, and temperament, Wallace would make a fine plainclothes policeman. No one would notice him.

He oughtn't complain about teaching Wallace. But poor Eliza needed the patience of a saint as she struggled to correct his wife's screeching tones. Higgins closed his eyes and counted to twenty, trying to blot out the sound of the woman's voice coming from the next room.

"'ow many 'airs would a 'airbrush brush if a 'airbrush could brush 'ares." Mrs. Wallace looked confused. "It don't make sense to me."

"I shall light this candle for you to practice the aitch sound at the back of your throat, blowing air," Eliza said. "Ha. Ha, ha, ha. There, do you hear it?"

"Aye, miss, I does!"

Higgins gripped a tuning fork until his knuckles whitened. The ambitious Ivy Wallace had married James a month after he'd come into his inheritance. While her speech was dreadful, she was clearly no fool. Before she met her husband, Ivy spent long hours working in a bottling factory. Higgins did admire the desire to improve herself; however, her atrocious accent made his eyes cross.

He rubbed his forehead with a heavy sigh. Higgins had slept badly last night, unable to banish the sight of Harold Hewitt being trampled. Far worse was finding Diana's lifeless body in that horse stall, along with the bloodstained pitchfork.

A quick glance at the mantel clock told Higgins the lesson was mercifully over. With a visible sigh of relief, he shooed Wallace into the foyer. Pickering arrived at that moment and brought in a hot breeze from the street. He set his hat on the rack by the door. When the young man caught sight of the Colonel, he automatically reached up to tug his forelock.

"No, no, no," Higgins told Wallace. "You may not be his equal yet, but remember you own a business now. Act like it. And practice addressing your peers twice daily. Enunciate properly, or I shan't bother to waste another minute teaching you anything."

"Thanks, Professor. My missus will help. She's a right corker."

Higgins rolled his eyes upward. Thankfully, Eliza had also finished her lesson with Ivy Wallace. After the young couple left, Pickering followed Higgins into the laboratory, a newspaper tucked under one arm.

Eliza trailed after them and plopped down on the sofa. "I'm so happy we're done until Monday."

"I say, Henry, you two usually take Saturday morning off," Pickering said.

"We made an exception. Mr. and Mrs. Wallace have *much* to learn."

When the mantel clock chimed eleven, Eliza jumped to her feet. "Blimey, I have to change my dress. Jack and his fiancée will be here any minute for brunch."

"What the devil is wrong with what you have on?"

"It's a uniform in a way, much like your raggedy sweater." At the sound of a loud knock on the front door, Eliza rushed out of the room. "Oh no, they're here already. Do try and be sociable for a change, Professor. Promise me, please." She took the stairs two at a time.

Higgins rocked back and forth on his heels while he tapped the ashes from his pipe.

"Pick, would you say my sweater is raggedy?"

"Hardly, old chap."

"It's comfortable. New enough, too."

Higgins packed fresh tobacco into his pipe, wondering why women always complained about something. Even his exemplary mother did so on occasion. The rattling of a hansom cab and a motorcar's piercing horn on Wimpole Street, plus the housekeeper's firm voice, could be heard from the laboratory.

"Do come in, Inspector Shaw," Mrs. Pearce said. "I shall ring for Miss Doolittle right away. Mr. Higgins and Colonel Pickering are in the drawing room."

Higgins set his pipe on the mantel. A young woman entered the room ahead of Eliza's cousin. Jack quickly set about making introductions to his fiancée. Higgins noted that Sybil Chase wasn't beautiful, but her gray blue eyes, arched brows, and classic English roses-and-cream complexion gave her a striking appeal. And Higgins rather approved of her bow-shaped mouth, which now curved in a charming smile.

Jack pumped the Colonel's hand as his gaze swept over the laboratory's stack of wax cylinders, gramophone, and bookshelves. Jack had been here so often, the room and its inhabitants were a familiar sight. Mrs. Pearce waited patiently until he remembered to hand over his trilby hat.

"Thank you for inviting us, Professor," Sybil said.

"Oh, I didn't invite you. Eliza did. Mrs. Pearce, will you tell the rude girl that her guests are here?"

"She's upstairs, sir. I'm certain she will be down any minute."

The Colonel pulled out a chair for Sybil and then sat on the sofa's far end. Jack took the armchair closest to his fiancée.

"I'm sorry we didn't see you at Ascot, Miss Chase." Higgins didn't care at all whether she'd been to the racing event. He only wanted to hear more of her speech patterns to ascertain where she was born.

"I didn't feel it was proper to attend the race so soon after Miss Davison's funeral," she said. "But Jack told me what happened during the Gold Cup. And of course, the newspapers speak of little else but Mr. Hewitt and poor Diana Price. My friends in the suffrage movement were quite shocked someone ran onto the racetrack again."

"The police feared there might be a copycat," Jack said. "But we expected it to be a woman, not a man. We haven't even determined if Harold Hewitt is a member of any suffrage group."

"No one in the Women's Freedom League ever heard of him," Sybil said, "but I've yet to ask anyone in the WSPU."

From that brief exchange, Higgins deduced Sybil had been raised in Kingston-upon-Thames in southwest London. She might have attended some college, due to her precise enunciation, but resided now in South Kensington. Queen's Gate, perhaps near the new petrol station built for the incoming flux of motorcars. And he noticed that she wore her badge of loyalty to the suffrage movement with a green sash tied around her waist and lilac flowers adorning her straw hat.

Eliza entered the laboratory at that moment and rushed to greet their visitors. Higgins thought the two young women could be sisters. Both boasted dark, upswept hair, impertinent profiles, and an obvious fondness for white lace dresses.

"I'm so happy to meet you, Sybil. Jack brags about you all the time," Eliza gushed. "Shall we go in to brunch? Mrs. Pearce said she's ready to serve."

"Allow me, Miss Chase." Pickering held out his arm to Sybil. She accepted with a delighted smile.

Jack escorted Eliza, leaving Higgins to trail after them like a spare tire in the boot. He frowned. Maybe he'd pinpointed the wrong end of Queen's Gate. Perhaps Miss Chase hailed from a flat south of Cromwell Road.

Once they were seated around the table, Eliza poured tea while the maids brought in full platters of bacon, eggs, and kippers.

Clearly not shy, Sybil began the conversation by regaling them with the tale of how she and Jack met at the police station when she was twenty-three. "There I was, dripping wet with a group of other Women's Freedom League members. It rained that hot August day. And the police took pleasure in dragging us through every puddle on the way to Scotland Yard. Our hems were a muddy mess. But all we did was block Prime Minister Asquith from getting into 10 Downing Street. If I'd known he was going to have us arrested, I would have hit him over the head with my picket sign." She shrugged. "In for a penny, in for a pound."

Jack laughed with the others. "That would have gotten you in worse trouble. The police figured you'd chain yourselves together if they didn't get you away from there."

"Oh, what a good idea. I'll have to suggest a chain of protesters to Mrs. Garrud. Writing articles is getting deadly dull for us both."

"Do you write for the newspaper of the Women's Social and Political Union?" Eliza asked. "I've read several articles about the cause. They're not dull in the least."

Sybil smiled. "Thank you. *The Vote* is put out by the WFL, and they're against the violence condoned by the Pankhursts. I've also written articles for *Votes for Women*. Sadly, most days fighting for the cause is like watching a slow trickle of water."

"Ah, but water brings life to the least expected places." Pickering shook out his linen napkin. "How did you get involved in the organization so young?"

While Sybil explained how she'd joined the WFL, Higgins tucked into a second helping of grilled tomatoes and fried mushrooms. Eliza split open a Bath bun and slathered on orange marmalade.

"I met Sylvia Pankhurst during a class at the Royal College of Art. She then introduced me to her sister Christabel and the WSPU group."

"Were you ever force-fed in prison?" Eliza asked. "I've read about that."

"No, Jack paid my fine to release me. He explained in great detail what force-feeding was like, and I lost my nerve." She smiled at him in gratitude. "Writing articles is mischief enough. Also he made me promise not to get arrested again."

"I had to promise him not to chase down murderers after what happened at the Drury Lane." Eliza gave her cousin a stern look. "Although he forgets that the murderer was chasing me."

"I'm only trying to keep both of you out of trouble," Jack protested. "Even if I'm having little success at it."

"Speaking of murder, is there anything new about the Diana Price investigation?" Higgins asked the detective.

"We discovered Hewitt's revolver was never fired. Our expert at the Yard is checking the pitchfork for fingerprints."

"Such a gruesome end." Pickering sipped from his teacup.

"According to the coroner, Miss Price was struck on the right cheek, which left a visible bruise. We believe she fell back and hit her head against the stable wall. That was a minor injury, however. Only a slight concussion. The killer used the pitchfork to make certain she was dead."

Eliza looked horrified. "Did you learn anything about Harold Hewitt?"

Jack nodded. "He's the eldest son of the late Charles Archibald Hewitt, who was a deputy lieutenant of Herefordshire and a justice of the peace. His father died two years ago. The family has an estate at Hope End, although Hewitt's lived in both Canada and Switzerland. And he's a forty-year-old bachelor."

"I knew it." Higgins snapped his fingers in triumph. "How odd that both our given and surnames begin with the letter 'H,' and we're the same age as well."

"He also stayed at the Kingsley Hotel in Bloomsbury the night before the race," Jack went on.

Sybil set down her fork. "The hotel near St. George's church? That's where Emily Davison's funeral took place before the procession."

"Probably not a coincidence," Eliza said. "He must have watched the funeral at some point, or even paid his respects at the church. Did you read the diary Harold Hewitt was carrying? Was anything interesting in there?"

"Oh, quite a bit. Strange things like 'all the pretty girls but none for me.' Hewitt is a religious fanatic," Jack added with a hint of exasperation. "It was torture having to read his ramblings. He hates horse racing, that came through loud and clear. He's also a Fellow of the Zoological Society and an anti-vivisectionist."

"An anti what?"

Sybil answered Eliza's question. "It's a term for people who oppose surgical experimentation on animals. As a Quaker, I also believe such scientific practices are inhumane. Did Hewitt write about his support for women's rights? He carried our flag, after all."

Jack shrugged. "He mentioned attending Miss Besant's lecture in an early entry, but I haven't finished reading the diary yet. Remember that Hewitt is not the only suspect in the investigation. I'd like to find out exactly where Lady Saxton and Mrs. Turnbull were while Diana Price was being murdered."

"I suppose looking for their spouses isn't much of an alibi," Pickering said. "At least I'm glad you don't have to ask Higgins for an alibi in this crime. We had quite enough of that this past spring."

"I can attest that it's not pleasant being the prime suspect in a murder case," Higgins said. "Who is on your list of suspects this time, Inspector?"

"Everyone except you, Eliza, Uncle Alfred, and his wife."

"Could the ladies really be suspects in such a violent murder?" Sybil asked. "You once told me that women who kill usually choose poison. Stabbing someone with a pitchfork seems a far cry from poisoning a victim's soup or wine."

"True, in most cases. But Gordon Longhurst and both ladies had a strong motive to commit murder due to the adulterous liaisons of their—"

"Eliza, thank heaven you're all right!"

Freddy Eynsford Hill had pushed past Mrs. Pearce and rushed into the dining room. Higgins set down his teacup with a loud clatter. Freddy's sister Clara, her cheeks flushed with embarrassment for interrupting their meal, stood in the doorway. But Freddy drew Eliza into his arms and kissed her full on the mouth in front of everyone.

Irritated, Higgins threw a buttered crumpet at Freddy. The mutton-headed dolt.

———

Eliza pushed Freddy away, her face flaming as pink as Clara's. She wanted to box his ears. Instead, she snatched up the napkin that had fallen at her feet.

"I'm fine. Really I am, Freddy."

"I was so worried, darling." He ran a hand through his wavy blond hair. Despite his ridiculous behavior, Freddy's adoring expression melted her heart. "The papers said someone was trampled during Ascot, just like at the Derby. I thought you'd been hurt."

"Don't be silly. You'll never see me running out in the middle of a horse race," she said with a laugh. "That would be pure suicide."

"I also read a woman got stabbed with a pitchfork!"

"And that would be murder," Higgins said with a growl.

Freddy ignored him. "I am quite relieved you survived Ascot, darling. Who knew that going to the races was so beastly dangerous? And you look beautiful as always. I missed you."

Eliza couldn't help but smile up at him. "I missed you, too. But why are you both back so soon from the wedding in Brighton?"

"I insisted we return early." Clara walked over to the table. "Not that I wanted to go in the first place."

Eliza introduced Freddy and Clara to Sybil. "You both know my cousin Jack, of course. He and Miss Chase are engaged."

Clara, who was desperate to find a husband, seemed crestfallen at the news.

"Congratulations." Freddy cast a longing look at Eliza. "If only we could agree to set a date."

"Hush, Freddy. Not now."

Mrs. Pearce directed several maids to bring tableware and silver for the new arrivals now seated between Pickering and Eliza. Eliza shook Freddy off at last and poured the rest of the tea. Clara only nibbled at the full plate the maid placed before her, but Freddy ate everything with ravening speed as if he'd skipped meals for a week. They both looked a bit sunburnt from their seaside visit to Brighton.

Although the Eynsford Hill family possessed the manners of the gentry, they lacked the money to truly play the part. Eliza noticed that Clara's pale blue linen dress had seen its fair share of summers, while her hat ribbon was frayed. And Clara's shell brooch, painted to resemble bluebells, looked cheap compared to Sybil's amethyst leaf-shaped pin. She felt a wave of pity for Freddy's eighteen-year-old sister. Eliza was fortunate that Colonel Pickering had outfitted her beautifully from the moment she arrived last year at Wimpole Street for speech lessons. And because she charged an impressive fee for giving her own lessons now, Eliza had added even more expensive items to her stylish wardrobe.

Although Clara had a difficult time keeping up with the latest fashions on her family's small inheritance, Freddy appeared quite the dapper gentleman. Today he looked smart in a light gray suit and silk waistcoat, even if his striped blue and white Ascot tie was a bit crooked. Eliza loved the way a lock of blond hair fell over his forehead, like in the painting she'd seen of Lord Byron.

"Did the wedding go off without a hitch?" she asked.

"Everything was perfect!" Clara's eyes lit up. "The bridal gown was white tulle, lace, and silk. Her bouquet was exquisite, all orange blossoms and white roses. And she wore the most adorable French-heeled pumps. The wedding breakfast wasn't much to speak of, though."

"Tell them how much you enjoyed the champagne punch." Freddy winked at Eliza. "Clara indulged in three cups before breakfast was over, and two afterward. We were both a bit tipsy."

"The cups were tiny," she said with a pout. "Mother didn't feel at all well, since the weather turned warm and humid. It rained the whole time until the wedding itself, when it finally stopped. We didn't mind coming home early."

"Only because it was so cramped staying at Cousin Edith's." Freddy tore another chunk off his bun. "There weren't enough bedrooms, and I was forced to sleep on the parlor hearth."

"At least you had a pallet of blankets. I rolled off that rock-hard sofa half a dozen times during the night. Not that I could sleep anyway. You snore worse than a foghorn."

"I do not snore!"

Eliza laughed at their customary bickering. "Enough, you two."

Sybil cocked her head at Freddy. "I'm curious how you and Eliza met."

"Oh, it was love at first sight. Professor Higgins's mother kindly invited my family to tea this past spring. Eliza was so funny with her new small talk. I'd never met anyone like her. She told the most amusing stories, especially about some aunt who bit the bowl off a spoon when everyone thought she was dying."

"I remember that," Jack said. "Uncle Alfred poured gin down her throat."

"We don't need to hear that story again." Eliza shook her head at him. "In truth, I first saw Freddy when he bumped into me in the rain at Covent Garden and knocked over my basket of violets. He rushed off without paying, too. He still doesn't remember I was the flower girl who sold them. Of course, I looked and spoke differently then."

"I only recall I couldn't find a cab that night," Freddy added.

Sybil turned to Eliza. "Jack said you and the Professor also met that same evening. While you were selling flowers, you heard him tell everyone where they came from by listening to them speak."

Eliza and Higgins both smiled. "Oh, he was performing his usual tricks, amazing us all with his phonetics genius. So much so, that I came straightaway the next morning and asked to pay for lessons. I wanted to speak like a proper lady."

"And I was gracious enough to teach her," Higgins said. "Pick challenged me to pass her off as a duchess at a society event. A bet I obviously won."

"With grudging thanks for my efforts." Eliza shook a finger at him. "Anyway, we now teach elocution here at Wimpole Street. The delightful Colonel Pickering keeps us company. He's a true gentleman and a renowned scholar of Sanskrit."

"And you've become a real lady, Eliza," he said with pride.

"Now tell me what happened at Ascot, darling." Freddy wiped his mouth. "What about your father's horse? Did it win?"

He and Clara sat enraptured while she told them about the Donegal Dancer's victory and her winnings, how Tracery trampled Harold Hewitt, and the awful discovery of Miss Price in the stables. Higgins added a few details. Jack fielded questions from Colonel Pickering since he had left soon after the body was discovered.

Freddy grabbed Eliza's hand. "Darling! Do you realize how thrilling this is?"

She pulled away in shock. "Murder isn't thrilling."

"No, no, I didn't mean that. But with your winnings at Ascot, we now have enough money to marry and set up a flower shop." He smiled at everyone around the table. "It's long past time since we announced our formal engagement."

"For the last time, Freddy, I never agreed to marry you."

"But darling—"

"No. I mean it."

"But you got yourself into such danger with that awful murder business in May. I only want to keep you safe."

"I'm perfectly safe. And don't look so crushed. I'm simply not ready to marry. We discussed the matter before you left for Brighton. Besides, nothing happened to me at Ascot." She looked over at Clara. "Lady Saxton was so disappointed you weren't there. The Viscountess wants to introduce you to a few suitable gentlemen."

Clara gasped with delight. "Tansy said that?"

"Yes. Rich ones, too."

She trembled with excitement. "Oh, oh! How wonderful to be a rich man's wife!"

"I know a score of rich men's wives who would disagree with you," Sybil said with a weary sigh. "A man with money and influence tends to be more arrogant than his less fortunate brothers. And far more disagreeable, too."

Eliza was pleased by her remark, since she agreed. Lord Saxton was certainly no prize.

Clara appeared baffled by what Sybil said. "The worst fate is to remain a spinster. Especially for a woman without means. For the rest of her life, she is nothing more than a burden on her relatives. And an object of pity." She shuddered. "I'd rather be dead."

"In this day and age," Sybil said, "with opportunities to work outside the home, a spinster need not be a burden on anyone."

"She would still be unmarried," Clara protested.

"I would gladly have remained unmarried and free of household duties, but I met Jack. Then again, he's far more enlightened and intelligent than most men." She blushed. "Handsome, too, which is why I'm looking forward to our wedding in August. I'm also lucky he agrees with my views on women's rights."

"You can still support the cause by writing articles," Jack said, "as long as you don't get arrested again."

"Arrested? Suffrage sounds too much like suffering to me." Clara sipped her tea. "I'll take marriage and an adoring husband over voting rights any day."

Eliza was tempted to mention Lady Tansy's unhappiness with her unfaithful drunkard of a husband. Then again, why dash Clara's hopes? All young women had romantic dreams. Harsh reality would eventually intrude. Meanwhile, if Lady Tansy wanted to set her up with a rich gentleman, so be it. Eliza had her hands full fending off Freddy.

Thankfully, Sybil changed the subject back to Harold Hewitt. "I don't understand why he carried a suffrage flag onto the track."

Jack shrugged. "He wrote in his diary about attending Miss Besant's lecture. But who can say why? Hewitt seems to be a confused and unstable man."

"He must be," Pickering said. "I'll never forget seeing Tracery run the poor fellow down. How remarkable he wasn't killed."

"Several suffragettes witnessed Emily Davison's death." Sybil lowered her gaze. "It wasn't suicide. She had a return railway ticket and planned to help her sister in France care for her new baby. Emily felt strong in her views, though."

"At Ascot, people booed when Hewitt was carried off the track," Eliza said. "Especially since he carried that flag."

"We often encounter hostility. One suffragette at the Derby was chased and beaten by a mob. She would have been killed if not for a railway porter who hid her at the Epsom train station. The police didn't help at all."

"For good reason," Jack said. "They were outnumbered. People were downright livid after they lost their bets on Anmer."

"Rotten luck," Colonel Pickering said. "Like losing out on seeing Tracery beat Prince Palatine. Lost a guinea or two myself."

Jack drew a photograph from his coat pocket and handed it to Sybil. "I meant to show you this earlier. Do you recognize this man? From a suffrage meeting or the funeral?"

She studied the photograph. "He seems familiar."

"It's Harold Hewitt. We had the newspaper print blown up using the magic lantern, but it's a bit grainy in quality."

"Did you find any connection between Hewitt and Diana Price?" Eliza asked Jack.

"We're still looking into that."

"Since she was a former Gaiety Girl, there are all sorts of stories circulating now about her," Pickering said. "I heard Lord Cavendish drank champagne out of her slipper during a party at the Griffin Club. Shortly after, she married that Longhurst chap."

Sybil tapped an index finger on her teacup's rim. "The WSPU asked her to sing at the suffrage rally once, but she refused. She actually laughed in Christabel Pankhurst's face. That didn't endear her to anyone. The actress Lena Ashwell did a dramatic reading instead. Good thing, too. She's far more sympathetic to the cause."

"I read in the *Times* that Miss Price was quite vocal about how ridiculous the suffragettes are, smashing windows and the like," Eliza said. "It seems she once gave an interview to the paper about her opposition to them."

"She was right." Clara lifted her chin in defiance. "They're silly women."

Ignoring Clara's careless remark, Sybil turned to the others. "I wonder if Mr. Hewitt read that article in the newspaper. If he was so obsessed about Miss Davison's death, that might have tipped him over the edge."

Jack shrugged. "We can't prove that without questioning him."

Eliza wasn't convinced. The conversation then split into two. Higgins, Pickering, Jack, and Sybil discussed the latest suffragette violence, while Eliza focused on Clara's and Freddy's plans for the summer season.

"You'll come watch me at the next rowing practice, won't you?" he asked Eliza. "I'm so worried the club will throw me off the team. I missed twice due to that blasted wedding, but if you and Clara come, they wouldn't dare. Will you wear our colors? You'd look wonderful in blue and white stripes."

"Of course." She squeezed his hand.

"Practice isn't much fun. It's bound to be hot, and there's no shade."

"We'll bring parasols." Eliza caught the drift of conversation between Jack and Higgins and shot them a quick question. "By the way, how is Mr. Hewitt?"

"Doing quite well, even though a surgeon at the Royal Victoria Nursing Home removed a piece of bone from the base of his skull," Jack said. "It seems his injuries were not life threatening. We'll question him once the doctors allow it."

"And arrest him to stand trial for murder," Higgins said with satisfaction.

"I only hope our fingerprint expert finds something on the pitchfork's handle. Otherwise, we won't be able to prove Hewitt used it."

Pickering nodded. "How do they go about checking for prints?"

Jack leaned forward eagerly to explain. Eliza could see that Sybil was enchanted with him. That pleased her. They would be a good match. She wanted Jack to be happy and hoped Sybil would be, too, given the many hours his bride would spend waiting for him to come home.

"The latest magnifying glasses have become indispensable in our work," Jack said. "Especially since Sir Edward Henry's system proved more reliable a decade ago."

Higgins and Pickering asked other questions, but Eliza grew bored with all this talk of murder, fingerprints, and women's suffrage.

"—no question he has a long-standing aversion to suffragettes."

"Who's this?" Eliza asked Sybil.

"Jonathon Turnbull. He's quite a character."

"I met him at Ascot. He's one of the Donegal Dancer's owners. I hated him on sight. Why do you think he's a character?"

"He's one of the strongest opponents to women's suffrage," Sybil explained. "Mr. Turnbull hires thugs to cause trouble at our events."

"How do you know so much about him?" Eliza asked.

"I'm friends with Ruth Lowell, who used to be a Women's Freedom League member. She quit after her marriage to Reverend Henry Lowell, but over the last few years she became involved with the WSPU. The militant faction."

"Militant? Has she been arrested?"

"Many times. Earlier this year, Ruth was arrested for destruction of property after the suffragettes smashed shop windows. She carried a ball-peen hammer, but claimed she hadn't meant to throw it."

Colonel Pickering clucked his disapproval. "Did it hit anyone?"

"Diana Price."

Eliza and Higgins looked at each other in surprise. "That's interesting," he said.

Sybil sighed. "I suspect Ruth knew that Diana was in the shop, but she won't admit it. Anyway, Ruth threw the hammer and hit her in the shoulder. It was only a glancing blow, but Diana swore she aimed for her face."

"Blimey," Eliza said. "Do *you* think Ruth meant to hit her?"

"I do. And not only because of Diana's opposition to the cause." Sybil glanced at Jack. "We haven't had much of a chance to talk since before Ascot, or else I would have told you about Ruth and what she did to Diana."

Jack looked puzzled. "Why should I care about Ruth Lowell?"

"Because Ruth is Rachel Turnbull's sister."

FIVE

Eliza fanned the latest fashion magazines in a half-circle on her bedroom carpet. With the Henley Regatta the following week, she had to go clothes shopping. She needed two more outfits for the regatta; as Freddy's sweetheart, it was her duty to wear the blue and white colors of the London Rowing Club. How dreadful if they'd been the green and purple racing silks of her father's horse.

Last week she had bought a white lawn blouse and slim blue walking skirt from Selfridges. During that same visit to the Oxford Street department store, she'd also purchased the loveliest white cotton dress trimmed in a blue silk that matched the LRC blue perfectly. However, that still left two more outfits to assemble for the four-day event. Her straw hat with the blue organza band would match everything. Still, she could afford to buy another. How wonderful being able to purchase a fancy wardrobe with her own money. For too long Eliza had depended on the generosity of Colonel Pickering, who looked on her as a daughter. But since this past spring, her teaching fees, coupled with her winnings at Ascot, had allowed Eliza to buy her own wardrobe.

She flipped open the July issue of *Vogue*. Yes, a new hat was a good idea. After all, she didn't want to embarrass Freddy in front of his rowing club. Maybe she should pay a visit to Harrods, too. Luckily there was no matchmaking scheduled for Clara today.

Lord Saxton's wife had kept her promise about finding a suitable husband for her old schoolmate. In the past week, Clara had taken tea with the Saxtons five times in order to meet yet another eligible bachelor. Eliza was not happy when she and Clara's mother were also invited. The conversation was dull, and the bachelors even duller.

Thank heaven the Saxtons planned to attend something called a gymkhana at the Ranelagh Club. And it was also Friday. She never scheduled lessons on Friday since she loved to attend the cinema. The whole day was free to spend more of her glorious Ascot guineas.

Someone knocked on her bedroom door. "Eliza, are you decent?" Professor Higgins said in an impatient voice.

"Decent enough for the likes of you."

The door flew open. Eliza was startled at the sight of Higgins wearing a neatly pressed gray suit and magenta silk tie—a far cry from his usual attire of rumpled sweaters, faded tweed jackets, and trousers with coins in their pockets.

"And where would you be going so dressed up?"

"To the asylum." He gave her a sly grin. "And you're coming with me. So you'd best put on something more ostentatious than that plain brown dress."

She sat back on her heels. "I am not going to any asylum. But don't let me upset your plans. If anyone deserves to spend time in an insane asylum, it's you."

"Very funny." He pointed at the fashion magazines. "Put on something that resembles the silly ladies in those illustrations. The fancier and sillier, the better."

"I told you, I'm not going off to any asylum. And if either of us were stupid enough to do so, why would we need to get dressed up? Did you get an invite to a cotillion they're throwing for all the crazy people?" She chuckled.

"I only wish they gave out invitations to the asylum. It would be easier to get inside." Higgins threw himself down on the cushioned window seat. "Especially since your cousin refuses to let me visit Harold Hewitt. That's where we're going, by the way. Claybury Asylum in Middlesex."

Eliza put down the copy of *Vogue* and picked up *The Delineator*. "I'm not going to Middlesex or the asylum. I am off to Harrods for a day of shopping. Whiteleys too."

"You already have more dresses than Marie Antoinette. We could open a dress shop with the contents of this room alone, let alone the trunks stored in the spare bedroom. No, you and I must go to Claybury Asylum today. The hospital in Ascot transferred Hewitt to Claybury four days ago. According to Jack, he's already recovered from the surgery. And there's talk that Hewitt's family want to transfer him to Herefordshire."

She shrugged. "Let them. I don't see how it's any of our business."

"Oh, you don't? Why, you supercilious little monkey."

"If you want a favor, you may want to leave off calling me names."

He let out an exasperated sigh. "Whenever I must involve a woman in any enterprise, I find myself forced to flatter and toady and make myself sick with self-disgust."

"I didn't hear you complaining when I saved your toadying self from being thrown into prison for murder."

"You will never let me forget that."

Eliza kept her attention on the magazine. "You're right. I won't. And since I saved you from being arrested only a few weeks ago, it's no use pretending you've forgotten." She finally looked up at him. "If you're done with this latest tantrum, please leave my room. I need to change. Although this dress is not brown, it's ecru. And it costs more than the sorry contents of your entire wardrobe."

"Eliza, I am going to the asylum with or without you. But it would make things easier if you accompanied me."

She studied him. "I know you think you could have prevented both Diana Price's murder and Hewitt's running out on the racetrack. But even if you'd told the police about the gun hours earlier, Jack said it probably would have made no difference."

"Perhaps. But I need to talk to Hewitt. If he did murder Diana, I bear part of the responsibility for her death."

"Rachel's sister might have killed her. At brunch Sybil said Ruth threw a hammer at Diana. If she is the murderer, you have no reason to feel guilty."

"I spoke with Jack last night while you were out with Freddy. Ruth Lowell was leading a WSPU parade past Westminster on the day of Diana's murder, and there are over a hundred witnesses to confirm it. No, it's Hewitt who seems mad enough to kill someone." Higgins seemed uncharacteristically earnest. This meant a lot to him.

She slapped the magazine down on the floor. "Why do I have to go with you?"

"Because I rang up the asylum and asked about their visitation rules. Only doctors, police, or relatives are permitted to see the residents." The hint of a smile appeared on his face. "But solicitors may also visit if accompanied by a family member."

"Let me guess. I shall pose as Hewitt's relative, while you play family solicitor."

"Exactly. You always were my cleverest pupil."

"If Jack hears about this, he won't be happy."

"Then let's not tell him." Higgins sprang to his feet. "Now hurry and put on the most pretentious outfit you own, Eliza. Pick one of those dresses that are so tight, you move like a Chinese woman with bound feet. Those make me howl with laughter."

"A hobble skirt?" She frowned. "A girl can barely walk in those awful things. One skirt fits tighter than a vise from my calves clear up to my waist. Makes me feel like a blooming mummy."

"Perfect." He snapped his fingers. "Wear that skirt."

"I can't breathe in it!"

"Even better. I need you to drip with disdain and hyperbolic haughtiness, Eliza."

"I don't need a tight skirt to do that."

"Yes, you do. You'll seem the most snobbish and useless of ladies. If I am to obfuscate the staff, I need a human smoke screen. So hobble yourself, Eliza. Pull out your tallest hat, your most expensive parasol, your costliest opera gloves." He bounded over to the bedroom door. "And be quick about it. I want to be at the asylum before lunch."

Eliza stared after him. If Higgins continued acting like this, the asylum doctors would never let him leave.

The closer to the asylum, the more imposing its complex of buildings appeared. Higgins had heard the grounds were extensive, so he hired a car to drive them from Wimpole Street to Claybury. Eliza could manage only the tiniest of steps. Having a driver deposit them at the main building saved time. Otherwise it might have taken an hour for her to walk from the front gate to the asylum's entrance.

It still took ten minutes for Eliza to mince her way to the reception area, and an additional five minutes to arrive at the Medical Superintendent's office. A solidly built man of middle years, the doctor wore a guarded expression. His navy blue suit was pressed as sharp as a razor, and he held himself like the guards outside Whitehall. Higgins also noticed he never took his eyes off Eliza, who moved as grace-fully, and as slowly, as a swan caught in the rushes.

Higgins was quite pleased with her costume. She resembled a young countess in a pink hobble skirt, short jacket, and parasol. Eliza's gloves matched the white lace blouse that covered her long neck. Even lon-ger was the brim of her pink flowered hat. It tilted vertically at such an angle, it added nearly two feet to her height. Thank heaven for the tall doorways at Claybury.

The Superintendent gestured to the two chairs near his desk. "Please sit down."

The men had to wait for Eliza. Her skirt fit like a second skin, and she could only descend by inches. With grim determination, she tight-ened her grip on the parasol handle for balance and lowered herself like someone sinking into a tub of boiling water. When she finally sat, Eliza threw Higgins a victorious look.

"I am Dr. Phillip Cullen, Medical Superintendent at Claybury." He glanced at the note his secretary had given him. "And you are Miss Elizabeth Hewitt and Mr. Henry Jones?"

Higgins nodded. "This is Mr. Hewitt's youngest sister, and I am the family solicitor."

"How do you do?" Eliza drawled in an exaggerated tone she hadn't used since he and Pickering were training her to speak like a lady.

Cullen raised an eyebrow. "We were not notified of your visit. As you may know, Mr. Hewitt was transferred here this past Monday. The hospital near Ascot deemed him well enough for the transfer, and he suffered no ill effects. But physical resilience is not the same thing as mental capability. If you came to inquire about his release, I must ad-vise against it."

"And why, pray tell, do you make such a statement?" Eliza enunci-ated each word as if it would be her last.

"Because your brother is not in his right mind, Miss Hewitt. He suffers from a number of mental disorders. Although he does experience moments of rational thought, he is easily confused and distracted. I'm afraid he may not recognize you at all."

Higgins almost crowed with delight. This would be easier than he thought. "Have you had to restrain my client?"

The doctor shook his head. "We rarely resort to physical restraint. Claybury is no ordinary institution, Mr. Jones. In fact, we were among the first asylums to include our own medical research building on mental illness. We were the first asylum to switch from gas to electricity."

"And why would electricity matter to a mental patient?" Eliza looked down her nose at him. "Unless you plan to give them a little shock now and again."

Higgins hurriedly cleared his throat. "What Miss Hewitt means is that she hopes her brother is receiving the best care possible."

"He could be in no finer hands. Not only is Claybury the best asylum in the Greater London area, it is the best in Britain. Currently we have two thousand patients in residence, most of whom enjoy considerable freedom within our walls and grounds." A note of pride crept into his voice. "Claybury contains fifty acres of woodland and ninety-five acres of open parkland. Many of the residents are allowed to walk about the gardens or sit by the ponds. I can't think of anything we lack."

Eliza sniffed. "Do you have a zoo?"

He looked startled. "Why, no."

She sat back. "There you are."

Higgins bit back a grin. Eliza was overplaying her part, and it was time to get her out of this office. "We've traveled a long way, Superintendent. Could we see Mr. Hewitt now?"

"Of course. He has been quite tractable since his arrival. Because he is a suspect in a murder case, the police have requested he be under observation at all times." Cullen smiled. "We explained that every resident in an asylum is always under observation."

"Have the police been here often?" Higgins asked.

"A Scotland Yard detective inspector visited Mr. Hewitt twice."

Eliza straightened. "Is he here now?"

"No, he visited earlier today. About half past seven."

Turning to Higgins, she said in her most elongated vowels, "As my aunt used to say, ain't that a stroke of luck."

"All right, then. I think we're done here." Higgins rose to his feet. "Thank you for speaking with us, Superintendent."

Cullen walked around the desk, and the two men shook hands. They watched as Eliza took a deep breath and began the laborious process of getting out of her chair. Higgins wanted to applaud when she finally stood up.

"One of our attendants will escort you to Mr. Hewitt." Cullen glanced at the wall clock. "Ten o'clock, so he should be in the chapel. Mr. Hewitt prays at this time."

When they reached the reception area, Cullen signaled a stocky young man in a white uniform. "Stevens will take you to Mr. Hewitt. Oh, and as you walk through the building, please take note of the carved wood paneling and stained glass windows. As I said, there aren't many asylums that are so beautiful as ours."

"You have convinced me, Dr. Cullen," Eliza said with a gracious nod. "If I ever become a lunatic, I shall ask to be taken here straightaway."

Since Hewitt was not in the chapel, the recreation hall, or even his private cell, Higgins feared the patients weren't as closely observed as

Dr. Cullen claimed. And Eliza moved so slowly, it took almost an hour before the erstwhile Mr. Hewitt was discovered in one of the Day Rooms. Apparently he had been reading there since breakfast and barely looked up from his Bible as they approached.

Stevens tapped Hewitt on the shoulder. "Your sister and solicitor have come to visit you."

Hewitt gave them a quick, incurious glance before he resumed reading.

"He likes his Bible, he does," the attendant said. "Maybe if you just sit here nice and quiet, he'll look up and say a few words." He gestured to the settees and armchairs scattered about, all of them padded in leather or carpet. "You'll have a bit of privacy. Everyone else is in the recreation hall or with the doctors. Have a nice chat, and don't worry. I'll be right by the door to keep an eye on things."

Higgins and Eliza waited until Stevens sat down in a bentwood chair by the entrance. He was far enough away that any conversation would not be overheard.

"Mr. Hewitt," Eliza said in a soft voice. "May we speak with you?"

No response. Hewitt sat in the middle of a green leather sofa, but Higgins thought the man might grow nervous if they sat next to him. He grabbed a nearby settee and dragged it over. After Higgins sat down, he gestured for Eliza to sit. She sighed and once again made her descent.

"Do you remember me?" Higgins asked. "We spoke at Ascot."

"The man with the notebook," Hewitt said, his eyes still fixed on the Bible.

Eliza and Higgins exchanged excited looks. "Yes, that was me."

"Best not write in your book here." Hewitt kept his eyes on the Bible. "They'll take it from you."

"We heard the police have your diary now," Higgins said.

Hewitt's jaw tightened. "They had no right. The diary belongs to me. My thoughts were in the diary. They stole my thoughts." He finally raised his head. "It's unforgivable."

"Perhaps we can persuade the police to return it to you." Eliza ignored Higgins, who shook his head. "They might once they're done with it. I mean, once the case is solved." She made a face at Higgins. "Why are you looking at me that way? I bet I'll convince Jack to give it back to him."

Higgins turned to Hewitt. "Please ignore her. That skirt makes all the blood rush to her head."

"But why should I ignore my sister?" Hewitt smirked. "Except my real sister is old enough to be this young lady's mother. A shame no one has informed the staff here." He narrowed his eyes at her. "Who are you besides a pretty girl? Do you wish me ill?"

"Oh no, we've come to find out what really happened at Ascot."

"What is there to tell? I ran in front of the horses. And I waved a flag that stands for a righteous cause. I hoped to draw attention to that cause."

"You also waved a gun," Higgins said.

"That, too, was meant to draw attention."

"But didn't you realize you'd be trampled like that poor woman at the Epsom Derby?" Eliza said. "You're lucky to be alive."

He took a shuddering breath. "Yes, the Lord spared me. I don't know why He did not spare Miss Davison. Perhaps He wanted her as one of His angels. In my eyes, she had long been an angel for truth and courage."

"Was Emily Davison a friend of yours?" Eliza asked.

"Only in spirit. I regret I never exchanged a word with her, though I heard her speak once. And I had the sad honor of attending the funeral." He gave Eliza a penetrating look. "Were you at her funeral?"

She shook her head.

"Of course not. You're a pretty girl. Pretty girls only know how to be pretty. They care about pretty things and pretty people. They have no use for serious ideas, or serious men like me." He sounded dejected.

"That's not true, Mr. Hewitt. I know plenty of pretty girls who care about such things, and plenty of ugly ones who are as dumb as brick."

Higgins held up his hand. "Before this pretty girl compels me to throw a brick at her head, I want to ask you a few questions about Ascot."

"What is there to say? I went to Ascot to protest injustice. Injustice perpetrated by the complacent, the greedy, the fearful and ungodly. I knew I would suffer for it, perhaps even die."

"But you weren't the only one on the racetrack," Eliza said. "You might have crippled one of the horses. Or even killed a jockey."

Hewitt sighed. "It was never my intention to injure the horses or the jockeys. I hoped they would see me and stop in time. But the horses were upon me so quickly. They ran faster than I thought possible."

"Of course they ran fast," Eliza said, clearly exasperated. "They're racehorses, you silly natters."

Higgins shot her a warning look. "Mr. Hewitt, are all your activities on that day recorded in the diary now in Scotland Yard's possession?"

He looked amused. "I fear I did not have the opportunity to record anything after I was trampled by the horses."

"You don't talk as if you were mad." Higgins regarded him for a long moment. "In fact, you appear quite rational."

Hewitt stared back. " 'I am but mad north-north-west.' "

"*Hamlet!*" Eliza cried in delight. "Act two, scene two. Do you know, I memorized the whole play last month right before we went to see it at the theater."

" 'When the wind is southerly—' "

Eliza finished for him. " 'I know a hawk from a handsaw'!"

"Don't you dare start quoting with him," Higgins grumbled. "If I have to hear you recite one more line from that play, I'm going to beg Stevens to stick me in a padded cell."

"Don't you see? He's only pretending to be mad."

"Unlike a certain Cockney girl who grows more unhinged by the minute."

"Do you know John Dryden, pretty girl?" Hewitt asked.

She glanced at Higgins. "Have I met him at one of your mother's teas?"

"Given that he was a seventeenth-century poet, Eliza, that seems unlikely."

"So your name is Eliza, not Elizabeth?" Hewitt sounded triumphant.

"How blooming stupid." She smacked Higgins on the shoulder. "Why don't you tell him that we both teach phonetics at 27A Wimpole Street? And that Colonel Pickering lives with us."

Higgins groaned. "I don't have to now."

She clapped a hand over her mouth. "Blimey."

"Mr. Dryden was a playwright as well as a poet, Eliza." Hewitt closed his eyes. " 'There is a pleasure sure in being mad, which none but madmen know.' " He opened his eyes and stared at them, as if waiting for a reaction.

"Not only pleasure, but safety," Higgins said wryly. "Mr. Hewitt, did you see who killed Diana Price?"

No emotion registered on Hewitt's face. "I do not know who Diana Price is."

"She was a singer in the theater," Eliza said. "But she started out as a Gaiety Girl, like one of those pretty girls you mention. You can't be a Gaiety Girl unless you're pretty. Diana Price was rather famous. I'm surprised you don't know her."

"The theater is nearly as foul with corruption as the racecourse. I haven't been to the theater since I was a boy."

Eliza turned to Higgins. "Poor man. I bet he hasn't been to the cinema, either."

"Following the Gold Cup, Diana's body was found in the stables," Higgins said. "She'd been run through with a pitchfork."

"How tragic." Hewitt opened his Bible once more. "I still don't know her. But I will pray for her immortal soul. I shall now read from the Book of Judges."

After several minutes of him reading aloud, an impatient Eliza interrupted. "Did you visit the stables while you were at Ascot?"

"I did not," Hewitt said, then resumed reading.

Higgins and Eliza waited until he finished the account of Samson and Delilah. But when Hewitt began the biblical account of Micah and the young Levite, Higgins lost patience. "Read the biblical injunction against spreading falsehoods. You just said you did not visit the Ascot stables. Yet jockey Bomber Brody and a young groom both claim they saw you there that morning. Since you weren't an owner or racing official, Brody had you removed from the premises."

"Perhaps I did." Hewitt closed his Bible. "I believe I arrived at the racecourse early in the morning. I may have wandered into the stables at some point. Remember I suffered a head injury at Ascot." He touched the bandage at the back of his head. "My memory may be faulty."

"But why go to the stables at all?" Eliza asked.

He was silent for a moment. Higgins guessed he was trying to concoct a convincing lie. For certain, Hewitt was a slippery fellow.

"I wanted to see the horses," he said at last.

"Why?" Higgins and Eliza asked in unison.

"I planned to run in front of them during the race and knew that might startle them. But if I showed myself to those horses scheduled to run in the Gold Cup—let them catch my scent, listen to my voice, note my appearance—perhaps they wouldn't take fright later."

Higgins snorted. That was the first irrational thing Hewitt had said. "Where did you go after we spoke? Did you go back to the stables?"

He remained silent, his eyes on the Bible.

"Tell us where you went."

Hewitt looked off into space. " 'If wishes were horses, blind men would ride,' " he chanted in a singsong voice, then stopped. "That's what you all are. Blind."

"Blind to what?"

But Hewitt's attention turned unexpectedly to Eliza's tight skirt. He pointed a stern finger at her. " 'Cast away thy sinful raiment.' "

"I will as soon as I get home," she replied. "I can barely breathe."

Higgins's frustration grew by the minute. "Mr. Hewitt, do you remember where you were between the time we spoke in the paddock and the start of the Gold Cup?"

"Now you sound like a policeman."

"Excuse me, gentlemen, but I cannot sit a minute longer." Eliza jabbed the tip of her parasol into the waxed floor and slowly pushed herself to her feet. "Bad enough I can hardly take a step. When I sit, it's like a giant snake is wrapped around me."

Hewitt looked solemn. "It's too pink."

"What? This is a lovely color. Freddy says pink makes me look like a ballerina."

"Who is Freddy?"

"Never mind about Freddy." With a sigh, Higgins stood up. He doubted they would learn anything more from this fellow. Hewitt wasn't mad. But he was stranger than most chaps. And probably more cunning than the asylum doctors realized.

"Did you go back to the stables after that first visit?"

"Why would I go back to the stables? There was evil in that place. And much falsehood." Hewitt closed his eyes. " 'He hath blinded their eyes and hardened their heart, that they should not see with their eyes, nor understand with their heart.' " He looked once more at Higgins. "John, chapter 12, verse 40."

"This is like being at Sunday service," Eliza said. "I wouldn't be surprised if Stevens comes by with the collection plate."

"What exactly are we blind to?" Higgins asked.

"That which seems hidden away, but is in plain sight. And you are not only blind but deaf. For I have seen *and* heard the truth. And it is a terrible truth indeed. One that I shall never reveal to the ungodly and the weak." He pointed at them. "That is what you both are."

"I bet he thinks you're the ungodly one," Eliza said.

Higgins shook his finger at the man. "Enough of this nonsense. If you saw or heard something suspicious in the stables, then by heaven you're going to tell me or the police."

Hewitt startled them both by springing to his feet. "Get behind me, Satan!" He shoved Higgins and Eliza, sending them both flying backward onto the settee. Higgins heard fabric ripping at the same moment Eliza shrieked.

Stevens rushed over. "There, now. It's time to say good-bye to your sister and solicitor. They have to leave." He grabbed the suddenly docile Hewitt by the arm. "As soon as I take him to his cell, I'll come back and escort you and the young lady out."

Higgins leaned over to examine the jagged tear along the side of Eliza's dress. The linen had ripped from her ankle to her waist. In fact, he could see the white cotton of her knee-length drawers through the bulging gap.

"That's one hobble skirt you'll never have to wear again."

Eliza grinned. "It was worth a visit to the lunatic asylum just to get rid of it."

SIX

Rainclouds threatened the final day of the Henley Royal Regatta, but not even a downpour could dampen Eliza's spirits. Although Diana Price had been killed only two weeks earlier, Eliza was thoroughly enjoying what Professor Higgins called the Carnival on the River. Murder was the furthest thing from her mind.

The town of Henley-on-Thames hosted the regatta and welcomed visitors by transforming into a fancy country fair. Every street held shops and cafés decked out in flowers, banners, and Chinese lanterns. Military bands performed long into the evening while illuminated houseboats drifted on the river. Rich attendees rented bungalows along the water for the four-day event, but Eliza traveled by train each morning. In fact, she looked forward to taking the day train from London's Paddington station and chatting with excited regatta fans.

Since all the festivities centered on the racing, the Thames naturally took center stage. Hundreds of onlookers clustered along the riverbank, with more on boats bobbing in the water. Despite its prestige, Henley was more casual than Ascot. Even lords and ladies sat on the grass or in punts, with food hampers piled around them. To Eliza, the regatta seemed like one long elegant picnic, and with boat racing besides.

Surprisingly, she found the actual regatta competition rather dull. The first race proved fun to watch; sculls floated expectantly near Temple Island, tense rowers and fans waited in anticipation for the starter pistol. But by the end of the first day, Eliza had wearied of the bewildering number of qualifying races. Each race—or "heat," as everyone called it—lasted only a few minutes. The handsome young men striding about in their rowing uniforms did catch her eye. Just as the horses were the focus of attention at Ascot, the oarsmen were the stars at Henley. Pride filled her since one of those dashing oarsmen was her devoted Freddy.

From her vantage point on the Thames's Berkshire side, she often glimpsed the London Rowing Club team members. Eliza had no problem catching sight of Freddy. Cor, but he looked handsome in the LRC blue and white colors. She'd never suspected his forearms and calves were so nicely muscled. At times like this, she wondered if Freddy was right. Perhaps they ought to marry—and quickly, too.

"My son makes a fine figure in his colors, doesn't he?" Mrs. Eynsford Hill said.

"Indeed he does. And the LRC has performed so well this week. Do you think they'll win the Diamond Challenge?" Eliza asked.

"I have no idea. But Freddy is quite pleased to be a member of the team. I've never seen him care about anything so much. Until he met you."

"He is a dear, isn't he?"

"If only his trust fund allowed us to send him to a university as fine as Oxford or Cambridge. He's missed making the sort of friends that would help him enjoy the life he deserves. The rowing team is like his second family, but I worry about my children."

"They'll be fine."

She didn't look convinced. Although Mrs. Eynsford Hill boasted the same blond hair and blue eyes as her children, she was a paler version of them. It was as if the anxiety she always carried about her like a shawl had drained her of color and vivacity.

"I hope so. You've been good for Freddy, but Clara is another matter." Mrs. Eynsford Hill frowned. "Her school friend isn't helping matters with her matchmaking."

Eliza agreed. Clara behaved as if she were nothing more than a piece of summer fruit waiting to be picked by any man with a title and a Mayfair address. Although she was only eighteen, the foolish girl feared she would soon be too old for the marriage market.

Since Ascot, Lady Tansy's matchmaking had progressed with a vengeance, requiring Eliza to see them both nearly every day. To make matters worse, her husband often joined them. Lord Saxton again insisted she call his wife "Lady Tansy"; Eliza now did so without thinking. The same lack of thought seemed to go into the choice of suitors for Clara. Each one had been unappetizing. One viscount was nearly seventy, with a body odor so strong, it would have knocked the Donegal Dancer to the ground. Eliza feared Lady Tansy had no intention of arranging a good marriage for the poor girl. Was she playing some sort of wicked game at Clara's expense?

Eliza suddenly spied Lady Tansy and Clara weaving through the picnickers on the lawn. They weren't alone. A stout young man walked between them. His crimson blazer and red-banded straw boater made him stand out.

"What about this latest gentleman Tansy introduced to Clara?" Mrs. Eynsford Hill pursed her lips in disapproval when the trio headed in their direction.

"Sir Giles is pushy and full of himself," Eliza said. "I don't like him."

"Neither do I."

"There you are!" Clara broke away from the man who clung to her arm. "We've been looking everywhere for you two."

"Eliza and I watched the last race from the bridge," her mother said. "We couldn't see anything from the bank."

"All the other boats were in the way," Eliza added. A sea of punts and vessels lined the watercourse. And while they looked lovely—especially the houseboats heaped with roses and daisies—they sometimes made viewing the race impossible.

"After my man arranges for a punt, I shall escort Clara there," Sir Giles announced. "You are welcome to join us for lunch. A hamper of food, pastry, chilled cider, and claret will be delivered within the hour. Only the best for Henley, of course."

"Sorry," Eliza said quickly. "I promised to visit friends at the Remenham Club."

Lady Tansy flashed her a jaundiced look, as if to say, "What a pretty lie." Despite her habitual haughty expression, the young viscountess had an innocent girlish air about her today due to her sprigged white cotton dress and wide-brimmed straw hat with bright pink streamers.

"Please come with us," Clara whispered to Eliza and her mother. "Tansy is lunching with the syndicate owners, and I don't wish to be alone with him in that punt."

Mrs. Eynsford Hill slid an arm around her daughter's waist. "I shall be happy to join you, Sir Giles," she said loudly. "Thank you for your gracious invitation."

He raised his hand in acknowledgment.

"You don't have to go," Eliza whispered. "Tell the Baronet and his punt to shove off."

Clara shook her head. "Tansy is trying so hard. I couldn't possibly offend her or Sir Giles. And as the fashion magazines say, 'Better dead than unwed.'"

Eliza rolled her eyes, wishing Sybil would take Clara in hand. A week spent with a suffragette might do the girl a world of good.

Clara stepped back. "Do I look all right? It's the last of my good summer dresses."

The hem of her cream and ivy patterned dress seemed a bit worn. But the low neckline made her appear more alluring than usual, especially paired with the green silk belt and feathered hat Eliza had lent her. She brushed a stray blossom from Clara's shoulder. She decided they both needed a shopping excursion. With her winnings from Ascot, Eliza could now afford to buy an outfit or two for Clara as well.

"You look wonderful," Eliza said in a soft voice. "Far too good for the likes of him."

Clara gave her a quick kiss on the cheek before heading back with her mother and the pushy baronet. Eliza beckoned to Lady Tansy, who showed disdain at being summoned.

"I'm glad the mother will be on that punt," Lady Tansy said. "Giles has a tendency to overplay the romantic swain. And I wouldn't want Clara to be embarrassed."

"Then stop fixing her up with these blighters." Eliza gave her a hard stare.

"I beg your pardon?"

"You know blooming well not one of the chaps you've thrown her way since Ascot is marriage material. Unless one wants a total bore or an idiot for a husband."

"My dear, all husbands are bores or idiots. And finding her a rich one isn't easy. Clara has little to entice them with."

"She's a lovely girl. Any young man would be grateful to have her."

Lady Tansy smirked. "Clara is attractive, but she doesn't possess the sort of beauty to make men lose their heads or empty their bank accounts." Her expression grew stony. Eliza suspected she was reminded of Diana Price. "Even her pedigree is threadbare. Clara has nothing to offer but a string of bankrupt paper mills on one side of the family and a headmaster or two on the other. Not a family tree to interest a duke or marquess. If not for a generous aunt, all the Eynsford Hills would be selling cod and violets at Covent Garden."

Eliza stiffened at the veiled insult directed at her former occupation. "At least selling fish and flowers is an honest way to earn a living. Better than selling yourself to some bloated baronet or viscount."

"Have a care, Miss Doolittle."

"No, *you* have a care." Her temper flared. "I make my own way in the world, and I don't need your good opinion or your help. But Clara is a fool thinking you're her friend. Instead, you're toying with her like a bored cat teases a mouse! Isn't it enough you were born with a title, and are a viscountess by marriage? Why humiliate the girl by raising her hopes and then parading these fools in front of her? For pity's sake, any barkeep in Spitalfields has better manners than most of these peacocks with a title. And that includes titled women."

"You have no right to speak to me like that." Lady Tansy's expression grew hard.

"I have every right. I'm fond of the Eynsford Hills. Don't think for one moment I'll just sit back while you hurt them. If you don't find a better class of gentleman for Clara, then leave off. Or I'll trot out some pretty lady for your husband to slobber over."

Lady Tansy's mouth fell open. However, the Viscountess surprised her by bursting into laughter. "Now I understand how you caught a murderer at the Drury Lane, Miss Doolittle. You probably shamed the villain into confessing."

"Not exactly," Eliza muttered. "I had to use a sword."

That sent Lady Tansy into another gale of laughter. "I'm sure you did." She dabbed her eyes with a snow-white handkerchief. "You may be as impertinent as Becky Sharp, but I do respect an honest woman. Heaven knows, I've met very few of them."

Eliza made a mental note to ask Colonel Pickering who Becky Sharp was.

With a last chuckle, Lady Tansy tucked her handkerchief back into her beaded purse. "I'd best find my husband before he drinks himself into a stupor. But you have my word I shall give a good deal of thought about Clara's next suitor, for your sake more than hers. Her expectations are abysmally low, but I would hate to disappoint you."

The Viscountess of Saxton sailed off, the long pink streamers on her hat bouncing with each step.

"Blimey!" Eliza wondered if everyone with a title was balmy on the crumpet, except for the King. Then again, she'd never met His Majesty. He might be balmy, too.

———

Higgins wasn't certain if coming to the regatta had been wise. Of course, he enjoyed cheering on the sculls of Eton and Oxford; he usually spent a day or two at Henley every July. But enjoying riverside picnics and boat races seemed rather frivolous so soon after the events at Ascot.

Scotland Yard was no closer to solving Diana Price's murder. The visit to Claybury Asylum had left him with more questions than answers. Was Hewitt a cold-blooded killer? Of course, the man claimed to be unaware of Diana's death. But a patient in a mental asylum would never confess to murder, not if he had the slightest hope of walking free one day. And what was all that nonsense about evil in the stables? What did Hewitt see or hear?

What little interest Eliza had concerning the murder vanished after their asylum visit. She'd spent all her time either giving elocution lessons, shopping for regatta clothes, or running off with Clara and Lady Saxton. Was he the only person who still cared that a woman had been brutally murdered at Ascot? Then again, he'd caught a glimpse of Lord Saxton wearing a mourning armband earlier at the Phyllis Court club.

Higgins ought to crash the Wrexham Racing Syndicate's luncheon this afternoon. One of the owners might reveal some useful information about Hewitt or Diana Price. Unfortunately, he'd promised to join his mother and Pickering for lunch at the Remenham Club. That normally wouldn't stop him from canceling, but Mrs. Higgins had also invited the Duke and Duchess of Waterbury.

He would never admit that he had a soft spot for Lady Helen. But she had captivated him the moment he saw her eighteen years ago. An American heiress, Helen Marsh was only twenty-one when she arrived in England to marry the powerful duke. Higgins was scarcely much older when he was hired to rid Helen of her Boston accent. In the intervening years, he had become the most celebrated elocutionist in Europe, and she the most admired of the American heiresses who married into the aristocratic families of England. All these years later, Lady Helen still boasted a confident energy that put his fellow Englishwomen to shame.

A slender figure in blue and white suddenly came into view. He smiled. Not all English ladies were quite so decorous. Eliza Doolittle waved, and Mrs. Higgins waved back.

"It's Eliza," his mother said. "I do hope she's decided to lunch with us after all."

The party waited until Eliza hurried over. She looked quite nautical this morning in a white walking suit with blue stripes and a fashionable version of a white sailor cap. Pinned to the jaunty cap was the LRC's blue badge.

After introductions, Eliza cocked an inquisitive eye at Lady Helen.

"The Colonel told me about a young heiress from America who studied with the Professor years ago. Was that you?"

"Indeed, Miss Doolittle." Lady Helen smiled. "We have much in common, given your background. No doubt Boston vowels and Cockney idioms were equally difficult to eradicate. We should compare notes about our teacher, too." She shot Higgins a mischievous look. "Does he still fling tuning forks about when he loses his temper?"

Eliza laughed. "I finally hid them."

The Duke of Waterbury cleared his throat in disapproval at such informality. Higgins wished Helen had married a more affable blueblood. "I see you wear the colors and badge of the London Rowing Club, Miss Doolittle," the Duke said.

"Yes, my young man is a team member. Freddy won't be racing in the finals, however. But he tells me Pinks is sure to beat that fellow rowing for the Tasmanians."

Higgins turned to Eliza and silently mouthed "Your Grace." He wanted to let her know she'd forgotten to use the correct honorifics when addressing a duke and duchess.

The Duke turned to Higgins. "What do you think of the LRC's chances, Professor?"

"Better than last year, *Your Grace*." Higgins emphasized his title. But Eliza was busy admiring the organza ruffles on Lady Helen's pale blue dress. "There's a strong current today and little wind blowing off the Berks shore. It should favor Pinks, not McVilly."

"Will you be joining us for lunch, my dear?" Mrs. Higgins asked Eliza.

"No, ma'am." She tore her attention away from the Duchess's ensemble. "Dad's racing syndicate meets today, and Freddy and I plan to join them." She smiled at the Duke and Duchess. "My father is an owner of the Donegal Dancer. He won at Ascot."

"Give him my congratulations," Lady Helen said in delight. "How grand to own a horse that wins at the Derby or Ascot. We have yet to manage it."

"It was grand, but things got a bit muddy after the Gold Cup."

"Yes, we saw that terrible man run out on the racecourse." Lady Helen looked at her husband. "I believe the papers said his name was Harold Hewitt."

"That was not the only unfortunate occurrence at Ascot, *Your Grace*." This time Higgins elbowed Eliza in the ribs.

"Oh, I'm sorry." She bit her lip. "Should I call both of you 'Your Grace'?"

The Duke nodded, while Lady Helen replied, "Of course not."

Higgins grinned at Eliza's puzzled expression. "Miss Doolittle's father is part of a racing syndicate. One of its members was killed in the stables that day."

"Quite tragic," the Colonel said. "She was so young."

Eliza leaned closer. "Stabbed with a pitchfork."

"Oh my!" Lady Helen paled. "The papers said that a music hall singer had been found dead at Ascot. We assumed she was murdered by this Harold Hewitt."

"He seems the likeliest suspect," Higgins said. "But not the only one."

Mrs. Higgins cleared her throat. "This conversation is turning rather lurid, so I shall take my leave. Colonel, if you will please escort me to the club."

After they departed, the Duke turned to Higgins. "Given the obvious danger this Harold Hewitt poses to society, how is it the Metropolitan Police failed to keep him in custody?"

Eliza's mouth fell open. "Hewitt is free?"

Higgins didn't like this news at all. "They released him from the asylum?"

"He escaped," the Duke said. "I only learned about it an hour ago. Several suffragettes selling their tiresome magazine near the bandstand were discussing Hewitt's escape."

Eliza and Higgins exchanged glances. She clearly shared his apprehension. "Jack will get in trouble for this," she murmured.

"Who is Jack?" Lady Helen asked.

"My cousin. He's a detective inspector at Scotland Yard." Eliza paused. "Your Grace."

"We'd best go, my dear." The Duke held out his arm for his wife. "I shall see you at the club, Professor." He gave a brief nod. "Miss Doolittle."

"Lovely meeting you, Miss Doolittle. And I quite like your hat." Lady Helen held up a warning finger. "Now don't be late for lunch, Henry."

After they left, Eliza whistled in surprise. "She calls you Henry? Aren't we on cozy terms with the upper crust. You'll be throwing back a pint with Queen Mary next."

"Be quiet, you impertinent girl. I've known the Duke and Duchess for almost as long as you've been alive." Higgins lowered his voice. "What do you think about Hewitt escaping?"

"He's a clever dodger. Bet he's on his way to Dover or some other city where he can take ship and flee England."

"What if he doesn't intend to leave the country? He may kill someone else. After all, if he escaped, he must have murdered Diana. Maybe he *is* mad."

"I don't think it's mad to escape. If I were locked away in a lunatic asylum, I'd bloody well try to get out, too."

"He had no reason to escape. His family has influence. Jack told me the Hewitts were working to get him transferred to Hope End, the Herefordshire family estate. They arranged for a private nurse, which means he'd basically be a free man. So why escape? Especially if the police can't find enough evidence to arrest him for murder. It makes no sense. He's made himself look guilty." He snapped his fingers. "Unless . . ."

"Unless what?"

"Unless he saw who murdered Diana. If Hewitt witnessed the murder, he must be afraid the killer will come after him. That's why he's running for his life. Who knows what he'll do next?"

"Maybe he'll go somewhere like France or Canada. That lets Jack off the hook."

"Damnation, Eliza. Whether or not it's Hewitt, a killer remains at large. And all you're worried about is your cousin's career."

"Excuse me, but Jack is getting married. He can't lose his job. How can he support a family if he's out of work? Ask my dad. It's not easy."

"I may as well be discussing this with the pigeons in Hyde Park."

Eliza straightened her hat. "Go ahead, talk to the pigeons or those ducks over there. I have better things to do than listen to you natter about Hewitt again. Freddy is meeting me at the syndicate luncheon, and I don't want to be late."

Higgins caught her by the elbow. "Promise me you'll be careful. One syndicate member has already been killed."

She shook off his hand. "If you had seen Freddy in his rowing uniform, you'd realize he's well able to protect me. He's got the muscles of a circus man, he does."

"Good grief."

"And I'll be lunching at the Henley Regatta in full view of hundreds of people," she said airily. "What in the world could possibly go wrong at a picnic?"

Although headed in the syndicate picnic's direction, Eliza first needed to find Sybil. If one suffragette at Henley knew about Hewitt, perhaps they all did. She'd run into Sybil every day of the regatta so far, but the packed crowds along the Berks shore seemed greater today. Probably due to the trophies being awarded that evening.

She should have asked that pompous duke which bandstand he was near when he overheard the suffragettes, but he seemed a right cold stick. At least his lovely green-eyed wife was all charm and warmth. And a woman had to be charming indeed for the Professor to act so polite in her presence. Eliza wondered if he'd been sweet on her all those years ago. Higgins couldn't have always acted such a rude old bachelor.

Eliza scanned the crowd. Most suffragettes who sold their weekly magazine wore white dresses with green and purple sashes. She caught sight of their colors on the other side of some boisterous men in Oxford blazers. Was it Sybil? If anyone knew the truth about Hewitt's escape, it was the fiancée of a Scotland Yard detective.

Hang good manners. Eliza cupped her hands around her mouth and shouted, "Sybil! Sybil Chase! Sybil!"

"Are you looking for someone, Miss Doolittle?"

Jonathon Turnbull stood behind her, a boater shading his razor-sharp gaze. He struck quite the elegant figure in white linen pants, yellow and blue striped tie, and navy blazer with yellow piping. She was surprised by his jaunty air. Had he forgotten that the woman he professed to adore was recently murdered?

"I'm looking for a friend," she said. "A suffragette."

He tipped his hat to get a better look at her. "Why in the world would you associate with those unnatural creatures? Are you one of them? If so, prepare to be a withered old spinster."

"I don't know where you get such silly ideas about suffragettes,

Mr. Turnbull. Mrs. Pankhurst was a wife and mother, and our own Duchess of Carbrey has had two husbands. My friend Sybil is also engaged to be married."

"I hear my name yet again." Sybil appeared before them, her arms filled with magazines. "You were calling my name a moment ago, Eliza, am I right?"

"Of course." She kissed the young woman on the cheek. "Sorry. For a second I felt like I was back at Covent Garden. But I had to find you before lunch."

"Is everything all right?" Sybil shot Turnbull a suspicious look. "I hope this gentleman is not bothering you, Eliza. If so, I will gladly rescue you."

"She needs rescuing from the likes of you," he snapped.

"Sybil, this is Jonathon Turnbull."

"I am acquainted with Mr. Turnbull. Or at least the men he hires to break up our rallies."

He snickered. "If women want to get involved in politics, they had best be prepared for a little roughhousing."

"Really? I wasn't aware that men with clubs regularly invaded the halls of Parliament."

"They might have to if females ever get the vote."

Eliza held up her hand. "Let's not debate women's suffrage right now. I only wanted to ask about a rumor. The Professor and I just learned Harold Hewitt escaped."

Turnbull looked shocked. "What the devil! That cannot be true."

"I'm only repeating what the Duke of Waterbury told me." Eliza turned to Sybil. "Since he heard it from suffragettes, I thought you might know more."

Sybil took a deep breath. "Our organization leaders learned that Mr. Hewitt escaped shortly before dawn today."

Turnbull whipped off his hat. "This is incompetence of the highest order. Are the police all drunkards and simpletons? How could they let that lunatic walk away? Everyone in Scotland Yard should be put in asylums themselves."

"I don't know how you can blame Scotland Yard for Mr. Hewitt's escape," Sybil said angrily. "Once committed to Claybury, he became the responsibility of the asylum officials. Or perhaps you believe the Metropolitan Police ought to stand guard at every mental hospital in the country!"

"They should certainly be guarding a man suspected of murder!" He looked disgusted. "That fanatic killed Miss Price. You're probably glad she's dead, aren't you? And don't pretend to be outraged. I know your leaders asked her to perform at one of your rallies. Diana naturally refused, and that put a target on her back."

"Are you *quite* mad, Mr. Turnbull?"

"I am not mad, Miss Chase. But the man sent by your organization to kill her obviously is. And I wouldn't be at all surprised if the suffragettes are behind his escape."

"But how would they get him out?" Eliza asked. "It would be most difficult for anyone to sneak a patient past the attendants."

"I don't know how they did it. But these women are mad as hatters. Several of them are sure to be inmates there."

"And what would we do with Mr. Hewitt once we set him free?" Sybil asked in an exasperated voice. "Have him speak at our public rallies? Send him to assassinate the Prime Minister? And men accuse *us* of being irrational and emotional. It might be best to give women the vote, and take it away from men."

Eliza bit back a chuckle. "She has you there, mate."

"You're both insufferable. I refuse to continue this absurd conversation." Turnbull gave them a last scornful look before he stalked off.

Sybil held up one of the magazines. "Don't forget your copy of *The Suffragette!*" she shouted at his retreating figure.

Eliza laughed. "Garn, but you have more brass than that band playing by the river."

"Because of men like him, we've formed a band of female bodyguards for protection."

"Female bodyguards? I've never heard of such a thing."

"Violence towards us is growing. The esteemed Mrs. Garrud has trained thirty women on how to use Indian clubs and the art of ju-jitsu. In our recent run-ins with the police, our Bodyguard came in quite handy." Sybil leaned closer. "Don't tell Jack, but I almost joined them."

Eliza looked at the petite young woman in surprise. Even with the suffragette sash across her dress, Sybil was the picture of a proper English lady. Closer inspection revealed a sunburnt nose and cheeks, as well as tousled brown curls coming loose from her chignon. She obviously did not spend hours each day fussing over fashion and face powder. Still, Sybil didn't seem robust enough to stand her ground against a burly policeman.

"Cor, but you might get hurt."

"Don't worry. I decided against it, and not because of being manhandled by police. It would damage Jack's position at the Yard if his future wife was arrested for braining one of his men with an Indian club." She winked. "If you like, I could teach you how to flip a brawny man over your shoulder without getting your skirt wrinkled."

"What fun." Eliza giggled at the thought of tossing Professor Higgins to the floor.

"I'll take you to our next rally. The Bodyguard are sure to attend."

She glanced up. "Sybil, I think that gentleman by the lemonade vendor is Gordon Longhurst. Why in the world is Diana Price's husband at a boat race so soon after her death?"

"He looks very out of place," Sybil said.

Indeed, Longhurst made a grim figure in his black suit, black gloves, black tie, and black hat. Eliza was surprised to see him in full mourning, something men rarely wore after the burial service. Because everyone else at the Henley Regatta sported bright summer colors or white linen, Longhurst seemed like an ominous raven amidst a flock of tropical birds.

He appeared oblivious to the curious stares directed his way. Instead, he gazed about as if searching for someone. The moment he spied Eliza, he hurried over.

"Thank goodness," Longhurst said when he reached them. "I have been trying to find anyone connected to the Wrexham syndicate all morning."

Eliza introduced Longhurst to Sybil, but he paid no attention to her.

"Miss Doolittle, Sir Walter sent a message last night inviting me to the luncheon meeting today. I was grateful to realize that neither I nor my poor wife had been forgotten. Diana may no longer be with us, but that is no reason to treat her as if she never existed. It comforts me that I can be here as Diana's representative."

"Of course. But how can I help you?"

"Where are they meeting during the luncheon interval?"

Eliza pointed toward the Henley Bridge. "Walk past the fellow selling raspberry ices, then turn left at where the Hungarian band is playing. Then turn right at—"

"Can you take me there yourself?" He paused. "*Now*, if you would."

Eliza shrugged at Sybil. "We'll speak about the rally later."

As Sybil took off in the opposite direction, Eliza led Gordon Longhurst through the crowd. "Turnbull had best not say a single thing to me or I won't be able to control myself," he muttered. "And the same goes for Saxton. At the funeral, he carried on like a figure from an

Italian opera. I was mortified beyond belief. One nasty aside from either of them, and I fear we may come to blows."

Eliza sighed. Higgins was right. This picnic might not be so carefree after all.

SEVEN

W hat the devil is he doing here?" Lord Saxton muttered as he threw back another glass of claret. The Duchess of Carbrey sat on a cushioned bench beside him. Her expression seemed troubled.

"He's dressed like the Ghost of Christmas Yet to Come." Lady Tansy lounged on a pillow a few feet away. "All we need are some rattling chains."

Eliza suspected everyone agreed with the Saxtons. When she arrived at the luncheon site with Longhurst, the syndicate members had looked as if she'd brought the Grim Reaper into their midst. The black-garbed widower made everyone uneasy. But not even the sad Mr. Longhurst could spoil Eliza's first fancy picnic.

Since the Saxtons had outfitted their Ascot private box and brought refreshments, it was now the Turnbulls who played host to the syndicate. Three of their servants—a maid, footman, and chauffeur—set up a lavish picnic. Tartan blankets were spread over the freshly mown grass, with large gold and navy pillows scattered on top of them. They'd provided benches for those who did not care to sit on the ground, but only the Duchess and Longhurst chose to use them. Everyone else sat or reclined on the blankets and pillows.

Wicker food hampers sat open in every corner, from which the servants pulled out an endless array of cold chicken pies, walnut and celery salad, Stilton cheeses, deviled turkey, curried eggs, potted pâtés, cucumber sandwiches, and more. Even better was the hamper of sweets. Eliza almost made herself ill from an excess of tea cakes, dates stuffed with ginger and nuts, pineapple ices, sugared berries, and tarts.

Claret, aerated water, lavender lemonade, and champagne quenched everyone's thirst. To keep the champagne chilled, bottles were wrapped in wet newspapers. A Primus stove heated water for tea beneath the nearby tree. But it seemed too warm a day for hot beverages, and only Jonathon Turnbull drank the tea that carried his family name. Despite the overcast sky, the air grew increasingly humid and still. A brief rain shower made everyone cry out. Once it stopped, the picnickers settled back to enjoy the lazy summer day.

At some point, Eliza exchanged happy looks with her father, who held a chicken pie in one hand and a glass of champagne in the other. Rose leaned back against two pillows, her attention focused on her third pineapple ice. Eliza felt someone kiss the top of her head, and she looked up and gave Freddy her sunniest smile. With a contented sigh, she nestled against him.

Freddy had changed into an LRC blue and white striped blazer, which emphasized his dazzling blue eyes. But he still sported his white knee-length rowing shorts, allowing everyone a good look at his muscled legs. Lady Tansy, the Duchess, and Rachel Turnbull snuck appreciative glances his way. Even Dad looked like a proper swell in his straw boater, deep violet blazer, cream-colored trousers, and purple and green striped tie. Unfortunately, the same could not be said for Rose, who wore a lilac dress boasting too many flounces.

This was the best luncheon Eliza had ever attended, and not only because of the food. To think she was an invited guest at the Henley

Regatta! And not escorted by Professor Higgins or Colonel Pickering, either. She was especially proud that Dad and Freddy had invited her. Who would have dreamed her sweetheart or father had a legitimate reason to attend the Royal Ascot and the Henley Regatta.

And she couldn't imagine a prettier spot for a picnic. In every direction, she spied brightly colored blazers, picnickers laughing on the wide green lawn, brass bands, rose and blackberry bushes, regatta flags, and the countless punts, barges, canoes, and boats floating on the Thames. She sipped her lavender lemonade. Cor, it tasted better than champagne.

"I must say I envy you, Miss Doolittle."

Eliza looked over in surprise at the Duchess. "Me? Whatever for?"

"You have the appetite of a dray horse, my girl," she said with a laugh. "But you're as slim as the orchids Sir Walter grows in his greenhouse. If I ate a tenth of what you did for lunch, I'd be larger than my champion mares."

Before Eliza could reply, her father chimed in. "My daughter gets it from me, she does. Doolittles don't run to fat. Glad I am of it now, seeing a feast like this." He finished off his chicken pie with gusto, followed immediately by a loud belch.

"As I said, I envy you." The Duchess raised a glass of claret in her direction. Eliza thought the older woman had a fine figure; her waist in the coral-hued gown was nearly as tiny as Lady Tansy's. Then again, the Duchess only nibbled at her food.

Eliza didn't explain that her slimness wasn't because of the Doolittle ancestors. Growing up, she often ate one meal a day, and a meager one at that. The year she turned eight, her father broke his leg and couldn't work at all. It was a bloody miracle they didn't starve. Now she was always hungry, especially for sweets, which she rarely got as a child. Poverty had left its mark on her; the result was a perennially slim figure. But years of gnawing hunger and desperation was a high price to pay for a wasp waist.

"I sympathize, Your Grace," said Bomber Brody. He sat cross-legged between the pails of champagne and a small table holding a tea chest, pots of honey, sugar cubes, and lemons. "One tea cake can put me over the regulation weight and knock me out of a race."

The dark-haired fellow was actually thinner than Eliza and taller than average for a jockey. She was a bit surprised Brody still raced, since he was well into his thirties. However, he looked younger than his years, with a raffish charm enhanced today by his emerald green blazer and white trousers. Certainly the buxom brunette he'd brought as his guest, a girl named Patsy, couldn't take her eyes off him.

"You can retire after our Dancer wins a few more times, Brody," Eliza's father said. "With each race, the purse will grow. Your share as the winning jockey gets you closer to taking off those racing silks for good."

Longhurst cleared his throat, and everyone turned in his direction. For the past hour he had not touched any of the food or drink at the luncheon, but only sat staring at the ground in silence. "Since the discussion has finally turned to racing, could we please get down to business? I believe this luncheon has gone on long enough."

"What the devil are you talking about?" Turnbull stood in front of a wide bramble bush, a teacup in his hand.

Turnbull's wife Rachel looked worried. "Jonathon, please."

"Please what? This chap comes uninvited to our luncheon and then orders us about. The nerve of the fellow."

"I invited him," Sir Walter said sternly. "We have syndicate business to discuss, and it's fitting that he be here."

"I'm not sure why," the Duchess murmured. "This seems a bit odd."

"As odd as Mr. Longhurst here." Lord Saxton chuckled and sipped his glass of claret.

Eliza threw a nervous look at Freddy. The poor boy had only just met the syndicate members. He had no idea how unpleasant they could be.

"Please excuse us, Mr. Longhurst," Rachel said in a quiet voice. "This picnic must seem rather frivolous considering your recent loss, but the business meeting was going to go forward regardless. My husband and I thought we should make it as pleasant as possible. Our staff shall remain at the site until the fireworks tonight, so you may stay as long as you like."

Eliza was stunned. This was the most she had ever heard Rachel Turnbull speak.

Turnbull looked disgusted. "Why don't we invite him home as well, my dear? I'm sure he has nothing else to do but trail after us. Too bad he wasn't following his wife around at Ascot. Diana might still be alive if he had."

Everyone gasped.

Longhurst grew pale. "How dare you say such a thing to me?"

"And how dare you come here? You have no place among us now that Diana is gone."

Sir Walter cleared his throat. "Gentlemen, you are making a spectacle of yourselves."

As Longhurst shot to his feet, the Duchess quickly turned to Freddy. "Mr. Eynsford Hill, you must be pleased at the LRC's victories yesterday against the Thames Rowing Club. And with Pinks and Wise both winning by four lengths."

Freddy nodded. "It was ripping, I must say. And I believe we have the Diamond Challenge safely in hand. It helps that the prevailing wind is not coming from the Bushes side."

"I don't think the Bushes wind prevailed last year either," the Duchess added. "Of course, storm clouds are gathering now. That could change the direction of the—"

"You beastly cad," Longhurst said between clenched teeth. "As if I would ever harm a hair on Diana's head! I did everything to make her happy, even if it meant looking the other way when she dallied with pigs like you and Saxton."

"See here, chap, I'm not drunk yet," Saxton said loudly. "Say one more word, and I'll chuck you into the Thames."

Waving a delicate painted fan, Lady Tansy gave an exaggerated sigh.

Amazingly Eliza's stepmother defused the situation. Rose Doolittle wagged a ringed finger at the men. "Look here, gents. You want to box each other's ears, fine by me. Only take it behind the boathouse. Where I come from, it's bloody bad manners to be scrapping over the lunch dishes. 'Specially if you got guests. So either take yourselves off, or put your blooming arses back in your seats." She adjusted the violet satin and gauze hat pinned atop her red curls. "Me and Alfie came here for a picnic, not to watch you swells have a dustup."

Alfred kissed his wife on her freckled cheek. "Ain't she a marvel?"

"First thing she's said that made a drop of sense," Eliza whispered to Freddy.

Saxton, Longhurst, and Turnbull broke eye contact. Longhurst sat down on the bench, while Lord Saxton drained his claret. Turnbull paced in front of the bramble bush. After an uncomfortable silence, Sir Walter struggled to stand up. At his age, a bench might have been the wiser choice than sitting on the ground. Still, he looked remarkably vital in his boating tie, socks, and blazer, all of which matched Lord Saxton's claret.

"This is our first business meeting since the tragic events at Ascot sixteen days ago."

With a groan, Longhurst buried his face in his hands.

"I did not wish to offend anyone, but postponing this meeting would have been unwise. The Eclipse Stakes are less than two weeks away. We must deal with a few business details before then," Sir Walter continued. "Of course, those of us who placed individual bets on the Donegal Dancer have already claimed our Ascot winnings."

Freddy leaned close to Eliza. "You lucky girl."

She grinned at the thought of those additional sixty guineas in her bank account.

Sir Walter pulled several thick sealed envelopes from a leather valise near his feet. "As per the Wrexham Racing Syndicate bylaws, I have calculated the various expenses incurred by our racehorse since our last business meeting. They are explained in detail, along with the dates of the aforesaid expenditures. You will also find a check made out to each owner for his or her share of the Ascot purse." He smiled. "The Dancer is now officially undefeated this season."

"Hear, hear." The Duchess clinked her glass with Lord Saxton's.

Sir Walter walked around the circle, distributing envelopes. He stopped at Brody and handed him an envelope as well. "Although Brody is not an owner, he did ride our colt to victory. According to our bylaws, he is entitled to a jockey's share of the purse."

Brody tucked the envelope inside his blazer while his young lady cuddled closer.

"Brody isn't an owner?" Longhurst appeared puzzled. "I thought these meetings were only for owners and their families."

"It is illegal for jockeys to own a racehorse, Mr. Longhurst," the Duchess explained. "They are not allowed to bet on the races, either. It's a conflict of interest, you see."

"My record is a pretty stellar one, so I do all right," Brody said to Longhurst.

"I bet you do, lovey." The young brunette smiled up at the jockey.

"You're the luv, Patsy." He grabbed her hand and kissed it. "That you are."

When Sir Walter closed his valise, Longhurst got to his feet again. "Wait a minute. Where is Diana's share? Her death doesn't make her less of an owner than all of you."

"Actually it does," Saxton said.

"What are you talking about? Diana was a part owner of the Donegal Dancer, and I am her lawful husband. That means one of those checks should be handed to me."

Sir Walter looked uncomfortable. "As I feared, your late wife did not apprise you of the particulars spelled out in the syndicate's contractual agreement. If she had, you would know that the shares each owner holds cannot be passed on to anyone else. They can only be sold."

"What!"

"Yes, we thought it best if only the owners could lay claim to any of the shares. That means they are not transferable. Not even in cases of an owner's death."

"He's quite right, Mr. Longhurst," Lady Tansy said with a shrug. "If my beloved husband were to die choking on his kippers at tomorrow's breakfast, I would have no legal claim on that horse. Not that I ever cared a farthing about owning a racehorse."

"Exactly," Sir Walter said. "For this accounting period, the other owners will pay Miss Price's share of the expenses that have been incurred since the last meeting. But they will also share her profits from this last race, divided according to the proper percentages."

"But I'm her husband, and the law says I inherit whatever belongs to her."

"The law may say that, but not the contracts signed by each of the owners of the Donegal Dancer. Those owners are Turnbull, Saxton, the Duchess, Doolittle, and myself." Sir Walter frowned. "Tragically, your wife is no longer an owner."

Longhurst flung his hat to the ground. "I'll see the lot of you in court!"

"Go ahead," Turnbull said. "Waste your money—and our time."

"I do wish this had been handled privately, Sir Walter," the Duchess said.

"I thought it only right that he be informed as soon as possible," he replied. "And I hoped the public setting would curtail any histrionics."

"Histrionics? I'm angry, and rightly so. You're cheating me!"

Lady Tansy rolled her eyes. "It appears there will be histrionics after all. I was also surprised by your appearance here today, Mr. Longhurst. I do believe you are officially in mourning." She looked pointedly at his black suit.

"He looks like a damn undertaker," Saxton muttered.

"I am grieving for my sweet wife. It's the decent thing to do. Shows a lot more respect for her memory than you," he said to Saxton. "Sitting there in your fancy gold blazer and silly white pants. Do you think you honor my wife's memory because you stuck a black armband on your sleeve? You filthy hypocrite."

Saxton pushed himself to his feet.

"Maitland, really. Behave yourself."

He ignored his wife. "Don't call me a hypocrite! I cared about that woman. I still can't believe she's gone. And for what? Her murder makes no sense. Unless we listen to the papers who claim the killer is some lunatic supporter of women's suffrage."

"We don't know Harold Hewitt is guilty," the Duchess said.

"I don't think it was that madman. I suspect someone else did the deed." He narrowed his eyes at Longhurst. "It wouldn't be the first time a jealous husband was driven to murder."

Eliza agreed with him. At least three people at the picnic might have wanted Diana dead.

With a growl, Longhurst lunged at Saxton. Although his sudden attack threw the taller man off balance, Saxton kept upright. The two of them gripped each other's arms and pushed like battling stags. Freddy and Brody hurried to pull them apart.

"Stop this right now!" The Duchess smacked both men with her parasol.

Freddy held Saxton's arms, while the wiry jockey managed to pull Longhurst off to the side. "Just like a Saturday night at the Ten Bells, ain't it, Lizzie?" Her father winked.

Eliza thought it best to leave before the next fight began. "We should go, Mrs. Turnbull," she said. "The luncheon interval is almost over, and Freddy must get back to his rowing team."

"No, please." Rachel Turnbull rose to her feet. She smoothed down her silvery gray skirt. "I do not want the luncheon to end in such disarray. Please release Lord Saxton, Mr. Eynsford Hill. I think we can trust him to keep his composure now."

After Freddy obliged, she whispered something in Saxton's ear. Like a disobedient pupil told to return to his desk, he sat back down on the blanket next to his haughty young wife. Eliza stared wide-eyed when Rachel approached Longhurst next.

"I apologize for the harsh words that have been spoken this afternoon. You have been dealt a bitter blow, and are deserving of our sympathy. Not our censure."

Longhurst's face crumpled at her gentle words, and he bent over sobbing. Rachel led him back to his cushioned bench. He collapsed onto it, one hand covering his eyes.

"I think we all need to calm down before the races resume," Rachel said. "There is another hamper with more sweets, and I encourage everyone to drink something. The day is warm, and a bit of lemon-ade, tea, or water may help bolster our spirits." She looked over at Lady Tansy. "Would you care for a cup of tea?"

"Thank you, but it's too beastly hot for tea." She fanned herself faster.

"I'll have another cup." Turnbull snapped his fingers for the maid. "Be more generous with the cream and honey this time."

While the maid headed to the silver tea urn with his cup, Rachel turned to Longhurst. "Would you like a cup of tea as well?"

He shook his head violently. "I'd rather die of thirst. Any tea bearing the Turnbull name is no better than swill."

That remark seemed to hurt Rachel, so Eliza gestured to the nearby footman. "I'd like a cup of tea, please. Cream, three lumps of sugar."

She elbowed Freddy, who piped up, "Me too. Only lemon with mine."

An uneasy but welcome silence followed. It was so quiet, Eliza could hear the Leander Rowing Club singing by the shore, accompanied by the chatter of chickadees. Brody's friend Patsy looked at what remained of the food and drinks.

"Are there any dates left? Or some sugared berries? And I might have a bit of tea as well," she said. "Cream, honey, *and* one lump, please. I do like it sweet."

Eliza smiled at her and sipped her own tea.

"How can you drink hot tea in this weather?" Lady Tansy fanned herself with a weary expression. "It's as warm and humid as the Amazon jungle. All we need are toucans."

Brody suddenly jumped back, waving his hands in front of him. "Damned bees! They're attracted to the honey pots. Do you have lids to cover them?"

Rachel signaled to the maid, who rummaged about in a hamper.

"I never liked bees." Brody eyed the tea table nervously. "Had a horse stung by a bee during practice once, right above the eye. He reared up and threw me over the paddock fence."

"Let's sit somewhere else, luv." Balancing a teacup in one hand, Patsy struggled to get to her feet. Several bees swarmed over her cup, and she froze.

"Watch out, Patsy!" Brody waved them away.

She let out a tiny scream before dropping the cup. Tea spilled all over her crisp white shirtwaist. "My beautiful new dress!" Patsy howled. "It's ruined now."

"I'll get you a new one, darling. Never you mind." Brody handed Patsy his handkerchief to dab her wet skirt. "But that's the last time I sit near honey pots."

"That's what men were like around Diana," Longhurst said suddenly. "Like bees drawn to honey. They couldn't resist her." He looked at both Saxton and Turnbull. "And one of those bees stung her to death, didn't they?"

"Not again," Lady Tansy murmured.

"I got something to say to the other owners." Alfred stood up. "I was right nervous to hear about these horse thieves snatching champion horses the last five years. So I says we all fork over some winnings and hire proper security for the Dancer." He shoved his boater to the back of his head. "'Cause any thief what lays a hand on my horse, I'll hunt him down. And when I find him, I'll stick him and his mates beneath a headstone in Kensal Green."

"He does have a point," the Duchess said to the others. "Only grooms and stable hands guard the Dancer now."

"Right you are. Let's hire a few brawny fellows to guard our colt."

Sir Walter nodded. "We can put it to a vote now, if you like. Although we must agree on how much to pay for the extra protection."

"The horse? You're worried about the horse?" Longhurst looked at them in disbelief. "Why didn't anyone worry about protecting my Diana?"

"I've had enough of this," Turnbull said to Longhurst. "I want you out of here now."

"The whole lot of you are cold, unfeeling monsters. Every one of you should be dead, not Diana." At Longhurst's hateful words, Eliza felt a chill down her spine.

Turnbull yanked the man up by the collar. "I said get out!"

Longhurst slapped his hand away. "And I said you all deserve to die. Especially you and that drunken sod of a lord over there."

"Go to the devil," Saxton spat out.

"Bad enough you both treated Diana like a toy you'd bought at Harrods. Now you steal her money when she's barely cold in her grave. Don't think you'll get away with this. I don't care how many titles Saxton and the Duchess have." He jabbed his finger at Turnbull's chest. "Or how much tea your bloody company crams down people's throats. I will have justice."

"Don't threaten me. You weren't even man enough to warm your wife's bed!"

"Bastard!" Longhurst swung at Turnbull. The punch landed squarely on his jaw.

Reeling from the blow, Turnbull fell against Brody. The jockey fought to keep his balance before he also tumbled backward onto the tea table. He and the table crashed to the ground. A nearby picnic hamper was knocked over, sending tarts spilling onto the grass.

Before anyone could help Brody, Longhurst spun on his heel and charged off into the crowd. Dozens of people stared after him.

Lady Tansy broke the awkward silence. "What a pity he smashed the lovely tea things. I had just decided I wanted a cup of tea." She smiled coolly. "I suppose I must settle for champagne instead."

———

The storm that had threatened all day let loose with a fury during the distribution of the regatta prizes. After the ceremony, the rain mercifully slowed to a drizzle. But it was near dusk, and the rain had dissipated the afternoon's earlier warmth. Chilled, Eliza shivered so hard that Freddy draped his LRC blazer over her shoulders.

He looked up at the roiling sky. "We won't know if there'll be fireworks for at least an hour. They'll make a decision when the sun sets."

"If there are fireworks, I'm not watching them during a thunderstorm." She pulled his blazer tight around her. "Besides, we saw enough fireworks at the luncheon. Let's find your mother and Clara so we can return to London."

Freddy scanned the milling crowd. "I haven't seen them since the end of the Diamond Challenge. But if we find the Saxtons, we're sure to find them. They drove up together."

"They'll probably drive back with them as well. Freddy, let's you and I catch the next train. But first we must thank Mrs. Turnbull for inviting us to the luncheon." Given the furor after Longhurst threw that punch, Eliza had never had a chance to extend her gratitude.

However, Eliza wondered if they'd ever find Mrs. Turnbull in this teeming throng, much less Freddy's mother and sister. A virtual sea of dripping parasols and umbrellas surrounded them on all sides. She didn't see a single familiar face.

"Why don't we return to the picnic site?" Freddy suggested. "The servants will be there."

He was right. Mrs. Turnbull had mentioned the servants would remain in that spot until after the fireworks. Eliza hoped so. With luck, there might be something left in those hampers. She wouldn't mind another chicken pie and a steaming cup of tea. Blimey, right now she'd settle for warm claret and a few curried eggs.

As she and Freddy walked toward the luncheon site, people scurried in every direction. Some headed to Henley and a dry roof over their heads; others clustered near the private boating clubs or the bandstands where musicians continued to play. No doubt the Professor and Colonel Pickering were warm and dry at the Remenham Club. Eliza had enjoyed her first regatta, but she couldn't wait to settle into a train compartment and kick off her damp shoes.

"Miss Doolittle!" The Duchess and Sir Walter waved at them from the boathouse.

"Do you know where the Turnbulls are?" Eliza asked after they joined her and Freddy. "We want to make our good-byes. I have no wish to get wetter, not even for fireworks."

"I haven't seen Rachel since the end of the Visitors' Challenge Cup. I did see Jonathon about an hour ago." The Duchess frowned. "He looked rather awful. Pale, shaky, feverish. I suspect he's caught a chill."

"Too much damp river air," Sir Walter added.

"If Mr. Turnbull is ill, we should find his wife," Eliza said. "She may not realize he needs her. We'll check the picnic site. Would you like to come with us?"

"I'm sorry, but my driver is getting the car. If this drizzle worsens again, the roads may become too muddy to navigate."

Sir Walter nodded. "Her Grace has been kind enough to offer me a ride." After a tip of his straw hat, he and the Duchess disappeared into the crowd.

Eliza frowned. "I'm not all that fond of Mr. Turnbull, but I hope he's not really sick. If we can't find Rachel, we should send the servants to search for her."

But when she and Freddy reached the site of the picnic luncheon, it was deserted. Perhaps they'd lunched on some other grassy hill bordered by bramble bushes and a large tree. Then Eliza caught sight of Lady Tansy's sodden paper fan.

"This is the right spot." Eliza saw smashed tarts among the grass blades, along with a few shards of broken china and a stray sugar cube. Aside from that, the area had been swept clean. Not a hamper, blanket, or servant in sight. "I suppose the Turnbulls decided not to stay for the fireworks either."

"Such a shame about the weather." Freddy wrapped his arms around Eliza from behind. "I wanted you to see the fireworks. They put on a ripping good show at Henley."

She turned and snuggled against his chest. "I don't need fireworks. My four days here have been wonderful. Thank you for being an oarsman in the London Rowing Club." Eliza peeked up at him. "A winning club, too."

He laughed. "That we are."

When someone moaned, Eliza and Freddy froze. "What was that?" he asked.

"I don't know." Another moan, weaker this time.

"Is anyone there?" Eliza slowly turned in a circle but only saw wet grass, the bramble hedge, and the dripping tree. "Who's there? Are you hurt?"

"Help me."

The rasping voice came from behind the bramble bush to the left of the tree. Once they rounded the hedge, Eliza cried out. Jonathon Turnbull lay slumped on the muddy ground against the tree trunk.

Hair plastered to his face, eyes wide open, he stared at them in despair.

Eliza and Freddy knelt on either side of him. She noticed vomit on the grass. "You poor man. What happened?"

"It hurts." Turnbull clawed at his chest with a trembling hand.

"Maybe he's having a heart attack." Freddy took his wrist. "I'll check his pulse."

"When did you fall ill, Mr. Turnbull?" She brushed wet hair out of his eyes.

"Can't—move—my legs," he gasped.

"His pulse is damnably slow," Freddy said. "He needs a doctor."

"Mr. Turnbull, where is everyone? Have the servants gone for help?"

But the man couldn't reply. Instead, his eyes rolled toward the back of his head.

"Freddy, run down to the boathouse. And yell for a doctor all the way there. Hurry!"

She spent the next few minutes shouting for help while trying to revive Turnbull. The brass bands playing loudly from different ends of the Berks shore drowned out her voice. Who could make themselves heard with that blooming racket?

Turnbull shuddered as if he were having a seizure. Eliza wept with frustration.

"The doctor's coming! Don't worry. The doctor is almost here." But by the time she heard the approach of a group led by Freddy, it was too late.

Jonathon Turnbull was dead.

EIGHT

Higgins glanced up at the arched entrance to Chelsea Old Church with foreboding. "We'll soon learn if my brother was right. He swore lightning would strike if I ever visited this church again."

Eliza looked startled. "You have a brother?"

"Two of them, actually. I'm the *second* spare."

"I say, Professor, do you have sisters as well?" Freddy stood on the other side of Eliza as they waited to enter. "If so, why haven't we heard about them before now?"

"Because my siblings are none of your business." Ignoring their obvious curiosity, Higgins led the way inside the brick church. "And that is enough about my family tree."

Although he did not attend regularly, he appreciated the history of the place, which dated back to the twelfth century. Chelsea's Lord of the Manor had once owned the north chapel, and the south chapel served as Sir Thomas More's private domain. In fact, Higgins's older brother James was ordained here in an interminable ceremony that he had been forced to attend. His mother had been quite mortified at Higgins's caustic remarks about the vicar who presided over the ordination.

She'd refused to attend church with him ever since. Hopefully a new vicar had replaced the doddering old one.

"Did you know Henry VIII married Jane Seymour in this church?" he said.

"We're here for Jonathon Turnbull's funeral, not a blooming history lesson." Eliza tugged at his sleeve. "And the service has already started, so keep your voice down."

Their footsteps echoed on the aisle's stone floor. Jack Shaw sat in the back pew. The Inspector shifted in his seat as they walked past. He had an eagle-eyed look about him, as if suspicious of everyone at the funeral—even them. Higgins noticed that Freddy put a protective hand at Eliza's waist.

As for Jonathon Turnbull, Higgins didn't give a damn about the wretched fellow. Indeed, he was surprised the church held so many mourners. Not that he believed most of these people had come to grieve. Turnbull's sudden death following so soon after Diana Price's murder had obviously drawn a horde of curious onlookers. And Higgins recognized at least three newspaper reporters. It was no secret that Diana was Turnbull's mistress, one of dozens he had kept over the years. Of course, many of the mourners today would also be the tea merchant's employees come to pay their respects. But from what Higgins knew of Jonathon Turnbull, there was little about the man to respect.

Eliza and Freddy still felt guilty about being unable to save Turnbull's life at the picnic. As for Higgins, he had his own guilt to contend with. And he wondered how Rachel Turnbull was responding to her husband's unexpected death. He remembered her recent horror at seeing Diana's body in the stables. He was surprised to see her in attendance today; most widows remained at home during the funeral service. But here she was in a jet-black gown and a hat shrouded with black netting. Rachel sat in the front pew between two elderly women also garbed in black. Her mother and mother-in-law, perhaps.

"Rachel Turnbull seems a bit subdued," Higgins said.

"She's a lady," Eliza whispered. "That sort know how to control themselves. Not like my Aunt Lottie, who wept and wailed like a banshee at her husband's funeral. Nearly tipped the casket right over." She adjusted the enamel tulip pin on her dress. "However, she was fine the next day and back to selling apples at Covent Garden."

Freddy sighed. "After Father died, Mother spent three years in seclusion."

Higgins settled back in the hard pew, nodding to the Duchess of Carbrey across the aisle. She looked regal in dark purple, her black straw hat crowned with a tulle bow. He spotted Sir Walter Fairweather in the pew behind her, his hands resting on a brass-topped cane. Lord and Lady Saxton sat near the Duchess. Saxton wore the proverbial black armband, but Lady Saxton sported a pale rose walking suit and an endless string of pearls that hung below the waist. Nestled on her coiffed curls perched a flat-brimmed hat; two pink plumes waved from its crown. Clearly she didn't feel the need to dress properly for the occasion.

Higgins thought that rather in bad taste. Eliza had chosen a simple black outfit without decoration or jewelry to set it off, save for the red tulip pin. Even Brody's lady friend wore a dark skirt and jacket, although her straw hat was banded in yellow ribbon.

When he caught sight of Alfred Doolittle and his wife, Higgins winced. They also arrived late for the service and hurried to grab a seat a few pews ahead of Higgins and Eliza. Although Doolittle wore a black armband, he forgot to remove his hat. If Higgins's mother had been here, she would have knocked it off his head. Not surprisingly, Rose Doolittle's bright floral gown was also in poor taste. He couldn't resist chuckling at the stuffed bird pinned backward to her wide picture hat. Its glass eyes seemed to stare straight at him.

Rose turned to her husband. "I've got an appointment, Alfie, remember—"

"Shh, woman," Alfred said in a loud voice. "You won't be late. Now shut yer trap."

Higgins leaned toward Eliza. "You should talk to your stepmother about her wardrobe."

She rolled her eyes. "Rose is a lost cause."

With a sigh, he focused on the high stone arches above the vicar's head. The church did not appear different from his last visit. Chandeliers still dangled above the mourners' heads. The wall and pillar plaques had not been moved, and the old carved musical cherubs flanked the arches. Higgins thought the eclectic mix a bit too much, although his mother loved attending every Sunday and listening to the choir warble out hymns.

Mother had been overjoyed to attend the ceremony here when his brother was appointed Bishop of St. Albans. Every Christmas, Higgins was forced to spend time with family, made more tedious by James carping about those who wallowed in a sinful life. His sanctimonious attitude invariably drove their oldest brother Charles into the study, where he spent the holiday smoking, drinking, and playing cards. Higgins often joined him in the latter, or shut himself in Charles's library, away from the women, children, and Bishop James.

Luckily the ancient vicar of Chelsea Old Church was long gone, either dead or retired. The younger man who replaced him now held the prayer book in a viselike grip. His round spectacles glinted in the sunlight streaming through a window overhead.

"Forgive us our sins and those of our dearly departed brother . . ."

"A tall order. St. Peter is probably still reading through his list of

Turnbull's sins and vices." Higgins winced when Eliza elbowed him in the ribs. "There's nothing wrong with telling the truth."

"Hush. This is a church, not a pub."

"Lord, hear our prayers and comfort us."

"Hm. I believe our vicar is from Norfolk—Yarmouth, on the coast. One of the lesser streets," he mused. "Although I'm not certain. Not until I hear a little more."

"Renew our trust . . ."

The vicar's strong voice echoed into the high rafters, drowning out the clacking noise from Lady Saxton. Visibly bored, she played with her long rope of pearls, back and forth, back and forth. *Snickety-snick.* Higgins was tempted to throttle her with them.

"Strengthen our faith that Jonathon Michael Turnbull and all who have died in the love of Christ will share in his resurrection . . ."

"It's rather comical." Higgins chuckled. "The man pronounces 'share' like 'shah,' as if he's talking about a Persian king. That definitely places him from Norfolk."

". . . blessed us all with the gift of earthly life. He has given to our brother Jonathon his span of thirty-six years and gifts of character . . ."

Higgins snorted so loud that everyone, especially the syndicate owners, turned to stare. "I wasn't aware Turnbull had any character."

His whispered remark started a flood of murmurs from the other attendees. Higgins strained to hear what everyone was saying. It seemed a combination of gossip about Turnbull interspersed with heated talk about the Irish Home Rule Bill passing once again in the House of Commons.

"I hear Turnbull often visited opium dens—"

"The Prime Minister opposes it, as he ought. You know the House of Lords will be bound to cut it down. There will never be a free Ireland."

"Didn't he own a brothel in Spitalfields? I believe he kept it for his gambling cronies and business partners' exclusive use."

"It's passed the Commons before and never made it further."

"Turnbull was no gentleman, no matter how popular his tea is."

"Look what you started," Eliza hissed. "Your mother warned me you couldn't behave."

Higgins fiddled with a loose button on his jacket. "Did you know this is the only church in London with chained books? The Homilies of 1683 are here, plus two volumes of the Book of Martyrs."

"You'll be the next martyr if you don't keep quiet," she muttered.

"The 1717 Vinegar Bible is also one of the chained books, and clearly you must have read how thieves tried to make off with it during Victoria's reign. Ouch!"

Everyone turned in his direction again. Cursing under his breath, Higgins rubbed his left forearm, which stung like the devil. Eliza shot him a satisfied grin and stuck her hatpin back into place.

"That was bloody uncalled for."

"I warned you."

"The service is over." Freddy looked worried they might start to argue in earnest.

The mourners noisily got to their feet. As the church organist played "Nearer, My God, to Thee," pallbearers carried the white lily-draped wooden casket up the aisle. Rachel followed, her arms linked with the elderly women's. The other family relatives trailed behind. The rest of the congregation exited through the doors in time to watch the pallbearers lift the casket into the hearse. Five black horses waited in their caparisoned purple and gold harness. The lead horse had a postilion rider in a formal black coat, a black cap, and purple breeches.

Higgins saw no evidence of damp cheeks nor heard sobs from anyone. A sorry epitaph for Jonathon Turnbull. Not even Rachel seemed upset by her husband's death, although he'd given the poor woman little reason to mourn his passing. Pickering had related a bit of Turnbull's background. The tea merchant had avoided marriage until his family insisted he take a wife, if only to stop the scandalous gossip surrounding him. But Higgins wondered what made the titled Rachel agree to marry someone like Turnbull. Perhaps the Duchess of Carbrey knew more about the match. Minerva was privy to every scandal and shameful secret of the British upper class.

The hearse ambled its way toward the street while church bells tolled a mournful dirge. Rachel and the older matrons headed to a closed carriage behind the hearse, but Jack Shaw stopped them. Meanwhile Higgins walked over to the Duchess, Eliza and Freddy close behind.

The older woman greeted him with a kiss on his cheek. "You rogue. I heard you prattling in there like a rude schoolboy bored at his lessons. Although Turnbull certainly didn't deserve much respect, alive or dead. Still, that's no reason to hurt Rachel's feelings. She's suffered enough, mostly while she was married to that scoundrel."

"That's what I wanted to talk to you about," Higgins began.

"Beg pardon, Your Grace." Jack Shaw suddenly appeared at Higgins's elbow. "I've asked the syndicate members to meet in the garden. I need you to join us as well, Professor." He nodded at Eliza and Freddy. "And the two of you."

Jack herded them toward the group gathered by the ironwork fence. Rachel stood between the two older ladies who'd flanked her at the funeral service. Higgins planted himself beside Sir Walter and the Duchess. Lord Saxton immediately started complaining to his indifferent wife. Brody and his lady friend stood near Alfred and Rose Doolittle; Rose was fussing with the stuffed bird on her hat.

Eliza looked at her father. "Dad, did Gordon Longhurst have a funeral service for his wife?" Higgins leaned closer to eavesdrop.

"That he did, but it was very hush-hush and private. Me and the little woman would've paid our respects since Diana was a syndicate member. But we didn't hear a thing about it till it was all over."

"The headlines were full of Diana's murder at the time," Higgins added while Jack conferred with his detectives. "I imagine Longhurst wanted to avoid more publicity."

Jack rejoined them. "Some news has come to light that all of you should know. Especially since the newspapers have gotten hold of it and will be publishing these revelations later today."

They all stared at each other in alarm. "Jack, what in the world has happened?" Eliza asked.

He turned to Rachel Turnbull. "I am sorry for what I have to tell you, but we received a preliminary report from the coroner. Your husband did not suffer a heart attack after all." Jack paused. "He was murdered."

The group let out a collective gasp. Rachel grew even paler. The two older women on either side pressed close to her, as if fearful she might faint.

"Every syndicate member who attended both Ascot and the Regatta is therefore a suspect, as is Harold Hewitt," Jack continued. "I need all of you to prepare a list of where you were during both events. Please include anyone who can support your alibis."

"This is preposterous!" Sir Walter sputtered in protest. "I'm a Senior Steward at Ascot. It's impossible to recall everyone I saw or every spot I visited during my time there."

Jack threw him a stern look. "I expect everyone's full cooperation. Half of you may come to Scotland Yard later today for questioning. The rest of you I expect to see tomorrow. Of course, I will call on Mrs. Turnbull at a more convenient time, and extend that same courtesy to you, Your Grace."

The Duchess raised her eyebrow at him. "I am perfectly capable of coming to Scotland Yard in person, young man. No need to treat me like a feeble-minded dowager."

He nodded. "Very well, Your Grace. But I intend to question everyone who was at the Henley Regatta picnic as soon as possible."

"Are you going to tell us what he did die from?" Saxton demanded. "Or is that going to remain another mystery Scotland Yard can't solve?"

"Yes, how was my husband murdered?" Rachel Turnbull asked in a quiet but steady voice. Higgins found her composure admirable.

"We're still waiting for several more test results from the coroner. But the toxicologist is certain about his conclusions." Jack's expression was grim. "Jonathon Turnbull was poisoned."

NINE

Walking along the Victoria Embankment, Eliza and Freddy had only a short way to go to reach Scotland Yard. She wasn't looking forward to the visit. Far too many hours were spent in the red granite building this past spring trying to clear Higgins of murder. And from the glum expression Freddy wore, he obviously felt the same. The only time he'd been to Scotland Yard was after they stumbled upon a murder victim.

"Don't know why your cousin couldn't take our statements at the funeral," Freddy said when they walked inside. "It's a damnable nuisance ordering us to come here."

"Turnbull's death is official police business. Jack can't be seen treating family members differently than anyone else." Eliza stopped at the front desk.

The sergeant on duty checked their names off a list, then handed her a slip of paper. "Third floor, miss." He turned his attention to the ledger book in front of him.

Once they got to the third floor, Eliza looked over the common room. Each desk held a detective hunched over paperwork, some with a nervous person sitting across from him. Phones rang from every corner, and everyone seemed to be talking at once. She knew that the adjacent corridor led to several holding cells where suspects and witnesses were interrogated. Eliza's memory of her own experience still gave her chills.

"Here we go, then." Eliza pushed through a swinging gate that led to Jack's office.

Before they could get too close, a policeman barred their way. He gestured for the paper she held and scanned it. After giving them a suspicious look, he rapped on the glass of the closed office door. A muffled voice answered, and the policeman stuck his head inside to say something. Security had been heightened since she was last here.

"The Inspector says you can go in," the policeman said.

Once she entered, Jack gave her a great bear hug.

"Is that your new guard dog out there?" Eliza and Freddy sat down in the chairs directly in front of a large cherrywood desk. "He seemed fierce."

Jack plopped down in his own chair with a sigh. "New regulations. Two PCs were found murdered within a mile of the Yard. And we have no end of bomb threats by the suffragettes, though Sybil swears not from any woman she knows. We had another bomb threat just this morning. The Commissioner feels extra protection is in order." He shrugged. "Don't know why he's feeling nervous all of a sudden. Danger's always been part of a policeman's job. When construction workers were putting up this place in '88, they found the dismembered body of a woman. Still haven't solved that one."

Freddy's face turned a bit green. "I say, I don't know how you fellows spend your days hunting down villains."

"If we didn't, Londoners would be running for their lives every time they left the house." Jack rearranged the files and pencils on his polished desk, although it was the picture of neatness and order. "Let's get down to why I asked you both here. I questioned the Duchess yesterday, along with Sir Walter and Brody. I also spoke with the jockey's lady friend." He glanced down at his notebook. "A Miss Patsy Wilkins from Putney. I interviewed the Saxtons about an hour ago, and your father and Rose should be here before teatime."

"I don't know what we can say about the picnic you haven't already heard," Eliza said. "As for what was served for lunch—assuming that's how Jonathon Turnbull was poisoned—it would be the Turnbull servants and Rachel who could best tell you."

"I plan to visit Mrs. Turnbull as soon as possible. Not that I'm removing her from my list of suspects. But if she is innocent, I'd hate to upset her further."

Eliza nodded. "She has one of the best motives, though I hate to say it."

"Jealousy is a powerful motive, one shared by Gordon Longhurst. Of course, Lady Saxton's husband also cheated, but I can't see that young lady committing a crime of passion. She seems to possess the steely nerves of a cat burglar."

Freddy leaned forward, his gloved hands clasped over an ivory walking stick. "Are you certain Mr. Turnbull was poisoned? It looked like he suffered a heart attack that day at the regatta. He wasn't able to say much, but he did complain of chest pains."

"Freddy's right, Jack. And according to the Duchess, Turnbull appeared ill at least an hour before he died."

"Poisons can kill instantly or take a long time to shut down the body. Sometimes weeks."

Freddy bolted upright with a stricken look. "Maybe we were poisoned. Eliza, we might be dead by the end of the day."

"Jack means a poison can take time to act if it's given on a steady basis." She patted his hand. "The costermongers at Covent Garden put out strychnine every week to kill the rats."

"I'm sure you're fine, young man," Jack said. "Our chemists have determined that the poison was botanical in nature, although they have not yet identified the exact plant."

She thought back to the scene of the picnic. "There were lots of flowers and bushes everywhere at Henley. And we sat right under a big tree. Don't know what kind, though."

"My detectives examined the site. It was a hawthorn tree. And hawthorn tree berries are poisonous."

"Maybe some of the berries accidentally fell into the food, or got mixed up with the sugared berries that were served. The Turnbulls brought strawberries and raspberries."

"They served tarts as well," Freddy added. "Most were lemon, but I saw at least a half-dozen raspberry tarts."

"The hawthorn tree isn't the only possible culprit," Jack said. "That bramble hedge near the tree also has poisonous berries."

"Blimey," Eliza said. "I'm such a city creature. Good thing I was never taken to the country when I was a child. I'd have eaten every poisonous berry in sight."

"Since no one else at the picnic became ill, it is likely Turnbull was the sole target. He could have been poisoned after the lunch, perhaps by something he consumed that afternoon. He died a good six hours after all of you had eaten, and the day was warm. He would have had no problem finding something to drink at the many venues at Henley. If someone followed him, the murderer may have waited for the best opportunity to administer the poison." Jack raised his eyebrows. "Unless Turnbull ate or drank something at the picnic which no one else did."

"I don't think so." Eliza remembered all those delicious goodies in the hampers. "You know me, Jack. I ate and drank a little bit of everything."

Freddy finally smiled. "A little?"

"Well, I was hungry."

When she listed everything she'd eaten, Jack nodded. "That matches what everyone has told me so far. And dessert?"

That would be easy. Eliza never forgot a single sweet she had eaten. "Those tarts Freddy told you about. Tea cakes and sugared berries, of course. Then those lovely pineapple ices. Oh, dates stuffed with ginger and nuts, too. I think that's everything."

Jack chuckled. "Sounds like more than enough."

"And they had lots to drink," Freddy said. "Champagne, claret, tea, aerated water."

Eliza sighed at the memory. "And such wonderful lavender lemonade."

"Think carefully. Did Jonathon Turnbull eat or drink anything that no one else did?"

Freddy and Eliza looked at each other. "No," they said at the same time.

"He drank more tea than the rest of us," Eliza added. "His own tea. Apparently that's what he always drinks, but he wasn't the only one. Freddy and I drank tea as well. That Patsy woman asked for tea, too. Lady Tansy wanted tea later, but by then Longhurst had started another fight and knocked the tea table over."

Jack scowled. "Turnbull's death was first judged to be from natural causes. Unfortunately, the food from the picnic lunch was never brought to the Yard and tested."

"It seems to me Turnbull and Diana Price were killed because of their affair," Eliza said. "Which makes Longhurst the most likely suspect. He made quite a scene at the picnic, as everyone there can tell you." Her eyes widened. "I just remembered that Longhurst refused to eat at the picnic. He wouldn't drink anything, either."

"We've already had Longhurst here twice for questioning. Worse for him, since he doesn't have a convincing alibi for the time leading up to his wife's death at Ascot. Oh, he placed a bet on Tracery like she asked, but no one remembers seeing him after that."

"There you are, then." Freddy looked satisfied. "You have your killer."

"Do we? Rachel Turnbull doesn't have a good alibi for Miss Price's death, either. And she was responsible for the food at the picnic." Jack rose and walked over to the window. He stared out in the direction of the Thames. "Then there's the missing Harold Hewitt. Is it a coincidence that he escaped from the asylum the very day Turnbull was poisoned? And both Turnbull and Price were opposed to the suffrage movement. Leaves me to wonder if this is a murder of jealousy and passion, or a crime motivated by politics."

Eliza thought a moment. "I vote for jealousy."

Jack turned and gave her a knowing look. "Did you make that decision based on your conversation with Hewitt at Claybury Asylum?"

Her cheeks grew warm with embarrassment.

"You went to see that madman at the lunatic asylum?" Freddy sounded horrified. "What in the world were you thinking? You might have been killed."

Sometimes Freddy was more melodramatic than her favorite cinema heroines. "The Professor believed we should have a talk with him, seeing as how he spoke with Hewitt at Ascot. I knew the Professor still felt guilty about what happened at the races, so I thought, what harm can there be in one little visit?"

Freddy looked speechless, but Jack was not. "Lizzie, you must have known I would learn about it the next time I saw Hewitt."

"I hoped the asylum officials would forget to mention it."

"Well, they didn't. In fact, they were pleased that his sister and the family solicitor paid a call on their patient for the first time."

"He seemed to enjoy the conversation," she said in a small voice. "Most of it, anyway."

"I'd enjoy hearing the particulars of that conversation, too." He flipped open his notebook.

After she was through relating the details, Jack continued to scribble. Eliza stared in silence at the large map of London on the wall, which was dotted with colored pins. Each one denoted a crime. The red pins indicated a murder. She noticed far too many of that color. She couldn't imagine having a job where every day revealed yet another butchered corpse. Trying to figure out who killed Turnbull and Diana Price was difficult enough. What must it be like to solve hundreds of such crimes? But she was proud of her cousin for doing just that.

"All right, then." Jack put down his pencil. "I'll have a word with your Professor and see if he has anything to add. And I will tell him—as I am telling you now, Lizzie—I want no more interference in this case. These murders are not like the one this past spring. You and Higgins were in the thick of it then, and had reason to be involved." He narrowed his eyes. "Even if it did almost get you killed."

"Don't worry. I have no interest in tracking down any more killers." Eliza stood and straightened her collar. "In fact, Freddy has promised to take me to the cinema this afternoon. We're going to see *The Lady and the Mouse*, starring Dorothy and Lillian Gish. They're sisters, you know. Usually I go to the cinema on Friday or Saturday, but Sybil and I have plans."

"Yes, I have heard about those plans," Jack said in disapproval.

"Why the stern face? Sybil wants to introduce me to her suffragette friends. She says there will be a few speeches, maybe by a Pankhurst. I've never been to a suffragette rally or parade. It should be interesting. Fun, too, I hope."

"Fun? It will be damned dangerous." Freddy tapped his walking stick on the floor. "My dear Eliza, I must put my foot down. Bad enough you run off to horse races where you might be trampled. Then you visit lunatic asylums to talk with madmen. Now you plan to march with suffragettes. You'll be throwing bricks at windows next."

"Don't be daft," Eliza said. "And I'm not marching. I only want to listen to what the ladies have to say. No one will know I'm there, I'll be so quiet." She gave Jack her most innocent smile. "And with Sybil to act as my chaperone, too. Unless you don't trust your own fiancée to keep us out of trouble."

"I do not trust either of you. But you're both bullheaded enough to do exactly what you want, no matter what I say." Jack pointed at Freddy. "You have your hands full with this one. I don't know if you're up for it."

Freddy bit his lip. "I don't know if I am either."

"Don't get arrested at the rally. I can only bail Sybil out of jail so many times."

Eliza laughed. "We'll be fine." Of course, she had no intention of telling him about the female Bodyguard, or how she hoped to convince them to teach her ju-jitsu.

Jack kissed Eliza on the cheek. "Have fun at the cinema, but stay out of trouble at the rally." He turned to her at the door. "Oh, and keep an eye on your dad as well."

The sudden note of concern in Jack's voice made her pause. "Dad? Is something wrong? He's not ill, is he?"

"I'd like an extra pair of eyes looking out for him until this whole case is solved."

"I don't understand."

"Lizzie, aside from adultery and the suffrage movement, what else do Diana Price and Jonathon Turnbull have in common?"

Eliza thought a moment, then nearly smacked herself on the head. "Blimey, they both owned the Donegal Dancer! Why didn't I see that before?"

"Because the other connections are stronger, and more likely to be linked to their murders. However, I can't overlook anything. It's possible the murderer is killing off the racehorse owners, which makes your father a potential target. So watch out for him. I'd hate to learn the next murder victim is Uncle Alfred."

By the time she left Scotland Yard with Freddy, Eliza's plans for the day had changed. Time enough to enjoy the cinema after her father was safe from harm. She had a murderer to track down.

TEN

Higgins hoped to spend a delicious afternoon listening to recordings sent by a colleague in South Africa. Although English was Higgins's main passion, the lexical influences of the Afrikaans language were fascinating. But two hours ago, Eliza had burst into his phonetics laboratory at Wimpole Street; she'd demanded he accompany her to White Flower Cottage, the Essex home of Sir Walter Fairweather. Since he'd dragged her off to the lunatic asylum, Higgins thought it churlish to refuse.

Although he complained during the entire train ride from London to the Burnham-on-Crouch station, Higgins looked forward to the adventure. Colonel Pickering, who had also been dragooned into this excursion, was not so eager.

"Dash it all, is this a wise idea?" Pickering asked as they drove in the car hired to take them to the cottage. "We are intruding upon the man's privacy."

Eliza hung her head out the car window, enjoying the warm summer air and the verdant scenery. "That's why I asked you to ring him up before we left London. He invited us."

"A phone call informing him that we would be in Essex an hour later to see his gardens is hardly an invitation. He was simply too polite to refuse."

"Nonsense," Higgins said. "Fairweather is obsessed with gardening. He probably revels in visitors who come to admire his nasturtiums and orchids."

He didn't add that he and Eliza were curious to hear Sir Walter's opinion on the recent deaths of Price and Turnbull. Higgins was relieved that Eliza finally showed real interest in trying to solve these murders, and he had Jack Shaw to thank for that. Eliza had returned from her morning visit to Scotland Yard convinced her father's life was now in danger. He didn't agree—he still believed Hewitt was somehow behind the deaths—but if it prodded Eliza into helping him solve this mystery, so much the better.

"You have a perfect right to drop by for a visit, Colonel," Eliza said. "After all, you're Sir Walter's friend."

"We are acquaintances, not friends. I've met him a total of eight or nine times, usually at a lecture. Hardly a relationship that allows me to barge in on him with the pair of you in tow."

Higgins and Eliza both laughed. "We'll behave," she said. "Besides, I want to see White Flower Cottage. It sounds lovely."

But when the car pulled into the long gravel drive, the two-story red house that awaited them looked nothing like a cottage. Eliza whistled. "Cor, it's a proper mansion. Why is it called a cottage?"

Pickering sighed. "My dear Eliza, if your father was the third Baronet of Horning and your mother a fifth cousin to the Swedish King, this would seem as humble as a cottage."

When the motorcar rolled to a stop, Higgins jumped out to get a closer look. The attractive house, built in the Queen Anne style, boasted red brick with stone groins. A black iron balustrade ran up both sides of the sweeping stone staircase leading to the ebony black front door. Potted topiaries sat on every other step. Blue hydrangeas bordered the house, along with white and pink rhododendron. Petunias spilled over the second-floor window boxes. He only now realized the gravel drive was lined with white verbena, impatiens, and wild ginger. Higgins suspected the gardens at the back of the house were just as breathtaking.

"Seems like the work of Sir Edwin Lutyens," Higgins said.

Pickering nodded, but Eliza gave him a curious look. "Sir Edwin is the most celebrated architect in Britain," he explained. "If you have a fat bank account and want a country house, Sir Edwin is the man to call." The front door swung open. "Our arrival has been noted."

The balding butler on the front step bowed slightly. "If you will kindly follow me. Sir Walter will join you on the back terrace."

On the way, they enjoyed a brief peek at White Flower Cottage's interior. Each elegant room was floored with terrazzo tiles and decorated with botanical wallpaper. Framed drawings of herbs and plants hung every three or four feet; tubs of small fruit trees and vases of fresh flowers were scattered about in such profusion, it resembled the orangery at Kew Gardens. Their heady fragrance permeated the air, making the cottage as perfumed as a harem boudoir.

Apparently Sir Walter also had a fondness for Staffordshire pottery, in particular porcelain horses. Every mantel or table displayed yet another china figure. Higgins was somewhat surprised at the graceful decor. He expected a more masculine look for an aging bachelor such as Fairweather. Then again, a man who spent most of his time surrounded by lush gardens had probably developed a taste for exaggerated beauty.

But even Higgins was struck speechless when they stepped onto the expansive flagstone terrace. Stretched before them in all directions were flower beds, ornamental trees, flowering shrubs, hedges, grasses, and topiaries. Off to the right, glass sparkled in the afternoon sun—one of Sir Walter's greenhouses. Water splashed from a nearby cherub statue, the centerpiece of a marble fountain; endless rings of Queen Anne's lace, phlox, and lilies of the valley circled its base. Tall stands of purple, white, and blue larkspur bordered the steps leading to the lawn, while beds of lilies in every possible color guarded the stone path to the topiary garden. From where they stood, Higgins could see several topiaries pruned to resemble racehorses.

"It's almost as big as Kew Gardens." Eliza's voice was filled with wonder.

The day grew hotter by the minute. Higgins took off his hat and fanned himself. Thankfully, he had worn a lightweight Panama cloth suit, as had the Colonel. And he had Pickering to thank for his revamped summer wardrobe. After years on the Indian subcontinent, the Colonel was well versed in dressing for hot weather.

"I see now why Sir Walter retired early from the university," Pickering said. "If I owned property like this, I doubt I would ever leave."

The butler cleared his throat. He had allowed them a moment to appreciate the glorious vista, something he probably did for all first-time visitors. "Sir Walter is occupied with a business associate in the study. He will join you shortly." The rather florid fellow gestured to a black wrought-iron table and chairs a few feet away. "If you will be seated, tea shall be served."

"On a day like this, a pity it won't be lavender lemonade," Eliza said jokingly.

"If you prefer, we can bring you a pitcher, miss." The butler waited.

Eliza sat with a big smile. "Lemonade will be lovely. Thank you."

Higgins and Pickering joined her at the table. "I agree, it's too warm for tea. Lemonade for me also," Higgins said. Pickering nodded.

Once the butler left, Eliza leaned forward. "Even if Sir Walter doesn't have a clue as to how Turnbull was poisoned, I'm glad we came. I don't mind canceling my date for the cinema. Cor, I haven't seen so many flowers in one place since I left Covent Garden." She took a deep breath. "I smell gardenias."

Higgins pointed at several enormous pots on the terrace. "There you are."

"I say, once we've taken the garden tour, what do the two of you plan on asking Sir Walter?" Pickering pulled out a handkerchief and mopped his forehead. "I hope you don't think he had anything to do with poisoning Jonathon Turnbull."

"Who else at the picnic had more knowledge of plants and poisons than Sir Walter?" Higgins asked, only half joking.

Pickering looked grim. "I will be most offended if you accuse our host of murder."

"He doesn't have a motive, Professor," Eliza said in a stage whisper. "At least not one that I can figure out. Unless Sir Walter wants the Donegal Dancer all to himself. But according to my dad, he already owns three horses. And Sir Walter has no gambling debts. He doesn't even bet heavily. Why would he start killing people over a horse?"

While Sir Walter had no apparent motive, that didn't mean there wasn't one yet to discover. Higgins had to admit the man wasn't an obvious suspect. Neither was the Duchess. That left the Saxtons, Gordon Longhurst, and Rachel Turnbull. Along with the missing Harold Hewitt.

"Can we agree that someone at the Henley Regatta poisoned Jonathon Turnbull?"

Eliza looked exasperated. "Over a thousand people were there, so that doesn't help us."

"The murderer is someone with a connection to both Turnbull and Diana Price. And that person was at Ascot *and* Henley."

"Maybe it's you." Eliza chuckled.

Higgins's sarcastic reply was cut short when the butler brought out a large lacquered tray. With practiced ease, he quickly set down several glasses, a beaded pitcher of lavender lemonade, a platter of watercress sandwiches, and a silver bowl of fresh strawberries.

For the next few minutes, they quietly enjoyed the refreshments. Higgins hadn't realized how thirsty he was until he filled his glass for the third time.

Eliza raised an eyebrow. "If Sir Walter poisoned the lemonade, you're in trouble. You've drunk over half the pitcher, Professor."

"Perhaps he has a death wish," Pickering added with a smile. "I know there's a family wedding next month he is loath to attend. I wouldn't be surprised if our Henry has chosen suicide over matrimony."

Higgins drained his glass in a show of defiance. "Now that I know the topic of poison is cause for merriment, I shall bring it up at the next stultifying dinner party. We'll begin the appetizer course with a joke about arsenic, then move on to soup and strychnine."

"Talk of poisons on such an exquisite day. Whatever prompted such a subject?" Sir Walter Fairweather strode onto the terrace.

Pickering and Higgins rose to shake his hand. Sir Walter inclined his head at Eliza, who stood as well. He smiled at them.

"I was most pleased to receive your call today, Colonel. I have long wanted to give you a tour of my gardens. And how delightful that you brought Miss Doolittle and Professor Higgins. Like myself, they have seen one too many dead bodies this past month. My flowers may help to banish such sordid memories."

They all made proper replies about the terrible murders, and how they hoped the victims' respective spouses were bearing up well. Sir Walter looked younger than his sixty-two years and more relaxed than he had at Ascot and the funeral, where he'd dressed conservatively and worn a serious expression. His white Dundreary sideburns and mustache emphasized the deep blue of his eyes. And today his figure looked almost boyish in his summer suit and straw boater.

Sir Walter seemed to read Higgins's thoughts. "Yes, I cut a different figure here in my gardens. Although visiting my horses at the Windsor farm is almost as relaxing."

"Could you give us a tour, Sir Walter?" Eliza opened her parasol and set it twirling on her shoulder. "The flowers look magnificent."

"And so they are." Sir Walter offered Eliza his arm before the pair descended the terrace steps. Pickering and Higgins followed close behind.

Halfway through the tour, Higgins wondered if the gardens might really be as large as those at Kew. It felt like they'd been walking for miles, although Sir Walter assured them his gardens only covered six acres. They explored every inch of it from the three greenhouses to the small man-made lake. Eliza couldn't stop oohing and aahing at each of the topiaries—the rabbit-shaped privet was her clear favorite—and even Pickering lingered before several elaborate plant sculptures. As for Higgins, Sir Walter's replication of an Elizabethan garden most impressed him. He also enjoyed the tropical greenhouse, beehives, and elegantly designed Poplar Walk.

The entire estate seemed perfect: kitchen gardens, herb gardens, spring bulb gardens, vegetable gardens, and separate gardens devoted to particular colors. Not surprisingly, the beds devoted to white flowers took precedence. Moon gardens, Sir Walter called them, and Eliza was enthralled by his description of how the white flowers glowed in the moonlight.

At first, Higgins suspected Eliza's excited interest was feigned. Then he recalled how she once told him that walking through Covent Garden's flower market each morning was the happiest part of the day.

No doubt those flowers were the only natural beauty a poor Cockney girl ever enjoyed. He hoped one day Eliza had a country house and flower gardens of her own. With luck, she wouldn't be sharing it with the simple-minded Freddy.

By the time they headed back to the house, Higgins had slung his jacket over one arm. Pickering was visibly perspiring, but Eliza and Sir Walter seemed untouched by the heat. In fact, Eliza resembled a moving part of the garden herself in a celery green skirt and blouse and a wide-brimmed straw hat with white flowers. He certainly envied the lacy sun parasol she held above her head.

"You've done a remarkable job here, Sir Walter," Higgins said.

"Thank you, Professor. I consider it a labor of love. One of the reasons I retired at the age of fifty was my father's death. As a younger son, I didn't expect to inherit the baronetcy, but I did receive enough to buy this property." Pride and pleasure mingled in Sir Walter's words. "The past thirteen years have been devoted to White Flower Cottage. Being a retired botanist with such gardens and greenhouses at my disposal allows me to continue my research."

"What exactly were you knighted for, Sir Walter?" Eliza asked.

"For my work in mycology. Specifically my discovery in the role that fungi play in lichen symbioses."

Higgins smiled when Eliza remained silent after that answer. "I'm curious where your interest in horses came from."

"Possibly the Swedish side of the family. My mother, Charlotte Andersson, was a distant cousin of the King. Several relatives raised Swedish half-blood horses for the Royal Mews, too."

"Are you saying the love of horseflesh is inherited?" Pickering asked with a chuckle.

"Perhaps, but I spend most of my time in the world of plants. Things grow slowly in my quiet gardens. Sometimes a man needs excitement and like-minded people. Racehorses move quicker than vines and give me a welcome infusion of energy."

"Money, too. At least if you win," Higgins said. He and Pickering moved to stand under a shady oak.

"I've been lucky since I bought my first horse. But I don't lose my head when it comes to betting. There's no need to resort to desperate wagers. One of my prize fillies had a winning season that netted me seven thousand quid."

Eliza whistled. "That's a lot of money. A gambler might be willing to kill for a sum like that. Or a horse that good."

"Perhaps you're thinking someone was even poisoned?" He raised an eyebrow at her. "And over the Donegal Dancer, no less."

"Why not? Two of the horse's owners have been murdered."

"It's a bit premature to start killing people for the Donegal Dancer. The season isn't half over. Yes, the Dancer has won all his races so far, but that's no guarantee he'll win another. And without an exceptional record at the track, a horse isn't worth much when it comes to breeding or stud fees. Why get rid of the owners of a horse that may lose before October? Best to wait before taking such lethal measures."

"But Diana Price was killed at Ascot," Eliza said. "And Turnbull was poisoned. Why?"

Sir Walter sighed. "As we all know, they both engaged in scandalous behavior. I may be a lifelong bachelor, but I know that betrayal in love often turns deadly. I only wish I'd been with you when Turnbull was dying. I might have ascertained how he was poisoned, or administered an antidote."

"What sort of antidote could you have given him?" Pickering asked.

"In many cases, people ingesting poison can be saved if they are forced to empty their stomach. A speedy dose of syrup of ipecac acts as an effective emetic." He looked unhappy. "Of course, one doesn't normally carry such things around."

"I advise you to start doing that. Especially anytime the syndicate members are together," Higgins said. "You may look amused by the suggestion, Sir Walter, but two owners have already been murdered. I would not be surprised if there is a third attempt."

"I would be stunned if someone else was killed, Professor. As an old bachelor whose only passions are gardening and horses, what jealous spouse would come after me? Now if I *was* going to be killed over a horse, it would make more sense to target me due to one of the three other horses I own by myself. One is enjoying a splendid season." He shrugged. "But the Dancer has not yet proved himself, like I said."

"Hewitt," Higgins said. "It must be Hewitt who is behind the murders."

"But how did he manage to poison Turnbull at the regatta?" Pickering asked.

"Jack said the tree by the picnic area was a hawthorn. A hawthorn tree has poisonous berries." Eliza looked inquiringly at Sir Walter. "The bramble bush also had poisonous berries. If someone wanted to kill Turnbull, he could have used either."

Sir Walter seemed amused. "First, the tree *and* the hedge at the picnic site were hawthorns. That genus can be grown as both."

"But they are poisonous, aren't they?" Eliza persisted.

"It's true the seeds contain cyanide. But the berries themselves are perfectly acceptable due to their high pectin count. Hawthorn berries are sometimes used in jelly. And I ate both the lemon and the raspberry tarts, as did you, Miss Doolittle. I think we can both agree that neither of those tarts had seeds in them. I don't see how the poison was derived from the hawthorn tree or the hedge."

Higgins saw that Eliza looked as frustrated as he felt. "Did either of you notice any other flowers or plants around the picnic area that could have been used as a poison?"

Sir Walter laughed. "Oh my, I sometimes forget most people are not botanists. Every garden harbors an arsenal of poisons." He pointed at a flower bed to his left. "Those pink, lavender, and yellow flowers are foxglove, which contains digitoxin. Any part of the plant will produce convulsions, stomach distress, and cardiac arrest. Growing around the fountain are lilies of the valley. They suppress the nervous system, blur vision, and alter heart rate."

He marched along the stone path. The others scrambled after him. "Now here's a lethal specimen: the oleander. A single leaf would be enough to kill. Merely inhaling the smoke from one of its burning branches could make you ill. In fact, eating anything made from the nectar of oleanders, rhododendrons, and azalea can be fatal."

Sir Walter next pointed at a herbaceous plant. "If you want to avoid poisonous berries, Miss Doolittle, those from *Atropa belladonna* are the most dangerous. That's why it is known as deadly nightshade." He nodded toward another plant. "Avoid picking the seed pods of *Helleborus niger*, commonly called Christmas Rose. The sap can cause paralysis and burning."

Higgins noticed how Eliza took care to keep her skirt from brushing against any leaves or flowers while Sir Walter described the deadly inhabitants of his garden.

"These little purple flowers are periwinkle. They cause stomach difficulties and heart palpitations. If you nibbled on the larkspur by the terrace, you'd grow weak, nauseous, and possibly die from an irregular pulse. Over there is the English yew, which has killed so many people, it's known as the graveyard tree."

He lovingly brushed a hydrangea bush when he passed. "Hydrangea, iris, daylilies: all toxic. The Caribbean manchineel tree causes rashes and skin irritation if you simply stand beneath one that drips in the rain. And eating its fruit will close up your throat within minutes."

Eliza now huddled beneath her parasol, as if expecting an aerial assault by an elm or ash tree at any moment.

Sir Walter seemed unstoppable. "Be wary of more than flowers. Never eat the leaves of a rhubarb plant. It impairs breathing, violently upsets the stomach, and might lead to death. Take care to cook your elderberries. Like hawthorn seeds, elderberries contain cyanide. And I haven't begun to warn you about the wide array of deadly mushrooms."

Higgins held up his hands. "We surrender, Sir Walter. You have convinced us that a typical English garden is best explored with great care and an expert botanist in tow."

"I'll never look at the flowers in Covent Garden the same way again," Eliza said.

"Nonsense. Nothing is more exquisite than a flower. You must simply take care not to eat any of them, at least until you have consulted with me." Sir Walter gave her a wink.

"You've confirmed what I told my friends earlier," Higgins said as they approached the back terrace. "No one at the picnic possessed as much knowledge about plants and poisons as you, Sir Walter."

The older gentleman smiled. "Does that mean you believe I murdered Mr. Turnbull?"

Higgins stood his ground. "Did you?"

"I say, Henry, what a deuced rude thing to ask," Pickering protested.

But Sir Walter seemed amused. "I was not the only person at the regatta picnic who had a clinical knowledge of poisons and their chemical properties."

Higgins and Eliza looked at each other in surprise. "Who?" she asked.

"Why, Gordon Longhurst, of course."

"Longhurst?" Higgins asked in disbelief. "I knew his late father. He presided over one of the oldest firms on the London Stock Exchange. And I recall when his son joined the family business. Like his father, Gordon is a stockbroker and investment banker. What do bankers know of chemistry and poisons?"

"Probably nothing, but young men with medical degrees certainly do. Gordon Longhurst graduated with a medical degree from the University of Edinburgh."

"Excuse me, Sir Walter, but Diana Price told us at Ascot that her husband was a runner when he was at Cambridge," Eliza said. "You must be mistaken."

"True. Longhurst graduated from Cambridge, but he started his medical studies at Edinburgh soon after. During my last year as professor there, Longhurst was in my Plant Pathology course. My best student, I might add, which is why I remember him. He was quite worried that his father would stop paying for his medical education. It seems Longhurst Senior had no wish for a doctor in the family."

"If he graduated with a medical degree, then his father did pay for the rest of his schooling in Edinburgh," Pickering said.

"Indeed. I happened to be at his graduation several years later to receive an award from the university. I assumed he went on to become a doctor, until I read in the papers about Gaiety Girl Diana Price marrying stockbroker Gordon Longhurst. This past spring, Turnbull brought Diana into the syndicate, but I didn't meet Longhurst again until Ascot. So much happened that day, we had no time for a real conversation." He frowned. "Poor fellow. Such a waste of a fine scientific mind. Coupled with a disastrous marriage."

"This doesn't look good for Mr. Longhurst," murmured Eliza.

"Motive, opportunity, and an expert knowledge of poisons," Higgins agreed. "If Jack doesn't know about Longhurst's medical background, we had best tell him."

"If it was Longhurst, I would be most interested in learning how he poisoned Turnbull," Sir Walter said. "I haven't been able to figure it out."

Higgins put his hand on the older man's shoulder. "I was being quite serious before. The next time you meet with any racing syndicate members, be on your guard. Never wander off alone. And bring that ipecac syrup, just in case."

"Don't see the need, Professor. As I said, who would want to kill me?"

"I'm sure Diana Price and Jonathon Turnbull thought the same thing," Higgins said in a grim voice. "Now they're both lying dead in a graveyard."

ELEVEN

Higgins would never understand the Doolittles. He'd known Eliza over a year, and every time she and her father met, they spent the time arguing. But after Jack warned that Alfred might be a potential murder victim, she'd become unbalanced in her display of filial devotion. Last evening Eliza had invited her dad to Wimpole Street for dinner in order to watch over him. To prove how worried she was, Eliza even included her stepmother in the invitation. A decision that bordered on madness.

His ears still rang from the awful racket during dinner. Pickering never made it past the soup course. Right before Mrs. Pearce brought in the lamb cutlets, the Colonel uttered an excuse about meeting someone at the club and fled, a napkin still clutched in his hand. Higgins wrote down a few Irish and Cockney curses he hadn't heard before, so the evening wasn't a total waste. But he was not prepared to spend another day guarding Alfred.

Salvation seemed to arrive at breakfast when a black-bordered card was delivered from Rachel Turnbull. She requested that both Eliza and Higgins call on her that afternoon. An intriguing prospect, since neither he nor Eliza had any idea what the widow of Jonathon Turnbull wished to discuss. But if Higgins thought he would be spared having to fret over Alfred Doolittle, he was sorely mistaken.

Although the Turnbull residence was in Knightsbridge's Rutland Gate, Eliza believed it made perfect sense to stop along the way at her father's house in Pimlico.

"Why not swing by Salisbury as well?" Higgins asked when they exited the tube station. "Fine day to see Stonehenge, don't you think?"

"Oh, it isn't *that* out of our way," Eliza said. "We've got a good three hours before we have to meet Rachel. There's no reason we can't stop by and check on Dad."

"If I must spend the next three hours with your family, start looking for some oleander or nightshade to eat. Because that would be a damned sight more enjoyable than listening to your Madame Defarge of a stepmother."

Eliza climbed the porch steps of the house where Alfred and Rose now lived. She lifted the doorknocker shaped like a horse's head. "I don't know why you keep calling her that. You know her name is Rose Cleary Doolittle."

"To me, she will always be Madame Defarge," Higgins said with mock seriousness.

After Eliza knocked ten times, the door swung open at last. Higgins was surprised to see Rose Doolittle glaring at them. Alfred's three thousand pounds a year was more than enough to pay for a servant or two. Obviously Eliza felt the same.

"Why are you answering the door?" she asked. "What happened to the maid?"

"Upstairs putting out the blasted fire." Rose looked like she was on fire herself, freckled cheeks aflame and red hair wildly askew from its pins.

"Fire?" Higgins cast an alarmed look at the upper floors. "Have you called the brigade?"

Rose smirked. "Now what would I be needing the fire brigade for? All they'd be good for is tramping over my new carpet, and soaking the drapes and coverlet in the bedroom."

"Is the whole house on fire?" Eliza peered over Rose's shoulder, but she moved to block her view.

"Just the bedroom," Rose said as if such things happened every day. "My brother's youngest was playing with a box of cigars and matches. The little devil wanted his morning smoke, but set the bed on fire instead."

Eliza looked shocked. "You mean Danny? The boy's only eight."

"What if he is? The child likes a cigar now and then, and if his dad and ma don't mind, it's no concern of yours."

"If he keeps this up, it may be the fire department's business," Higgins warned.

"Now see here, Rose," Eliza said. "You've got about twenty relatives living here, some of them even younger than Danny. If there's any danger of the fire spreading, you have to get everyone out now. And if you don't, I'll call the brigade myself."

Rose crossed her arms. "Don't you be telling me what to do in me own house."

Eliza tried to push her aside, but the older woman was as immovable as a brick chimney. "Dad! Dad, it's Eliza! Are you all right?"

"Your dad ain't here right now. Now back off, or I'll be throwing your arse right into the street, I will!"

Since fisticuffs seemed imminent, Higgins took Eliza by the elbow to hold her back. "Mrs. Doolittle, is everyone in the bedroom safe?"

"'Course they are. I told ya, the maid went up there and put the fire out. But there's a right mess to clean up, and I don't have time to be wasting on the sorry likes of you."

"Blooming witch," Eliza said, her eyes flashing with anger. "Where is my father? I need to talk with him."

"For the last time, he ain't here." Rose looked down her nose at them and said airily, "He's at a business meeting."

"With the Wrexham syndicate?" Higgins grew worried.

"Whenever Dad says he's going to a business meeting, that means he went to the pub." She took another step toward Rose. "Which one is he at?"

Rose sniffed. "The Hand and Shears. Not that he'll be any happier to see you."

"You're such a rude cow."

Higgins pulled Eliza off the porch. "Time to go."

"And you'd better keep those children in your house safe!" Eliza shouted as Higgins dragged her away. "Bad enough they're learning manners from you, like never taking a bath and eating biscuits with their feet!"

Rose slammed the door so hard, all the windows rattled.

By the time they reached the Hand and Shears in Smithfield, Higgins was in desperate need of a pint. By Jupiter, these Doolittles were exhausting. Eliza hadn't stopped railing against her stepmother since they left Pimlico. He prayed she'd lose her voice soon.

"I can't believe out of all the so-called stepmothers I've had, that's the one he finally marries," she fumed. Higgins held open one of the curved pub doors. "I swear, I'd rather see him in prison than tied to the likes of her. It would be quieter in prison. And now that's he's got money, she'll never leave him. Oh, she has her claws in him now."

"Eliza, cease this babbling or I shall throw you in front of a double-decker bus."

When they entered the small pub, Higgins inhaled the delicious smell of fish and chips. Ale, too. A dartboard hung on a matchboard wall, and there seemed to be more than one bar area. Since it was noon, the pub was filled with people. At least a half dozen were women, but the ladies all sat at tables along the wall. He and Eliza pushed through the crowd and spied Alfred Doolittle with two men at the polished wooden bar.

When Doolittle saw them, he broke out in a wide grin. "Lizzie, my girl. What are you and the governor doing here?" He waved at them. "Come join us."

His two companions looked like they had been drinking since dawn. One of them quietly sang the old sea shanty "Hanging Johnny" under his breath.

"The Professor and I can't stay." Eliza pointed toward a small adjacent room with tables. "But we need to have a few words with you in private."

Higgins was grateful when her father rose with a grunt. No doubt Alfred had downed a few pints already. He was in his shirtsleeves, with one suspender hanging off his shoulder. Plus his eyes looked red. However, he acted as clearheaded and sharp as ever.

"Can I be getting you a drink, governor?"

"I wouldn't mind a pint." Higgins noticed that Eliza looked over at him with disapproval. "It promises to be a brutally long day."

Doolittle waved at a barmaid who walked past, her hands filled with empty glass mugs. "Ellen, the Professor here will have a pint of Robinson's Old Tom." He sat down at the table next to Eliza. "Now what brings the two of you to the Hand and Shears? I'm betting it's not for the fine ale and conversation."

"Dad, I told you last night that Jack and I are worried about you. These murders may be connected to the Donegal Dancer. Every owner of the horse is in danger."

"And what do you want me to do about it? Hide under the bed until Scotland Yard finds the killer?" He sipped his ale. "It's like I said yesterday at dinner. Diana and Turnbull were killed because they was fiddling around and didn't care who knew it. I'd bet a year's worth of pub bills that either Diana's husband or Turnbull's wife did them in. Let me tell you, if I got caught foolin' around, Rose would put a knife through me heart before I got past the front door."

"I'm sure she would," Eliza said in a grim voice. "However, it is possible Turnbull and Diana were murdered over the horse. You need to be extra careful."

"I'm always careful. I didn't spend all those years in the East End without knowing how to look after myself."

"Please stay home for a while. And don't let any strangers in the house."

Doolittle slammed his glass down, splashing ale onto the table. "Are you daft? Every day another relative of Rose's comes knocking on my door, suitcase in one hand and a bawling child in the other. I tell you, there's no peace to be found in that fancy house I bought. See what money and respectability has done to me? Killed my free and easy ways. Now I got to take care of every Cleary that loses their job, and that's the whole lot of 'em! A sad day it is when a man is forced to become responsible for other people."

Higgins took pity on Eliza. "Alfred, be careful whenever you're around any of the racing syndicate members." The barmaid set down a glass of ale before him. "Since you probably won't see them until the Eclipse Stakes next week, you should be safe until then."

"Oh, I'm seeing them all before that," Doolittle said. "Tomorrow, in fact."

"What do you mean?" Eliza asked. "It's not time for another syndicate meeting."

"No, but we all talked after Turnbull's funeral and decided to check out the security measures at the Windsor farm what stables the Donegal Dancer. With the Eclipse Stakes set for next Friday, we can't risk any thieves making off with our colt."

Eliza shook her head. "Absolutely not. You can't go to the farm tomorrow. It's too dangerous."

"I'm going, Lizzie, and don't you be trying to stop me. There's never been a Doolittle born who can be talked out of doing a fool thing once they've set their mind to it."

"Amen to that," Higgins muttered.

"Can't you go to the farm on Sunday? If you go then, I can come along and keep an eye on things."

Higgins's curiosity was piqued. "Where exactly are you going tomorrow? Really, Eliza, if you are putting the cinema ahead of your father's safety—"

"Don't be ridiculous. I promised Sybil to attend a suffragette rally with her."

Alfred groaned. "Girl, you better not be chaining yourself to no fences tomorrow."

"I'm not going to chain myself. Lord, you're as bad as Freddy. I promised Sybil I'd be there, and it will be a perfect time to ask the suffragettes about Harold Hewitt and Turnbull. As well as Diana Price." She gave Higgins a cynical look. "They certainly wouldn't open up to you. Besides, I also want to learn some ju-jitsu moves from the Bodyguard."

"What?" Higgins thought he must have misheard that last part.

"Never mind." Eliza turned back to her father. "Dad, can you reschedule the visit to the stables for Sunday?"

Doolittle burped. "Nope."

She drummed her fingers on the table for a minute. "All right, then.

The only solution is for the Professor to go to the stables with you tomorrow. He'll keep an eye on things."

"I beg your pardon," Higgins said.

Doolittle grinned. "If the governor wants to come to the stables, it's fine by me. We leave at eight."

"I'm glad that's settled," Eliza said in obvious satisfaction.

Higgins grabbed the glass of ale in front of him and drank it straight down.

———

Eliza hoped she was dressed appropriately for their visit to the widowed Mrs. Turnbull. She'd first donned the same black ensemble she had worn to the funeral two days ago, but decided it might be presumptuous. After all, she wasn't a family member or even a friend. She finally settled on a printed silk dress of dove gray, devoid enough of color, and bordered in black silk with a summer neckline of gray and black flowers.

"You should have put on an armband," she whispered to Higgins as they stood on the front steps of the Turnbull residence. A large black funeral wreath hung on the door.

"Whatever for?" Higgins idly scanned the long row of white stucco houses in one of Knightsbridge's finest neighborhoods. The trees in the park across the street afforded welcome shade from the July sun, as did the elegant colonnaded porch of the Turnbull mansion.

"To show proper respect for the dead," Eliza replied. "And if not for Turnbull, then out of consideration for his widow."

"I haven't even been formally introduced to Rachel Turnbull. And I couldn't give a hang that her husband is dead. Besides, I think you're looking mournful enough for the two of us." He raised an eyebrow at her black-feathered hat. "The hat is a bit much, and a gray parasol would have sufficed. Not a black one."

Before Eliza could fret about her outfit, a tall maid in a black uniform opened the paneled door. A moment later, she ushered them into the drawing room.

Rachel stood at a writing desk by the window. She greeted them with a smile. "Miss Doolittle and Professor Higgins, how kind of you to accept my sudden invitation. Please sit down." She gestured toward a gold brocade divan. "We'll have tea, Lucy." The maid curtsied before scurrying away.

The sunlight streaming through the tall windows showed that Turnbull's widow looked quite rested, almost rejuvenated. Indeed, the plain-featured Rachel looked rather attractive today. Her black silk dress enhanced her creamy complexion. And for the first time, Rachel wore her wheat-colored hair piled fashionably atop her head, a few curls spilling around her ears. The new hairstyle combined with her dress's high gauze neckline made her appear swanlike.

"No doubt you were both surprised to receive my message this morning." She sat across from them in a maroon velvet chair. "As you know, it is not customary for the recently bereaved to receive guests other than close family for the first few months."

Before she could continue, the phone on the writing desk rang. With a murmured apology, Rachel answered it. She stood facing the window while she spoke, her voice too low for Eliza to hear any of the conversation.

The interruption gave Eliza and Higgins time to examine the drawing room. Considering the late Jonathon Turnbull's domineering personality, Eliza wasn't surprised by its masculine decor, maroon walls, and dark wood trim. Although crystal vases of white roses were placed in every corner, the room felt oppressive. A towering grandfather clock loomed over them. Eliza was grateful the thick velvet draperies had been pulled back to let in light. The room needed all the fresh air it could get, what with the cloying scent of those funeral roses.

"Please forgive the interruption." Rachel sat back down with a sigh. "Turnbull relatives I have never heard from before are now eager to make themselves known. I should hire a secretary to handle the calls and letters, along with all the legal matters forced upon me." She smiled. "As I was saying, you must be curious why I asked you here."

"I'm glad you did," Eliza said. "I wanted to tell you how sorry I am about your husband's death. I would have spoken to you at the funeral, but I didn't want to bother you or the family."

"It is I who should have spoken to you earlier. After all, you were the only person with Jonathon when he died. My dear Miss Doolittle, I want to thank you for trying to help my husband, and for seeing to it that he wasn't alone at the end."

"I only wish Freddy and I had found him sooner. We might have been able to save him. If there is anything the Professor and I can do, you have only to ask."

"Please tell me exactly what happened. I need to know how Jonathon died. Was he able to speak at all? Did he have a message, either for me or anyone else?"

Eliza took a deep breath before describing the final minutes of Jonathon Turnbull's life. Rachel listened intently. But at no point did she seem close to tears.

"I see," she said in a soft voice. "No message, then."

"I'm sorry," Eliza added. "But the poor man was in a bad way when we found him. It's a wonder he could speak at all."

Rachel glanced at Higgins, who had already been silent for longer than Eliza expected. "Professor, you must be wondering why I wanted to see you as well."

Higgins shrugged. "I do admit to a little curiosity, Mrs. Turnbull. I wasn't with Eliza when your husband died. And the only time I ever met him was at Ascot."

"Lady Saxton told me that you suspect Harold Hewitt murdered both my husband and Diana Price. I would like to know why you think Hewitt is responsible. Many people believe it was Mr. Longhurst."

Eliza wasn't surprised when Higgins eagerly complied. He'd been convinced since Ascot that Hewitt was the murderer. The Professor described his conversation with Hewitt at the racecourse and their subsequent visit to Claybury.

"But what was his motive for the murders?" Rachel asked when he was done.

"It appears Mr. Hewitt championed women's suffrage," Eliza said.

"Ah, I see," Rachel said. "And my husband did not. In fact, he was an outspoken opponent. My sister Ruth was most offended by Jonathon's efforts to derail their movement. I think she was even more upset with me for not being able to restrain him. But no one could control Jonathon." She sighed. "Least of all, a woman."

"My cousin's fiancée is a member of the Women's Freedom League," Eliza said. "Their leaders were insulted when Diana refused to sing at their rally. She made things worse by giving an interview in the paper in which she mocked the women."

"I heard no end of that from Ruth. Of course, she also had a grievance against Miss Price for other reasons." Rachel's smile was bitter. "After all, it is common knowledge that my husband and Diana were lovers. Another situation I could do nothing about."

"We heard your sister threw a hammer at Diana Price," Higgins said.

"Ruth is impulsive, but I can't fault her loyalty. Or her courage."

They were again interrupted, this time by the maid carrying in a silver tea tray. Everyone waited until tea had been poured and biscuits offered. Once the maid left, Eliza turned her attention back to Rachel.

"If Mr. Hewitt did murder your husband, how was he able to poison him at the regatta picnic? I watched the servants unload the hampers from the cars and set everything up. When would a stranger have had the opportunity to poison anything there?"

"I do not believe Jonathon was poisoned by anything he ate or drank at the picnic. After all, each of the luncheon guests sampled everything."

"Except for Gordon Longhurst," Eliza reminded her.

"True, but I don't think Mr. Longhurst came to the picnic with the intention of harming anyone. He wanted his share of the winnings, and only grew upset when he learned it was not forthcoming. I find it unlikely he had poison hidden on his person for just such an occasion."

Higgins agreed. "It's possible your husband was poisoned between the end of the luncheon and the award ceremony. He might have been followed."

"I'd like to believe that is what happened. After all, Mr. Hewitt is not only a madman but a total stranger. If he didn't do it, the murderer of my husband and Miss Price is someone we all know." Rachel shuddered. "That is a chilling thought."

"Did you see Mr. Turnbull with anyone suspicious after the luncheon interval?" Higgins asked. "A man you didn't recognize, perhaps?"

"I spent the rest of the day with friends at the Leander Club. I never saw Jonathon again after the picnic." She paused. "Not alive, that is."

"Then the crucial thing is to discover what your husband was doing during that time."

"Oh, I know what he was doing, Miss Doolittle." Rachel wore an unhappy expression. "He was placing bets on the races. Jonathon wagered on everything from horses to parliamentary elections. I am ashamed to confess that he gambled away nearly everything his father left him."

"A person who is a heavy gambler takes great risks," Higgins said. "And if he doesn't honor his bets, there's usually an angry man or two willing to make him pay."

Rachel took a long sip of tea before answering. "Jonathon was not a kind man, nor a cautious one. I have no doubt his enemies were legion and their grievances justified."

"Forgive me if this is a rude question, but why did you marry Mr. Turnbull?" Eliza asked. "Your husband had a dreadful reputation long before he met you. Were you unaware of it?"

Rachel stared down at her teacup, as if the answer lay swirling in its steaming surface. "I had no choice in the matter, Miss Doolittle. Our respective families wanted the marriage. Although the Turnbulls were the wealthiest of merchants, they craved a titled lady to add to their bloodline. And my father was weary of marrying off five daughters. He never forgave my sister Ruth for choosing a vicar."

"Becoming the wife of a vicar hardly seems scandalous," Higgins said with a grin.

"But she married for love, and to a common churchman besides. Father never spoke to her again. Afterwards, his matchmaking efforts became quite ruthless. By the time he got around to me, he only cared about the bank account of my groom, not his character."

Eliza marveled at these highborn ladies who appeared to have been sold by their families to the highest bidder. As poor as the Doolittles were, they were above that sort of thing in the East End. And as hard as her life was, Eliza learned how to fend for herself—no thanks to any man.

"Your father must have known of Jonathon Turnbull's reputation when the marriage was arranged," Higgins said. "I am not one for society gossip, but even I was aware of the stories circulating about your late husband for many years."

Rachel looked weary. "Certainly Father knew, but I was never informed. I spent much of my girlhood in France, and heard none of these rumors."

Higgins snapped his fingers. "I thought I detected a French cadence in your speech. You lived in the region of Provence-Alpes-Côte d'Azur. The town of Grasse?"

The young widow seemed impressed. "Correct. My mother's family is from Grasse. My grandparents worked in the perfumery business, and I spent several years with them. I wish I had been allowed to remain there. Grand-père and Grand-mère taught me how to create scents by using the flowers and oils of the region. But Father had other plans for me."

"I can't believe your father married you off to a man notorious for his violent behavior, especially towards women," Higgins said with disgust.

"From a parental standpoint, it seemed a beneficial arrangement. The Turnbull tea merchants got a baron's daughter to add to their family tree, and the Sturbridges disposed of the last of their unwelcome daughters. A fine deal all around." While Rachel twisted her wedding band, her voice hardened. "Except for the bride and groom."

"Then Mr. Turnbull did not want to marry either?" Eliza asked.

"Heavens, no." She looked aghast. "Jonathon viewed the match as a prison sentence. What need did he have of a wife, when so many loose women were at his beck and call? And the idea of children filled him with horror. When I suffered a miscarriage, I thought it was a tragedy. I could not have another, you see. But looking back, I realize it was a blessing. Children would only have been additional targets for his cruelty."

Higgins and Eliza exchanged looks. They must be thinking the same thing. Rachel had excellent reasons for wanting her husband dead.

"Given the state of your marriage, Mrs. Turnbull, no one would blame you for not grieving over your husband," Higgins said.

She set her teacup back on the tray with a clatter. "What you actually want to know is if I had anything to do with his murder. After all, I planned the whole picnic lunch. But do you really believe I raced to the stables and stabbed Diana with a pitchfork? The very idea of such a gruesome death is abhorrent to me."

"Mrs. Turnbull, we don't mean to be rude or unfeeling," Eliza replied. "But the police are looking for motives in the deaths of your husband and Diana. And you and Mr. Longhurst were both betrayed by your spouses."

"You cannot compare me with that poor man. He was in love with his wife."

"And you no longer loved your husband?" Higgins asked.

"I thought I was clear. Jonathon and I never loved each other. At best, we were civil in public. And after the miscarriage, we were little more than enemies." Rachel looked at them as if they were idiot children. "I forget I am dealing with a middle-aged bachelor and a girl of twenty. What do either of you know of marriage, especially an unhappy one?"

"We know enough to realize people may kill to escape such a marriage."

"And why would I do that, Miss Doolittle? What do you think I have gained by my husband's death? Yes, Jonathon was a cruel man, but is it less cruel to find myself his widow?"

Puzzled, Eliza glanced at Higgins. "I don't understand."

"While my husband lived, he knew how to fight off his creditors. Now they are literally baying at the door. I have spent every hour since his death fending off attempts by either his relatives or his bankers to wrest control of Turnbull Tea away from me." Rachel clasped her trembling hands. "If I lose it, how will I live? Jonathon's gambling debts are so onerous, it seems I must sell off every property, including this house. Where can I possibly go? My father would see me starve before he would help me."

Eliza was moved by Rachel's sudden show of vulnerability. "There's your sister. I'm sure she would help you. Or your grandparents in France."

"My grandparents are dead. And their perfumery business is now owned by others. As for Ruth, she doesn't deserve to have a penniless sister thrust upon her."

Higgins put down his teacup. "I know several influential bankers in the City. Your financial situation may not be as dire as you believe. Allow me to arrange a few meetings. It's possible your husband's debts may be discharged without the estate being totally lost."

For the first time, tears welled up in her eyes. "Thank you, Professor. I am only grateful that racehorse is no longer my concern. Jonathon borrowed heavily to buy the Donegal Dancer, a rash decision on his part. One of many." She took a ragged breath. "This has been a trying week. Perhaps a part of me *is* grieving for my husband, despite our history. After all, Jonathon and I were forced into this marriage. Maybe both of us should be pitied."

Eliza got to her feet and gestured for Higgins to do likewise. "I'm sorry if we upset you, Mrs. Turnbull. It was not our intention. Like you, we only wish to discover the truth about these deaths. Two people have already been killed, and I'm worried there might be another."

Rachel dabbed at her eyes. "I will have no peace until I know who is responsible for Jonathon's death. Perhaps Harold Hewitt is guilty, Professor."

"Perhaps," Higgins said. "Anyone clever enough to escape from Claybury Asylum and remain undetected is clever enough to have committed these murders."

"I shall ask Inspector Shaw about Mr. Hewitt when he arrives," Rachel said.

"Inspector Shaw is coming here today?" Eliza asked in alarm.

"I expect him at any moment. He called this morning to ask if he might visit me after tea. It seems he has questions regarding the regatta picnic. At least he had the good manners to wait until after the funeral."

"We must be going, Mrs. Turnbull."

Eliza rushed out of the drawing room before Rachel could ring for the maid. Higgins and Rachel quickly followed her into the foyer. Jack would not be happy to discover that she and Higgins had questioned the widow before he did.

"Miss Doolittle, are you by any chance wearing *Fleurs de Juillet*?" Rachel took a step closer and sniffed. "I thought I smelled that scent in the drawing room, but the funeral bouquets overpowered it. Ah yes, I recognize the bergamot and lavender, along with an undertone of lily of the valley. It must be *Fleurs de Juillet*."

"It is," Eliza said proudly. "My young man gave it to me last week. He said it was the perfect time to wear the perfume because it's called Flowers of July."

Rachel smiled. "And so it is. I helped create that fragrance over ten years ago. But most of the credit should go to my grandmother, Madame Aubertin. She was a truly gifted perfumier." She gave her an unexpected hug. "You have reminded me of my dear Grand-mère. I thank you for that, Miss Doolittle."

Somewhat abashed, Eliza stepped onto the front porch with Higgins. "May I ask you one last question, Mrs. Turnbull? Seeing how you speak French and all."

"Of course." Rachel waited at the entrance to her Knightsbridge mansion.

"I have a friend that keeps calling my stepmother Madame Defarge."

Rachel seemed concerned. "If a friend calls your stepmother that, it is not meant as a compliment."

"Eliza, really," Higgins muttered. "There's no need to bring this up now."

She ignored him. "Why? Who is Madame Defarge?"

"Madame Defarge is a disagreeable character from *A Tale of Two Cities*, a famous novel by Charles Dickens. She's bloodthirsty, vengeful, unjust, and violent. A most dreadful villainess. I'd hate to think your stepmother resembled her in any way."

Eliza gave a dramatic sigh. "Actually, she sounds just like her."

TWELVE

Eliza ran up the steps from the underground station. How dreadful if she was late and missed all the fun at the upcoming rally. Dodging the tube crowds below street level on Saturday morning was never easy, but today the congestion seemed even worse. She literally battled her way around a group returning from Tower Hill. Oblivious to anyone else, they chattered about the crown jewels and the executioner's block.

Near the bronze statue of the Duke of Wellington on horseback, she scanned the milling pedestrians. Sybil's early morning telegram had instructed Eliza to meet her here. Jack's fiancée was nowhere in sight among the dozens of suffragettes. Dressed in white and wearing sashes of green and violet, they flocked about the stone steps of the Royal Exchange. Several held crudely lettered signs with VOTES FOR WOMEN and SUPPORT SUFFRAGE painted on them. Two ladies waved a cotton banner that said FREE PANKHURST.

"Eliza! Over here!" Sybil waved from across Threadneedle Street. She wore a bottle green walking suit, quite dark for a warm summer day, but a sprig of white and violet flowers decorated her jaunty boater.

Eliza hurried over to join her at the Bank of England's balustrade.

Although impressed by the Bank's imposing six stories and massive pillar columns, she'd heard that a ghost called Sarah haunted the grounds. Eliza reminded herself to return another day when politics didn't demand so much of her attention. After all, ghosts were just as interesting as votes for women.

"I thought there'd be a huge number of suffragettes," Eliza said.

"This is a small demonstration," Sybil replied in a matter-of-fact tone. "We know the police will show up, since Lloyd George is supposed to arrive by eleven o'clock. Ladies have been posted on every block to give the signal once he's spotted."

"David Lloyd George, the politician?"

"The Chancellor of the Exchequer himself. Excuse me, I must speak with Mrs. Garrud."

Sybil rushed across the street. Eliza's excitement grew as she recalled how Sybil had told her Edith Garrud was secretly training female bodyguards in ju-jitsu to protect the WSPU's leaders and speakers. A pity Eliza hadn't had a few lessons when she lived in the East End. Ju-jitsu might have come in handy when pickpockets tried to nick her meager earnings.

"Everything's ready, but we'd better keep our distance," Sybil said when she returned.

"What about Mrs. Pankhurst's daughter?"

"Which one? Christabel fled to Paris to escape imprisonment. And Sylvia doesn't approve of our tactical use of violence. Look, there's Annie Kenney in disguise." She pointed to a slight man who wore a shabby suit, scuffed brogans, and a flat cap. "Annie looks quite nice as a young man, don't you think? The police never suspect, either. She uses the disguise to avoid being arrested and force-fed in prison again."

"Who was the woman you spoke with a few minutes ago? The one wearing dark purple. No taller than five feet, I'd say."

"That's Edith Garrud. She and her husband teach at the Palladium on Argyll Street." Sybil waved at Annie Kenney, who had lifted her cap in a signal. "I believe Lloyd George's automobile has been spotted. Watch carefully, Eliza. You'll see the suffragettes in action."

Loud chants rose up from the Royal Exchange, along with shouts of "Votes for women!" and "Free Pankhurst!" The women in white with their suffragette ribbons, signs, and banners began to march in formation. One woman climbed the building's steps and hushed them.

"There's Flora Drummond," Sybil told Eliza. "We call her 'The General.'"

"Ladies, we are at war!" Flora's ringing voice carried across Threadneedle Street. "The government has instituted the Cat and Mouse Act, a cruel punishment for voicing our opinions! We have been beaten, assaulted, dipped in horse ponds—"

"You deserve it!" A man who shouted near the bronze statue was immediately drowned out by women chanting, "Down with Parliament!"

"Yes, we've smashed windows and set fire to buildings," Flora Drummond went on, "but we have no other recourse! How else are we to bring attention to our noble cause? If damage occurs to certain politicians' property, then they ought to listen instead of fighting us!"

Sybil chuckled. "She's referring to Lloyd George's new house, which was mysteriously vandalized during construction. Of course, Jack agrees with Sylvia Pankhurst. He believes militant violence hurts the movement. But the politicians leave us little choice. And despite fears that Miss Davison's funeral would cause rioting, the event was peaceful. We know how to honor one of our own."

"It's too bad Harold Hewitt made things worse for the suffragettes with his stunt at Ascot," Eliza said. "A pity the Queen isn't a supporter. People might listen to royalty."

"That will never happen. For now, we must be content with a few ladies of the gentry, like Lady Constance Lytton and Lady Astor."

Eliza half listened to Flora Drummond's speech, since she'd read a handbill relating the cause's history and recent events. Annie Kenney climbed the steps and stood near Flora, and the suffragettes chanted whenever she paused. Eliza caught sight of groups of men in suits and trilby hats by Wellington's statue. A few of them wore rough coats and caps, patched trousers, and soiled collarless shirts. Flora raised her voice when their angry voices grew louder.

"I can attest to inhumane treatment in Holloway Prison!" she shouted over the men. "Women warders held down my arms and legs while a doctor forced a tube down my nose and throat. I could not breathe—"

"You deserved it, ya silly tomrig!"

Men cursed or yelled, "Women belong in the kitchen," but Flora ignored them. Their taunts and catcalls only mounted after the suffragettes began marching again, largely in an effort to prevent any men from breaking through their line.

"Give women the moat, I say," one ruffian shouted. "Drown 'em!"

"Here now, shove off." A tall man in work clothes pushed the heckler back. "Those women fed me family during the strike. Go on, find a job and be useful."

"My job right now is to take you out, you bloody sod!" He punched the worker in the face and laughed in triumph.

The two men fell to wrestling, kicking, and biting, egged on by the ruffian's friends. A group of policemen swarmed up from the underground station but didn't bother to break up the fight. Instead, they made a beeline for the suffragettes. Outraged, Eliza was about to join the marchers when she spied a long, sleek automobile inching its way from Queen Victoria Street. She caught a fleeting glimpse of the man sitting in back, no doubt Chancellor Lloyd George by his high fore-head and thick mustache. Eliza recognized him from a recent news-paper caricature.

The politician raised his fist at the women, who yelled back; many suffragettes now pulled out objects from their pockets or bags. The police formed a protective ring around the vehicle. That didn't stop the women from chucking rotten tomatoes, vegetables, and fruit at Lloyd George's car. The spoiled vegetables splattered both the vehicle and the policemen, who ducked and cursed.

Sybil held Eliza back from joining the melee. "Jack was right. It's gotten dangerous, and neither of us wants to be arrested."

The air was filled with whistle blasts, men's shouts, and women's screams; the *chooga-chooga* of the automobile's horn only added to the chaos. More policemen rushed into the street and grabbed the ladies roughly by the arm or waist. Screams, horn honks, and whistles min-gled with the din on the streets. Suffragettes surged in every direc-tion, trying to escape the police in close pursuit. Eliza ducked at a deafening crash overhead. She looked up to see a broken window in the Bank of England's broad facade. Luckily no shards of glass rained down on their heads.

"Blimey, that scared me half to death!"

Sybil pulled her around the corner. "None of our women threw that rock, but we'll get the blame. No doubt those hecklers did it. Better clear off while we can."

Eliza looked back to see tiny Mrs. Garrud flip a policeman who'd flailed his billy club at the marchers. Holding Eliza's arm in an iron grip, Sybil tugged her across the street. Along the way, they dodged two men who tried to block them. Eliza jumped aside, then nearly fell as the other man tripped her. Sybil gave the man such a shove, he went flying. Hand in hand, Eliza and Sybil sprinted to safety.

Annie Kenney and Flora Drummond joined them, both panting for breath. Several angry bobbies chased after the two WSPU leaders; Eliza kicked the kneecap of the one who grabbed Flora's arm. With a howl, the policeman let go. Flora ran, followed by Annie, whose flat cap fell off, letting her long hair stream behind her. Sybil and Eliza raced in the opposite direction to the nearest alley, headed up to Threadneedle Street, then ducked over to Old Broad Street.

Out of breath, Eliza finally stopped. She'd run so fast she had a stitch in her side.

Sybil gasped for air, too. "Oh, good show, Eliza!"

"If Jack ever learns about this, he won't be happy. Where to now?"

"The nearest underground station." Sybil glanced around at the pedestrians on the street, the carriages, carts, and double-decker buses. "Where are we?"

"I know this area. Follow me." Eliza linked arms with her and hurried to catch the nearest bus. Once they climbed the curved stairway to the top, she plunked their fare into the box and sank onto a narrow seat. "That was a bit more excitement than I bargained for."

"Rallies bring out the worst types, I'm afraid," Sybil said. "We certainly didn't expect so many policemen to show up. At least they didn't arrest Annie or Flora."

"Thank goodness Mrs. Garrud escaped." Eliza smiled when she spotted the tiny woman sitting up ahead. The suffragette turned to nod at her. "She's a blooming wonder, she is."

All three women got off the bus at Liverpool Street. Eliza and Sybil followed Edith Garrud to the underground station. They kept a discreet distance from her so as not to attract notice. Luckily her dark purple outfit and straw boater helped distinguish her from the other ladies in their dresses of summery pastels. After they'd purchased tickets at the platform, Sybil introduced them.

"Eliza is my fiancé's cousin, Mrs. Garrud."

"I saw how you handled yourself, Miss Doolittle," Edith said with an admiring glance. "You would make an ideal ju-jitsu candidate for our Bodyguard."

Surprised speechless, Eliza smiled in delight.

Sybil laughed. "Jack would fly into an unholy temper if she did."

"Let him," Edith said with a wave of her hand. "But I'm serious. Miss Doolittle, I can teach you to flip a six-foot bobby who outweighs you by ten stone."

"I saw you," Eliza blurted. "I never would have guessed a woman your size could do such a thing."

"My small height is an advantage. Men never expect defeat, yet what they don't realize is that they defeat themselves. Ju-jitsu is not about overpowering, but using your opponent's strength against him."

The underground train whooshed and then rattled to a stop. The women scuttled inside before the doors shut. An older businessman rose to his feet and offered Eliza his seat. She motioned to a dour-faced matron in shabby black to sit instead. With a weary sigh, the woman sat. Muttering under his breath, the businessman moved farther along in the moving car.

"That ain't no gent," the matron said as she cradled a heavy basket in her lap. "But I thanks you, miss. You have proper menners, giving a poor woman a chance to tek a load off. Been up since t'ree this morning, and me with old shoes what pinch me toes till they bleed."

"You're welcome." Eliza recalled her own sore feet after long hours of standing at Covent Garden or the Opera, selling flowers. She would have slipped the woman a few pence but didn't have less than a fiver. Such a large sum might insult her.

Looking around, she noticed several other women who wore white or gray with the suffragette colors. One held a rubber mallet, which reminded her of Rachel's sister.

"Sybil, what else can you tell me about Rachel Turnbull's sister?" Eliza asked.

"Mrs. Lowell? She's been involved with the WSPU far longer than I have."

Edith Garrud shifted as the train swerved. "Ruth has a devil of a temper."

"Yes. Remember when she threw a hammer at Diana Price? Of course, that wasn't a political gesture. She was angry at Diana for cheating with her sister's husband," Sybil said. "I can't say I'm sorry Jonathon Turnbull is dead. He was no friend to the movement. But now that he's gone, I'm sure some other wealthy man will hire hooligans to break up our rallies."

"And bribe the police," Edith added.

The train screeched to a stop. Passengers surged out of the doors and double the number surged inside, making further discussion impossible. At Oxford Circus station, Eliza led the way out of the train and up the steps. She blinked in the bright sunshine, her stomach rumbling.

Sybil smiled. "We'll soon have lunch at the Palladium with the other suffragettes."

Eliza stared at a fish and chips stand, her mouth watering from the smell of fresh-fried cod and potatoes wrapped in newspaper cones. Sybil pulled her away, however, and quickly guided her down Oxford to Argyll Street. From there, it was less than a block to the Palladium.

Relieved she'd made it to the theater without fainting from hunger, Eliza followed Sybil and Edith into the Palladium. Sandwiched into a row of white stone buildings, it looked oddly similar to the Royal Exchange, except on a smaller scale. Once inside the lush vestibule, they joined women wearing the suffragette colors. The chatter seemed deafening.

"Did you see that big brute, the one who pushed me to the curb?" one woman asked, and shook her dirty skirts. "I should have kicked him where it hurts."

"He punched me on the arm," another said. She rubbed her shoulder. "It hurts so bad, I'll have a bruise for a month. Don't know how I'll be lifting boxes next week at the shop."

Flora Drummond appeared out of nowhere and stopped to chat with Sybil. While the two women conversed, Eliza admired the Palladium's colored marble flooring, rose-hued granite walls, and gold-painted columns. She loved theaters, especially if they showed moving pictures.

A line began to form. Eliza followed the others to a room where she prayed there would be food. She wanted to clap her hands when she saw the spread that awaited the suffragettes: teapots, trays of ham, toasted cheese and roast beef sandwiches, scones and thick jams, large china bowls of clotted cream, tea cakes, and cookies.

"Cor, look at all this!"

Sybil laughed. "The Palladium manager, Mr. Gulliver, is a supporter of our cause."

"He sets a lovely table, too."

"We have friends in many places. Like at Ascot. The police did not want us to hand out our latest edition of *The Suffragette*. But Lord Churchill gave his approval."

Annie Kenney joined them. "That's surprising, since he doesn't believe women should vote. In fact, he's the reason I was arrested up in Manchester."

"The politicians will come around to our way of thinking before long."

"Let's hope we aren't long in the tooth when it happens," Edith said. "Or in the grave."

The others all laughed. Meanwhile Eliza filled her plate with two sandwiches, two scones, and a thick slice of seed cake during the discussion. One of the suffragettes, taller than the others, nibbled on a slice of toasted cheese. Her dark hair was swept back on either side of a heart-shaped face, and she had a pleasingly plump figure. Eliza recognized her as the maid at the Henley Regatta picnic. She hadn't spoken to the girl, as the servant was busy following Rachel Turnbull's instructions all afternoon. But it was definitely the Turnbulls' maid.

Eliza approached the young girl. "Excuse me. I'm Eliza Doolittle, and my father is a member of the Wrexham Racing Syndicate. I saw you yesterday when we took tea with Mrs. Turnbull. And you were at the Henley Regatta picnic. It was dreadful what happened that day."

"That was terrible, wasn't it?" The maid introduced herself as Lucy and dropped her voice to a whisper. "But I don't think Mrs. Turnbull is all that upset. Not that I blame her. Master Turnbull was a hard man."

"I'm sure you know he was poisoned."

She sighed. "Been in all the papers, it has. Don't know how it happened, though. I was serving that day. Looked to me like everyone tasted a little bit of everything. So how did the gentleman get poisoned?"

"I have no idea. Did the other servants eat or drink anything at the picnic that afternoon, or feel ill afterwards?"

"Oh, we aren't allowed to eat the food meant for guests," Lucy said quickly. "Mrs. Turnbull would be most upset if we did. That could get a servant dismissed."

"Eliza, come and meet Mr. Garrud," Sybil called out. "He's agreed to teach you."

Although she was eager for a ju-jitsu lesson, Eliza regretted losing the chance to learn more from Lucy. She excused herself and followed Sybil down the sloping aisle of the theater auditorium. The warm red plush seats and ornate tasseled hangings in the private boxes were breathtaking, along with the white and gold trim. The stage was bare. Its wooden boards echoed with the swift movements of two men fighting. She hesitated. The men seemed quite aggressive as they attacked each other with long sticks and well-placed kicks.

"Come along, then." Sybil led the way up the narrow side stairs, skirting the orchestra pit, and into the stage wings. Edith Garrud met them. One of the men, who sported a tapering mustache turned up on each end, groaned after a vicious kick to the ribs.

Edith clapped her hands. "Your time is up, gentlemen!"

The man with the mustache bowed to his opponent. The younger, clean-shaven man bowed lower as if in deference, then departed. Edith's husband turned to the ladies. "What you've just seen is a demonstration of bartitsu, which is a combination of ju-jitsu techniques, kickboxing, and stick fighting. My wife and I instruct men, women, and children in the art."

"You also appeared in a film, didn't you?" Sybil asked Edith.

"Yes, back in '07. We perform in exhibitions all over London. And Sir Arthur Conan Doyle used bartitsu when Sherlock Holmes grappled with Moriarty at Reichenbach Falls. Sir Arthur was most intrigued after we showed him the technique."

Sybil looked impressed. "I didn't know. I shall have to reread that story."

Eliza made a note to read it as well. She'd only recently begun to read Sherlock Holmes and was in the middle of *The Hound of the Baskervilles*. Edith went on to explain what happened at the rally today near the Royal Exchange. William Garrud grew somber at the news, especially when she described how the police targeted the suffragettes.

"To keep us from getting hurt in the future, both Eliza and I would like to learn ju-jitsu," Sybil said. "I may even pass these moves on to my fiancé. He's been in more than a few fights with criminals. Jack might sustain fewer injuries if he knew the techniques."

"He would indeed," Edith said. "Now let's get started. And fear not for your clothes, ladies. You won't get more than a speck of dust on them."

Without warning, William rushed his wife. Edith calmly twisted her husband's arms and threw him to one side. He sprawled on the stage at her feet. Rising quickly, he rushed her from behind; she bent forward and tossed him over her shoulder. After William landed on the wooden boards with a grunt, he tried another frontal attack. Edith crouched, rolled him over her head, and sent him flying.

"The trick, ladies, is to utilize the opponent's own momentum and energy. It saves you from expending your own," Edith explained. "Now, Miss Doolittle. Are you ready to try it?"

Eliza felt uncertain. "I wouldn't know how to start."

"We'll go slow, we promise," William said with a wink.

He approached her with caution. Eliza gave a nervous laugh, which spoiled her focus, and William easily overpowered her. "Most women show surprise at an attack since they don't expect it," he said with a wry smile. "But you can learn to be prepared in any situation."

"I am sorry."

"Don't apologize." He spun about and grabbed Sybil around the waist. She shrieked. "You see? Women need to be aware of the ever present threat of danger."

Sybil nodded. "I understand, Mr. Garrud. Please, try again."

"Slowly, and I'll show you how to grasp his forearms." Edith advised Sybil how to brace her feet, bend a certain way, and then push so that William rolled over her back.

He landed on his feet and then rushed Eliza. Although she didn't expect him to attack her, she threw the heavier man over her shoulder. He landed on his back with a grunt. William quickly twisted and launched himself at Eliza. She leaned over, elbowed him in the groin, and stood when he fell backward on the stage.

Eliza grinned from ear to ear. "How's that?"

"A bit inventive," William gasped out, still on the boards.

"If an opponent approaches from the side, you can also pinch him near the kidneys," Edith said. "That will take him down, too. You're a fast learner, Miss Doolittle."

"Please, it's Eliza."

"Eliza, then. Let's try again."

Edith, Sybil, and Eliza practiced for another hour. A cluster of women had gathered in the auditorium, clapping whenever they subdued William and groaning if they failed. Eliza's confidence grew each time she succeeded.

"It's a shame you can't act as Bodyguards," Edith said.

"I don't think we're ready for that," Eliza said with regret.

Edith smiled. "But you will be ready the next time the police get rough with either of you. Just remember the skills we've taught today. They could save your life."

After Eliza and Sybil thanked the Garruds, they fetched their hats and gloves and headed outside. The afternoon sun beat down, and the summer heat shimmered in the air.

"That was fun, wasn't it? I can't wait to demonstrate those techniques to Jack."

"I hope he's made progress in these murders," Eliza said. "And it would help if we knew where Hewitt escaped to."

"Do you really think Hewitt's the murderer?"

"No. But the Professor does. Of course, none of us knows anything for certain. But two syndicate members have been killed, and I don't want the third victim to be my dad. That's why I told Higgins to watch over him today. They're visiting the stables where the Donegal Dancer is kept." She frowned. "The other syndicate members will be there as well."

Sybil patted her arm. "I'm sure your father will be fine."

"If not, I'll use these ju-jitsu techniques on whatever blighter causes him harm. And the Professor had best keep my dad safe. Or I'll flip *him* all the way to Dover."

THIRTEEN

By the time Higgins jumped out of the cab at Bay Willow Stables, he felt like he'd completed a journey on the Orient Express. The Doolittles seemed to possess more energy than the monkeys at the London Zoo. Eliza's father had not stopped talking during the entire train trip from London, except to knock back a few sips from his brandy flask. How in the world could the older man look fresh as a daisy after such a long journey? He had entertained Higgins nonstop on the train, cracking jokes, telling stories, charming the ladies with a wink and a lift of his hat. Even on the cab ride over, Alfred kept chattering. Higgins understood now why he was so successful as a speaker for the Moral Reform League. Doolittle's talents had clearly been wasted as a navvy and dustman in London's East End for too long.

Still, Higgins did not take his duties lightly. It wasn't only Eliza who worried about what might occur during their visit to Bay Willow Stables. If a murder took place each time the syndicate members met, then Higgins would do everything possible to protect Eliza's father.

At least the setting was enjoyable. Higgins gazed about with approval. The horse farm looked green and refreshed from a light morning rain. The grass beyond the fences sparkled in the sunshine, although the July heat would soon change that. He breathed fresh air deep into his lungs.

"Couldn't ask for better weather, ain't that right?" Doolittle asked.

Higgins watched the grooms brush or wash down the horses, while stableboys raked hay into piles. He and Doolittle strolled down the lane toward the paddock. Thank goodness Rose Doolittle had decided not to tag along today. She planned to torture the store assistants on Oxford Street with her presence instead. Doolittle seemed as relieved as Higgins by her decision.

"Come along then, governor. Sir Walter has some fine horseflesh for us to inspect today. Maybe I can get the Wrexham syndicate to buy another future champion like our Dancer."

"Good lord, not another horse!" Higgins feared Alfred would be up to his ears in debt within the year. And the fellow seemed to forget that most horses did not win every race.

The Duchess of Carbrey stood in the stable yard conversing with Lord Saxton and Brody. A few feet away, Gordon Longhurst fidgeted and scowled, hands in his pockets. Eliza had told Higgins how Longhurst came to Henley dressed in full mourning. Thankfully, the widower chose a gray summer suit today.

"Good morning," Sir Walter sang out as they approached. He was dressed nattily in jodhpurs, a light jacket, and shiny brown boots. When Doolittle and Higgins joined them, he shook their hands. "Good to see you, Alfred."

Doolittle puffed out his chest. "Did you hire the guards like I suggested?"

"Yes, I did."

"Glad to hear it. We don't want no bloody horse thieves stealing our colt."

"It's good to see you too, Professor," the Duchess said. "What a perfect day to be out in the countryside."

Higgins tipped his hat to her. "Indeed it is, Your Grace."

Saxton eyed Higgins with displeasure. "Who invited you? You're not part of the syndicate."

"Neither am I," Longhurst said before Higgins could respond. "But Sir Walter insisted I come. I only hope it was not to suffer more abuse. I had enough of that at the regatta."

"Water under the bridge, old chap." Sir Walter clapped him on the back. "We're glad you decided to come. To be truthful, Lord Saxton and I have been feeling a bit guilty over what happened. We hope the Duchess and Mr. Doolittle will agree with us."

"About what?" Longhurst asked. "You already said you refuse to sign over Diana's share of the Donegal Dancer to me."

Sir Walter sighed. "I'm afraid the ownership rules in the contract are set in stone. But I found a way to get around that clause. After all, your wife was not killed until *after* the horse won at Ascot. So it would be perfectly legal—and proper—to award Diana's share of the prize money to her husband. That is, if Alfred and the Duchess agree to it."

"Sounds fair to me," Doolittle said. "And sporting, too."

"I have no problem with this." The Duchess sent Longhurst a polite smile.

Longhurst stood speechless, as if he didn't believe it. Sir Walter pulled an envelope from his inner coat pocket. "I kept your wife's share in her account until we could decide the matter. Come now, Gordon, you mustn't harbor hard feelings. It was quite a shock to all of us."

When he didn't move to take the envelope, Sir Walter stepped closer to him. "As the agent for the Wrexham syndicate, I am pleased to act on their behalf and offer you this check for Diana's share of the

Ascot purse. It's rather a nice amount, enough to invest in a horse of your own. If you're interested, I can recommend a few here at Bay Willow."

Longhurst snatched the envelope, quickly peeked inside, then stuffed it into his own coat. "I'll think about it. Death taxes are very dear, as you know."

"Of course." Sir Walter hesitated. "I'm afraid there's a bit of bad news to share. It appears we hired the guards just in time, Alfred. Last night, around three in the morning, thieves broke into the stable—"

"What's this?" Doolittle huffed in outrage.

"If our horse has been stolen, I'll whip every last man who works at this stable!" Saxton's face flushed with anger.

Sir Walter held up his hand. "Please, let me finish. The Donegal Dancer is safe and unharmed. The fellows we just hired prevented any trouble."

The Duchess snapped open her parasol. "Hiring the guards was well worth the expense, then. How fortuitous that Alfred suggested it."

"Indeed yes." Sir Walter wiped his damp brow with a handkerchief and replaced his hat. "Shall we tour the stables? There's a two-year-old filly I'd like you all to see."

Higgins followed the others toward a traditional block of three long outbuildings with a croft roof. Inside, their footsteps echoed on the tile floor; dim sunlight streamed through high windows. He noted the neat tack room and admired the gleaming harness and saddles. The group strolled on to inspect the stalls with the usual half-doors and mounted rails, already mucked out and filled with clean straw. The horses inside looked well groomed. They peeked into one stall that held a glorious black stallion, but he charged the half-gate and they quickly moved on. The Duchess soon made friends with a much gentler horse that nickered and eagerly succumbed to her stroking his nose.

"What a magnificent darling," she crooned. "I'm sorry I don't have a lump of sugar."

"That's Jester, one of the four-year-olds. He's fast as a bullet on the final stretch." Sir Walter polished a brass nameplate fixed on the door with his sleeve.

When the group headed outside, Higgins trailed after them. In the distance stood a brick building plus several cattle barns. Sir Walter herded them next to the paddock to watch the grooms exercise the horses. Higgins wished he were back at Wimpole Street with the morning paper and a cup of tea. Fresh air and exercise were fine in small doses, but this had already grown tedious.

The Duchess fell into step beside him. "This horse-thief ring seems quite bold."

"They've probably stolen more horses than anyone knows. Wonder what they do with the ones they can't ransom."

"Most likely they're sold to America, Canada, or South America." She smiled at Higgins's questioning look. "Remember the Jersey Act was signed earlier this year. It was designed to prevent horses from outside Britain from being registered in the Stud Book."

"Ah, yes." Higgins guided her around a pile of fresh horse dung. "The specter of all those unregistered American horses tainting the bloodlines of our English breeding stock. If you ask me, the only thing that should matter is how fast the blasted animal can run."

"I don't agree. The Act protects the British racehorse and increases their value as well. Not that there isn't deceit in English racing circles. Whenever there's gambling involved, there's corruption. Look at Turnbull and Saxton. Throwing away half their fortunes on a race or a boxing match. Idiots."

They halted at the paddock gate, where Alfred Doolittle admired a filly prancing on the oval track. She was a spirited chestnut beauty with a white blaze and one full white stocking on her left back leg. While everyone watched, a groom led the horse toward the group, stroking her until she stood quiet. Doolittle paced back and forth, his excitement clear.

"Larkspur, did you say?" he asked. "How did they come up with that name?"

"Her dam is Lark, and the sire is Hotspur."

"That makes sense," Brody said with a laugh. "I'd love to ride her."

"She'll be a winner, you can tell that by her long legs." Sir Walter gestured to the groom, who led Larkspur around and back again. "By the way, the men I hired to protect the Dancer are Melling, Keene, Ingleby, and Owens." He pointed to the groom. "Samuel recommended them."

"How d'ye do?" Doolittle wrung the groom's hand so hard he nearly spooked the horse. "We're interested in this little filly. She's a real looker."

"Aye, sir. Now't kin hold a candle to that yan."

Higgins perked up at the young man's dialect. He hadn't been through northwest England since he was a boy on holiday, heading for Lake Windermere. Aunt Mary lived near Shrewsbury, and they'd taken the train north from there. In fact, he'd first been inspired to study dialects by listening to residents in the area. Even Oxfordians sounded different from Londoners.

Sir Walter waved over the two other burly men who led the Donegal Dancer after his workout. A sheen of sweat marked the Dancer's blood-bay coat. One man rubbed the colt down while the steward introduced them as Melling and Keene, two of the guards they'd hired.

"Owens and Ingleby take the night shift. So Melling and Keene weren't here when the thieves tried to break in."

"If we had been, we would have caught them blighters for certain," one of the men said.

Higgins was struck by the fellow's thick hair streaked with brown and white. And his Manchester accent was almost as thick as his hair.

The steward frowned. "That's enough, Keene. The gentlemen didn't ask for your opinion." He turned to the groom. "Samuel was here last night. Tell everyone what happened."

Doffing his cap, the groom launched into his story. Higgins sensed most of the syndicate members didn't understand half of what he said, given his heavy dialect. Thankful he hadn't forgotten to grab a fresh notebook when he left home, Higgins quickly wrote down every word.

"An' once t'were mizzlin, we heard scrapping t' the back. Owens gaes ou' an' around, while us kept waitin' t' see. Scared me half t' death when th' boyos let out that skrike, from when Owens caught 'em claten and flailed his kebbie! I near lowped out of me skin. They nashed off an' Ingleby chessed 'em—wha ya de'yan, mon?" Samuel stared at Higgins.

He glanced up from his notebook. "I'm an expert in phonetics. Go on, don't mind me."

"Us nivver 'eard of owt like fan-et-ekes."

"By your speech alone, I can place you in Cumbria. Not as far east as Sedbergh, nor as far west as Kendal. I'd say, perhaps Old Hutton. Yes, I thought so." He gave a cheerful nod at Samuel's shocked expression. "Is Kirkby Lonsdale still there, farther to the south?"

"Aye, 'tis. Whis'tha agin?"

"Professor Henry Higgins of Wimpole Street, London."

The groom inched backward without another word. A second, younger groom brought Larkspur closer. While the others discussed the filly's prospects. Higgins closed his notebook and stuffed it away with his pencil. Too bad he'd scared off the groom. He could have listened to Samuel all day. Perhaps he could catch the young man unawares later this morning.

"I recommend bidding on Larkspur before someone else does," Sir Walter said.

Lord Saxton appeared doubtful. "I'm not sure we're ready for another big investment so soon after buying the Dancer."

"If the others are not interested, I shall buy her myself," the Duchess announced.

"What about that horse we saw back in the stables? The fine black one?" Doolittle asked.

"The Black Baron?" Sir Walter shook his head. "I wouldn't put money down on that two-year-old. During transport, the train he was riding on had an accident. The horse has been wild ever since. The rescue and his injuries have made him fearful of people. A horse never forgets, you know. Anyone who approaches him needs to know how to handle an overly skittish horse."

"He looked like he had good lines, though."

"That he does, Alfred. You have a good eye for horseflesh."

The Duchess frowned. "I'd stay away from a colt like that. Too unpredictable. And the training costs would be high. Surely there are other horses here who are as suitable as Larkspur."

Sir Walter gave her a slight bow. "Of course, Your Grace. Follow me."

Higgins noticed a young stableboy hand a note to Doolittle. Eliza's father scanned it, then shambled over to Sir Walter before the group moved on.

"The missus is on the telephone. I'll catch up with you in a moment."

Higgins started to follow Doolittle, but someone tugged his sleeve from behind. He turned to see Brody. The jockey squinted in the bright sunshine.

"Professor Higgins? I'm sorry to bring this up, but I have an important question. I hear you're friends with that Scotland Yard detective. Inspector Shaw."

"I am. What about it?"

"Well, I answered all his questions after the regatta. Then he called me in again with my lady friend. Now Patsy's worried to death she's in trouble. I wish I hadn't taken her to the picnic. We weren't even there when your Miss Doolittle found Turnbull—"

"She is not my Miss Doolittle. Eliza is a fellow elocution teacher."

Brody shrugged. "Sorry, I meant no harm. But ever since Inspector Shaw told Patsy that Turnbull was poisoned, she refuses to eat. And he keeps hounding us about what happened."

"Did he specifically say you and your lady friend are suspects?"

"Oh, no. He just keeps asking us to remember if anyone besides the Turnbull servants went around the picnic hampers. The Inspector drove Patsy to tears."

Higgins began to follow the group now returning to the paddock. "No one else became ill from eating or drinking, so Patsy can gorge herself from dawn to dusk if she likes. And she has nothing to worry about from Inspector Shaw. Your lady friend is a most unlikely suspect."

"I tried to tell her that," Brody said. "Patsy's a bit nervous about everything, though. Whenever I'm scheduled to ride, she has nightmares that I fell and broke a leg—"

Higgins looked toward the stables. "What's that noise?"

Loud frenzied squeals rose from the nearest stable building. Higgins and the jockey broke into a run, but Sir Walter, Saxton, and Gordon Longhurst beat them there. The Duchess hurried behind them.

Once they were inside the stable, Higgins rushed toward the stalls and the horse's cries. Now that he was so close, Higgins also heard faint moans. Peering through the bars atop the half-door, he saw the wild horse known as the Black Baron. His wide eyes rolled and his nostrils flared. Ears flattened, the colt reared and stamped, tail arched over his back.

"Bloody hell!" Higgins saw Alfred Doolittle lying motionless on the straw. Everyone crowded against the half-gate. Their cries joined that of Higgins.

He tugged and pulled at the latch. "It won't budge!"

"Someone get that horse under control, for God's sake!" Saxton said. "Where are the trainers and grooms?"

Brody rushed into the next stall while Higgins kicked the locked gate in frustration. He turned to Longhurst. "Find someone who can unlock this. We must get Doolittle out of there!"

Longhurst disappeared. Higgins now saw that Brody had grabbed a halter and climbed the adjoining stall's side. The jockey leaned over the bars and tried to slip it onto the Black Baron's head. The colt reared and stamped perilously close to Doolittle's still and bloodied body. Brody managed to get half of the harness over the animal's ears, only to watch it fall to the straw below the flailing hooves. Samuel and Longhurst suddenly appeared behind Higgins. With practiced ease, the young groom unlatched the complicated lock.

"Divn't do that, mon, ye canna calm him! Gae back wi' ye."

Brody jumped down from the wall and joined Longhurst in the aisle. The groom made soothing sounds and slowly opened the gate. Samuel stepped over Alfred Doolittle's body, one arm raised to protect his head. The Black Baron reared once more and then stood, trembling and sweating, pawing the ground with his ears back. Higgins and Sir

Walter dragged Doolittle out of the stall to safety before Samuel backed out and closed the gate.

"Is'tha kaylied then, ya daft horse?"

"Is he dead?" the Duchess asked, one hand on her throat.

Higgins knelt down and felt for a pulse. "No, thank God."

He detected a flutter in the injured man's neck and saw the slow rise and fall of his chest. Higgins cursed himself. Doolittle looked terrible. Bright blood coated his head and face and stained his clothing. Tearing off his jacket, Higgins rolled it into a pillow and nestled it under Alfred's head. Guilt and anger welled up in him. How the devil had this happened? Eliza's father knew this horse was dangerous.

"Fetch a doctor," Sir Walter ordered Samuel.

"Who was the stableboy that brought the note to Alfred?" Higgins asked.

"Toby." Sir Walter glanced around, as if the boy would materialize out of thin air. "You, Melling! Search for Toby. Don't stand there gaping. Go fetch him!"

The man bolted, his boots clattering on the tile.

The Duchess seemed close to tears. "Why ever did Doolittle go into the Black Baron's stall?"

Higgins had stanched most of the blood from a deep cut on Doolittle's head, but the bleeding had not stopped. A head injury was always serious. He knew that from listening to his father's stories of medical emergencies. Higgins dreaded to think how Eliza would react to this dire situation, especially if Alfred never revived.

Longhurst slammed a fist against the railings. "This can't be another accident."

"If he dies, only three members of the syndicate remain. Well, I've had enough." Saxton whirled to face Gordon Longhurst. "If you're still interested in owning a share of the Dancer, I'll sell. I'm not going to be stabbed, poisoned, *or* trampled to death over some damn horse!"

"Really, Maitland, stop fretting about your own skin," the Duchess chided. "We have Alfred to worry about. Where's the nearest hospital, Walter?"

"We'll have him transported there as soon as possible. And Saxton, I must caution you against such a hasty decision. It may be exactly what it appears—an accident."

"This was no accident," he shot back. "Alfred went off to take a phone call. How did he end up in a stall with a wild horse? No, someone is knocking off the syndicate members one by one, and by heaven I won't be next. I repeat my offer, Longhurst. If you want my share in the Dancer, let's shake on it."

A heartsick Higgins looked up to see Longhurst and Lord Saxton shake hands. Higgins agreed with Saxton. Someone had tried to kill Alfred. But because of the attack, Gordon Longhurst had gotten what he wanted: a share of the Donegal Dancer.

Although not a religious man, Higgins prayed Alfred survived. If not, he would blame himself even more than he did over Hewitt and Diana Price. And what would he tell Eliza? He was supposed to guard her father, who now lay bloody and broken on the stable floor.

Whether Alfred lived or died, Higgins feared he would be the next one killed. Only this time Eliza would land the deadly blow.

FOURTEEN

A last sunbeam from the high window brightened her father's wan face. Eliza fought back tears at how helpless the old man looked. It was a blooming miracle he was still alive. Then again, he had more energy than someone half his age. But not even a prize boxer could hope to survive a round with a rampaging horse. Somehow Alfred Doolittle had.

At the sound of another loud moan, Eliza looked up. She was in the men's ward of the King Edward VII Hospital. All around her were patients who groaned or snored in their sleep; one played solitaire on a tray, his cards slapping in rhythm. Eliza loathed the odors in the room: antiseptic, sulfur, and laundry soap. They cleaned continuously here. She watched as yet another staff member, known as a "scrubber," entered the ward with a mop and bucket. A headache pounded inside her skull. Eliza rubbed the bridge of her nose, wishing it away.

Her bum also ached after sitting for hours. Taking pity on her, the nurse had placed a wooden chair by Alfred Doolittle's bed. While Eliza appreciated the matron's reassuring words and her promise to watch over Dad all night, she didn't intend to leave his side.

It would take at least that long to control her anger so she wouldn't kill the Professor on sight. She knew Higgins too well. While Dad was being attacked by the horse, he was probably jotting down a stable-boy's new slang words. Bleeding idiot. As if a new turn of phrase were worth more than her father's life. More fool her for trusting Higgins to keep Dad safe.

The unconscious Alfred moved, exposing the bruises on his bare shoulder. Eliza tucked the sheet and blanket over him and sat back. Of course, she was as guilty as Higgins. To think she'd been at the suffragette rally while all this was going on at the stables! She'd been enjoying lunch at the Palladium and playing about with ju-jitsu lessons. She was no better than the Professor. Instead, she should have been at Bay Willow Stables with her father.

Eliza felt ill again, remembering how Mrs. Pearce had told her the news as soon as she returned to Wimpole Street. She nearly passed out from shock at learning her father was lying close to death in hospital. Eliza somehow found her way to Paddington station and boarded a train to Windsor. She wept all the way, wondering how something so terrible had happened. And she still didn't know much. The police had detained everyone at the stables for questioning.

"Dad?" She leaned forward when he murmured in his sleep.

Even unconscious, her father kept raising a hand in a jerky motion, as if warding off a blow. He seemed so weak lying there in his narrow bed. And where was that blooming idiot he married? On second thought, she hoped Rose Doolittle wouldn't show up. Her wails would disturb every last patient in the hospital.

Rubbing her arms, Eliza paced around the bed. The doctor had explained that her father was found unconscious in a locked stall—a stall with a wild horse. Dad was brash, but not even he was fool enough to get close to a crazed beast. Someone had locked him in! Who was evil enough to trap him there? It had to be a syndicate member. But which one?

Gloomy dusk deepened the shadows in the ward. Her father shifted in his sleep. Eliza turned at the sound of clattering footsteps. Her stepmother's shrill voice echoed from the hall outside the ward. "I'm looking for Alfred Doolittle! Where is he? Where's me poor husband?"

"Please, ma'am, you must calm down."

"Get out of the way." Rose fought past a nurse and rushed to Alfred's bedside. She let out a shriek that could have been heard in France. "Oh, blessed Jaysus! He's dyin'! Poor Alfie, all swaddled like a blooming corpse!"

Eliza stamped her foot. "Don't say such a thing. He's not going to die."

Rose ignored her. "I'm too young to be a widow! We ain't been wed a year yet." She threw herself down on the bedside chair and wailed like a banshee.

"Hush," Eliza hissed. "The other patients here are trying to rest."

"How can you be so heartless? Your da's lyin' there, half dead if not all dead—"

"He's not dead!"

The matron hurried from the ward's opposite end. "Ladies, please. You must keep your voices down. You're disturbing the other gentlemen in the ward."

"They look bloody fine compared to my Alfie." Rose sniffled into a handkerchief. "Any minute, he'll be tellin' a joke to St. Peter at the pearly gates. And who's to blame for all this, I'm askin' ya? It was her!" She jabbed a finger at Eliza.

"Why blame me? I didn't talk him into buying a racehorse."

"D'ye think I did? All that money what come from lectures, it swelled Alfie's head. And how did he get it? Because you been keeping those fancy gents warm on Wimpole Street!"

"Ah-ah-oh-ow! That's a lie, you old cow! I'm a good girl, I am. Not like you. When all that money come in, you forced Dad to marry you."

Rose shrieked louder. The matron tried her best to hush the woman, but soon gave up and marched away in defeat. Eliza sighed with relief when she spied Higgins, Sir Walter, the Duchess of Carbrey, Lord Saxton, and Brody enter the ward. She was surprised to see Gordon Longhurst among them. Eliza struggled to control her temper. This wasn't the place to have a dustup with Higgins. But it would be difficult to wait until they got back home.

Hands on her hips, Eliza stared at Higgins. "All right, Professor. You've got five minutes before I start punching you. Tell me what 'appened. I mean, happened."

He looked more miserable than she had ever seen him. And so he should. "Eliza, you must know how sorry I am."

"Sorry, are you!" Rose huffed in disgust. "What was me husband doing in a stall with a bleeding crazy horse? Was it some kind of daft game you gents were playing?"

"This was no game." A somber Jack Shaw joined the group at the foot of the bed. "Your husband was told there was a phone call from you, madam. He went off to the stable office to speak with you. No one suspected anything until the horse set up a racket. When everyone got there, Alfred was already unconscious."

"Alfred must have wanted a closer look at the Black Baron," Sir Walter added. "I don't know why he went into the stall. I warned him to stay away from that horse."

"How many times do I have to tell you? The latch was fastened from the outside." Higgins seemed as angry and frustrated as Eliza. "He'd been locked in. Alfred couldn't escape."

Rose knocked over the chair in her haste to stand. "Someone locked him in, on purpose?"

"Of course someone locked him in," Saxton said. "The same scoundrel who killed Diana and Turnbull. Who else could it have been?"

"We've not had time to investigate this latest incident," Jack said. "So we don't know exactly what transpired. But it seems the same person is behind the deaths and the attack today."

"It had to be a trap!" Rose yelled so loud, Eliza winced. "Set by some fiendish murderer! You said Alfie went off because I rang him up. But I never called. I was shopping, I was. Didn't know what was goin' on till I got home and the maid sent me here."

Eliza didn't care what Rose prattled on about. Instead, she stood toe-to-toe with Higgins. He focused on his feet, too ashamed to meet her gaze. "Why weren't you with Dad when he went to the stables? You promised to watch over him."

He finally looked at her with a guilt-stricken expression. "When your father slipped off, I started to follow him. But Brody stopped me. He had questions about the investigation."

"That I did, Miss Doolittle." Brody looked grim. "The Professor meant to go after your dad, but I held him up with my fool questions. I apologize. It's my fault."

Higgins hung his head again. "No, it's my fault. My fault and no one else's that Alfred was almost killed. And I'm sorrier than I can say, Eliza. I don't expect you to ever forgive me."

"It's my fault, too," Eliza said with a bitter sigh. "I should have been there."

Her dad moaned once more, then mumbled something. It sounded like "Help, help me." She couldn't be certain because Rose drowned his words out with her caterwauling and clutched his arm, which made him groan louder.

"He's dyin'! Listen to him," Rose cried out. "Oh, Alfie, don't you be leavin' me."

The Duchess cleared her throat. "Perhaps one of these gentlemen could escort you home, Mrs. Doolittle."

"And why should I be doin' that? Me husband was nearly murdered!"

Sir Walter glanced around at the other syndicate members. "It makes no sense. I can't see why any of us would want to lock poor Alfred into a stall with that wild colt."

"Maybe one of the grooms," Jack said, "or the stableboy. I ordered the local constable to question Toby and the entire Bay Willow staff."

"Toby is twelve or thirteen, for heaven's sake. No more than a mere boy."

Jack continued as if he hadn't been interrupted. "Toby said he found the note on a table in the tack room, Sir Walter. It was sealed and addressed to Alfred Doolittle. The telephone box is nowhere near the Black Baron, however. Someone must have intercepted him and dragged him to the stall."

Eliza scrutinized the members of the syndicate, looking for any sign of guilt or nervousness. Unfortunately, all of them looked equally miserable.

"Professor, did anyone leave the group after Doolittle did?" Jack asked.

"No. We were all by the paddock fence watching the horses or conversing. None of us suspected any trouble until we heard the commotion from the stables."

Jack turned to Sir Walter. "What about the owner of Bay Willow?"

"Mr. Rowling is well respected, and he hires only the best men to work at his farms."

"Rose," a voice croaked. Eliza turned around to see her stepmother smothering her father's face with kisses. He looked over at his daughter. "L-Liza, izzat you?"

Eliza rushed to kneel on the other side of the bed. "Yes, Dad, it's me."

"Alfie, what happened at the stables today?" Rose asked. "Tell us who did this!"

Her father opened the one eye that wasn't swathed beneath the gauze bandages and then squinted. "Wha-wha 'appened?"

"Don't you remember, Dad?" Eliza said. "They found you in the stall with the Black Baron. The wild stallion, the one they warned you to stay away from."

He glanced around in obvious confusion at the group gathered about the bed. Eliza motioned them to step back, while Rose continued to weep and clutch at her husband's hand. She wanted to kick her stepmother, who now crawled onto the narrow bed. She'd smother the poor man if she crept any closer.

A nursing matron ran over. "Give him air, Mrs. Doolittle, please. And you must not get into bed with him. Your husband suffered multiple bruises and several fractures. Every time you touch him, you only cause him pain." With a firm hand, the matron grabbed Rose by the collar and pulled her away. "Must you all be here? The patient needs to rest."

"We'll only be a few minutes more," Jack said. "Uncle Alfred, what do you remember after receiving the note about the telephone call?"

Eliza clasped her father's other hand. "Take your time, Dad. Think hard."

"I-I followed the boy. To the stable."

When he licked his dry lips, Eliza jumped up to fetch him a glass of water. The matron had beaten her to it, however. She motioned everyone aside, helped lift her patient, and then held the glass to his mouth. He sipped a few times, then closed his eyes and fell back.

"M'all right," Alfred mumbled. "Now. Thass be'er. The boy left me at the door. I walked inside. A bit dim, it was. An' then I fell. Flat on me face."

"Did you trip?" Jack held a hand up to prevent anyone else from speaking.

"I don't remember. Nothin' else, till I woke up here."

"He's got a lump the size of a plum on the back of his skull," the matron said.

Jack reached a hand behind his uncle's head. "I think someone knocked you out, then dragged you into the Black Baron's stall."

"It seems clear the blasted attack on Alfred is connected to Turnbull's and Diana Price's murders," Higgins said. "Not even I believe this has anything to do with Harold Hewitt or women's suffrage any longer."

Jack nodded. "It does appear the Dancer's owners are being killed off one by one."

Eliza noticed how the syndicate members took a step back from each other, as if worried one of them might be murdered at any moment.

"But why?" the Duchess asked. "Because of the Donegal Dancer?"

"Open your eyes," Eliza said with exasperation. "Of course it's about the Dancer. Someone wants the horse all to themselves. And I believe Harold Hewitt saw or heard something in the Ascot stable. When we visited him at the asylum, he kept saying we were blind, that there was evil and lies there. Perhaps that's why his family arranged for his escape. They thought he was in danger, too."

"We don't know his family was involved, Lizzie."

Eliza whirled on her cousin. "If the police had done their job properly, they'd have found out what Hewitt knew before he escaped. Maybe then Dad wouldn't be lying here in pain."

Jack backed away, surprised by her outburst.

"These murders are not about cheating spouses or a woman's right to vote," she went on. "They're about greed, pure and simple. And it's all connected to the Donegal Dancer."

"This means one of us is the culprit." Saxton shot Gordon Longhurst a suspicious look. "Alfred's attack so unsettled me today that I sold my share in the Dancer to Longhurst a few hours ago. He's been hounding us for money since his wife's death. This latest incident has given him exactly what he wanted."

"Are you saying I'm the murderer?" Longhurst's face flushed dark red, from his neck to the roots of his hair. "That's ridiculous, and a damned lie!"

"You do seem the obvious choice."

He launched himself at Saxton, but Higgins managed to grab him by the upper arm. Jack quickly squeezed himself between the two men. This latest outburst brought the matron rushing over once more.

"I have had quite enough of this. I insist you all leave the ward."

"I am sorry, but we're almost done here." Jack flashed his official badge.

With an offended sniff, she walked off to tend to a patient begging for laudanum.

"Jack, if the killer hired a man to do his dirty work at the stable, he could waltz in here at any time. Dad's still not safe." Eliza gently stroked her father's forehead.

"I shall have him immediately transferred to a private room," the Duchess said with a kind smile. "And I will arrange for round-the-clock nurses to care for him. Sister Eleanor is an old friend of mine, as is the hospital superintendent."

The matron marched over once more with a tall older gentleman. "Dr. Plummer, they've been nothing but trouble the whole time they've been here. They must leave."

"I'm afraid Matron is right." With a forbidding expression, Plummer herded the Wrexham syndicate members away from the bed. "Mr. Doolittle needs to rest."

Higgins followed the others down the aisle. Several patients sighed loudly in relief when Dr. Plummer shut the door after them.

With a weary look at Eliza, Jack pulled Rose off her husband's bed. Ignoring her earsplitting sobs, he dragged her out of the ward. "Uncle Alfred will be fine, no need to worry. You can visit again tomorrow."

"How do I know he'll be safe?" Rose wailed.

"If the Duchess promised, then it's sterling."

Once the others left, Eliza knelt by the bed. The staff was busy with a feverish patient at the ward's other end. She gently placed a hand on her father's arm, trying not to startle him. She smiled when he opened his eyes. "Dad. I've a favor to ask."

"Not a good time," he said with effort, "to be granting a favor, lass."

"It's important or I wouldn't ask. I need you to sell me part of your share of the Donegal Dancer. The killer won't expect another new owner. It might frighten him into taking a risk that exposes him. We have to find out who did this to you before anything worse happens."

He sighed. "Seems dangerous, girl, but I'm hurtin' too bad to argue."

"Good. I'll have the papers drawn up for you to sign—"

His snores resumed rattling the ward. Eliza kissed his cheek. She'd stay on guard until they moved him to a private room. No one would harm her father again. She was done waiting for Scotland Yard to do their job. By becoming a part owner of the Donegal Dancer, Eliza had made herself a target.

That might be the only way to draw out the killer.

FIFTEEN

I love when the Bohemians scandalize everyone," the Duchess of Carbrey announced. "Say what you will about Mr. Diaghilev and his company, they know how to set the ladies to fanning themselves. After the uproar that ensued at the Paris premiere, I made certain to buy a ticket for their London performances." She pointed at her ensemble. "I even ordered an outfit inspired by Mr. Bakst's costumes for *The Firebird*."

Higgins now understood why the Duchess sported a burnt orange satin dress decorated with reddish-gold birds. To complete the dramatic effect, a gold turban covered her hair.

Mrs. Higgins sipped her tea. "Jemima Hobbes saw the production in Paris. She said she didn't understand a thing the dancers were doing onstage. And she despised the music. Who was the composer again? Some Russian fellow."

"Igor Stravinsky," Higgins said.

When he had asked his mother yesterday to host an impromptu tea at her Chelsea flat, he didn't expect them to converse for an hour about a Hungarian operetta called *The Marriage Market*. Now the conversation had moved on to Vaslav Nijinsky's shocking choreography for *The*

Rite of Spring. Following the riot at its Paris premiere, the Ballets Russes had brought the production to London for four performances.

"Mr. Stravinsky's music sounded positively savage." The Duchess gave a delighted shudder. "Of course, we must remember the Russians are an uncivilized race. Not a decent painter among them, and their novels are far too long. Still, I haven't spent such an enjoyable evening at the Drury Lane in years. Then again, I missed all the excitement in May. I heard it was an extraordinary production of *Hamlet*."

Higgins sighed with relief. Once talk moved on to the Shakespearean fiasco when Eliza caught a killer, it wouldn't take much to nudge the conversation to the most recent murders. "Yes, it was the most entertaining *Hamlet* I had ever seen."

"Certainly unique," his mother added. "A pity you were in Bath, Minerva."

The older woman looked disappointed. "Oh, were you all there? Even you, Colonel?"

Pickering finished his tea sandwich before answering. "Of course. And the Drury Lane will not see another one like it again." He paused. "Thank goodness."

"I am glad you brought up that production, Minerva." Because Higgins and his family had known the Duchess of Carbrey for decades, they were on a first-name basis when in the privacy of their homes. "Eliza and I had been on the trail of a murderer for weeks. We were fortunate the crime-solving stars aligned that night. I am hoping they do so again."

She cocked her head at him. "So it is not the theater you wish to discuss, but murder."

"Given what happened to poor Alfred, the discussion is long past due."

"I agree. How shocking to make such an attempt in broad daylight with all of us nearby. We are dealing with a criminal whose boldness is matched only by his madness." Minerva frowned, which was the only time any wrinkles could be discerned on the sixty-year-old duchess.

Although she was never regarded as a great beauty, Minerva's intelligence and humor had dazzled many men since she was a girl. London society was shocked when the 6th Duke of Carbrey married the Baron of Sefton's daughter. But the Duke was an astute man who valued Minerva's wit and vivacity over a pretty face and empty conversation. He remained devoted to her until his death. She inspired an equal amount of devotion in her second husband, a wealthy business owner and racehorse breeder twenty years her junior. And the redoubtable duchess had not lacked for male company since his death nine years ago.

"I am glad you mention the madness of these acts," Higgins said. "That is why I believed Harold Hewitt was behind the murders. But we'd be fools to think that now."

"Then you agree with Miss Doolittle. A syndicate member is the killer."

"Exactly. All of you were together at Ascot, Henley, and at the horse farm. Because of the crowds at the races and the regatta, an outsider could have done the deed there. But damned few of us were at the horse farm on Saturday." Restless, Higgins walked over to the windows overlooking the second-floor terrace. The rain streaming down the glass obscured his view of the flowerpots outside, as well as the river Thames below. "The murderer was among us that day. And that narrows the list of suspects by a considerable margin."

Pickering cleared his throat. "Racing attracts desperate characters, and two disreputable men were part of the racing syndicate. One is gone. The other remains."

"What? You mean Lord Saxton?" Minerva let out an amused guffaw. "Don't be absurd."

"The Colonel never trusted either man," Higgins said.

Minerva rolled her eyes. "I don't trust most people I meet in the course of the day. That doesn't mean they're killers. Good heavens, I know both fellows gambled away their fortunes like drunken sailors on a sinking ship. In fact, Turnbull Tea was run so atrociously, I've heard rumors the bank will soon take it over. But stupidity is not the same as murder."

"You should not make excuses for these wastrels," Pickering said with a stubborn expression. "I see no reason to speak ill of the dead. I will not bring up Turnbull's many vices, but Saxton is alive and well. The gentlemen at my club say he has gambled away over half his inheritance. That makes a man desperate."

"My dear Colonel, rich men have been gambling to excess since before the time of Nero," Mrs. Higgins said. "It is not a rare occupation among the wealthy."

"Exactly," Minerva said. "And it grieves me to see how much Maitland drinks. Have you noticed his yellowish pallor? A sure sign jaundice is setting in. He'll be thirty-one next month, but at this rate he won't live to see forty. Such a handsome, likable fellow, too."

"I say, this is really too much." Pickering got to his feet. "Since I fear this conversation will only agitate me further, I must take my leave." Before Mrs. Higgins could ring for Daisy to show him out, the Colonel bowed over their hands and departed.

"Does Maitland owe him money?" Minerva asked in bewilderment.

Mrs. Higgins hesitated. "I do not wish to betray a confidence, but during my past conversations with the Colonel, he has mentioned a family member with a drinking problem. That time in his life left painful memories, and little tolerance for such behavior now."

Higgins turned and stared at his mother. "The man has been living under my roof at Wimpole Street for over a year, and I have not heard a word about any of this. When are the two of you having these confessional tête-à-têtes?"

She raised a haughty eyebrow. "Whenever you are not around."

He felt a bit nervous. Was there some sort of clandestine romance between his mother and friend going on behind his back?

"Unless Colonel Pickering's drunken relative is a secret member of the syndicate, I see no reason to jabber on about it. Nor do I see any purpose in suspecting Lord Saxton." Minerva sat back with a sigh, one hand stroking her necklace's amber pendant. "I've known Maitland and his family for years. He is not a vicious brute like Jonathon Turnbull. The poor fellow wanted to be a painter and spent his youth in Paris. But the Bohemian *artiste* had to make his way home to become a viscount. I heard he drank at university and in France. From all accounts the drinking worsened when he returned to England."

Higgins wished Eliza were here. He knew she would be unable to hide her scorn. All this pity expressed over a privileged young man who had to leave off painting in order to become even richer and more privileged.

"I find him an unlikely suspect as well," Higgins said. "It seems obvious he cared deeply about Diana Price. I cannot see him murdering her."

"Goodness, no. I'd never seen Maitland so enthralled with any of his other showgirls, although I never understood why. Diana may have been pretty, but she was such a stupid creature. I felt a bit sorry for Maitland, watching how he mooned after that golden-haired simpleton. And he spent a fortune buying her furs and jewels. At times, they reminded me of a drunken version of Samson and Delilah."

Higgins whirled so fast, he nearly tripped over the Persian carpet. His mother looked at him in dismay. "Whatever is wrong, Henry?"

"That's the Bible story Hewitt quoted when Eliza and I visited him at Claybury Asylum. Hewitt read the entire story from the Book of Judges."

Minerva snorted. "Anyone who peppers their conversation with Bible verses usually wants to justify some bad behavior they committed—or plan to."

Higgins paced between the fireplace and piano. "Eliza was right. Hewitt tried to tell us what he'd seen at Ascot. And the Delilah he referred to was Diana Price."

"Diana looked like a harlot at Ascot in that green sequin dress," Minerva said.

"Hewitt could have been in the stables when Diana was killed. Brody and a groom found him there early that morning and threw him out. But what if he went back? Maybe he wanted to find a hiding place before the Gold Cup started. Hewitt probably saw Diana Price's murder."

Mrs. Higgins sighed. "If so, he took the secret with him when he escaped."

"That he did," Higgins said in frustration.

"Leaving us with the question of who is responsible for killing off the syndicate members," Minerva said. "We can cross Maitland off our list of suspects. Oh, he drinks and gambles, but he's a good man. I don't even fault him for his affairs. That wife of his is a chilly piece of business."

Mrs. Higgins frowned. "I'd be chilly myself if I was married off to a drunkard ten years my senior. A drunkard with a ruinous gambling habit and a penchant for greedy loose women."

"Fair enough. But the girl must warm up enough to give him an heir and a spare. After that, she can spend what's left of his money while enjoying dalliances with men younger and more sober than her husband."

"We are getting off the point." Higgins wondered what sort of colorful conversations women had in his absence. "Saxton is not a likely suspect. Doolittle certainly isn't one. That leaves Sir Walter and Gordon Longhurst."

"Yes, and Longhurst has what he wanted," Minerva replied. "Maitland promised to sell him his shares of the Donegal Dancer."

"What better way to eventually own the horse outright than by killing off the syndicate members one by one." Higgins paused. "Or scaring them into selling. Which is exactly what led Saxton to sell."

Minerva narrowed her eyes. "We ought to look closer at Sir Walter. When I visited White Flower Cottage, I was struck by the size of his estate. He attributes it to the money left by his late father. If so, the third Baronet of Horning was remarkably generous to his younger sons."

"I met the Baronet twenty years ago, along with his Swedish wife," Mrs. Higgins said. "They both seemed kind and level-headed. It doesn't surprise me that Sir Walter's father made certain to provide for all his children, not merely the firstborn."

"Besides, why would an aging botanist start killing people?" Higgins asked. "For one thing, Sir Walter is much too old for such an ambitious series of murders. The fellow is sixty-two. He's fit for little more than afternoon naps and pottering about the garden."

His mother and Minerva both shot him withering glances.

He raised his hand. "My apologies, but Sir Walter is not in debt, and his interest in horse racing appears almost cerebral. His true passion seems to lie in gardening. Now if someone were threatening to destroy his orchids, I've little doubt he'd beat the wretch to death with a rake."

"Or poison them," Minerva said. "Inspector Shaw said the poison that killed Turnbull was botanical. Who better than a botanist to prepare such a poison?"

"A doctor." Higgins informed both women about Gordon Long-hurst's medical education in Edinburgh. "Therefore, two people in the syndicate have expert knowledge of poisons."

Minerva bit her lip. "Actually, there are three."

"Who's the third?"

"Rachel Turnbull." She shook her head at his skeptical expression. "Henry, really, how can you look so surprised? I know Rachel invited the pair of you to visit her shortly after the funeral. I assumed you asked inappropriate questions as you do of anyone you run across. If so, you would have learned her grandparents were perfumers."

"She did mention she spent some years in France, helping to create scents." Higgins smacked his head. "Of course. She created scents from flowers and oils! She'd have to know a great deal about plants and flowers to do that, including which ones were poisonous."

"Exactly."

Mrs. Higgins rang for the maid. "I find it distasteful that either of you suspects the widowed Mrs. Turnbull."

Higgins waited until after Daisy had removed the tea tray. "Mother, it makes sense. The first victim was her husband's mistress. The second was her philandering husband."

"And the third murder attempt was directed at a former Cockney dustman," Mrs. Higgins said sharply. "Where was the motive for her to kill him? Or have you forgotten that once her husband died, Rachel was no longer a legal owner of the Donegal Dancer? At least not according to the syndicate contract, which you have described to me in exhausting detail."

Damnation. Higgins flung himself down on the nearest chair so hard, the legs creaked.

"If you break my Chippendale, I may be driven to murder as well," Mrs. Higgins warned.

"Then Rachel Turnbull is not a suspect," he said finally.

"Oh, I think she is." Minerva wore an uneasy expression. "Since April, I have seen Gordon Longhurst and Rachel together in London. Three times."

Startled, Higgins straightened up. "Where?"

"I spotted them at Harrods during the last week of April. They were at the glove counter and seemed most companionable. At the time, I assumed they'd run into each other accidentally. I was on the way to an appointment and never stopped to greet them. I didn't think much about it until I saw them a second time."

"When was that?"

"Right before the Epsom Derby in June. I went with a friend to the National Portrait Gallery. There was an exhibit he was very keen to see."

Higgins and his mother exchanged amused glances. It was common knowledge the sixty-year-old Minerva was romantically involved with an art gallery owner from America. Said to be both handsome and erudite, Ambrose Farrow was also her junior by nearly thirty years.

"So you saw Longhurst and Rachel at the museum?" Higgins asked.

"They were arm in arm. And pressed so close together, it left little room for daylight. This time I deliberately avoided them, but followed at a distance to satisfy my curiosity. I observed no clandestine kisses or furtive embraces. However, they seemed most content in each other's company."

"Why shouldn't they be friends?" Mrs. Higgins protested. "After all, Rachel's husband was off rendezvousing with Longhurst's wife. I don't wonder they became allies."

"You said you saw them three times." Higgins leaned forward. He was interested in these sightings, even if his mother wasn't happy to hear about them. "When was the third time you saw them together?"

Minerva raised an eyebrow at him. "Yesterday morning."

He hadn't expected that. "Where?"

"Hyde Park. I go riding there on Sunday mornings when I'm in London. My friend Mr. Farrow is a fine horseman, and we often ride together. Since there was a light rain yesterday, I knew there would be fewer pedestrians. That suited me. It meant I could gallop now and again without fear of running over any tourists gawking at the deer."

"But you saw Rachel Turnbull and Longhurst?"

"Yes, from a distance at first. They were too far away for me to identify them. I did note that the woman was dressed entirely in mourning."

"How do you know it was Rachel?" Mrs. Higgins asked.

"Mr. Farrow and I had ridden close to where the couple stood. But they were deep in conversation, and no doubt thought they enjoyed a private moment. Suddenly a deer darted from the shrubbery and ran across our path. We reined in the horses. Just as we were about to ride on again, the couple turned. I recognized Rachel instantly. Then the gentleman took off his hat, leaving no doubt it was Longhurst."

Higgins held out his hands. "That's it?"

"No. They exchanged a most passionate kiss. Afterwards, they embraced, both of them oblivious to the rain or to any riders on the horse path."

He let out a low whistle. "Rachel and Longhurst are lovers, then."

"It would appear so," Minerva said. "I would never have said anything, because I didn't see how it could be connected to the murders. After all, the two of them certainly deserve some happiness after their dreadful marriages."

"That is the first thing you have said I agree with." Although his mother wore a sand-colored lace dress, Higgins thought she only needed a white bench wig and scarlet robe to complete her impression of a stern judge. "Neither Rachel Turnbull nor Mr. Longhurst has ever had a word of gossip spread about them, except in connection with their morally bankrupt spouses. If they have found comfort in each other's arms, I applaud them."

"Mother, they are murder suspects."

"More than once, I have run across Rachel at a soiree or tea. And try as she might to conceal her bruises, I could see the marks left by that brute of a husband. And everyone in society knew he forced her to ride on a foxhunt when she was five months with child. I think he did it deliberately, knowing she might fall and lose the baby. Which she did."

"No one blames her for wanting Jonathon dead," Minerva said. "To be frank, if either of my husbands had treated me like that, I would have run them down with my fiercest stallion. And then dragged them behind me until the very flesh was scraped off their worthless bones."

"Remind me to never get on your bad side," Higgins muttered.

"If the law won't protect women, they'd best learn how to protect themselves," she said with feeling. "It's why I have given so much of my time and money to the cause of women's suffrage. But the vote won't stop wives from being abused by their husbands. Not if they don't fight back, or publicly expose them."

"Perhaps Rachel did fight back, along with the assistance of Gordon Longhurst," Higgins said. "I know she is being hounded by creditors. If her financial situation is that dire, acquiring a champion racehorse might look like salvation."

"I don't believe it." His mother stared back at him.

"But someone involved with the syndicate is the murderer. Who, then?" Minerva asked.

His mother sighed. "Why not that Brody fellow? The jockey."

Minerva shook her head. "Jockeys are barred from racing if they own a racehorse. No matter how many syndicate members die, Brody cannot own the Donegal Dancer. I doubt he cares. Brody won the St. Leger Stakes when he was only seventeen and became a racing hero at twenty with a stunning upset at the Derby. The prize money from his winning mounts has been considerable. I heard he recently bought a flat here in Chelsea. Quite a big one, too."

"Then who is left?" Mrs. Higgins sounded perplexed.

"Me, for one. After all, I am a syndicate member. Although I own twenty racehorses, I certainly would enjoy having the Donegal Dancer all to myself. Therefore it makes sense to include me on your colorful list of suspects. Or don't you think I'm capable of murder?"

Higgins smiled. "You may joke about trampling any man who would dare strike you, but I doubt you'd go that far."

Minerva patted him on the hand. "My dear boy, anyone is capable of murder."

"Even you?"

"Especially me." Minerva sat back with a laugh.

Higgins and his mother laughed as well, but he couldn't help wondering if he was sitting across from the murderer right now.

SIXTEEN

If there was a heaven, Eliza hoped it looked like Selfridges. Renowned for its excellent service, fine merchandise, rooftop terrace, and five floors boasting a hundred departments, the store cemented its premier status with artfully designed windows. Eliza gazed in admiration at the current window, which showed a lady's boudoir peopled by elegant mannequins draped in silk and satin dressing gowns. Tall potted ferns arched over brocade divans, a marble fireplace, and two stuffed Persian cats. On a lacquered table sat glass atomizer bottles of French perfume, each one in varying shades of purple, rose, and blue.

She heard Clara clear her throat. The girl was obviously restless. Eliza didn't blame her. Both of them had waited far too long for Lady Tansy.

"Let's go inside," Eliza said. "The perfume counter is right in front. This way your friend can't miss us when she finally arrives." She frowned. "If she ever does."

"Thank you for coming with me," Clara said. "Though if she introduces me to another widower today, I shall scream. Literally, I will scream right in his face."

"I spoke to Lady Tansy at Henley about these gentlemen. She promised to come up with a potential suitor who didn't turn everyone's stomach."

"One of them had rotting teeth from the cigars he smoked. And all he talked about was his hunting hounds. I hate hounds. They frighten me." She shivered. "He did, too."

The two women walked past the uniformed doorman into Selfridges. As always, Eliza delighted in the magnificent high ceilings and bright chandeliers that added to the natural light pouring through the windows. Today, colorful red, white, and blue bunting hung everywhere. Must be some sort of national holiday. Dozens of customers strolled along the spacious aisles. And polished glass counters displayed every type of goods imaginable: men's waistcoats and other attire, soaps and toiletries, parasols and feather boas, brooches and earrings in costume jewelry, shoes of all kinds, silk and linen handkerchiefs.

Best of all, perfume and cosmetics were on display front and center. One of the female shop assistants flashed a winning smile at them. Her smart navy dress had an ecru lace collar, making her look as stylish as the customers. The young woman focused her attention on Eliza.

"May I help you, madam?"

"No thank you. We're waiting for someone," Clara blurted out, but Eliza shushed her.

"I'd like to choose a new perfume." She glanced around the display, uncertain. "The scent I have is a bit flowery. Very nice, but something different might be more to my taste."

"May I suggest Houbigant's *Quelques Fleurs*?"

The sales assistant selected a pale bottle, removed the stopper, and dabbed a bit on her own wrist. After she motioned for Eliza to extend her arm, she demonstrated how to rub her other wrist against the tiny smudge of scent. She waited as Eliza breathed in the heady citrus mix of orange and lemon, with a musky undertone.

"It's wonderful. Thank you, I do like it."

Lady Tansy suddenly appeared. "I assumed you both would wait for me outside."

Eliza bit back a curt reply at the young woman's haughty tone. She also thought her plum gown was too regal for daytime, with its sheer lace sleeves and tasseled sash. As for Lady Tansy, she didn't bother to conceal her sharp interest in Eliza's blue and white pinstripe dress and white plumed hat. Perhaps the young viscountess was a bit jealous of her new summer outfit, which was all the rage in Paris. Poor Clara's pale pink ensemble couldn't compete with either of them. But the girl's wide-brimmed hat festooned with rose satin bows and ribbons was perfect. Eliza had bought the expensive chapeau for Clara only last week.

Lady Tansy shook her head at the shop assistant. "That perfume is much too old-fashioned for her. Try a bit of my *Nuit de Chine*, Clara. 'Chinese Night' is the translation, quite exotic. Sandalwood and civet."

"The perfume is for me, not Clara. And I find the scent delightful." Eliza leaned toward the sales assistant behind the counter. "Please box it for me."

The young woman nodded. "Shall I put it on Colonel Pickering's account, Miss Doolittle?" Eliza shopped here so often, the staff knew her by name.

"Not this time. I recently opened my own account. Charge it to that one." When Eliza looked around, Lady Tansy had whisked Clara away to examine parasols.

"Thank goodness we're here today, and not tomorrow." Lady Tansy inspected a carved parasol handle. "No one comes on Wednesdays except 'value' shoppers from the suburbs."

"Their money is as good as anyone else's," Eliza said. If only the Viscountess didn't take on such airs. It was quite maddening. No wonder Lord Saxton drank so much.

"Next you'll be showing sympathy for the unionists."

In dismay, Clara mouthed a "Please don't," as if the problem were Eliza and not Lady Tansy's snobbish attitude. "What shall we look at first, Your Grace?" Clara asked.

"I've told you to call me Tansy. We're old school friends. And Lord Richard Ashmore is my second cousin on my maternal side. If you do marry him, we'll practically be sisters."

Eliza tried not to laugh at the woman's attempt to make her jealous. Ever since Lord Saxton had insisted she call his wife "Lady Tansy," she noticed it irritated her whenever Eliza did so. If she imagined Eliza had any interest in what Clara called her, she was mistaken. Clara could call Tansy "sweetheart" for all Eliza cared.

"Who is Lord Ashmore?" Eliza asked as they strolled over to view the gloves.

"He has lately returned from India," Lady Tansy said. "His brother, the fourth baron, died last year of either pleurisy or some other inconvenient illness. Richard's a captain in the King's Hussars. He was, that is, until he resigned his commission to inherit the barony."

Lady Saxton prattled on about the Ashmore estate in Kent, a Jacobean house known as Banfield Manor. When she was done with her exhausting description of its extensive gardens, she went on to discuss every aristocratic guest at the shooting party she'd attended last autumn at the manor house. This went on for the better part of an hour.

By the time they reached the topmost floor of Selfridges, Lady Tansy was explaining how Richard's oldest brother died in a car accident two years ago. If this went on much longer, Eliza would fling herself over the fifth-floor balustrade.

"Are we done hearing about your cousin?" Eliza didn't bother to hide her exasperation. "Or are there a few details you've left out? Like his shoe size and what he eats for breakfast."

Lady Tansy shot her an offended look. "Richard will join us for lunch, and I thought it proper for Clara to know all she can about him."

That set off Clara's nerves. "What if he doesn't like me?"

"I know my cousin. He'll adore you, darling."

Eliza halted by the hat display, her eye caught by a new design for fall, but Clara dragged her away. Thirty minutes later, the women had finished exploring the fifth floor. They headed for the lift, where Lady Tansy continued to extol the virtues of Lord Ashmore. They hadn't even met the fellow, but Eliza was already sick of him. When Eliza announced her plan to return downstairs to Cosmetics, Clara gushed in excitement.

"I'd love to try a bit of color. It's all the rage now. Powder and rouge, I mean."

"Whatever for? Your complexion is like cream and roses," Lady Tansy protested.

"Clara's rather fair." Eliza carefully exited the lift. "Besides, it might be fun to try it."

"I imagine Richard will be surprised by all the changes since he's been away from England. Cosmetics, women driving motorcars, the nightclubs. It's all too much."

"I've never driven a motorcar," Clara said wistfully.

Eliza led them to the cosmetics counter once more. "You've never attended a nightclub, either. Not that I would expect you to. By the way, I think this pale pink rouge would be perfect. And you'd only need a hint." She picked up a tin of powder. "What is this made from?"

"Finely ground safflowers. Brush on a dab rather than pinching your cheeks." The saleswoman smiled at her.

Although Lady Tansy rolled her eyes in disapproval, Eliza could tell she applied color to brighten her complexion. Clara swept the lightweight powder just below her cheekbones. The effect lent a sparkle to her eyes. Next she picked up a long metal tube, and the saleswoman demonstrated how to apply a tiny amount on her lips.

"It's wonderful," Clara said with enthusiasm.

Eliza decided to buy it for her. She was actually grateful for this little shopping expedition, since it gave her a reprieve from sitting at her father's hospital bedside. He was recovering nicely in a private room, with nurses at his beck and call. The train trip back and forth to Windsor was tiring, however; so was the crowd who visited her father, from the old neighborhood as well as his new friends. Her stepmother's family also visited, shoving and pushing to sit on the few chairs. They even dragged their children along despite the staff's pleas to leave them home. The brats climbed all over "Uncle Alfie." Her father didn't seem to mind the bantering and fussing, as long as it didn't go on for too long.

Her father's recovery had lifted her spirits. Now she needed to find a moment to ask Lady Tansy about Longhurst's friendship with Rachel Turnbull. Higgins expected her to confirm the information he'd gleaned yesterday from the Duchess of Carbrey.

"How old is Lord Ashmore?" Clara sounded worried.

"Twenty-eight," Lady Tansy said. "I haven't seen him since before he left for India."

"Are you sure he's not a confirmed bachelor?"

She laughed. "You will find out for yourself soon enough. But I rather doubt he'd agree to meet you if he was, don't you think? Now stop worrying. He's an excellent catch."

Clara seemed rattled by the upcoming meeting. "Oh dear. My hat is coming loose from its pins." She stood before a counter mirror and fussed with it.

Eliza took Lady Tansy aside. "Given what happened to my father, I imagine you're relieved your husband sold his share of the Donegal Dancer."

"Heavens, yes. The last thing I want is to be widowed because of that fool horse. Maitland is no prize, but he is useful in his own way. Now that he's sold his share, he should be safe. At least until he drinks himself to death."

"Who do you think is behind these murders and the attack at the stables? Gordon Longhurst, perhaps? He could very well have killed both Diana and Turnbull out of jealousy."

She shrugged. "If so, he ought to be knighted for it. I may not agree with the methods for their eradication—murder is a messy business—but neither of them will be missed."

"I had tea with Rachel Turnbull the other day. She didn't seem at all heartbroken."

"And you're surprised by that? I wouldn't blame her if she threw a party to celebrate."

Eliza lowered her voice even more. "There is talk that she and Longhurst are lovers."

"Don't be ridiculous."

"Why is it so unbelievable?" Eliza wondered if she should reveal what the Duchess had mentioned to Higgins.

"Rachel is no more capable of romantic passion than one of those mannequins over there." She cast a wary eye at Eliza. "You're full of questions today. Are you playing police detective again, as you did this past spring? If so, you no doubt suspect Maitland *and* me."

"I believe someone wants the horse all to themselves. Since Lord Saxton sold his shares, he no longer has a motive. Forgive me for saying so, but you don't seem all that interested in passion either. Nor did you show any jealousy of Diana at Ascot. Just wounded pride."

That prompted a bitter smile. "Although Maitland chases after the dregs of womanhood, I would not risk my own neck to murder him. Trust me. I have other ways of punishing my husband for his bad behavior." She leaned closer to Eliza. "I ordered a lavish new wardrobe for fall from the Paris salons. Along with a ruby ring the size of a cherry. That's what hurts him the most—my spending habits. It's less money to gamble away, or spend on his latest paramour."

"Aren't you afraid Lord Saxton will cut off your allowance one day?"

Lady Tansy seemed amused. "He's not that stupid. Maitland knows I would not kill him over some dreadful woman. But if he ever cuts off my clothing and jewelry allowance, he'd best sleep with one eye open."

———

Fragrant bouquets of red roses, lilies, and carnations filled two tall Chinese vases near the door of the Palm Court restaurant. The headwaiter welcomed them and led the way through the room. Selfridges proved an ideal lunch spot for Londoners. An orchestra played softly, taking care not to drown out the conversation of the patrons. A small bud vase of roses and ferns decorated each linen-draped table, while leaded glass chandeliers glittered overhead. Waiters in black tie and tails swept around guests, filling water goblets and serving plates of braised lamb chops, cod cakes, or luscious desserts.

At one table, a nervous young gentleman waited to greet them. Eliza was pleasantly surprised by his appearance. Tanned and good-looking, with green eyes and wavy brown hair, Lord Richard Ashmore stood just shy of Clara's taller than average height in her low heels. And his light gray linen suit fit his trim figure well. Once Lady Tansy finished the introductions, he pulled all the ladies' chairs out, Clara's last, with a courtly bow.

Eliza's feet ached from hours of wandering through the store. And she worried Lady Tansy's cousin might prove as talkative. But Lord Ashmore was a quiet, soft-spoken gentleman. He fielded questions about his Army career, the Indian subcontinent, and Banfield Manor with a hint of nervousness, which Eliza found endearing. It proved he was as anxious about this meeting as Clara. While the others conversed, Eliza enjoyed a fine Darjeeling tea and lemon chicken cutlets over savory rice. Her flagging spirits revived when their waiter brought custard tarts with fresh raspberries for dessert.

"Does your family hail from Eynsford, perchance?" Lord Ashmore asked Clara. "It's a small village southeast of Swanley."

"I-I'm afraid I don't know."

"There was a Norman castle built there in 1088, but it was ransacked in the fourteenth century. The Ashmores are great lovers of history, you know. In fact, both my father and grandfather funded archaeological excavations in Asia Minor and India. We have quite an extensive antiquities collection at Banfield Manor. Perhaps you would like to see it one day."

"I would be honored, Your Grace." Clara batted her eyelashes at him.

He touched her hand. "Call me Richard, please. I'm not accustomed to any title save that of Captain. Until this moment, I didn't realize how much I missed England. My years in India caused me to forget how beautiful my countrywomen are."

"Thank you, Your—Richard," Clara said, blushing pinker.

"How is the Dowager Baroness?" Lady Tansy asked. "I haven't seen your mother at any London dinner parties or charity functions this season."

"I assume Mother is fine. We take care not to spend too much time together."

Lord Ashmore's terse answer and quick change of subject spoke volumes about possible family troubles. Eliza wondered if his mother had been shocked by the deaths of her older sons and had not yet recovered. Or was she disappointed that her youngest, and perhaps not her favorite, child would become the 5th Baron Ashmore?

"Tell me about your family, Miss Eynsford Hill."

"Clara, please." She giggled. "I have a mother and older brother."

"Splendid. Tell me all about them, your home, your childhood, everything."

Pleased by Lord Ashmore's manners and good nature, Eliza sensed Clara might be a perfect match for him. He seemed taken with her modern "small talk," copied from Eliza, of course. Thank goodness he was a cut above the rest of the men Lady Tansy had thrown Clara's way. And he clearly wanted a wife.

Eliza hoped Clara allowed herself enough time to become acquainted with Lord Ashmore before doing anything rash. The girl so wanted a ring on her finger. Eliza must ask Mrs. Higgins what she knew about the Ashmore family. For the sake of Clara's future happiness, it wouldn't hurt to make a few discreet inquiries.

She was puzzled that Lord Ashmore seemed keen on marrying someone who might not measure up to his mother's aristocratic standards. He was young, attractive, and agreeable. Add his title to that, and it was a wonder half the debutantes in London weren't chasing after him. Yet he seemed genuinely delighted by Clara. Not that Clara wasn't a pretty young woman. But she had no dowry, and her family tree was bare of any titles or distinguished ancestors. The fact that Richard agreed to this meeting at all was astonishing. Why wasn't he pursuing the daughter of a fellow lord, or a rich American heiress?

Still, they seemed to hit it off. It touched Eliza's heart to see how after an hour's conversation, they already teased each other and laughed at the same silly jokes. This might be a match made in heaven, even if it was the sardonic Lady Tansy who engineered it.

He whispered something in Clara's ear, which sent her into a gale of giggles. Eliza finished her tea, while Lady Tansy turned sideways to greet a friend at the nearest table.

"Miss Doolittle? May I have a private word with you?"

Startled, Eliza looked up to see Gordon Longhurst. "Excuse me?"

"I've been following you all day."

She drew back in alarm. "Why are you following me?"

"Please, I must speak with you. It's urgent."

Lord Ashmore and Clara had fallen silent and sat listening. Lady Tansy looked uneasy. Eliza had misgivings as well, but she had questions for Mr. Longhurst, too. This might be the best time to get answers.

She stood. "I am not leaving this restaurant, Mr. Longhurst."

"I am not asking you to. Join me at that table by the window." Longhurst gently took her elbow. "Everyone will be able to see you there."

After they walked to the window table, Eliza quickly sat down. Longhurst settled himself in the opposite chair. "Apparently you don't trust me."

"Don't know why I should, given what happened to my father at the stables."

"I had nothing to do with that." Longhurst's voice grew as hard as steel. "I know your cousin is Detective Inspector Shaw. Perhaps you're not aware that he's been hounding me. Asking questions about my late wife, about the Henley Regatta picnic, and about the Donegal Dancer, too. Let me assure you I've done nothing wrong."

"Then you have nothing to fear."

"As if that means anything to a policeman. Did you know Shaw visited me where I work? Twice! And he questioned the other stockbrokers. Now they're treating me as if I'm a murderer. And I answered all his questions when I was at Scotland Yard. He had no right to ask my employer about my private life outside of work."

Eliza couldn't think of anything to say that would reassure him. Especially since she suspected he might actually be the killer. She didn't blame Jack for snooping around after him.

"If he continues, I will lose my position. What will I do then?" Longhurst seemed oblivious of the restaurant patrons who glanced their way. She also grew uncomfortable with every nervous twitch and clench of his fists, his reddened cheeks, and his forceful tone.

"Surely it won't come to that."

"I implore you, Miss Doolittle, make him stop!" Longhurst banged his hand on the table, upsetting a half-filled teacup. A pale stain spread over the linen. "The police have also been at Mrs. Turnbull's home. How can they trouble a new widow who is in mourning for her husband? It's an outrage, I tell you. Not only did Inspector Shaw barge into her home to interrogate her. He also demanded she report to his Scotland Yard office today."

Eliza swallowed hard. "But why?"

"Don't you see? He's trying to catch her out about that damned fool picnic. Rachel—Mrs. Turnbull is such a gentle soul, a virtual angel. She wouldn't hurt a fly, much less kill two people." Longhurst shook his head. "They're treating us both in a monstrous fashion, Miss Doolittle. I insist you have a word with Inspector Shaw."

"I have no right to interfere in his investigation. And he wouldn't listen to me anyway."

"You can broach the subject at least."

"How do you know all this about Mrs. Turnbull? Like you said, she's been in seclusion as a widow. Did Rachel ask you to speak to me?"

"Of course not. But I've heard from mutual friends that Mrs. Turnbull is being most dreadfully harassed by the police. By your cousin, in fact."

She took a deep breath. "And I have heard from mutual friends that you and Mrs. Turnbull share a special friendship. A romantic one, in fact. One friend even claims to have seen you embracing the widow in rather a familiar manner."

Longhurst turned purple. "That is preposterous and untrue!"

He stood so quickly, the table overturned. Eliza jumped back as the teapot, sugar bowl, and creamer crashed to the floor. The ladies at the next table gasped when he stormed past them out of the Palm Court. The waiter rushed over.

"Madam, are you all right? I do apologize."

"No need. The gentleman was rude, not you."

When Eliza rejoined Clara, Lord Ashmore, and Lady Tansy, they stared at her with stunned expressions. "I say, Miss Doolittle," Lord Ashmore said. "That man seemed a bit mad."

"I agree." Eliza pushed her teacup aside. She'd pay two quid for a glass of champagne right now. "And if Longhurst ends up in the asylum, I refuse to visit. I don't care what Higgins says. Once was quite enough."

They looked even more bewildered, but Eliza didn't bother to explain. Her only concern was that Gordon Longhurst seemed as unhinged as Harold Hewitt. And perhaps—just perhaps—she should not have mentioned that he and Rachel had been seen embracing in public. She had spooked him for sure. Not a wise decision.

If Longhurst was the killer, he was now more dangerous than ever.

SEVENTEEN

I hope murder isn't on the menu," Higgins said as they exited the taxi. The blare of a dozen horns and the cries of a bus conductor greeted them. At half past twelve, the streets teemed with pedestrians, horse-drawn wagons, and motorcars.

"I wouldn't joke about something like that." Eliza gave him a disapproving look. "My dad is still lying in a hospital bed, with a jaw so swollen he can barely swallow oatmeal."

"I wasn't joking." In fact, he looked upon the upcoming Wrexham Racing Syndicate luncheon with trepidation.

Such a pity, too. The lunch was being held at the Criterion, one of his favorite dining spots in London. Although the opulent restaurant and its adjacent theater sat in bustling Piccadilly Circus, the outside world slipped away the minute patrons stood beneath its fabled gold leaf ceiling. In addition, the Criterion had an excellent kitchen and a fine wine list. The only thing he had to worry about was another murder.

As they walked toward the entrance, a gleaming blue Daimler pulled up to the curb. Inside he glimpsed not only a uniformed chauffeur but the Duchess of Carbrey and the Saxtons. Higgins hurried Eliza through the doors of the Criterion. He had little patience with either Saxton. Conversation could wait until the appetizers had been served.

As soon as they were inside, Eliza pointed down the wide hallway. "There's Jack."

Jack Shaw and his detectives marched ahead of them, a maître d' trailing in their wake. At least the police would keep a close eye on things this time. Only the brashest of killers would dare strike with four Scotland Yard detectives scrutinizing everyone's movements.

Eliza straightened her hat, a small white Tam o'Shanter with but a single black aigrette feather. She was dressed more conservatively than usual in a white and black houndstooth skirt and matching jacket. It gave her a brisk businesslike appearance. Higgins thought she was taking her responsibility as representative for her father quite seriously.

Sir Walter appeared from around the corner. "How glad I am to see you both. Almost everyone is here. Brody and Miss Wilkins are already upstairs, and I see the Duchess and the Saxtons dawdling outside. Mr. Longhurst was twenty minutes early."

"The police are here, too," Eliza said.

"Yes, I spoke with them. A shame your father is still recovering. He so enjoys the syndicate luncheons." Sir Walter smoothed down his linen suit coat. "Excuse me while I greet the Duchess. I believe she's speaking with Lord Gosley. One of his horses won at Ascot. If I don't hurry them along, luncheon will never be served."

After he left, Higgins nodded at the adjacent room. "That is the Long Bar. You're reading Sir Arthur Conan Doyle, so I trust you know what it's most famous for."

Eliza had been quiet all morning, which worried him. But at the mention of Conan Doyle, her eyes sparkled. She peeked at the long polished bar as they passed, a wide grin on her face. "That's where

Dr. Watson first heard about Sherlock Holmes. A friend of Watson's told him that an eccentric fellow was looking for a roommate."

"Exactly." Higgins beamed at her. Eliza was still his best pupil.

"I wish Watson and Holmes were here right now. We need someone's powers of deduction aside from our own."

"I think we're doing rather well."

Eliza smirked. "Really? Two people have been murdered, while someone tried to kill my father four days ago. Yet we haven't a clue who the blighter is."

"After yesterday's encounter at the tearoom, I thought you had settled on Longhurst."

"So I have, which means Rachel Turnbull is probably part of the murderous scheme, too. What we don't have is proof. That's why we need Sherlock Holmes to reason it out for us."

As soon as they reached the second-floor dining rooms, Eliza hurried off without a backward glance. Higgins stared after her as she greeted Jack and his detectives. What was going on? He'd expected her to chatter his ears off on the taxi ride over, but she seemed lost in thought. At breakfast, Eliza ate in total silence, her attention focused on the latest issue of *The Suffragette*. Had she become an active member of the WSPU? He hated to sound as silly as Freddy, but was she about to start throwing bricks through windows or chain herself to No. 10 Downing Street?

When Higgins reached the luncheon table, he noticed that Gordon Longhurst avoided looking at either of them. Eliza sent him a cold stare, however. Higgins knew that if she could prove Longhurst was behind the attack on her father, a brawl might ensue during lunch.

To keep things calm, Higgins sat between them. Her resentment toward Longhurst might explain why she seemed so distracted. Eliza had never been inside the Criterion before. Normally she would have

delighted in the sheer grandeur of the restaurant: the expansive mirrored walls and curved ceilings of golden mosaic, the marble floors,
the neo-Byzantine arches studded with semiprecious stones. But she
acted as if she sat in the Hand and Shears pub.

Brody's girlfriend plopped down across from them. "Ain't this a
blooming lovely place?" she whispered in delight. "So happy Jimmy
asked me along." She reached over the water glasses. "I'm Patsy. Me
and Miss Doolittle were at the picnic. And we met at the funeral."

Higgins shook her hand. "I remember."

"Hope I'm dressed fancy enough." She smoothed her butter yellow
dress.

"You look fine," Higgins assured her. Eliza loved fashion, and he
expected her to comment on Patsy's dress and velour hat. Instead, Eliza
threw caustic glances at Longhurst.

"The Duchess is here." Brody suddenly appeared behind Patsy's
chair.

Everyone looked over as Sir Walter escorted the Duchess to the
table. Thankfully, she appeared less Bohemian this afternoon in a
beaded blue outfit. The Saxtons, however, looked like dress mannequins from the windows at Selfridges. They had donned nearly identi-
cal outfits; he sported a white shirt, jacket, and pants, while his wife
wore an ivory skirt and bolero with her white blouse. Higgins had
never seen Lady Saxton look so jubilant. And the two-foot-high white
plumes on her hat bobbed with every movement.

The reason for her joy became evident once she reached the table.
Lady Saxton stood before them, both hands clasped on her parasol's
carved ivory handle. "This is the last meeting of the Wrexham Racing
Syndicate that either Maitland or I shall ever have to attend." With a
victorious smile, she sat in the chair Lord Saxton drew out for her. "I
insist on drinking the first glass of champagne to celebrate."

Her husband sat down beside her with a glum expression. Higgins suspected Saxton would buy another horse as soon as possible, albeit one without murderers involved.

As agent for the syndicate, Sir Walter took his place at the head of the table. Gordon Longhurst sat directly to his right, the Duchess to his left. Brody sat at the other end of the table. He winked at Patsy, and she squeezed his hand in reply. Higgins wondered why the jockey was here. Then again, everyone probably wondered the same about him.

Once all the guests were seated, Sir Walter tapped a spoon against his water glass for attention. "The recent unhappy events at the Bay Willow Stables have prompted this meeting. Normally the syndicate would not meet until after the upcoming Eclipse Stakes, but much has happened over the past few days."

"Far too much, in my opinion," the Duchess said.

"Agreed. I spoke with the hospital this morning, and am happy to report that Alfred is recovering nicely. He may be released as early as next week."

"Has there been any further news about who attacked him?" Saxton asked.

Sir Walter pointed to the detectives who ringed the table. "As you can see, Scotland Yard will be joining us this afternoon. Inspector, perhaps you would like to say something."

Jack walked over. "We have questioned everyone who was at the stables that morning, including some of you. At this time, Mr. Doolittle cannot remember the attack. We hope his memory improves and he will give us a piece of crucial information."

"Which means you don't know anything more than you did on Saturday," Saxton said with obvious contempt.

Jack's expression grew steely. "I know enough to realize that someone at the stables that day was responsible. Until the culprit—or culprits—are found, everyone remains a suspect."

Lord Saxton swore under his breath. His wife leaned over and whispered, "Ignore him. He's just a policeman."

Higgins bit back a chuckle when Eliza shot an icy glare at Lady Saxton.

"Not only are you suspects, you are all possible murder victims," Jack continued. "That is why my men and I are here this afternoon. If another attempt is made to kill one of you, at least it won't take the police long to respond." Jack tipped his hat. "Enjoy your lunch."

"Yes, well. Ahem. Thank you, Inspector." Sir Walter took a deep breath. "Before we proceed, Mr. Brody will relay some pertinent news about future breeding opportunities for the Donegal Dancer."

After giving a self-conscious tug to his navy blazer, Brody droned on for five minutes regarding recent offers to breed their horse with various prize mares. Higgins heard Eliza's stomach growl. He was more than ready for lunch, too. And Lord Saxton looked most unhappy that Sir Walter hadn't yet asked the waiters to uncork the champagne.

At long last Brody sat down. Sir Walter stood again. "No doubt everyone is aware that Lord Saxton sold his shares of the Donegal Dancer this past Saturday to Mr. Longhurst. My solicitor drew up the proper papers, and both men signed them yesterday. I have the original documents with me for anyone who cares to inspect them. I also made copies for each of the owners." He held up a sheaf of legal documents.

At a nod from Sir Walter, one of the waiters lifted a magnum of champagne from an ice bucket. "Let us toast the arrival of a new member of the syndicate, as well as bid farewell to one of our original owners." Sir Walter lifted his full glass.

After the rest of the glasses had been filled, even Higgins took a few appreciative sips. It was an excellent vintage, although he preferred a good port.

Still holding his champagne flute, Sir Walter smiled at Eliza and Higgins. "A pity Alfred could not be here. With the Eclipse Stakes only two days away, he would be feverish with anticipation. Obviously he could not attend, nor his wife, who is staying by his side in hospital. But his daughter Eliza is here today to represent him. Given the alarming outcome of recent syndicate meetings, she has brought along Professor Higgins for moral support."

Eliza set her glass down. "I am here not only to represent my father's interests," she said. "I am also representing my own."

Curious, Higgins watched her reach for her handbag, a larger one than she normally carried.

After Eliza withdrew several papers, she stood. "I have decided it is too dangerous for my father to remain the only Doolittle in the Wrexham Racing Syndicate. If another attempt is made on an owner of the Donegal Dancer, then by heaven, we need more members."

"What in blazes are you talking about?" Higgins asked.

"The more targets, the harder they are to hit." Eliza shook the papers at Sir Walter. "I am the latest syndicate target. My father sold me part of his shares in the racehorse."

Startled cries rose up from everyone at the table.

"My dear girl, you didn't!" The Duchess looked aghast.

Saxton's wife sighed. "You ninny. Now you'll have to wear those awful colors."

"Are you out of your mind, Lizzie?" In an instant, Jack appeared at her elbow. Without asking, he grabbed her papers and scanned them.

What had the impulsive girl done? Higgins groaned. Eliza wasn't there at the stables to see how close her father came to dying. She didn't seem to understand that whoever was behind these attacks was utterly ruthless. And she had just offered herself up as a sacrificial victim.

"What a foolish thing for you to do." Higgins joined Jack in examining the documents.

"Not as foolish as waiting for this devil to make another attempt on my father's life." Eliza lifted her chin in defiance. "And I don't care what any of you think. I am now a part owner of the Donegal Dancer. I had papers drawn up by Sibley & Moffett, and the lawyers and I visited Dad in hospital on Monday so he could sign them."

"Sibley & Moffett?" Higgins shook his head in frustration. "You not only went behind my back to do this, you used my family's solicitors?"

She shrugged. "I had to use somebody. Anyway, the papers are all in order. Everything has been witnessed and the money transferred."

Higgins cursed under his breath. Damnation, Eliza had bought the shares with all her winnings from Ascot. Once again, she had bet everything she owned. If Eliza kept this up, she'd be back to selling violets at Covent Garden by the time she was twenty-five.

Sir Walter looked as concerned as Higgins and Jack. "If I may see the documents."

Handing them over, Eliza sat down once more and ignored both Jack and Higgins.

"You've put a blooming bull's-eye on your back, girl," Jack whispered in her ear.

"Better me than Dad. And if you solve these murders, none of us will have to worry anymore, now will we?"

Jack swore under his breath. With a last furious look at his cousin, he stomped back to rejoin his detectives near the mirrored wall.

Higgins leaned over her shoulder to say something, but Eliza put up a hand. "Not a word, Professor. Not a single word. All I asked you to do was keep an eye on my father, but he almost got trampled to death because you were talking, as usual. So I am done listening to what you or Jack have to say."

He felt cut to the heart, especially since her accusation was true.

"It appears Miss Doolittle's papers are in order." Sir Walter folded them and returned them to her. "Therefore, the Wrexham Racing Syndicate now has two new members." He lifted his champagne flute. "To Miss Eliza Doolittle, the latest owner of the Donegal Dancer."

Higgins refused to join in the toast. Eliza was not only the latest fool to own that blasted racehorse, she could very well be the next murder victim.

———

Eliza was pleased. Things had gone better than planned. As expected, Jack and Higgins carried on for a bit, but it could have been worse. It might be wise, however, if she spent all her free time with Freddy until the Eclipse Stakes. Otherwise, Higgins and Jack would lecture her nonstop.

She had worried for days about their reaction after learning she was now a syndicate member. Although she wasn't good at keeping secrets, this one was too important to divulge. Those papers had to be legal and signed before she breathed a word of it to anyone. Of course she had put herself in danger. But it was the right thing to do. If Higgins and Jack were this upset, imagine how disturbed the killer must be now that another owner stood between him and the Donegal Dancer!

For the hundredth time, she wondered if Longhurst was the murderer. When she announced the news, she made sure to catch his reaction. He seemed surprised and upset. Then again, so did everyone else. Especially Higgins.

Clearly she had unsettled the Professor. He barely touched his lunch, odd since he was always going on about how much he loved the

Criterion's food. For her part, she quite enjoyed the pickled oysters, Norwegian anchovies, oxtail consommé, and fillets of beef. She'd eaten two servings of the boiled new potatoes, and almost asked for a second of the plover on toast and cress salad. Now and then she worried a bit of poison might have been included on the menu. But Jack and his detectives shadowed the waiters, inspecting every single dish they served. Four more detectives reportedly stood guard in the Criterion kitchens. How in the world could the food be poisoned under such scrutiny?

When dessert was served, Eliza debated between the iced pudding, apricot fritters, or raspberry nut shortcake. Perhaps a little of all three.

As she savored her first delicious bite of shortcake, Higgins muttered, "You're eating more than all the syndicate members at this table, Eliza. If any of this food is poisoned, you will be the first one to drop dead."

"If there's poison in this cake, it's the best blooming poison I've ever tasted."

"I do not find that amusing."

"When would this food have been tampered with?" she asked, enjoying her next forkful. Quite rude to talk with her mouth full, but Higgins spent half his life being ill-mannered. "The police have done everything but peel the potatoes."

"At least stop drinking any more tea," he whispered in her ear. "Remember how much tea you said Turnbull drank at the picnic."

"A lot of us drank tea that day." This cake was heavenly. Eliza wondered whether the nuts it contained were pecans or almonds.

Higgins grumbled. "Why you don't weigh fifteen stone, I will never understand."

"If you spent twenty years on the edge of starvation, you'd be able to eat as much, too." Pushing aside her empty cake plate, she reached for a fritter. "Instead, you've been well fed and pampered like a prize poodle your entire life. I wonder you don't have two chins and a belly to go with it. You *are* rather fond of blancmange."

"I must have been thinking with the brains of a poodle the day I agreed to teach such an insolent cabbage leaf." Higgins took a sip of his port.

Across from her, Patsy seemed to be enjoying the desserts as much as Eliza. "I don't know if I've ever tasted anything so lovely as these fritters."

Brody looked up from his dessert bowl with a grin. "Wait till you taste the pudding."

"No wonder gluttony is one of the seven vices," Higgins said. "And a damn dull vice at that." He finished off his glass.

Eliza stiffened when Longhurst spoke. "Would you care for some more port, Professor? Sir Walter and I have been drinking far too much of it, I'm afraid." He held up the bottle that had been placed in front of him.

She was glad Higgins sat between her and Longhurst. If she knew for certain he had harmed her father, that bottle of port would have been smashed across his nose.

"Please do," Sir Walter said. "Mr. Longhurst has filled my glass three times. I really must stop drinking before I need help getting to a taxi."

Longhurst poured more port into Higgins's glass. Eliza wondered why the waiters didn't do that, until she noticed they were replenishing the platters of shortcake and fritters.

Higgins lifted his glass toward Sir Walter. "Superb tawny port. It's been aged in wood at least twenty years."

"Trust the Criterion to keep such a fine cellar." The older gentleman sipped from his glass, as did Longhurst. "You can taste the nuttiness, and the discernible scent of butterscotch."

Higgins nodded after his next taste. "Usually I prefer a good vintage port that has been aged two years, but this has a satisfying mellowness."

"Blimey, keep your knickers on," Eliza muttered. "It's only wine."

"Perhaps we should extol the artistry of fritters instead."

"Drunkard."

"Glutton."

"Are you all right, Sir Walter?" Longhurst asked in alarm.

She and Higgins looked toward the head of the table. Sir Walter set down his glass with a trembling hand. He leaned back in puzzlement. "I'm feeling a bit short of breath."

Eliza jumped to her feet. "Jack, something's wrong!"

As Jack and his detectives rushed to Sir Walter's side, Higgins looked down at his glass of port. "Damnation."

Her own heart nearly stopped. "You don't think the wine was poisoned, do you?"

Sir Walter's face broke out in a sweat and he gulped for air.

She grabbed Higgins by the shoulders. "Can you breathe? Do you feel sick?"

He looked grim. "I feel fine, at least for now."

"Thank heaven we didn't drink the port." Lady Tansy pushed back from the table. Her husband did likewise.

Eliza's heart sank when Sir Walter began wheezing. She noticed that Longhurst suffered no such symptoms, but he looked as fearful as Higgins.

"Get an ambulance," Jack barked at one of the waiters. The man knocked over a serving trolley in his haste, and the clatter of falling dishes rang through the dining room. The other diners now scrambled to their feet. Some craned their necks to get a better look; others gathered gloves and parasols to make a hasty retreat.

Once he'd loosened Sir Walter's cravat, Jack pointed at the people who now streamed out of the dining room. "Whitfield and Bryce, see that no one leaves the restaurant." The two detectives hurried off.

Sir Walter started to choke. Eliza clapped a hand over her mouth. This was like experiencing Turnbull's awful death once again. "Who else drank the port?" she asked.

"Not me." Brody stared in horror across the table.

"Me neither," Patsy added with a whimper.

The Duchess shook her head. Eliza crouched beside Higgins, who sat motionless in his chair. "That means only you, Sir Walter, and Longhurst drank the port. We'll take you to the hospital, too. If he drank more than you, your symptoms might start later."

Higgins took a deep breath. "A wise assumption."

His fatalistic calm frightened her even more. "When we get there, the doctors are sure to have an antidote."

That finally roused him. "Yes, an antidote." He jumped to his feet. His chair fell backward. "Sir Walter, did you do what I asked? Did you bring that syrup you told us about?"

But he was strangling for air, doubled over and on the verge of collapse. Jack supported him on one side while a terrified Longhurst held him on the other. When Sir Walter's face turned purple, Eliza let out a dismayed cry. How could this happen in front of everyone, including the police? What sort of monster were they dealing with? Again, she looked at Longhurst. If he was the killer, he was a fiendishly deceptive one. While frightened, he appeared determined to help Sir Walter.

Higgins now rushed over to where the older gentleman struggled for life. "Did you bring that bloody ipecac syrup? Sir Walter, did you bring it?"

The dying man leaned back with a shudder and gestured with his hand.

Eliza pointed. "Look in his suit jacket! Hurry!"

Both Higgins and Jack searched frantically through his pockets. With a muttered oath, Higgins pulled out a small glass vial from Sir Walter's vest. Eliza could barely breathe. Higgins fought to uncork the tiny stopper while Sir Walter gestured toward his mouth.

"Thank heaven he brought an antidote," the Duchess said as if talking to herself. "He is sure to be all right. He *must* be all right."

But Eliza wasn't certain of anything. Would the syrup be enough? Jack leaned Sir Walter back in his chair. The poor old man fought for every labored breath. Please make this work, Eliza prayed. Higgins's hand shook, but he managed to pour the liquid down Sir Walter's throat.

The entire dining room grew hushed as everyone waited to see what happened next. Eliza had no idea how long they all waited, frozen like statues. The only sound was Sir Walter's ragged breathing. Then the fellow coughed and threw himself forward. She had never seen anyone be so violently ill before. Surely that was a good sign. It meant the poison was leaving his body before it could do more harm.

Jack seemed to think so as well. He ordered the waiters to bring fresh linen napkins, and he and Higgins spread them over the table and the front of Sir Walter's shirt.

"How did he know to bring the antidote?" Jack asked Higgins.

Since Higgins seemed shaken, Eliza answered for him. "The Professor told him to when we visited Sir Walter at his home. We talked about poisons. And he mentioned that ipecac syrup might have saved Jonathon Turnbull if he had taken it in time. The Professor advised him to bring the syrup whenever the syndicate met."

She was relieved to see Sir Walter's face return to a normal hue, no longer purple. And his breathing had quieted. But Eliza remained worried about Higgins. "Jack, we have to get the Professor and Long-hurst to a doctor as quickly as possible. They drank the port, too, and we don't know when it will take effect."

Jack brushed the hair out of Sir Walter's face. "As soon as the ambulance gets here, all three men will be taken to hospital. How do you both feel?"

Higgins tried to smile. "Irritated that I ever developed a taste for port."

"And you, Mr. Longhurst?"

"Unsteady, and a bit ill." Longhurst's legs seemed to give out on him, and he collapsed onto a chair. "But I don't know if I'm sick from poison, or from fear."

Jack sighed. "We'll find out soon enough. Meanwhile we need to discover who brought the poison to the Criterion." He snapped his fingers at the three remaining detectives, who circled the table. "Search everyone's pockets, handbags, their hats, their umbrellas. Even their shoes."

"This is absurd." Lady Tansy frowned as one of the detectives unpinned her lofty hat.

"No, this is a crime scene," Jack said in a low threatening voice. "And I advise all of you to cooperate. Not doing so will be most unpleasant."

Eliza gladly handed over her pocketbook and hat. She slipped off her shoes as well. When he was done searching her, the detective moved on to Longhurst, who got to his feet with an audible sigh. A minute later, the detective cleared his throat.

"Sir, I think I've found something in this gentleman's outside jacket pocket." The policeman held up a small amber glass bottle.

Longhurst stared at the bottle in disbelief and tried to grab it. Another detective hurried over and pinned his arms behind him.

"Let me go!" Longhurst fought to wriggle out of the policeman's grip.

So Longhurst *was* the murderer. Eliza was filled with outraged horror at what this dreadful man had done. Higgins stared at Longhurst in obvious disgust.

Jack took the bottle and brought it close to the window. After he sniffed the stopper, Jack held it up to the light. "Half of the contents are still in the bottle. We can test it to make certain it's poison." He walked back to where Longhurst struggled with the detectives.

"This is madness." Longhurst looked desperate to free himself. "I poisoned no one. That bottle is not mine, I swear it!"

"Then how did it get in your pocket?" Eliza asked coolly.

"Yes, explain that, you damn murderer!" Lord Saxton's face reddened with rage.

"I don't know how in hell it got in my pocket," Longhurst spat back. "Most likely one of you put it there. You're all a pack of liars and scoundrels!"

Jack gestured to another detective, who pulled out a pair of handcuffs. "And you appear to be much worse than a liar and a scoundrel, Mr. Longhurst. I am placing you under arrest for the attempted murder of Sir Walter Fairweather, and the murder of Jonathon Turnbull. You will be taken immediately to Scotland Yard."

"But you can't do that!" Longhurst cried out when the handcuffs snapped onto his wrists. "I'm innocent. And I drank the port, too! I must go to the hospital with Professor Higgins. I'll die if you don't give me the antidote."

"He's right," Eliza said. "Besides, if he dies, you'll never learn the truth."

Jack smiled for the first time since the Criterion luncheon began. "Don't worry, Lizzie. I won't let him die. If he is the murderer, we'll show him more mercy and justice than he ever showed his victims."

"I hate the lot of you." Tears of anger sprang to Longhurst's eyes. "Everyone in the syndicate has always treated me like dirt. Now one of you is framing me for murder. I hope each of you suffers the horrors of the damned. And that includes your filthy Donegal Dancer!"

The Duchess of Carbrey whacked him over the head with her parasol. "Say what you like about the members of the syndicate, sir," she said. "But I'll poison you myself if you ever say an unkind word about our magnificent horse."

EIGHTEEN

Eliza and Higgins wound their way around the crowd at Sandown
Park. Luckily the early afternoon had not turned beastly hot—
yet. She missed her father. And he so wanted to be here for the Donegal Dancer's race at the Eclipse Stakes. Alfred Doolittle would be
buying drinks for his colleagues and friends, and predicting another
stunning win for the Dancer. Instead, he was still recovering in the
hospital. Poor Dad. He even got dressed early this morning, determined to attend the race. Despite his loud protests, the staff marched
him back into bed.

As for Higgins, he had remained at the London hospital only a few
hours following the Criterion lunch. Although he was given an antidote, neither he nor Longhurst seemed to have been poisoned. Now
Higgins and Eliza could relax and enjoy the Dancer's next win.

Eliza's excitement matched everyone else's at Sandown, but she also
sensed a growing uneasiness. Given the tragedies that occurred at both
the Derby and Ascot, she probably wasn't the only person who was
worried. What if something shocking happened here, too? Higgins
waved at Detective Jeremy, who stood guard near the stable entrance.
The policeman's grim expression didn't change. With Longhurst safely

in custody, Eliza wondered at the strong police presence. Did they fear an attempt by the horse thieves who remained at large? Or were they concerned about another demonstration by the suffragettes?

She nudged Higgins. "I see two more detectives. Jack has them out in full force."

"I doubt there will be trouble. Not with the number of policemen we've seen."

"Ah, but you were wrong about the syndicate luncheon," she said. "Murder *was* on the menu despite Scotland Yard's presence. If Longhurst had an accomplice, another attempt may be made here."

Higgins groaned. "Don't bring up Rachel Turnbull again. I don't think she was his accomplice. And if that woman is a murderer, I'll eat my hat."

She looked at his crumpled fedora. Unlike his rare appearance in formal dress at Ascot, Higgins wore his usual street clothes today. "Your betting form would be easier to digest."

"Don't look now, but you may be the one with indigestion. Here comes Clara."

Clara sauntered toward them with her new beau. She looked quite smart in a white linen skirt, white blouse, and a vest of marine blue. Her golden hair was piled beneath a blue straw hat, tipped at a fashionable angle, with a curled feather. Eliza suspected Clara's mother had borrowed money to buy such an expensive outfit. But the new dress wasn't responsible for Clara's smug expression, like a bird with a fat worm. Although Lord Richard Ashmore wasn't fat or wriggly, Clara obviously believed she'd caught him. The girl gazed at him with an air of ownership.

Eliza forced a polite smile when the couple drew near. She had already regaled Higgins with details about the shopping trip to Selfridges. While he found Longhurst's behavior quite telling, he had no interest in Clara's latest suitor. Eliza wished he did share her concern over the silly girl. Since she met Lord Ashmore, Clara had spent virtually every waking moment in his company. And she clung so possessively to the man's arm, Eliza was amazed he didn't wince from pain. But he seemed smitten, too. The couple were oblivious to everyone around them, which included Freddy and his mother. Behind them strolled the Duchess of Carbrey, accompanied by a younger gentleman Eliza didn't recognize.

When the group reached them, she introduced Lord Ashmore to Higgins, who shook the man's hand without much interest. Eliza had asked, but neither he nor his mother knew anything of the Ashmore family except for their enviable reputation for collecting antiquities.

The Duchess of Carbrey introduced her friend Ambrose Farrow with obvious pride. "We hope the Donegal Dancer wins today, but it may be a tough go."

"Especially with Belmont's Tracery in the field, and Louvois as well," Farrow said.

Eliza nodded. "Tracery would have won the Ascot Gold Cup."

"Such a shame." Farrow smoothed down his dark blond mustache. Eliza thought him an attractive fellow, and most impeccably dressed. She wondered if Higgins could place his American accent. Though the man looked no more than thirty, the Duchess cast flirtatious glances his way, which he returned. "Are you certain you don't want to see if the tent is ready, my dear?"

"No need. I've hosted events at Sandown before. My servants are well aware of how I like things arranged." She turned to Eliza and Higgins. "You may want to stop by, however, even though we won't be serving luncheon until after the race. Look for the white tent with the green and violet pennants. You won't be able to miss it."

The couple walked off through the excited crowd. Long after they had disappeared, Eliza could still glimpse the bobbing green feathers that towered above the Duchess's wide hat.

"I invited Mother to come today, Eliza," Clara said. "I hope you don't mind if she sits in the Duchess's viewing box with the other owners."

"Of course not." She smiled at Mrs. Eynsford Hill, who looked grateful. "And you and Lord Ashmore must join us, too."

Freddy had wrapped his arm tight around Eliza's shoulders. She recognized that besotted look in his eyes. Eliza blamed herself for that. Since the Criterion luncheon, she had spent a lot of time with Freddy. Although she only did so to avoid lectures by Jack and Higgins, it increased Freddy's romantic obsession to an alarming degree.

"My sweet, you are the most ravishing woman here," he said. "I don't know why you worried about wearing the horse's racing colors. You look divine."

Eliza was rather pleased with her outfit—a slim lilac skirt, a green bolero jacket, and a white blouse. She'd even dyed the ostrich feather green on her white straw hat. Despite her misgivings, it was possible to put together a decent green and purple ensemble.

"I hear you're from Kent, Lord Ashmore," Higgins said.

"Just east of Canterbury. I was born at Banfield Manor and spent my boyhood there."

Clara pulled her aside while the men discussed the Kentish countryside. Eliza suspected Higgins of trying to figure out where else Lord Ashmore had lived from his speech patterns.

Radiant with excitement, Clara whispered, "I'm going to marry Richard."

"You cannot marry someone you've known a mere four days! How do you know you're compatible? The man is a virtual stranger. And you should love whomever you marry."

"But I do love him. How could I not? And I want to marry him as soon as possible."

"He's an attractive titled gentleman of appropriate age." Mrs. Eynsford Hill joined them. "He adores my daughter, I could tell immediately. It's almost too good to be true. Clara will be a baroness. A baroness!"

"With twenty thousand pounds a year," Clara added in delight. "Surely you're not jealous, are you, Eliza?"

"No, only worried. How do you know he wants to marry you? Has he proposed?"

"Oh, I know how to convince him to marry me." Clara winked. "After all, he clearly finds me pretty. And a modern woman knows there are better ways to seduce a man aside from clever conversation and a fat dowry. I have it all worked out." With a smug smile, she waltzed back to rejoin her suitor. Her mother patted Eliza's arm, then followed her daughter.

Eliza stared at them in disbelief. Did Clara mean to seduce Lord Ashmore? Blimey, when did this eighteen-year-old turn into Lillie Langtry? And why didn't Mrs. Eynsford Hill dissuade her daughter from doing something so dangerously foolish?

"I need to talk to you," Eliza hissed in Freddy's ear. She dragged him away from the group, not caring if he was midsentence with Higgins and Lord Ashmore.

"I wasn't done telling the Baron about—"

"Oh, hush." Eliza glanced over at Clara and her soon-to-be lover. "Freddy, this is blooming important. You must help me before it's too late."

"What are you talking about?"

"Clara is so set on marrying Lord Ashmore, she plans to take him to her bed. You must stop her. You're her older brother, after all. Maybe she'll listen to you. Please discourage her from pursuing Baron Ashmore. What if he rejects her? She'll never recover from the shame."

Freddy shook his head. "Why should I? She claims he's the perfect man for her. I think Clara ought to marry him, and as quickly as possible. She'll be a baroness."

Had all the Eynsford Hills gone mad? "Freddy, you can't be serious."

"But I am." He clasped both of her gloved hands between his and dropped to one knee. "Marry me, darling. I want to announce our engagement before my sister and Lord Ashmore do. Please, we've waited long enough. You cannot hold me off forever, Eliza."

She quickly tugged him to his feet before anyone noticed. "Stop this!"

"We both love each other. I see no reason to wait any longer." Freddy hesitated. "And in case your father does die from his wounds, he'll know you and I are happily wed. He will die knowing I am taking care of you." He smiled. "And we'll have your Ascot money, too."

Eliza pushed him away, disgusted with both Freddy and Clara. She was glad she hadn't told him she spent her winnings on a share of the Dancer. "Don't follow me, Freddy. You've put me in a foul mood. One more word, and I'll brain you with this." She raised her parasol.

"Eliza, wait!"

She stalked off. He'd best heed her advice and stay away. As if Freddy knew anything about what her father wanted! Alfred Doolittle had never given a fig for Eliza's welfare. The last thing he would worry about was whether she married, happily or not. And Eliza had serious doubts she could ever be content as Freddy's wife.

At this moment, she was far more worried about Clara. Solving a murder would be simpler than convincing Freddy or Mrs. Eynsford Hill to be sensible about that girl's marriage plans. Eliza squinted when dust swirled up in the growing heat. She hoped Higgins soon caught up with her. He at least would agree about the lunatic behavior of the Eynsford Hills.

Someone bumped into her. Eliza turned to see Lord Saxton in a pale suit, his tie askew, and as usual half drunk.

"B-beg pardon. Oh, it's you, El-liza," he slurred. "Splendid. S'good to see you."

"I'm surprised to see you here. Especially since you sold your shares of the Dancer to Gordon Longhurst. Thank heaven he's in jail."

"True enough." Lady Tansy joined them. Beneath her Merry Widow hat, she looked quite sullen. "Maitland insisted we attend today. I truly believe he's lost his mind."

"You're just miffed that I want to buy another racehorse."

She waved a hand, as if dispelling alcohol fumes. "I hope you're not too drunk to negotiate a fair price. And choose a beast with agreeable racing colors this time."

He sipped from a silver flask. "Yes, I know. Anything but green and purple."

Lady Tansy brushed dust specks from the lapels of her deep marigold tailored suit. Two long, slender quail feathers adorned her curved hat.

"These colors are not as bad as I thought." Eliza smoothed her lilac skirt.

"You did your best, I give you that. But you looked far better at Ascot in that yellow gown, even if it was the tiniest bit garish." She sent Eliza a sly smile.

Eliza breathed a sigh of relief when the Saxtons sailed off to greet friends. Several young men walked past Eliza with admiring glances. She really ought to enjoy the race today. After all, she now owned a racehorse. And Jack had caught the murderer red-handed at the Criterion. Hang the Eynsford Hills! Eliza planned to cheer the Donegal Dancer to victory again, even if it meant ruining a new parasol on the railing the way she had at Ascot. Her stomach growled at the thought of the lavish spread awaiting them in the Duchess's tent afterward.

Yes, today might prove to be the loveliest day of summer.

———

Henry Higgins scribbled a few more interesting words and phrases he'd overheard from a couple discussing the Ascot Gold Cup race. "So Hewitt was 'dafter than a buzza' and they were 'mazed' to lose their bet," he muttered under his breath. "That must mean they were none too happy. Oh, excuse me, miss."

He had bumped into a girl dressed in white with a green and violet sash. "Aye, watch where yer goin', governor." She grinned at him when Higgins apologized a second time. "Since you stepped on me toes, p'raps you'll buy a paper?"

When she held up a copy of *The Suffragette*, he dug into his pocket for a coin. Eliza might want to read it on the return train. Higgins noticed a police detective keeping close watch from a distance; the man looked familiar. He might have been at the Criterion earlier in the week. Higgins stuffed the rolled copy under his arm and marched toward the grandstand's stairway. Eliza met him halfway.

"I've been stopped three times by Jack's men from the Yard. In fact, the same detective warned me away from the track just now. Bloody fools," she snapped. "I told 'em again and again I'm no suffragette."

"You're wearing green, white, and violet. Along with a green feather in your white hat. Those are the WSPU colors signifying 'Give Women the Vote,' remember."

"Blimey." Eliza held up her parasol. "This is white and green, too."

"You'll just have to ignore them."

Eliza looked over his shoulder. "Isn't that Rachel Turnbull's maid

Lucy?" She hurried off to greet the woman, leaving Higgins to trail behind.

"So you're selling *The Suffragette*?" Eliza asked her.

"Yes, I signed up the day of the march." Lucy gazed at Eliza's outfit with approval. "You're dressed in the proper colors today, miss."

"Actually, these are the Wrexham racing colors." Eliza gestured at Higgins. "You may remember the Professor from when we came for tea in Knightsbridge. So how is Mrs. Turnbull?"

"She must be fine. I saw her about an hour ago." Lucy smiled when a woman handed a coin over in exchange for a newspaper. "Thank you, madam. Votes for Women!"

"She's here?"

"Yes, with her sister."

He and Eliza exchanged worried glances. Why would Rachel attend the race? Her husband's death meant the Turnbull shares of the Donegal Dancer reverted back to the syndicate, according to the rules. And he was shocked a new widow would appear in public so soon after her husband's murder. Especially at a horse race.

"Excuse me, but do you believe your mistress poisoned her husband?"

The young woman seemed flabbergasted by his question. "That's the most ridiculous thing I ever heard, sir! You wouldn't accuse Mrs. Turnbull if you knew her like I do. She never even lifted a finger to defend herself against that brute she married."

Lucy plunged on, relating the terrible things she'd witnessed Jonathon Turnbull do to his wife: slapping Rachel for suggesting a change to the Turnbull Tea tin, throwing her into a wall for not answering a question fast enough, and locking her into a broom cupboard after the servants had gone on an outing. Lucy waved her stack of papers.

"Why, she couldn't even stand up to Mrs. Lowell, who asked her to come today in support of the cause."

"Where are they, exactly?" Eliza asked.

"Somewhere selling copies, same as me. And Mrs. Turnbull is even wearing a green and violet sash across her widow's weeds. She has courage, given all that's happened to her."

"Don't you think it's strange?" Eliza insisted. "After all, her husband was poisoned."

"Oh, it was such a hot day. They say the picnic food just spoiled. Some people die of food poisoning or get dreadful sick every summer."

"Then why didn't anyone else at the luncheon fall ill?"

Lucy looked around, as if making certain no one could eavesdrop. "I didn't say this before, but someone else did get sick that day."

"Who?" Higgins perked up at her revelation.

"I did." Lucy sighed. "We all sweated buckets setting up the picnic lunch, it was so hot. We needed five more pairs of hands. Me, the footman, and the chauffeur nearly died of thirst."

"When I saw you at the Palladium after the rally, you told me you didn't eat any of the food," Eliza said. "So you drank something at the picnic?"

"I only drank ginger water. That's all the servants were allowed to drink. But looking back, I realized I forgot something. Remember when the tea table was knocked over? I'm the one who cleaned up the mess. The honey spilled and I got a tiny bit on my finger. All I did was lick it off. Just a drop, mind you, but I was so sick after."

"Sick how?"

"Queasy, dizzy. I had to sit in the shade for a bit. The missus told me to rest until I felt better again, she was so worried."

"Was she?" Higgins and Eliza exchanged knowing looks.

"I blamed the heat for making me sick. And who's to say it wasn't?"

Lucy turned away when several women stepped forward to buy *The Suffragette*.

Higgins led Eliza over to the concession area, behind the queue of people waiting to purchase chips, sweets, or lemonade. "Remember what Sir Walter said at White Flower Cottage? That the nectar of a poisonous flower could kill a human. The poison had to be in the honey. And Rachel was worried Lucy would die from it."

Eliza nodded. "That means Rachel must be in on it. Freddy and I drank tea, but we sweetened it with sugar. Jonathon Turnbull was the only one who had honey in his tea. Patsy asked for honey, but she never got the chance to drink hers. The tea table was knocked over." She looked unhappy. "Rachel poisoned the honey."

"And Longhurst helped by distracting everyone. By George, that must be what happened." Higgins rubbed his hands together. "We've got to find Jack right away. The two of them carried out the murders of Diana and Turnbull, then tried to kill Sir Walter and your father. Even with Longhurst in jail, Rachel may intend to murder another syndicate member today."

Eliza's heart sank. "The Duchess!"

Higgins shot her a weary look and pointed toward the grandstand entrance. "You search for Jack or any of his detectives. I'll go in the other direction and find Rachel. I think it's very disturbing she came to Sandown today."

"What if I see her first?" Eliza asked.

"If you do, run and find a policeman." He frowned. "Remember you're an owner, too. And I have a bad feeling that you may be the next victim."

NINETEEN

The festive crowd pushed against the low railing along the track. Eliza sensed the growing excitement from the racing fans. She shaded her eyes from the sun. Where was Jack? A shame he wasn't dressed in an olive green suit and derby like Detective Jeremy. He might be easier to spot. And she certainly didn't see Rachel Turnbull in her widow's weeds.

"'Ere now, why haven't you got copies to sell?" An older woman planted herself before Eliza. She wore a crooked WSPU sash over her dark suit. The lady thrust a bundle of *The Suffragette* at Eliza. "Remember to thank whoever gives you a penny. Even if they give you less, best let 'em take the paper. We need all the supporters we can get."

"But I'm not part of your organization. These are my horse's racing colors." Eliza dumped the papers back into the woman's arms. "I do support the cause, however. I've already bought my copy."

"I saw you at the Palladium." A sprightly suffragette joined them. "I love your outfit, it's perfect for today. Someone get her a sash!"

"No, please—"

Three other women hurried over. "Aw, be a good sport," one said, and popped the sash over Eliza's hat. "Let's raise the grandstand roof! Give Women the Vote! Give Women the Vote!"

The older woman who had first approached Eliza shook her head. "No chanting. We've already got the authorities waiting for us to make the slightest bit of trouble. If we start shouting, the police and race officials will use that as a reason to throw us out of Sandown."

As the ladies argued, Eliza slipped away. At a safe distance, she tore off the suffragette sash and dropped it onto the ground. Eliza wondered if she should start chanting "Votes for Women"; that might bring the police running. But she'd already asked several uniformed bobbies where Jack was, and they kept pointing her in different directions. Since she and Higgins split up, she hadn't seen a single plainclothes detective, either. Where were the police when you really needed them?

Up ahead Eliza saw yet another small group of suffragettes. Rachel Turnbull was not among them, which was lucky for the widow. Male onlookers jeered at the women, whose loud singsong chants drowned them out. Bobbies pushed their way between them, trying to quiet the group, but a young woman fell to the ground. Her screams only added to the chaos.

Eliza decided to head back the way she had come, hoping to find Higgins. He might have had better luck in this teeming crowd.

"Eliza, darling!" Freddy called out. He was accompanied by Sir Walter Fairweather. The two nattily dressed gentlemen strolled toward her.

Amazing. The one person she was not searching for had managed to track her down.

"We've been looking all over the racecourse for you." Freddy pecked her cheek. She drew back. "You really should not have gone off in such a temper. It's deuced difficult finding anyone here."

"You are looking well, Miss Doolittle," Sir Walter said with a tip of his hat. "Everyone is heading for the Duchess's box. The race will begin soon, and you don't want to watch it in the middle of this crowd."

"I'm looking for a detective just now. Especially my cousin Jack. It seems that Rachel Turnbull is at Sandown today."

That had the same effect on Sir Walter as it had on her and Higgins. "My word, you don't say. How interesting. I don't like the sound of that."

"Neither do I. That's why we need to—"

"Dash it all, Eliza. We didn't come to the Eclipse Stakes so you can play at being Sherlock Holmes with the Professor." Freddy took her arm. "Can't we simply enjoy the races from the viewing box? If you want to run around afterward looking for clues or God knows what else, fine. But I didn't get all dressed up for this event to watch it alone."

Eliza counted to ten. "Freddy, Rachel Turnbull is very likely Longhurst's accomplice, which makes her a murderer. And catching a murderer is more important than watching a blooming horse race with the Duchess."

"She's right, young man."

He ignored Sir Walter. "You're probably still angry with me over my proposal, even if I don't understand why. We'll discuss that later. For now I insist you come with me." Freddy gripped her arm tighter. "I want us safely up into the grandstand, far away from any possible trouble. It is the only way to keep an eye on you. I would never forgive myself if you ran onto the track and got trampled by the horses."

"For the last time, I'm not going to run onto the track! How much of a ninny do you think I am?" Eliza shook off his grip. "Now I must find Jack. I'll join you in the stands once I do."

"But why are you getting involved at all? Let the police handle

Mr. Longhurst and Mrs. Turnbull. They don't need you interfering in things again."

Eliza gave him an icy stare. "I said I will join you later. But if you keep this up, you may not see me for the rest of the day." She paused. "Or the rest of the summer."

"Dash it! You're more stubborn than a hundred suffragettes, Eliza." Frustrated and red-faced, Freddy stormed toward the grandstand.

Eliza sighed in relief. "I'm sorry about that little scene. Freddy can be most persistent."

Sir Walter smiled. "No need to apologize, Miss Doolittle. The young man is only concerned for your welfare."

"I'm concerned for my welfare, too. But I must find my cousin."

"I believe Detective Shaw is making certain no one has tampered with anything in the Duchess of Carbrey's private tent. If another murder attempt is made today, it may occur at the syndicate luncheon."

That made sense. "I should head over there before Jack and his men leave."

"If you're right about Gordon Longhurst having a partner in crime, it's best you not be alone," he said gallantly. "I'll be happy to escort you there."

"Yes, please. I'd like that very much."

Eliza slid her hand under his proffered arm, although she knew the older gentleman would not be much protection against a murderer. After all, he'd been poisoned two days ago. Sir Walter had been lucky to survive.

She only hoped Higgins found Rachel Turnbull before it was too late.

Squinting from the bright sunshine, Henry Higgins caught sight of two women waving copies of *The Suffragette*. One of them wore black. He hurried across the grassy racetrack and climbed over the white railing. Too bad he hadn't known Rachel was on this side of the course, or he'd have found her earlier. He noticed how most of the well-heeled racing fans ignored the women. One man in a shabby suit bought a paper and then shredded it, laughing with his friends.

"You dollies better not be plannin' some fool trick like at Ascot and the Derby," he said loudly, "or me and my pals will make sure you're trampled good and dead."

"Here now, that's uncalled for," an onlooker said, but the ruffian's friends jeered him into silence. His wife hushed him, and they both hurried away.

The men next tossed the paper shreds onto the women's hats. Rachel looked miserable, but her sister Ruth stared them down. "This abuse is one reason why women ought to vote," she cried in a ringing voice. "We have every right to free speech and assembly."

"Take yer trash elsewhere!"

Higgins pushed the biggest bully aside. "Go on, you've made your point."

"And who the devil do you think you are? I'll mash yer face—"

The fellow lunged, but Higgins grabbed his wrist and twisted it. When Higgins finally let go, the man fell backward with a loud curse into his group of friends.

Offering his arm to Rachel and her sister, he escorted them a few hundred yards down the track. Luckily the crowd had scattered during the altercation, making it easier to maneuver.

"Where the devil is Scotland Yard?" he murmured. "Are you ladies all right?"

easily have hired men to arrange the attack on Alfred at the horse farm, all in a scheme to gain sole ownership of the Donegal Dancer."

Her gaze turned cold. "Someone slipped that bottle into Gordon's pocket to implicate him. It's circumstantial evidence, Professor."

"The police will determine that, along with a court of law. Meanwhile your friendship with him seems highly suspicious," Higgins said. "If Longhurst does have an accomplice, the most likely person is you."

Ruth Lowell again sprang to her sister's defense. "How dare you accuse her? You have no right to spout such nonsense!"

Aware of the other suffragettes muttering their disapproval, Higgins forced himself to listen to Mrs. Lowell's harangue. She insulted his intelligence and status as a gentleman, accused him of pandering to the police, and even questioned his involvement with the syndicate.

"Who's to say that you aren't the murderer?" Ruth said at the end of her tirade.

"Wasn't he the governor accused of killing that Hungarian fellow?" another suffragette asked. She shook a fist at him. "I read about it in the papers, I did."

"The police caught Nepommuck's murderer." He scanned the angry women now pressing close about him. "Ladies, I insist you allow me free passage. I will use force if I must."

"Do you mean to twist our hands like you did that bully's?" Ruth sneered. "I dare you!"

Higgins fought to keep his temper in check. "I mean you no harm. And I have no issues with your cause. I only want to ask Mrs. Turnbull a few more questions." He turned to where Rachel had stood a moment ago.

Damn, damn, damn. Rachel Turnbull had vanished.

TWENTY

When Eliza entered the tent, she smiled at the sheer size of the billowing white silk structure, along with the green and purple balloons floating above a long table. The Duchess had marked off an entire piece of Sandown Park as her own—at least until the end of today's races. However, despite being surrounded by colored balloons and bottles of champagne chilling in silver buckets, her cousin looked unhappy.

"Glad you're here, Lizzie. And I'm relieved to see you're not alone." Jack nodded toward Sir Walter. "But I thought Higgins or Freddy would be with you."

"I sent Freddy to join the others in the Duchess's private box. He's driving himself mad with worry that I'll somehow run onto the race-track."

"Where's Higgins? If he's off writing down people's dialects at a time like this—"

"The Professor is figuring out if there will be another murder attempt at Sandown. And we've discovered something that should interest you and your detectives."

Jack raised a skeptical eyebrow. "Which is?"

Eliza sank in a chair by the banquet table, hands clasped over her parasol handle. "Rachel Turnbull is at the racetrack today."

"Why would Turnbull's widow be at the Eclipse Stakes?"

"It does seem peculiar," Sir Walter chimed in, and pulled out a seat at the table.

"Rachel's maid is at the racetrack and claims that her mistress is here. The girl is selling copies of *The Suffragette* near the paddock. She says Rachel Turnbull is doing the very same thing. And wearing her widow's weeds, too. Now that is a sight I'd like to see."

"Then you and Higgins did not actually see Rachel?"

Eliza shook her head. "But Lucy swore her mistress is at the track selling the magazine alongside her sister Ruth. Higgins is looking for her. He wanted me to find you straightaway, and send you and your detectives after him."

Jack seemed troubled. "I hoped we could relax with Longhurst in custody. But if Rachel Turnbull is at the Eclipse Stakes so soon after her husband's murder, I have to ask myself why. The answer makes me uneasy."

Eliza noticed three policemen examining the hampers in the tent. "Are you checking the luncheon food for anything suspicious?"

"I'm taking no chances. My men and I have been through every basket, bottle, and champagne bucket in here. All the food is either safe in unopened cans or boxed up and taped shut. And the champagne is sealed."

"Blimey, I forgot the most important thing." Eliza leaned forward. "Lucy told me that one of the pots of honey spilled at the regatta picnic. When she cleaned it up, a drop got on her finger and she licked the honey off. Lucy swears she never ate or drank a single other thing from the picnic except that tiny bit of honey. She felt quite ill afterwards."

"I never thought about the honey."

"Higgins remembered right off what Sir Walter said when we visited his gardens. That even the nectar from poisonous plants is dangerous. Isn't that right?"

"Yes, indeed," Sir Walter said eagerly. "The ancient Greeks killed people by using the nectar from poisonous flowers. They often baked it into honey cakes. An ingenious method of poisoning. If more people at the picnic had asked for honey in their tea, half the syndicate members might be dead by now."

"I think the murderer knew very well who used honey and who didn't," Eliza said. "The same person who organized the picnic and planned the menu."

"Rachel Turnbull." Jack nodded. "It makes sense."

"And now she shows up at the Eclipse Stakes! Jack, I'm certain she's going to do something during the race. We must get to her first."

"Right, then. Both you and Sir Walter are to remain here." Jack waved for his detectives to head outside. "I'm hoping it's not too late to find Rachel. When I do, I'm putting her under arrest. Meanwhile, promise me you'll stay inside this tent. You too, Sir Walter."

"See here, Inspector. The Donegal Dancer's race is due to start in less than thirty minutes." Sir Walter rose to his feet. "I have no intention of staying here."

"Neither do I," Eliza protested. "We want to watch the race from the Duchess's box. I'd rather put up with Freddy lecturing me than miss the race altogether."

"Both of you will stay in this tent until I tell you otherwise. The Duchess's servants are right outside the entrance, which is where they shall remain with instructions that neither of you is to leave." Jack sounded grim. "When I find more of my detectives, I'll send them here. But I can't allow Rachel Turnbull to walk about free during this race.

And I have no time to worry about you. Now do I have your word that you'll stay here?"

Eliza shrugged, while Sir Walter muttered, "Damned presumptuous, I must say."

"Presumptuous, but wise. The pair of you can afford to miss one race. Or perhaps you have forgotten that someone tried to poison you only two days ago, Sir Walter."

He seemed abashed by that. "Very well, Inspector. I shall do as you ask."

Jack wagged his finger at Eliza. "And keep an eye on her, too. I should send Freddy to join you as punishment." Before he lifted up the tent flap, he turned back. "Even though we've checked all the food, don't eat or drink anything until I get back."

"Not bloody likely," she said under her breath.

After her cousin left, Eliza turned to Sir Walter. "How long should we wait before we head for the Duchess's box? I vote ten minutes."

"I suggest fifteen." He grinned. "Just to be safe."

Starting with Diana's murder, Higgins had been wrong every step of the way. For too long he'd been convinced Harold Hewitt was the prime suspect. Then he let Alfred Doolittle out of his sight at the Bay Willow Stables. Next he encountered the recently widowed Rachel Turnbull at a horse race. But instead of heading for the nearest detective, he stupidly confronted her. A brilliant move, one worthy of the nonsensical Freddy Eynsford Hill.

Now he'd made Rachel so nervous, she had vanished like a magician's rabbit. And the Donegal Dancer's race was due to start soon. Thankfully, he was a phonetics specialist and not a policeman. They would have had his badge three times over by now.

The crowd pressed about Higgins. He looked in vain for a glimpse of a dull black gown. With so many people milling around, he only caught a blur of movement here, a glimpse of something black there. Whenever he got a better look, the black was invariably a gentleman's top hat. Perhaps he should make his way over to the Duchess's luncheon tent. Eliza was most likely there by now, along with Jack.

Unfortunately, he was on the wrong side of the racetrack. Higgins gazed in frustration at the huge white tent in the distance. A purple and green pennant waved from one of its poles. He should have tried to get there ten minutes ago. The crowd grew larger by the moment, and police were beginning to keep people back. They'd never let him cross the track until after the race.

Even worse, he didn't recognize a single detective. It was like Ascot all over again, and look how that turned out. Higgins cursed under his breath. No, he refused to let another person be murdered during a race without doing all he could to prevent it. Damn it, Higgins would run across the track and reach that tent, no matter what.

"There he is!" a woman cried. "He's the man chasing after Rachel!"

Alarmed, Higgins spun about. Four women, all sporting WSPU banners across their chests, pushed their way through the crowd toward him. One was Rachel's sister Ruth, whose angry expression seemed worthy of a marauding Viking.

He held up his hands in mock surrender. "Please, I must speak with Mrs. Turnbull again. If not, the police will get to her first."

The women surrounded him in a half-circle. "I wouldn't doubt you already set the police on her," Ruth said in disgust. "My poor sister finally decides to support our cause in public, and you tell the police to arrest her."

"No, no! But I do need to speak with her before the police do, or they will arrest her."

Ruth glared at him. "I knew it. The police plan to haul her off to prison. They'll make a big show of arresting the widow of a man who openly worked to undermine the WSPU."

"And you're no doubt her dead husband's friend," another lady accused him. "That means you're up to no good."

A small woman dressed in men's clothes clapped her hands. "He wants to get us all arrested, he does. We can't let him do that, ladies!"

As if they had choreographed it, the four women lunged toward him. At the same moment, Higgins bolted in the opposite direction.

"Wait!" Ruth shouted. "Come back here, you coward!"

Higgins had no intention of stopping. As he shoved through the crowd, he glanced over his shoulder at the pursuing women. What did one call a band of angry suffragettes? He ran through the names of collective groups: a gaggle of geese, a pack of wolves, a leap of leopards.

Another quick look told Higgins he was being chased by a storm of suffragettes. And he'd better run fast before he got struck by their "lightning"—or their fists.

———

"I think we've waited long enough." Eliza traced designs with the tip of her parasol on the sandy ground. The white silk walls of the tent billowed softly about her.

"Hold on, let me take a look." Sir Walter stepped outside. A few moments later, he returned. "I'd wait a bit longer to be certain the Inspector is nowhere around."

"If we don't leave soon, we'll miss the Donegal Dancer."

"Never fear, Miss Doolittle. I promise that neither of us will miss that race." He sat once more at the table. "And I trust *our* horse will win again today. You must be excited. This is your very first race as an owner."

"Absolutely. But I feel terrible Dad will miss it. At least the doctors say he'll be released from the hospital soon."

"How remarkable that Alfred is still alive. Not many men would survive a frightened horse stamping on them."

"My father's tough, believe me."

"He does seem strong as a bull for a man his age. And luckier than most."

"If he'd been lucky, he never would've been attacked in the first place." Eliza tapped her parasol on the ground. "I wonder how Gordon Longhurst pulled it off at the horse farm. He and Rachel are obviously responsible for poisoning you and Jonathon Turnbull. I wonder if the poison you drank was the same one used at Henley."

He shook his head. "No. The poison I drank at the Criterion was tasteless. But the honey at the regatta would have tasted bitter."

"Why?"

"Blame the flower nectar. In this case, rhododendrons."

Eliza sat up straighter. "I don't remember Jack saying what sort of plant had poisoned Jonathon Turnbull. How do you know it was rhododendron?"

Sir Walter shot her an apologetic look. "Because it came from a hive in my garden."

Had she heard wrong? "What? From your garden? I don't understand."

He chuckled. "Oh, I think you do."

Eliza got to her feet. "If the poison came from your hives, then you killed Turnbull."

His smile chilled her. "It appears so."

"But *you* were poisoned two days ago." Once the answer dawned on her, she gripped her parasol in the middle, realizing she could wield it as a weapon. "Unless you poisoned yourself. Deliberately. That way the police would never view you as a suspect."

"There. See how easily you figured it out. You're quite intelligent, and far more clever than Inspector Shaw. How fortunate that I am more clever than either of you."

"Not too clever for me, mate!"

Eliza swung her parasol at his head. He ducked, however, and her blow only knocked off his hat. She raced toward the entrance. But she never got more than a foot outside. Two husky men, neither resembling any of the Duchess's servants, blocked her way. Grabbing her by the arms, the men marched Eliza back to her chair and literally flung her down.

"Who are these blighters? And where are the servants that should be right outside?"

"I informed the servants a few moments ago that the Duchess wanted them to enjoy the upcoming race. Therefore they had permission to leave the tent area in order to find a choice viewing spot along the track." Sir Walter sniffed at the white carnation in his lapel. "They won't be back until the race is over, my dear."

"But Jack told them to stay here!"

"And I told them they could leave. Please remember I am a close friend of their mistress, and also boast a knighthood. Whatever I say carries a lot more weight with a servant than an order from an underpaid policeman."

She pointed at the men now planted before the tent entrance. Both wore brown suits and crushed felt hats. "Who are they?"

"My racing associates. I have quite a few."

Worried, Eliza wondered how soon Jack would return. Could she fling herself at the tent wall and bring it all down? Would any of these men allow her to get to her feet again?

"Are you going to kill me, then?" She refused to show fear, although her stomach was doing sickening flip-flops.

"Of course I am not going to kill you." Sir Walter clucked in disapproval. "I am a man of my word, and I have already promised that you will see the race."

"I don't like this," Eliza said in a low voice. "What's your game?"

"My game is horses. Their ownership, their breeding, their races. I love them even more than I love my gardens."

"Apparently you love one horse enough to kill for him. That's what this is all about. To gain complete ownership of the Donegal Dancer."

Sir Walter looked over at the two fellows. "This is why men should oppose women's suffrage. Most ladies are far more intelligent than gentlemen. If we allow them the vote, the fairer sex may end up ruling the world one day. Not just Parliament."

"Look, I'll sell you my blooming shares of the horse if you want," Eliza said.

"No need for that, my girl."

"But you tried to kill my father for his shares."

"Not me." He lifted his silver-tipped walking stick at the two men. "Mr. Keene and Mr. Ingleby are responsible for that."

"On your orders, most likely."

"Of course. I am, as they say, running the show."

Rage built inside Eliza. Sir Walter had just admitted he ordered her father's murder. "And you poisoned Jonathon Turnbull, too."

He winked. "I have already confessed to being involved in that trivial matter."

"Trivial?" Eliza wanted to kick him in the head. "And you killed Diana Price."

"I most certainly did not." He sounded offended. "We have the short-tempered Mr. Brody to thank for that one."

"Brody?" This was too much to take in. Exactly how many people were involved with these murders? "What reason did Brody have for killing Diana?"

"Purely a business decision." He cocked his head, as if considering how much to reveal. "Mr. Brody and I have been partners for five years."

Eliza was confused. "Partners? Because he races some of your horses?"

"*Our* horses. While Brody has made a great deal of money as a jockey, he felt humiliated at being banned from owning a racehorse. When I realized how deep his bitterness ran, I offered to buy horses in both my name and a name we created for him to use. The arrangement worked well. In the case of the Donegal Dancer, however, I could not concoct a false owner according to the syndicate contract. Brody had to trust me."

"Trust you to do what?"

"I secretly sold him half my shares. This way, he not only earned a share of the purse as winning jockey, he also received a share meant for the horse's owners. And since I was the official agent for the racing syndicate, I handled all the paperwork and all the money." He laughed. "Not one of the owners ever raised a single question about my transactions. Which confirmed my low opinion of their intelligence. We figured it was only a matter of time before we convinced the other owners to sell their shares."

"Then why did Brody kill Diana Price?"

"The drunken fool wandered into the stables at the worst possible moment, at least for her. Brody was in a foul temper that day. The Dancer had just won another race. He feared I would cheat him out of his share. We had a rather heated discussion. I was trying to reassure him when Diana appeared."

"Wait a minute." Eliza held up her hand. "You murdered a woman because she learned Brody had a secret share in the Dancer? What a ridiculous reason to kill someone."

"Oh no, we didn't kill her over that. Goodness, if that was all she overheard, I would have simply bribed her. Diana was greedy *and* gullible." He took a deep breath. "No, Miss Doolittle. As I said, Brody and I were having a tense conversation, which led us to be indiscreet about private business matters which are not your concern. We didn't realize this foolish woman was listening until she burst in on us."

She looked at him in growing horror. "So Brody decided to murder her?"

"Like all great riders, Brody has lightning-fast reflexes, along with a fierce instinct for survival. Such skills are excellent when fighting for a pole position in the Derby, but they don't always serve as well off the track."

Eliza recalled what Jack had told her following the autopsy. "Diana suffered a blow to the head, but she was killed with a pitchfork. Why would Brody do both?"

Sir Walter crossed his legs. He seemed as bored as a theatergoer waiting for the curtain. "When Diana burst into the stall, she called us thieves—and at the top of her voice, too. Brody had to quickly shut her up, so he struck her. Despite his size, he's a powerful chap. The blow knocked her unconscious."

Eliza glanced over at the two men by the entrance. One fellow seemed indifferent to Sir Walter's tale, the other vaguely amused.

"Things had gone too far by then," Sir Walter continued. "We needed to act fast before someone walked by and discovered us, even though we were in the back of the stables. Without a word to me, he grabbed a pitchfork and stabbed her. A most unpleasant sight." He paused. "I don't care for killing women. It's unsporting. But Diana did not give us much choice."

A shout went up from the crowd. The horses were probably being led out onto the track. "Then Fortune smiled on us. The mad Mr. Hewitt ran out right afterward on the racetrack. And waving a loaded gun, too. Everyone—especially the police—turned to Hewitt as the murder suspect. That very night, Brody and I decided we had discovered the perfect way to acquire the Donegal Dancer for ourselves: murder."

"But you could only blame Hewitt if the police released him, or if he escaped." Eliza's mind raced. "You engineered that escape from the asylum, didn't you?"

Sir Walter beamed with pride. "I arranged for someone to pay two suffragettes who worked at Claybury to help Hewitt get away. After he ran out onto the track at Ascot with a suffragette flag in his pocket, Hewitt became a hero to many ladies in the movement. It wasn't difficult to find women willing to break the law to help him."

Eliza heard the distant music of a band above the crowd's roar. The air smelled of dirt, horse manure, and perfume from a hundred ladies. Outside this billowing tent, Sandown Park was filled with excitement, shouts, and laughter. It seemed miles away.

She fought to fit the puzzle pieces together. "You wanted him free that day, just as you made sure Gordon Longhurst came to the picnic. Even the Duchess thought it was bad form for you to tell Longhurst publicly that he had no right to the horse's winnings. You could have done it at any other time. But you needed him at the picnic."

"Please continue, Miss Doolittle. You're doing a splendid job."

"You planned to poison Turnbull that day, and made certain Longhurst was there to take the fall. And because you arranged for Hewitt to escape hours earlier, the police now focused on Hewitt *and* him. It's why you gave Longhurst his Ascot purse at the stables on Saturday.

You knew these two pigs were going to murder my father while he was there."

Sir Walter nodded. "If only I'd recruited you into our little group."

"As if I'd dirty my hands with the likes of you or your thugs."

"You don't know nothing about us, girl," one of the men replied. He swept off his hat and pointed it at her for emphasis. His hair, a bushy tangle of white and rust brown streaks, made him look like an angry badger. "We got more money than you'll ever live to see."

His companion chuckled. "Especially now."

Eliza clasped her hands in her lap to conceal their trembling. If they planned to kill her, what were they waiting for? If this continued much longer, Jack or one of his detectives would return. Then again, if these blighters wanted to be fools, the better for her. As soon as the Donegal Dancer's race finished, the other owners would make their way here, too.

She froze. The race! They were waiting for the race to begin, but why? The memory of both Emily Davison and Harold Hewitt being trampled flashed into her mind. Blimey, they wanted to push her in front of the racehorses. If so, they'd have to tie her up and drag her kicking and screaming through the crowd. Because she bloody well wasn't going to set foot on the track without one hell of a fight.

"Why so quiet, my dear?" Sir Walter's expression grew suspicious.

Eliza decided to keep him talking until she figured out how to escape. "Why not buy the Donegal Dancer from everyone? If you have as much money as your stooge implies."

"The name is Keene."

"As I said, if you're all so blooming rich, why not just buy the other owners out? Don't see the need for treating people like weeds in your garden."

Sir Walter tapped her on the knee. "What an apt analogy, Miss

Doolittle. I do indeed view them as weeds getting in the way. However, I did not start out this bloodthirsty. I had my eye on the Dancer since his foaling. I blame myself for waiting too long to buy him. By the time I realized he would be auctioned off, Turnbull had snapped up the colt."

"Turnbull," Keene said with contempt. "I wouldn't shed a tear over that one."

Sir Walter nodded. "Exactly. It galled me to see such a worthless fellow become owner of the Dancer. I knew Turnbull was in debt. I planned to wait until his financial troubles worsened and then buy the horse from him. Next thing I knew, he'd sold a share of the horse to his mistress, then joined up with the Duchess, Saxton, and Alfred. After that, the whole Wrexham Racing Syndicate was born, and I scrambled to become part of it."

"And decided to kill them all off, one by one," Eliza said with disgust.

"Not at first. I did inquire about buying their shares. Everyone turned me down."

Assuming she was as good as dead, Eliza was in no mood to placate this killer. "You play the gentleman scientist, but you're just a murderous dodger! A right rummy bastard is what you are. To think people call you 'sir'! And what exactly makes that horse so special, anyway?"

"Since you've chosen to insult me, I do not believe I will tell you why."

"Oh, bugger off. I don't even care." But Eliza did care about getting out of this tent alive. Screaming would do little good. With the start of the race imminent, the din of the crowd grew almost deafening.

"You care about your father, however," Sir Walter said. "I find that touching."

Eliza's terror grew. Once they got rid of her, Fairweather and Brody would go after Dad again. She must stay alive long enough to tell the police about Sir Walter's ruthless plans.

"If you admire me so much, you'll leave him alone."

"If things go as I suspect, Alfred will be so frightened that he will sell his shares straightaway. Just as Saxton has done."

She looked around for a weapon. Her parasol had landed in a corner. Her gaze fell longingly on the bottles of champagne cooling in buckets. If only she could get her hands on one. "And what will frighten my father so much that he'd sell?"

Sir Walter looked rueful. "If I told you, then *you* would be frightened."

Eliza's heart sank. "Fine. But how will you convince the Duchess to sell her shares if she's already turned you down?"

"Minerva has led a colorful life. Some episodes in her past are more colorful than others. But as unconventional as she is, I believe she will do anything to keep a few things hidden."

Eliza tapped her foot, ready to jump out of her seat. "And Longhurst?"

"What about him? He poisoned me at the syndicate luncheon. And the police found the vial of poison in his pocket."

"Except you planted it there. Must have been easy, too, seeing as how he sat right next to you the whole time. And then you brought along that ipecac syrup. Bloody convenient."

Sir Walter laughed. "I must thank Professor Higgins for advising me to have it on hand the next time I met with the syndicate." He shrugged. "Not that I took enough poison to do more than make me sick to my stomach. I was never in real danger."

"But poor Gordon Longhurst is in danger now," Eliza said.

"Indeed he is. I'm sure he'll have a date with the hangman before the year is out."

Another man stepped into the tent. Without sparing a glance for her, he said to Sir Walter, "It's almost time."

"Good. Tell Melling we'll get things started here."

As his latest "racing associate" turned to go, Sir Walter fished around in his jacket pocket. The two other men watched the third fellow leave. It was now or never. Picking up her skirts so she wouldn't trip, Eliza darted around the table.

"We have no time for this." Sir Walter pointed his walking stick. "Restrain her."

Eliza grabbed a champagne bottle and threw it at the man with the striped hair. It hit him on the shoulder, and he howled. She grabbed another bottle while pushing on the tent wall with her other hand. Although staked to the ground, the structure tilted for a minute.

"Stupid chit!" The other fellow vaulted over the table.

She swung the bottle, but he grabbed her arm and twisted so hard she dropped it.

"Let go of me!"

"Keep her still," Sir Walter ordered.

Suddenly both henchmen had tight hold of her. Kicking them had no effect. Eliza did manage one scream before they slammed her backward onto the banquet table. The blow knocked the wind out of her. As she struggled for breath, Keene pinched her nose shut. Eliza couldn't breathe at all now and gasped.

Sir Walter's face appeared above her. "Open wide, my dear." He held up a vial.

Both men pinned her down while Sir Walter poured a sweet liquid into her mouth. She fought to spit it out, but he clamped her mouth shut with his hand. If only she could make herself choke—anything to prevent the liquid from going down her throat.

Her eyes welled with tears as she felt herself swallow. Held fast to the table, Eliza could only look up. Green and purple balloons floated above her. What a strangely festive sight for someone who had just been poisoned.

TWENTY-ONE

Eliza waited to die. She lay motionless on the table while the three men stared at her with worried faces. Was she in shock? Was the poison taking effect? When they realized she had stopped struggling, Sir Walter and his colleagues stepped back. Still she lay there, fighting for every shaky breath.

Why hadn't she followed Higgins's advice to Sir Walter? Since today's race included the syndicate members, she should have brought ipecac syrup herself. Not that they'd let her drink the antidote.

"It's done." Sir Walter tucked the vial back into his suit coat pocket.

"You're a horrible man." Her voice sounded weak.

He looked solemn. "Yes, I suppose I am."

"Jack will find out the truth." Eliza slowly pushed herself up onto her elbows. The white tablecloth beneath her was in wild disarray.

"No, he won't. As I said earlier, the Inspector is not as clever as you are." When Sir Walter nodded, the two men helped her stand. In an oddly courteous gesture, Ingleby straightened Eliza's hat.

Relieved she remained upright even after they let go of her arms, Eliza blinked. "How soon before the poison kills me?"

"I chose a gentle poison for you, my dear," Sir Walter said. "Death will not come for hours, and you'll feel no pain. But you will grow dizzy, disoriented. Your hearing and vision may be compromised. And this poison does cause paranoia. If you don't know what that means, be prepared for a surge of unreasonable fear."

Eliza laughed bitterly. "Unreasonable fear? I've been held down and forced to drink poison. I think it's bloody reasonable to be afraid."

"You're an extraordinary young woman. I truly regret having to do this."

"I don't want to hear your regrets. Especially now."

"Keene, do you have the flag?" Sir Walter asked.

The man with the striped hair held up a folded cloth. "Got it right here."

"Good. Let's prepare her."

Ingleby pulled her toward the tent entrance. Too shocked to resist, Eliza watched Keene hand the flag to Sir Walter, who unrolled it. It was the green, purple, and white flag of the WSPU.

Once again, the two men grabbed her arms. Sir Walter folded the cloth into a triangle. Wrapping the flag tightly about her waist, he took care to knot it twice. Eliza looked down in dismay. The flag covered half her skirt.

"Perfect." Sir Walter gazed at her in approval. "I was irritated when the Duchess of Carbrey chose green and purple as the racing silk colors. Originally, the Dancer's colors were blue and red. But some lord with a connection to the royal family wanted those colors, and we had to re-register ours. Now I'm grateful the Duchess chose the suffragette colors."

Keene snickered. "She's even dressed like one of them."

Sir Walter smiled at Eliza's lilac skirt, white blouse, green-feathered hat, and pale green bolero jacket. "When the crowd sees her, they'll automatically assume she's with the WSPU. We don't really need the flag, but it's an excellent finishing touch."

"I'm not just going to walk in front of the horses." Eliza began to feel a bit queasy. Perhaps she could make herself ill and rid her stomach of the poison.

"We'll see." Sir Walter reached inside his jacket and pulled out a watch on a silver chain. "Make certain no detectives are in the area, Keene. We'll leave as soon as it's clear."

Keene hurried out of the tent.

Although Sir Walter had warned she would grow dizzy, Eliza still felt steady on her feet. If she didn't act now, she might not get another opportunity. Especially since they thought she'd been weakened by the poison. While Sir Walter tucked his watch into his vest pocket, Ingleby grabbed her by the elbow. When he turned her toward the tent entrance, Eliza tried to recall every minute of her ju-jitsu lessons with the Garruds.

As soon as Ingleby pushed her forward, she reached back with her free arm and grabbed his neck. An instant later, Eliza flipped him over her shoulder. He landed with a grunt at her feet. Then she promptly kicked him as hard as possible in the head.

Sir Walter let out a startled cry. Without hesitating, she grabbed his hand. Spinning about to face away from him, Eliza threw him over her shoulder. He fell on top of the half-conscious Ingleby. Before either man could move, she grabbed a champagne bottle and swung it at Sir Walter. He screamed as the heavy bottle smashed across his face. Blood gushed from his nose. When Ingleby's eyes fluttered open, she struck him as well.

But Eliza's heart sank when Keene's shadow fell across the tent entrance. Taking a deep breath, she ran through the tent flap, barreling right into him. They tumbled to the ground and lay side by side for a stunned second—just long enough for Eliza to remember the pain a kidney pinch could inflict. She reached out with both hands and squeezed hard. Keene yelled out. Eliza scrambled to her feet and flung herself into the crowd.

Although she dared not stop, Eliza shouted as she ran. "Help me! I'm being chased! Help me, please!"

Unfortunately, the flag wrapped about her waist caused everyone to view her with alarm or distaste. "It's one of those troublesome suffragettes," someone muttered.

"Stay away from her," a lady said. "The police are probably chasing her."

The sun seemed far too bright. Her vision blurred. Images grew clear, but clouded again a moment later. It made her unsteady on her feet, and she nearly fell. She pushed forward, not knowing where she was going or why she was so afraid. And why was a man with striped hair chasing her? Nothing made sense.

Eliza suddenly stopped and held her pounding head. Why did she feel so sick? And what had happened to her hearing? One second the noise around her seemed deafening, then it hushed to a whisper. She turned slowly in a circle. What had just happened? Where did all the sound go? It was as if she had turned down the volume on Professor Higgins's Victrola.

"Professor," she whispered. The image of a tall man with an impish grin appeared in her mind. But she couldn't remember who he was, or why the thought of him gave her comfort.

Dizzy and confused, Eliza rubbed her eyes. When her vision cleared, she saw the man with a white stripe through his hair heading in her direction. His mean expression frightened her.

"No! Stay away! Stay away!" Eliza turned and blindly groped past the crowd around her. She heard vague shouts. Someone shoved her hard. She had to keep going. She mustn't stop, not with that horrible fellow closing in behind her.

Confused, Eliza heard people shouting and pointing toward the left. What were they looking at? And where was she? She muscled her way to the crowd's edge. Ahead she saw only a single wooden railing and dirt beyond it. Far on the other side, other people stood waiting. Eliza only knew she had to escape from that vicious man. And one look over her shoulder revealed he was but a few steps away.

He pointed a finger and said something. She knew what he wanted—to kill her. Eliza ducked under the railing and ran. She almost wept with relief when he didn't follow. But the crowd along the railing now all pointed at her.

Coming to a halt, Eliza spun around. People were everywhere. They crammed against the railing, or jumped up and down in the stands. But she was totally alone. Why didn't the man with the striped hair follow? And why did everyone seem so upset with her? Several now pointed away from her, and she turned to see.

Eliza now realized she wasn't alone on this side of the railing. At least ten horses were here, too—and racing straight toward her.

Higgins suspected he had run faster than any of the horses that had burst from the starting gate. Good grief, those suffragettes must have legs of steel. He had dodged them for the past ten minutes. Their interference had caused him to miss his chance to cross the track and reach the Duchess's tent.

Somewhere out there, the Donegal Dancer was no doubt on his way to another victory. Higgins hoped the delay in reaching Jack would not be another cause for regret. Damnation, he had lost Rachel Turnbull, missed his chance to reach the police, and now he couldn't even watch the race. The track might be only fifteen feet away, but Higgins was exhausted. He'd have to push through the mob to reach the railing.

As he tried to catch his breath, a deafening cry rose from the crowd. Higgins felt the hairs rise on the back of his neck. That cry sounded exactly like the one he'd heard when Harold Hewitt ran onto the Ascot racetrack. More shouts followed, and women screamed. Good lord, would someone be trampled again?

Higgins shoved through the crowd in earnest. Before he reached the railing, a man yelled, "Get that woman off the track!"

It must be Rachel Turnbull! Higgins's heart sank. Could that be why the widow had come to Sandown? The misguided lady apparently wished to do more than help her sister sell copies of *The Suffragette*. She had decided to become a martyr to the cause like Emily Davison. By Jupiter, why had he ever let Rachel out of his sight? Pushing aside several agitated men, Higgins finally reached the railing. When he did, horror washed over him.

A young woman with a suffragette flag wrapped about her stood in the middle of the racetrack. Higgins reeled with shock. It was Eliza!

He must be mistaken. Why would Eliza wear a suffragette flag and run onto the track? But she stood motionless only twenty feet down the racecourse from him. And she stared with wide eyes at the oncoming horses.

"Eliza! Good God!" Higgins ducked under the railing and ran toward her. More shouts and screams rose up from every direction.

When he reached her, she seemed oblivious to his presence. Instead, she pointed in front of her and whispered, "Look. Horses."

Higgins didn't need to see them. He heard the cries of the jockeys, the whistling of the riding crops, and—worst of all—the pounding hooves. The horses were nearly upon them. It was too late to carry Eliza off the track. They'd never make it, not with more than ten horses racing like the devil right at them.

Grabbing Eliza by the waist, Higgins flung her to the ground. He threw himself on top of her. Between the crowd's roar and the labored pants of the horses, Higgins feared his eardrums would shatter, along with his terror-stricken heart. He stretched his body over Eliza, who lay beneath him without a struggle. Higgins could only hope he shielded as much of her as possible.

The horses were here. They were all around them. Higgins pressed himself hard against Eliza; the horses pounded an inch away from where they lay flattened on the ground. He bit back a cry as he felt first one set of hooves, then another, literally fly over his back. He heard curses from several jockeys. At least one horse gave a startled neigh. Clods of dirt showered his face and he pressed his eyes shut. The very earth trembled beneath them. At any moment, Higgins expected to be crushed by a thundering thousand-pound beast.

As suddenly as it began, it was over. Higgins felt weak with relief. Eliza's heart was still beating beneath him, and he didn't think either of them had been injured. He rose to his knees and looked down at her. Her eyelids fluttered open, but she didn't really see him. What in heaven's name had happened to her?

"Eliza? Are you all right?" He cradled her in his arms as a mob of people ran out on the track toward them.

"Where are the horses?" she asked in a weak voice.

Suddenly Jack was there. He looked white as a ghost. "Is she alive?"

"Horses?" Eliza repeated.

"What's wrong with her?" Jack's left eye twitched furiously. "Did the horses trample her? Any bones broken?" He snarled at the curious onlookers now swarming about. "Get back, everyone! Get back, I say! And call an ambulance!"

Higgins squeezed Eliza's arms and legs, but she didn't respond to the pressure. "I don't think any of the horses touched her. I covered her as best as I could. I wasn't hit either."

Jack shook his head. "The most amazing thing I ever saw. Those bloody horses swerved around or jumped right over your back. I thought I was going to die of fright."

Higgins suddenly spied a crumpled body in green and purple silks. He lay motionless with his eyes open. "Looks like one of the jockeys is dead. Is it Brody?"

"Dead?" Eliza opened her eyes. "Did I die?"

"No, but Mr. Brody did." Jack wiped the dirt off her cheeks. "He probably broke his neck after he was thrown from his horse."

"Watch out for Brody." She closed her eyes again. "He killed Diana."

"What!" Jack and Higgins said at the same time.

"Sir Walter told me. So I hit him with the champagne bottle." Eliza seemed to lose consciousness. Terrified, Higgins shook her until she opened her eyes again.

"That explains why we found Sir Walter and another man bloodied and unconscious in the tent," Jack said.

"Where did the horses go?" Eliza opened her eyes wider and tried to move.

Higgins helped her to a sitting position, but she slumped weakly against him.

"Eliza, did they give you something?" He felt equal parts rage and fear at the thought. "Is that why you ran out on the racetrack wearing that blasted flag?" He shook her again. "Eliza, stay awake. Please. Did you drink anything they gave you?"

She looked up at him, obviously disoriented. "Don't worry. Sir Walter said it's a gentle poison. I won't die for hours."

"Bloody hell!" Jack ran his fingers through his hair so wildly, it stood straight up. "I'll kill the lot of them, I will."

He shot to his feet. By this time, a half-dozen policemen had arrived. "Where is that damned ambulance? This young woman has been poisoned! She needs to be taken to hospital now!" Jack looked down at Higgins. "What the hell is that?"

"The antidote." Higgins held up the bottle he'd removed from his jacket. "You didn't think I'd attend another event with the Wrexham Racing Syndicate without bringing ipecac syrup, did you?"

As Higgins forced Eliza to drink the syrup, Jack fell to his knees. "You're a blooming marvel, Professor. Sybil and I will name our first child after you, even if it's a girl."

"Let's just get *our* girl back on her feet, shall we?"

Worried, Higgins stared at Eliza. Thank heaven she had swallowed it all down, but he had no idea if ipecac syrup worked for every poison.

The Duchess and the Saxtons appeared just as Eliza began to cough. "Is she alive? Have the horses killed her?" Lord Saxton asked.

"My heart stopped when I saw Eliza run onto the track," the Duchess said in a trembling voice. "I had no idea she was so fervent about the suffrage cause."

"She wasn't fervent, Minerva," Higgins replied. "She was poisoned."

Eliza suddenly jerked upright, leaned to one side, and became violently ill. Both Higgins and Jack held her while she vomited up the poison.

"I'm never coming to another horse race again," he muttered to Jack. "From now on, it's nothing but cricket matches for me."

Jack patted Eliza on the shoulder. "Sir Walter and his men must have put this damn flag on her. I'm glad now that Mrs. Turnbull came to the races. She's the one who found me and said something funny was going on at the tent."

Higgins wiped Eliza's face with his handkerchief. She slumped once more against his chest. "Funny in what way?"

"Rachel saw Eliza run out of the tent and knock down some man with a white streak in his hair."

"That sounds like one of the men hired to guard the Dancer at Bay Willow Stables."

Jack nodded. "A fellow called Keene. When Eliza ran away, Keene chased after her. Rachel peeked into the tent and discovered Sir Walter and another man lying unconscious. That's when she came looking for me."

"I'm going to buy that woman the most expensive bottle of French perfume I can find." Higgins smoothed Eliza's hair back. She had lost her hat. No doubt it had been trampled to pieces on the racetrack. "Do you feel any better, Eliza?"

"A little." Her color had improved. "But I might be sick again." Eliza's voice sounded stronger.

"Be sick all you want. The more you are, the less poison remains in your stomach."

As Eliza turned again to be ill, a horn sounded. Jack stood up. "It's the ambulance."

The orderlies rushed over with a stretcher while Freddy's voice rang out. "Where is she? Where is my darling? Let me pass! I'm her fiancé. You must let me see her. I am the only one who can help her. Where is my sweet angel? If I do not see her, we shall both die!"

Freddy burst upon them just as Eliza was lifted onto the stretcher. Grabbing her hand, he covered it with kisses. "My darling girl, you're alive. I was so worried. I had no idea you cared so much about women getting the vote. But you could have been killed!"

Eliza gave him a weak smile. "I'm fine. But very tired." The men carried her to the ambulance. Higgins started to follow, but Freddy caught his sleeve.

"How could you let her run out on the track?" Freddy accused Higgins. "I told all of you for weeks she'd be trampled if she ran in front of the horses. Of course, no one listened to me. Even though I am the only one here with any sense! Instead, you nearly got her killed, Professor. You ought to be ashamed of yourself."

Higgins took a deep breath. "Jack, have you taken Sir Walter into custody yet?"

"I left three detectives in the tent, with orders to restrain them when they revived."

"You're sure to find the bottle of poison on Sir Walter. When you do, I have a request."

Jack lifted his eyes in surprise. "What's that?"

Higgins pointed at Freddy. "See if you can get this fellow to drink what's left."

TWENTY-TWO

I don't believe it!" A startled Mrs. Pearce dropped the tiered pastry dish. She looked over at Higgins. "The girl must be ill again. Should we take her back to hospital?"

Eliza patted the housekeeper on the arm. "I only said I didn't want any scones."

"But you've refused everything but a boiled egg and tea. And you ate only consommé at dinner yesterday. Maybe you're running a fever." Mrs. Pearce laid a hand on Eliza's forehead.

"Oh, for pity's sake, she was poisoned two days ago. Give her a bit more time to work up an appetite. No need to fling our breakfast to the floor." Higgins bent to pick up the broken pieces of currant scones scattered over the carpet.

"The doctors advised me to eat nothing but soup, toast, and eggs for a few days," Eliza said. "By Friday, I'll be ready to wolf down every scone in your kitchen."

"I won't be happy until you're back to eating us out of house and home again." The housekeeper kissed Eliza on the cheek. "You gave us quite a fright."

Before Eliza could respond, Mrs. Pearce hurried from the room—

but not before Eliza glimpsed tears in the housekeeper's eyes. Eliza was a bit amazed herself that she had so little appetite. Then again, she had never had a vial of poison forced down her throat.

Higgins dumped the broken scones on the table. "Are we supposed to eat these, Pick?"

To Eliza's dismay, Pickering seemed as upset as Mrs. Pearce. He threw down his napkin, his face a mask of misery. "I cannot believe how close we came to losing you, Eliza. If only I had been at the racetrack. I might have been able to stop that scoundrel."

"I don't see how you could have done anything, Colonel. Sir Walter fooled us all."

"Do not call that monster 'Sir.' He is an affront to humanity, the lowest form of life to ever receive a knighthood. And to think we visited his home in Essex. Why, he might have tried to poison you there." His face reddened with anger. "He might have poisoned all of us!"

"Calm down, old man. Eliza has recovered, and Fairweather's facing charges of multiple murders." Sitting down once more, Higgins reached for a piece of toast. "And you didn't need to be at the racetrack, not while I was there. As everyone in the stands can tell you, I behaved with the utmost daring and courage. Saved the day I did, along with saving Eliza."

She felt such a wave of affection for the Professor, Eliza had to fight back tears. She blamed the poison for her uncharacteristic weepiness. "You should have been there, Colonel. I was flat on the ground and couldn't see anything. But everyone says it was a miraculous sight to behold. Higgins spread-eagled on top of me, while racehorses leaped over his back."

"I was quite magnificent," Higgins said with a wide grin as he buttered his toast.

Laughing, Eliza got up from her chair. Before he could protest, she gave him a quick hug. "Thank you again, you marvelous preening hero." She sat back down. "Maybe by Christmas you'll stop reminding me every hour that you saved my life."

Higgins seemed thrown by her unexpected embrace, but she knew he'd pretend it hadn't happened.

"Let's strike a bargain," he said. "I won't remind you that I saved your life, if you stop reminding me how you rescued me from prison this past spring."

Eliza slapped her hand on the table. "Done."

"Now I feel far worse." Pickering stood. "Both of you have been in deadly trouble the past few months, and I have been no help at all. None."

"Colonel, that's not true." It bothered Eliza to see how upset the dear fellow was.

Higgins leaned back in his chair. "How about this? The next murder case Eliza and I stumble across, we'll let you be the one who nearly gets killed."

Pickering shook his head. "I'm going to my club. All this talk of murder and poison is simply no way to start the morning."

"Don't be silly, Pick," Higgins called after him. "Come back."

Higgins and Eliza shrugged at each other when he didn't return. A few minutes later, voices rang out from the entry foyer. Eliza frowned. Neither of them was dressed to receive visitors. As always, the Professor wore a tattered bathrobe at the breakfast table; she had come down this morning in her most comfortable satin wrapper. Eliza hadn't even bothered to put her hair up. Instead, a thick braid hung halfway down her back.

With a flurry of greetings, Jack, Sybil, and Rachel Turnbull entered the dining room. Eliza was taken aback to see all three in their Sunday best.

"I wish you'd telephoned first," she said. "We're not properly dressed."

"Oh, hang that." Higgins snorted. "They're the ones being beastly rude. It serves them right to find us sitting here in our carpet slippers and bathrobes."

Sybil laughed. "True. Forgive our ill manners, but we won't stay long."

Higgins rang for Mrs. Pearce to bring in more coffee, scones, and eggs.

When everyone had taken a seat, Jack cleared his throat. "I thought you'd like to know that Sir Walter isn't the only one arrested for murder. Keene, Ingleby, Melling, and Owens have all been charged as accomplices."

"And Mr. Longhurst has been released," Rachel said. Although the widow wore a black mourning gown, she'd pinned a VOTES FOR WOMEN brooch to her collar. "I asked him to come with us today, but he's still unsettled from his past few days in jail."

"Please tell him how sorry I am for believing he'd poisoned Sir Walter." Eliza bit her lip. "I also apologize for thinking you poisoned your husband."

Rachel smiled. "I would have believed the same thing in your place. Let's not speak of it anymore. I'm only glad to see how quickly you've recovered."

"And I'm glad you saw me run out of the tent and found Jack. Sir Walter might have woken up and escaped if you hadn't."

"Highly unlikely, Lizzie," Jack said. "You broke his nose with that bottle. He was so disoriented from the blow, it took a solid day of interrogation before we got a coherent story out of him. Not that we needed it to arrest him. He still had the bottle of poison in his pocket."

"He confessed, I hope?" Higgins asked.

"Indeed he did. And to much more than killing off the syndicate members." Jack took a long sip of coffee. "We know now why Brody killed Diana Price at Ascot."

Eliza sat forward in anticipation. "I've been waiting to learn this. Sir Walter wouldn't tell me. What did she overhear that drove them to murder?"

Before Jack could answer, someone knocked furiously on the front door. Mrs. Pearce left the room with a worried frown.

"Who the devil is here now?" Higgins asked. "If that's your father and Rose, I'm going upstairs to take a bath."

"Don't be silly," Eliza said. "Dad won't be released until Wednesday."

"It's worse than I thought," Higgins muttered as Freddy rushed into the room.

Eliza had only half risen before Freddy crushed her to his chest. When he was done with his painful embrace, she realized he had also smashed the bouquet of daisies he held.

"I'm so sorry, I've quite battered these flowers. But they're to welcome you back home from the hospital, my darling."

"I was only there for a day, but thank you, Freddy." Eliza handed the bouquet to Mrs. Pearce. "Sit down and have some breakfast. Jack's brought news about the murders."

Luckily Freddy spotted fresh scones and jam preserves on the table. He sat across from Eliza without further protest and reached for a plate.

"As I was saying, we interrogated Sir Walter. I also sent men to his house in Essex, and to Brody's apartment in Chelsea. We found papers in both places confirming that Brody was a secret owner of the Donegal Dancer," Jack said. "And that wasn't the only horse Brody owned with Sir Walter. We uncovered documents exposing their other criminal deeds."

"I say, wasn't it a bit of ill luck the only jockey killed yesterday was Brody." Freddy stopped smearing his scone. "The Donegal Dancer swerved at the last minute just as he reached you and the Professor. Perhaps the horse knew you were there, darling, and didn't want to harm you. But the horse veered so abruptly, it sent Brody flying. A most alarming sight."

"It would have been more alarming had the horse trampled us," Higgins said.

"Of course, but I feel sorry for that lady friend of his. What was her name again?"

"Patsy," Eliza said. "The poor girl probably had no idea what Brody was up to."

"It doesn't appear so." Jack cleared his throat. "Now if I could continue."

"If you don't let him finish, that eye of his will start twitching," Sybil said with a grin.

"We shall be silent for as long as you want, Jack." Eliza winked at Sybil.

"We'll see how long that lasts," Higgins said.

"As I was saying, we found papers proving their joint ownership of several racehorses. We also found evidence that both men were part of the infamous horse kidnapping ring that has plagued the racing world for five years."

Eliza's mouth fell open. "The one my dad was so worried about?"

"The very one."

Rachel shook her head. "Sir Walter hired men to guard the Dancer, when all along the syndicate should have been protecting the horse from him."

"How big a part did Brody and Sir Walter play in the ring?" Higgins asked.

"Part? They ran the organization. We've found at least eleven men who worked for them. Melling, Owens, Ingleby, and Keene were only a few."

Eliza thought this over. "Sir Walter said he and Brody had been having an angry conversation at Ascot. Diana obviously heard them speak about the kidnappings. But was it really worth killing her over that?"

Jack looked at her as if she had just sprouted wings. "Worth killing for? Lizzie, these men were kidnapping champion racehorses and holding them for ransom. These horses are worth tens of thousands of pounds. Many of the thefts never even reached the papers. Owners paid the ransom without reporting it to the authorities for fear the horse—or they—would be harmed. However, several owners refused to pay. They either didn't have enough money, or they feared by paying the kidnappers, it would only encourage them to steal more horses. Regardless, those who didn't pay the ransom never saw their horse again."

"Did they kill the horses?" Eliza's anger built once more.

"Only one horse was killed, and we believe that was accidental. At least according to Sir Walter. If the horses weren't ransomed, the kidnappers bred them with other horses they had stolen. In fact, they often bred the horses even if the ransom *had* been paid."

"What would be the purpose in that?" Higgins seemed puzzled. "The kidnappers could never reveal the true bloodlines of these animals. If so, they'd be arrested."

"Don't you see?" The truth seemed clear to Eliza. "By racing them! They knew these young horses were the offspring of champions, and likely to become champions themselves. To avoid suspicion, Sir Walter probably sold these horses when they were first foaled. Then he bought them back under assumed names when they were old enough to race."

"By George, I believe she's right." Higgins chuckled. "I told you we didn't need Sherlock Holmes, Eliza. We figured the mystery out ourselves."

"What do you mean *we?*"

"Maybe you figured it out, but my detectives and I got the murderer to confess."

Sybil winked at Jack. "If you ask, Eliza might promise to let you solve the next mystery."

"And I promise she has no idea how valuable the Donegal Dancer really is," Jack said.

"Is he the offspring of one of the kidnapped champions?" Higgins asked.

"Not just one champion. Two." Jack made them wait while he took another sip of coffee.

Eliza snapped her fingers. "Red Glory and Maximus!"

Jack choked on his coffee as Freddy asked in confusion, "Who are they?"

"They're the champion racehorses Jack told us about when he questioned the syndicate members at Ascot," she said. "Actually, Brody brought it up."

"The girl does have a phenomenal memory," Higgins said.

"I don't know why I bother. Scotland Yard should just come to her with their next case."

"So the parents of the Donegal Dancer are two champions?" Freddy persisted.

Eliza nodded. "Brody said they stole Red Glory when she was pregnant. She was found a year later, unharmed, but her foal had already been born. No one knew what happened to the foal. I remember the Duchess was upset about that. But Maximus was taken the year before as well. The kidnappers must have mated them." She let out a whistle. "No wonder Sir Walter and Brody wanted the Dancer all to themselves. The horse hasn't lost a race in two seasons. Except for this last one. And I've never been happier to see a horse lose than I was on Friday."

Higgins pushed aside his plate and rested his elbows on the table. "Even if they couldn't use his real parentage to hike up the stud fees, the Donegal Dancer's winning record has already made the horse worth his weight in gold."

"Sir Walter told us they shipped the foal off to a horse farm in Ireland," Jack said. "The owner Ahearn Griffith was eighty and not well. Over the past five years, they had sold these 'secret' champions to Griffith, only to buy them back a year or two later at low prices. Using an assumed name, of course. They planned to do the same with the Donegal Dancer, only—"

"My husband bought the horse first," Rachel finished. "A pity Jonathon never learned what a prize the Dancer really was."

"What this all means is that the four members who remain in the Wrexham Racing Syndicate are likely to see substantial returns on their investment," Jack said. "That includes you, Eliza. Because we only have the word of horse thieves to back up the Dancer's true parentage, that won't be enough to get the Jockey Club to accept it. But given the horse's bloodlines, the rest of his racing career looks to be a glorious one. With a lucrative breeding career to follow."

"Cor, wait till Dad hears this." Eliza grinned. "We'll be rich in just a few years."

Jack nodded. "Extremely comfortable at the very least."

"We haven't told Gordon yet," Rachel said. "We're going there next."

"This is excellent." Freddy got to his feet. "Now that our financial future is secure, Eliza and I can marry and set up our own household."

"Freddy, please. I told you I'm not ready to marry."

"Eliza's right." Sybil gave Freddy a stern look. "Besides, you're both too young."

"Pardon me, Miss Chase, but you and the Inspector are planning to marry soon," Freddy said in an offended tone. "I hardly think you should be dissuading us from doing likewise."

"You're only twenty-one," Jack said, "and Eliza a year younger."

"But *you're* getting married," Freddy repeated.

"Jack is ten years older than you," Sybil said, "and I am twenty-six. We are old enough to know our own minds. However, you both need more experience of the adult world, especially you, Mr. Eynsford Hill. You should consider taking up a profession. I'd hate to think you plan to live off Eliza for the rest of your life."

Higgins sat back with a whoop. "I knew I liked you, Sybil!"

Freddy sank back down in his chair. "I've never heard anything so absurd. Eliza, tell them. I am a gentleman, not a member of the working class. And with your racing money, neither of us will ever have to work a day in our lives."

The stress of the past few days had taken its toll. Eliza wanted nothing more than to go upstairs and nap. She hoped Freddy would be gone when she woke up.

"I enjoy teaching, Freddy. And no matter how much money I have, I don't want to stay home all day while servants wait on me. I've worked my whole life. I plan to keep doing so."

"Hear, hear," Sybil said. "By the way, we'd like you to speak at our next rally."

Eliza perked up at that. "I'd love to. I especially want to thank the Garruds for those ju-jitsu lessons." She leaned close to Sybil. "They came in quite handy."

Freddy frowned. "Any woman would leap at the chance to marry a man who adores her. Clara can't wait for Baron Ashmore to propose. I wish you were more like my sister."

"God forbid," Higgins muttered.

Eliza poured herself another cup of tea. "Today is not about weddings. The murders of the Wrexham Racing Syndicate have been solved, and justice will be served. So let's celebrate." She raised her teacup. "A toast to the Donegal Dancer."

Everyone raised their teacups, even Freddy. "A toast to the Donegal Dancer."

Higgins turned to her. "And a toast to Eliza, a woman of independent means."

"To Eliza!" they echoed.

He was right. After a lifetime of privation and hunger, Eliza realized that blooming racehorse had given her something she hardly dared dream of.

Her freedom. How loverly.